Praise for *An Indiscreet Princess*

NO LONGER PROPERTY OF SEATTLE PUBLIC LIBRARY

"*An Indiscreet Princess* is a fascinating portrait of the life of Princess Louise, Queen Victoria's fourth daughter. Blalock powerfully depicts Louise's passions, struggles, and triumphs while effortlessly immersing the reader in the royal household and their personal lives. A glittering, poignant story."

—Chanel Cleeton, *New York Times* and *USA Today* bestselling author

"A royal princess determined to create a hidden love, and a demanding queen who vows to keep her in her place—I couldn't turn the pages fast enough. Rich in period detail, *An Indiscreet Princess* is a beguiling story of duty, power, and a young princess's passion for art and love. A thoroughly engaging read."

—Shelley Noble, *New York Times* bestselling author of *Summer Island*

"Meticulously researched and vividly written. Georgie Blalock paints a detailed portrait of Princess Louise and her refusal to bow to society's—or her mother's—expectations, from Louise's unusual admittance into the National Art Training School to her sweeping romance with a renowned sculptor. Fans of *The Crown*'s Princess Margaret will adore this look at Princess Louise, the unconventional daughter of Queen Victoria, as she bends all the rules to live a life on her own terms."

—Stephanie Marie Thornton, *USA Today* bestselling author of *A Most Clever Girl*

Received On:

JAN 28 2023

"Princess Louise was a woman out of her time: a creative freethinker with a strong will and a passion for living who was raised in the restrictive environment of her mother Queen Victoria's court. In Georgie Blalock's novel Louise steps out of history and into our hearts as she struggles to hew a fulfilling role for herself. It's a fascinating glimpse into the pressures of being royal in an era when princesses had few choices, and a portrait of a very likeable, relatable woman who lived 150 years ago yet feels incredibly modern."

—Gill Paul, bestselling author of *The Manhattan Girls*

"Georgie Blalock has delivered a mother-daughter story of immense proportions. Especially because the mother is Queen Victoria and the daughter is Princess Louise, a rebellious woman determined to pursue a life of art and forbidden love. *An Indiscreet Princess* is a must-read for fans of *The Crown*, Princess Margaret, and all things Royal."

—Renée Rosen, author of *The Social Graces*

"This is a brilliantly told tale that pits a royal princess's passionate desire to use her extraordinary talents and follow her heart against her duty to family, queen, and country."

—Lecia Cornwall, author of *That Summer in Berlin*

"Vivid and compelling, Georgie Blalock's *An Indiscreet Princess* tells the story of a passionate young artist who also happens to be a princess, and thus struggles to forge a meaningful life in the face of stifling convention. Louise's longing to live as herself, rather than the princess the world sees and expects, had me rooting for her from the first page. Brimming with forbidden love, artistic ambition, and the nuance of life in the royal family, this was a fascinating and memorable read."

—Kristin Beck, author of *The Winter Orphans* and *Courage, My Love*

an
indiscreet
PRINCESS

Also by Georgie Blalock

The Last Debutantes
The Other Windsor Girl

an indiscreet PRINCESS

A Novel of Queen Victoria's
Defiant Daughter

———— ❧ ————

GEORGIE BLALOCK

WM

WILLIAM MORROW
An Imprint of HarperCollins*Publishers*

This book is a work of fiction. References to real people, events, establishments, organizations, or locales are intended only to provide a sense of authenticity, and are used fictitiously. All other characters, and all incidents and dialogue, are drawn from the author's imagination and are not to be construed as real.

P.S.™ is a trademark of HarperCollins Publishers.

AN INDISCREET PRINCESS. Copyright © 2022 by Georgie Reinstein. All rights reserved. Printed in the United States of America. No part of this book may be used or reproduced in any manner whatsoever without written permission except in the case of brief quotations embodied in critical articles and reviews. For information, address HarperCollins Publishers, 195 Broadway, New York, NY 10007.

HarperCollins books may be purchased for educational, business, or sales promotional use. For information, please email the Special Markets Department at SPsales@harpercollins.com.

FIRST EDITION

Designed by Diahann Sturge

Library of Congress Cataloging-in-Publication Data has been applied for.

ISBN 978-0-06-308328-8

22 23 24 25 26 LSC 10 9 8 7 6 5 4 3 2 1

To W.C.R. I love you.

Chapter One

The Queen *must say* that she does feel *very bitterly* the want of feeling of those who *ask* the Queen to go to open Parliament . . . why this wish should be of so *unreasonable* and unfeeling a nature, as to *long* to *witness* the spectacle of a poor, broken-hearted widow, nervous and shrinking, dragged in *deep mourning*, *ALONE* in *STATE* as a *Show*, where she used to go supported by her husband, to be gazed at, without delicacy of feeling, is a thing *she cannot* understand, and she never could wish her bitterest foe to be exposed to!

—QUEEN VICTORIA TO LORD RUSSELL

London, February 1868

Princess Louise Caroline Alberta rose from the Sovereign's throne beneath the gilded canopy of state at the front of the House of Lords. She nodded to the sea of peers in their parliamentary red robes trimmed with ermine, and the MPs in their somber suits standing at the back of the chamber. They returned the bow, honoring her as the representative of her mother, Her Majesty Victoria, by the Grace of God, of the United Kingdom of Great Britain and Ireland Queen.

The Earl Marshall, the Duke of Norfolk, in his red-and-gold-braided coat, stepped forward and picked up the Imperial State Crown on its velvet cushion, signaling Louise to descend from the dais. The gathered lords and gentlemen stood so still, every rustle of Louise's long parliamentary robe carried by four Pages of Honor echoed off the Gothic wood walls. The ominous quiet rattled her more than when she'd entered the Lords Chamber and taken the throne to wait for the Gentleman Usher of the Black Rod to lead the Members of Parliament in from the Commons. She'd braced for a barrage of boos from the republican MPs, but even the ones who'd hissed at Mama during the last two openings had remained respectful. Of course, Mama had no one to blame but herself for their ire. If she'd willingly fulfill her duties instead of grudgingly appearing only when her children needed money for majorities and weddings, the republican MPs would have a great deal less to complain about.

The respectful quiet continued as Louise followed the Earl Marshall to the side door. She held her head high, maintaining the regal stance she'd spent days practicing along with Mama's speech. Lady Sybil St. Albans, her dearest friend, watched from her seat beside Lady Ely, one of Mama's Ladies of the Bedchamber. Mama had commanded both women to assist Louise today. Once Louise passed, they'd fall in behind her for the procession back through the Royal Gallery to the Robing Room, passing again the lines of Gentlemen at Arms standing watch in front of the dignitaries and officials gathered for the State Opening of Parliament. Lady Ely stared grim-faced while Sybil beamed as brightly as the diamonds in her tiara. Sybil's smile eased the air of responsibility hanging on Louise's shoulders like the long parliamentary robe. Today was a triumph and far from the disaster Mama had feared.

IN THE QUIET of the Robing Room, Lady Ely directed the Pages of Honor in the removal of Louise's robe. Louise sighed when they lifted the weight off her shoulders, and she rubbed her neck as she took in the large frescoes of King Arthur's Court by William Dyce hanging on the walls above them. Papa had commissioned the pieces during the rebuilding of the Palace of Westminster after the nasty fire thirty years ago. The knights and ladies stood among the ornate gilded high ceilings, their medieval air so different from Franz Xaver Winterhalter's regal portraits of Mama and Papa flanking the gold throne. Papa stood in his dark Rifle Brigade uniform, his Order of the Garter star shining on his chest. When he'd posed for the portrait, no one had known his death was only two years away. Louise closed her eyes, the warm feel of his large hand covering hers as potent today as it'd been the first time he'd led her through this room. He'd beamed with pride as she'd explained each image, knowing more about the Arthurian legends than even Mr. Dyce.

"You're a true artist," Papa had complimented, squeezing Louise's hand.

"Someday, I'll complete a piece to really make you proud."

His warm smile swelled her chest with adoration. "I have no doubt you will."

Are you proud of me now? Louise opened her eyes and

touched the smooth strand of pearls adorning her neck. They'd belonged to Papa's mother, Princess Louise of Saxe-Gotha-Altenburg, for whom she was named. His mother had been cruelly torn from him when he was five, her absence leaving an awful hole in his heart and life the way Papa's death had done to Louise.

"You were marvelous, Your Royal Highness," Sybil congratulated, fluffing out Louise's wide skirt and bringing her back to today.

"Her Majesty couldn't have asked for a better representative," the Lord Great Chamberlain, Baron Willoughby de Eresby, assured with a courtier's reverence. Lord Norfolk nodded his agreement before the two men fell into quiet conversation. Nearby, the Crown Jeweler and his assistant examined the Imperial State Crown to ensure none of the hired stones had come loose during the ceremony. In a few moments, Lord Norfolk would escort Louise to the Irish State Coach for the return to Buckingham Palace and the last leg of her journey through this exhilarating day.

"Do you really think I did well?" Louise asked as Sybil straightened the gold-and-diamond Order of Victoria and Albert hanging from a white satin ribbon on Louise's bodice.

"I could see from my seat the lords and MPs were quite in awe of you, weren't they, Lady Ely?"

The older woman froze as if caught prying a diamond out of Mama's crown.

"I couldn't tell," she mumbled, then returned to ordering the pages about.

"She's difficult today," Louise whispered to Sybil.

"She's always difficult." Sybil, the daughter of General

Charles Grey, Her Majesty's Private Secretary, had served as a maid of honor before her marriage to the Duke of St. Albans. She was one of the few young women Mama hadn't deemed too indiscreet and dismissed before they'd learned their way around the palace. She was also the only young lady allowed to assist Louise when the occasion called for it, and she'd caught the wrong end of Lady Ely's temper enough times to know the woman. "Don't think of her, think of them." She inclined her head toward the closed door and the mass of people waiting outside for Louise to reappear. "You were marvelous and they know it, and so will Her Majesty. After today's success, who knows what she'll allow you to do next?"

The door opened and Mr. Disraeli, the new Prime Minister, strode in, his lace cravat fluttering against his dark velvet coat lapels. His curled hair was pomaded smooth at the top and left wild along the sides, with a single curl artfully placed in the center of his forehead. He bowed, then straightened, and with a flourish produced a small red jewelry box from inside his coat pocket. "Your Royal Highness, you have enthralled everyone. Allow me to present you with a gift to commemorate your grand success."

Louise opened the box to reveal a gold butterfly with small onyx eyes, the details along the body as exquisitely rendered as the fragile gold wings. They were so finely wrought, they appeared as if they might flutter. "It's beautiful."

"As is Your Royal Highness. Her Majesty will be very proud of you."

Lady Ely snorted in disbelief and Louise snapped the box closed. How dare the woman try to humble her in front of these august men. She wouldn't be so bold if it weren't for

Mama's constant example. Louise wasn't about to let it stand. Today was a triumph for the Crown because of her, and Sybil was right, everyone knew it. "Her Majesty wasn't unable to open Parliament, Mr. Disraeli. She was unwilling."

The sharp intake of breath from Lady Ely matched the wide-eyed shock of Baron Willoughby de Eresby and Lord Norfolk.

Mr. Disraeli threw back his head and laughed.

THE CROWD ALONG the route to Buckingham Palace roared with applause. Louise waved to them, the borrowed diamonds adorning her wrists flashing in the sunlight. Her arm ached from holding it up to wave but she refused to lower it. Unlike Mama, Louise wouldn't deny the people the pageantry they'd spent hours queuing to see. "Isn't this grand?"

"It's marvelous." Sybil waved to a little girl in braids who tossed a red rose at the carriage. "They love you."

"I love them." Louise threw a kiss to a group of gentlemen who clutched their hearts in a fake swoon. "I'd do this every day if I could."

"Her Majesty isn't likely to trust someone so impertinent with such an important task again." Lady Ely sat stiff against the squabs, her mauve dress as unwilling to wrinkle as her forehead. With gray hair creeping in along her temples and marring the smooth black of her coiffure, she was losing her regal looks along with what remained of her humor. "You shouldn't have been so indelicate in front of Mr. Disraeli, Lord Willoughby de Eresby, and Lord Norfolk."

"I didn't say anything they didn't already know, not after

the last two Parliaments when Mama complained to anyone who'd listen how awful it was for a poor, fragile widow to be forced into public. What nonsense. Mama is as fit as a Highland heifer." Only her self-pity and ability to scold were more robust than her constitution. "If she listened to Bertie and simply drove through Hyde Park once in a while so her subjects could see her, she'd be a great deal better off. Instead, she carries on as if a ride were as strenuous as discovering the source of the Nile."

"Impertinent chit," Lady Ely mumbled.

Louise dropped her arm and pinned the woman with a glare cold enough to crack ice. "I am Her Royal Highness Princess Louise, and any opinions you have about my conduct or behavior will be kept to yourself. Do I make myself clear, *Lady* Ely?"

Lady Ely's lips drew tight, but she said nothing, the arrogance of her position matched by her ingrained reverence for station. "Yes, Your Royal Highness."

"WHAT WERE YOU thinking, saying such an ugly thing about me to the Earl Marshall, the Lord Great Chamberlain, and the Prime Minister?" Her Royal Majesty Queen Victoria demanded from across the large brass desk in the Bow Room of Buckingham Palace. She was swathed in her usual black, the color a marked contrast to the red-lacquered dispatch box before her and the yellow silk adorning the walls. Lenchen, Louise's elder sister, her stout figure filling out what waist the dressmaker had managed to add to the mauve silk frock, stood at Mama's elbow shaking her head in matronly disapproval. Through the open windows, the roar of the crowds outside the palace gates drifted in on the chill winter breeze.

Louise didn't look at Lady Ely, who stood by the unlit fireplace beside Lady Churchill, another Lady of the Bedchamber. Smug satisfaction radiated off Lady Ely, and Louise clasped her hands in front of her and took a settling breath. She'd gain nothing by flying off the handle or boxing Lady Ely's ears. "It was but one comment in a private room in the midst of a very public triumph."

"It was an impertinent remark from a thoughtless girl. I never should have allowed my ministers to talk me into appointing you to open Parliament." Mama leveled a thick, ring-clad finger at Louise. "You will write a note of apology to those gentlemen at once."

"I will do no such thing. Mr. Disraeli praised my performance and gave me this to thank me for it." She pointed to the butterfly pin on her bodice. Even with the curtains open there wasn't enough sunlight falling on this part of the palace to make the gold shine. "The people loved me. Listen to them, they're still cheering for me."

"They are cheering for me." Mama snatched a pen out of the silver stag inkstand, dipped the nib into the crystal inkwell, and resumed her never-ending correspondence, ready to return to work, but Louise refused to be dismissed.

"Then step out on the balcony and give your subjects what they're begging to see."

"I am not an animal in the Tower Menagerie to be stared at, but a queen who works tirelessly for her people. Lenchen, close the windows, the noise is straining my nerves."

"Yes, Mama." Lenchen slid the sashes down, dampening the last remaining excitement of Louise's glorious day.

"You can't shut them out forever and expect to remain Queen."

"Do not tell me what I can and cannot do," Mama snapped. "Since your official duties are complete, we will return to Windsor at once. Dr. Ellison and Dr. Jenner said I am too fragile to endure the noise and noxious fumes of Town, did they not, Lenchen?"

"They did, Mama."

"May I remain in Town another day or two with Bertie and Alix at Marlborough House?" Louise was loath to leave the life of London for the mausoleum of Windsor. "I'd like to visit the South Kensington Museum and view the new sculptures from Paris."

"Not after your behavior today. It is time you learned not to say every thought that flies into your head. Return to your rooms and prepare for our departure."

"Yes, Mama." Louise dropped a curtsey and backed out of the Bow Room, cursing her boldness. If she'd held her tongue, she might've been allowed to stay in London, but she hadn't been willing to simply stand there and watch her great triumph be reduced to nothing.

"How was she?" Sybil asked when Louise joined her in the Principal Corridor, the dust on the tabletops and the dingy walls evident in the daylight. Mama detested coming to Buckingham Palace and quite neglected it.

"Mama refused to even acknowledge what I did for her today." Louise twisted the string of pearls around one finger. "Papa wouldn't have been so cruel."

Sybil laid a comforting hand on Louise's shoulder. "I know."

Louise took her gloved fingers and squeezed them, appreciating her support. With Louise's younger brother Leopold at Windsor with his tutor, Reverend Duckworth, no one else was here to offer it.

"Lady St. Albans, your carriage has arrived," a footman announced, the black mourning band affixed to his sleeve breaking the bright line of his red-and-gold livery.

"I wish I could stay longer, but I must go. William and I are hosting a dinner tonight for the Liberal lords and everyone is eager to hear about today. I can't wait to tell them how grand you were."

"Was I?" With Mama's rebuke ringing in her ears, it was difficult to believe.

"You were. Don't allow anyone to make you think otherwise."

"You're too sweet. Now off with you. You have your husband and duties to attend to."

Sybil followed the footman down the length of the Principal Corridor, stopping at the end to throw Louise an encouraging wave before disappearing down the Ministers' Staircase. What Louise wouldn't give to follow her, but she couldn't. Mama's command to prepare for the return to Windsor had been given, and if she didn't obey, it'd mean another rebuke, or a stinger, as General Grey called the nasty little notes Mama sent on her black-edged writing paper. Everyone in the royal household had desk drawers full of them.

"Are you ready to change, Your Royal Highness?" Jane, the button-nosed dresser, asked when Louise entered her bedroom. She held a dark gray frock across her arms while a flurry of maids and footmen prepared Louise's trunks for Paddington Station.

Louise curled her lip at the dull, limp dress, not ready to remove the beautiful white one and see it condemned to the wardrobe to rot beside the bridesmaid's dress she'd worn for Bertie and Alix's wedding six years ago. "No, fetch my drawing supplies."

Louise had no idea where they were in the chaos, but she needed them and the serenity of sketching. She picked up a small statuette of her old dog, Flash, from the table beside her and turned it over in her hands, admiring how Mary Thornycroft, her sculpting tutor, had modeled his fluttering fur for the bronze casting. She wished she had her sculpting tools and clay to work until her arms ached and the tension inside her eased, but everything was at Windsor. Pencil and paper would have to suffice.

Jane returned with the well-worn green-and-black leather sketchbook and the silver gilt pencil box with Louise's initials engraved on the front. The box had been a gift from Leopold for her seventeenth birthday. She thanked Jane, then left, hurrying down the corridor to the Ministers' Staircase and the floors above. She was nearly to it when the door to Beatrice's room opened and her youngest sister stepped out.

"Where are you off to?" Beatrice demanded, blocking her way.

"The art studio." Louise tried to step around her soon-to-be eleven-year-old sister, but Beatrice slid in front of her, the wide skirt of her short dress swinging about her legs. Her thick blond hair, held back by a black ribbon, fell in waves over her shoulders.

"It's so dusty and dirty up there." She wrinkled her nose in disgust, the full-cheeked innocence Louise had sculpted for Mama four years ago beginning to fade. The years of isolation with Mama's grief and constant coddling had soured the once-sweet girl. "What will Mama say if you ruin your gown?"

"She'll be quite pleased, since she detests any color except black." Louise pushed past Beatrice and climbed up to the light-filled studio on the top floor. Despite the years of neglect, the sharp scent of oil paints, turpentine, and linseed oil permeated the air. Louise took a deep breath, memories of afternoon lessons with her siblings and Papa washing over her. He used to work beside them when his schedule allowed, guiding their brushes or charcoal, always praising their efforts and never belittling them. He'd encouraged their interests, hiring a watercolor tutor for Lenchen and a sculpting master for Louise. There'd been so much possibility and life back then. It'd died with him.

She wiped away the tears stinging the corners of her eyes. There wasn't time to cry if she wished to draw, and she must. If she didn't settle herself, she'd go mad during the train ride to Windsor or pick a quarrel with Lenchen.

She dragged a stool to the large windows overlooking the city, sat down, and balanced the sketchbook on her lap as she'd done a hundred times during tedious public outings or in Mama's dull Drawing Rooms. With quick flicks of her silver gilt pencil, she captured the smoke curling from the hundreds of chimneys, and the people, horses, and carts moving along the crowded streets. The faster she gave shape to the view, the more a sense of calm spread through her like the shadows creeping across the floor. In here, nothing mattered but the art, not Parliament, Mama, or even tomorrow.

She worked until faint lights began appearing in windows and Big Ben announced it was almost time to leave for Paddington Station. She closed the sketchbook, loath to abandon it. Today's glitter and pomp were only a brief respite from endless days trailing behind Mama like a well-trained and often-kicked spaniel.

She touched the pearls. *Papa, you wouldn't have made me so irrelevant.*

He'd have found a purpose for her, as he had for her elder sister Alice through her marriage to the Grand Duke of Hesse, or for her eldest sister, Vicky, the Crown Princess of Prussia. Louise had no desire to make a foreign marriage, and Papa wouldn't have forced her into such a match, but he wouldn't have left her to wallow in this muted existence either.

She removed the butterfly pin and traced the delicate gold wings with one lead-stained finger. The entire House of Lords and the Commons hadn't thought her impertinent or thoughtless, but important and worthy of respect and attention. Sybil was right, today had happened and nothing could take it away from her, nor stop her from achieving it again. She would be more than a shadowy figure behind the monarch, but a woman of accomplishment with a life of her own, even if she had no idea how she might achieve it.

Chapter Two

I am sorry to see all the trouble and anxiety . . . which reminds me of Louise a little. She is in some things very clever—and certainly she has great taste and great talent for art which dear Lenchen has not, but she is very odd; dreadfully contradictory, very indiscreet and, from that, making mischief very frequently.

—QUEEN VICTORIA TO HER DAUGHTER
THE CROWN PRINCESS OF PRUSSIA

Windsor Castle, February 1868

Mr. Rearden, the member from Athlone, intends bringing the subject before Parliament whether the government, out of consideration to her Majesty's health, comfort, and tranquility, and in the interest of the Royal Family and her Majesty's subjects throughout the empire, to advise her Majesty to abdicate in favor of his Royal Highness the Prince of Wales, or to introduce a bill for the purpose of establishing a Regency in the persons of their Royal Highnesses the Prince and Princess of Wales, in order to perform the duties incumbent upon the Sovereign during her Majesty's absence from the metropolis during these last seven years,'" Lady Churchill read from the *Morning Advertiser* to Mama and her women sitting in Windsor Castle's East Garden. Lady Churchill wore a black dress similar to Mama's and Lady Ely's, the rest of them attired in gray or mauve half mourning, giving the entire party the look of a murder of crows sitting on the lawn.

The tinkling water from the nearby lotus fountain became irritatingly loud in the silence greeting the article. Even Mama paused in her writing, and Lady Ely's face grew more pinched than usual. Louise kept her head bent over her sketchbook, practically choking on an unspoken *I told you so*.

"Parliament would not dare remove me. It is merely a few rabble-rousers eager to torment a poor, helpless widow." Mama rubbed the head of her black collie, Sharp. She was as in denial of the dangerous anti-monarch sentiments circulating among some MPs as she was of the bitter cold making everyone shiver. The Mexican revolutionaries had thought nothing of executing Emperor Maximilian last year, and with revolution brewing in France again, she was foolish to think it couldn't happen here.

"Would His Royal Highness accept the throne under such circumstances?" Lady Caroline Lyttelton whispered to Louise from where she sat sketching beside her on the stone bench. The round-faced blond was near Louise's nineteen years and had been a maid of honor for a mere six months before Lord Cavendish had proposed and she'd accepted. Mama had reluctantly accepted the coming end of Lady Lyttelton's tenure, irked as always at someone choosing a life and future of their own over slavish devotion to her.

"If it stopped a revolution, Bertie would leap on it, and

many would boost him onto it." Louise laced her fingers together and jerked them up, mimicking a groom hoisting a rider into the saddle. Lady Lyttelton laughed, breaking the steady rhythm of Lady Churchill's reading.

"Lady Lyttelton, as your service has not yet concluded, you will conduct yourself with appropriate decorum until your last day," Mama scolded from behind the small writing desk set on the gravel path between the topiaries. Sharp dashed off after a bird on the lawn.

"Yes, Your Majesty." Lady Lyttelton exchanged a weary glance with Louise, and both returned to their drawings.

Mama would order the birds to stop singing if she could. At least Lady Lyttelton had wedding plans and a future to occupy her. Louise smudged out her envy along with a line on the paper, selecting a thicker pencil from the case and adding a touch of shading to the crenellated parapets and Gothic windows adorning Windsor Castle's East Wing. Louise struggled through the deep cold to hold her pencil with her gloved fingers, refusing to abandon her drawing and endure the boredom making Lenchen nearly nod off where she stood behind Mama.

"Louise, assist Lenchen in preparing my letters," Mama commanded. "It is clear you need more occupation and fewer idle moments."

Louise closed her sketchbook and took the letters, envelopes, and sealing wax from a sallow-faced Lenchen.

"If you'd properly attended to your duties instead of constantly having to be asked, I'd be home with my children instead of here," Lenchen hissed.

"If you insisted on remaining home instead of meekly doing everything you're told, then you might be there." Louise snatched the envelopes out of her sister's hand while Lady Lyttelton continued sketching, pretending not to hear the royal tiff.

Lenchen returned to Mama in a huff, and Louise skimmed Mama's missives to Alice and Vicky before sliding them into their envelopes. There was no missing the scant mention of Louise's success before Parliament. One of the most important days of Louise's life had barely merited a few words, while the smell and congestion of London consumed pages.

"I received a lovely letter from the Duke of Argyll about his son, Lord Lorne," Mama announced as Louise struggled to heat the sealing wax over the candle Lenchen had set beside her. Mama abhorred warmth, convinced the bracing cold was best for her and everyone's health. She'd force them all out-side even on the coldest days, and only ever allowed meager fires to be lit inside, ones that failed to ease the pervasive chill. "The Marquess of Lorne has taken his seat as the Labor representative from Argyllshire in the Commons. A charming young man, don't you think, Louise?"

"I don't know him well enough to say." Louise pressed the royal seal into the hot wax. "I'm sure he's preferable to those old German pauper princes I met two years ago."

"On that we can both agree," Mama sniffed, indifferent to Lenchen's gasp of indignation, the only sound she was brave enough to utter in her husband's defense. Prince Christian of Schleswig-Holstein's only recommendations as a spouse for Lenchen had been his lack of money and responsibilities, and his willingness to live in England so Lenchen could remain in Mama's service. Louise would demand better when it came time for her to marry, and she intended to put that off for as long as possible, not ready to trade an imperious mother for a demanding husband.

"Lord Lorne is a great admirer of art," Mama added. "If only you would further develop your talents with the brush instead of sculpture. It is such a masculine art and I am not sure entirely suitable for a princess. I am of a mind to end your lessons with Mrs. Thornycroft and reengage Mr. Corbould to hone your oil painting skills."

Louise stilled the bronze seal above the wax, panic flooding her. Of all the mediums she'd mastered, none brought her the same joy and peace as sculpting. The movement of her hands and the full attention of her senses had eased the grief after Papa's loss. Engrossed in her work, it'd felt as if he were watching her and if she turned she might catch him standing behind her. His presence had of course been an illusion, but not the statues or the work. They were real and belonged to her alone. Losing them would sever the frail connection to the world she'd known before he'd died, the one where she'd been valued and encouraged to believe her life might someday have more meaning and purpose than being Mama's personal secretary. "Papa didn't think sculpting too masculine for me and always encouraged it. His time with Mrs. Thornycroft's father gave him the idea to employ Mrs. Thornycroft as my tutor, and allowed you to discover a delightful and talented sculptress."

Mary's statues and statuettes of horses, dogs, and Louise and her siblings and Papa filled every royal residence, but her position was no more guaranteed than any other royal servant's. Walter Stirling was proof of that. It hadn't mattered

how much the young tutor had done to help and encourage
Leopold, or how much Leopold had liked him. Walter had
been dismissed once Mama had taken a dislike to him, and,
much to her guilty shame, Louise had played no small part in
that unfortunate situation.

"Sculpture was dear Papa's favorite art form," Mama
mused. "He used to say he could sympathize with the sculptor in the fable who implored the gods to allow his work to descend from its platform." Mama's eyes began to glisten with
tears. "Every time I look at Mrs. Thornycroft's bust of him, I
wish it too."

Mama stifled a sob with the back of her hand and Lady
Ely handed her a black-edged handkerchief. Louise assumed
the same required sympathetic attitude as the others, but she
could almost hear their silent exasperation. Louise missed
Papa as much as anyone, but the last six years had softened
her pain. Mama enjoyed grief too much to relinquish it.

Mama dabbed her eyes with the silk, and handed it to Lady
Churchill. "You may continue your lessons because it is what
Papa would have wished, but I will end them if you display
more of the insolence of the Robing Room."

"Yes, Mama."

*The little statuette is really admirably modelled, and I
strongly advise you to continue taking lessons with Mrs.
Thornycroft as you certainly have great talent in mod-
elling, and may perhaps become some day an eminent
sculptress.*

—*Prince of Wales to Princess Louise*

"It's a fine piece," Mary Thornycroft praised Louise's bust of Arthur, Louise's younger brother. The Windsor Castle art studio was awash in late afternoon light that turned the gray clay a pale shade of goldenrod. With Mary's help, Louise had narrowed the bridge of Arthur's nose to make the image a truer likeness. "I'll arrange to have it sent to London and sculpted in marble."

"I wish I had the skill to do it properly, but I will once you teach me."

"I'm afraid you're reaching the limits of my instruction." Mary slipped off the cotton apron covering her dark gray frock, observing half mourning in deference to Mama's rules, the faint scent of her rosewater perfume filling the air.

"Impossible." Louise rinsed the clay from her hands in a ceramic bowl, worried by Mary's comment. "The daughter of a sculptor, the wife of a sculptor, an artist who exhibited at the Royal Academy when she was barely twenty-four years old must have more to teach me."

"There are better sculptors than me who could instruct you." Mary handed Louise a towel. "I must also consider my work. Her Majesty is a demanding patron."

"And your children need you." All five of them, and a husband whose sculpting career had not reached the heights of his wife's but who encouraged her because she supported them. Louise rubbed her fingers dry, the day she'd long feared much too close. "This morning Mama threatened to end our lessons."

"Perhaps Her Majesty has something better in mind for you." Mary took Louise's face in her hands, her long fingers rough and callused from years of working with stone and clay. She studied Louise with the same motherly affection Lady Sarah Lyttelton, the old governess, once had. Mary was everything Louise wished Mama could be but wasn't. "After our last lesson, I spoke with Her Majesty about enrolling you at the National Art Training School."

Louise jerked back. "You didn't."

"I did. I told her you're as gifted as Prince Albert, and how Mr. Millais and Mr. Boehm and other eminent men at the school could turn you into a first-rate sculptress."

"What did she say?" Louise twisted the towel between her hands in anticipation.

"She said she'd consider it."

Louise tossed the towel on the table. "That means she hasn't given it a thought since you mentioned it. She's certainly said nothing to me."

"Patience, Louise. You never know what image a stone will yield until you begin to work with it. This is no different."

"Mama isn't as malleable as marble."

"She isn't as hard as it either. Give it time. I believe Her Majesty will surprise you."

Louise shoved her spatulas, sgraffiti, and styluses into the pockets of the leather tool roll. "You're entirely too optimistic."

"A necessary skill for an artist, one you must develop if you hope to succeed in this brutal business. There are far more defeats than rewards."

"I'm not likely to have the chance to succeed. Mama would die of apoplexy if I dared to compete with professionals. Gift tables at family birthdays are the only places I'm allowed to exhibit."

"That could change if we find a way to convince Her Majesty to enroll you. The school will be honored to teach a member of the royal family."

Louise slowly spun the sculpting wheel, rotating Arthur's bust. She'd sculpted him in his Army uniform instead of Grecian robes, a classical rendering not right for a nearly eighteen-year-old young man obsessed with the military. Arthur was at the Royal Military Academy, Woolwich, pursuing his dream. Was it possible she might be able to pursue hers? "I don't want them to think I'm a bored princess in need of something to do, but a true artist."

Mary laid settling hands on Louise's shoulders. "Once enrolled, you can prove you're worthy of your place, but we must get you there first."

* * *

The scrape and tap of spoons against the side of soup bowls filled the Oak Dining Room. Lady Churchill, Lady Ely, and General Grey joined them for dinner, the clearing of throats or commenting on the weather the only acceptable conversation.

For once, Louise welcomed the quiet. The prospect of school had eased the gloom of Mary's departure, and not even assisting Mama with tedious government business had dampened it. She'd composed notes to ministers and foreign dignitaries while imagining attending classes and practicing new techniques. She'd dressed for dinner contemplating what she might learn from the professors and fellow students. They'd debate new movements, discuss their favorite masters and pieces, share new techniques, and perhaps even compete for places in the Royal Academy Exhibition.

Mama set down her spoon and the footmen sprang forward to whisk away the half-finished bowls of cock-a-leekie and replace them with plates of les filets de Soles à la Maréchale. Prince Christian softly grumbled at not being allowed to finish his soup. He sat across from his wife, both of them flanking Mama, who commanded the head of the table and fell on the next course with zest. He was thirty-seven, but Prince Christian's receding hairline and constant ennui made him appear much older. Life in Schleswig-Holstein must have been terribly dull for him to have willingly exchanged the boredom there for a life of pointlessness here, and Lenchen allowed it because Mama wished it.

That won't be my fate. Louise would find a way to convince Mama to send her to the National Art Training School.

"Arthur wrote to me," Leopold said from where he sat across the table from Louise, breaking the oppressive clink of silverware against the china. He was almost fifteen years old, with a smooth face, and a body nearly slender enough for the breeze to blow away. Mama hadn't allowed him to watch Louise from the Strangers' Gallery, afraid he might overexert himself and bring on another bleeding spell. He'd barely recovered from the last one that'd left him bedridden for nearly two months and still weak in one knee. "He wants to move into the barracks instead of living with Major Elphinstone at Ranger's House. It'd strengthen his camaraderie with his regiment."

"Certainly not." Mama handed a scrap to Sharp, who sat patiently beside her chair. "I will not have an innocent young man ruined by the Army's foul influence. Bertie's immorality in the barracks killed dear Papa. Imagine what Arthur's fall might do to me. That my children act against the values dear Papa instilled in them by debasing themselves with such common urges and people is most vexing."

"Leopold and Arthur are nothing like Bertie." Louise exchanged an exasperated look with Leopold, tired of hearing about Bertie's great downfall with the actress Nellie Clifden during his time with the Irish Guards, and his infecting Papa with the lethal typhoid. It wasn't typhoid that'd killed Papa, but something sinister that'd festered in his stomach for years. Louise didn't say so, as tired of that conversation as she was of black fabric, hushed voices, and the ever-present gloom. She also couldn't help but wonder if Mama's wailing about her children's vices behind their backs extended to her.

"We will not discuss the temperaments and temptations of young men." Mama motioned to Beatrice. "It is not an appropriate conversation for Baby."

"I'm not a baby," Beatrice complained, irritated at being denied more scintillating discussion than the weather. Mama kept the dinner conversation tepid, determined not to tempt Beatrice into wanting a husband, home, and children of her own someday instead of being Mama's old-age companion, a role the Queen had already earmarked for her.

"I should like to visit Arthur and watch him train with his men," Leopold pressed.

"The excitement would be too much for you, especially if they fire rifles or cannons. The explosions shatter my nerves whenever I hear them."

"A few days won't do any harm," Louise lightly suggested, trying to ease the tension growing as thick as the cold. It only made the air frostier.

"A few days could do a great deal of damage," Mama insisted. "He could have another bleeding attack or hurt himself on the training field. I won't allow it."

"What about what I want?" Leopold banged his fist on the table, making the plates rattle. Everyone stared wide-eyed at him, surprised at something interesting finally happening at dinner. "I need occupation, a purpose, a future."

"You will have no future if you rile yourself up and make yourself sick. Return to your room at once and think on it." Mama's hard glare killed the discussion.

Leopold threw down his napkin, snatched up his gold-handled walking stick from its place on the back of his chair, and rose, the hard bang of the tip against the floor telegraphing his anger.

"Louise, you will not encourage Leopold to endanger himself or contradict me again. As the mother of nine, I know better than you what is best for my children."

"Yes, Mama." Silence settled over the table as the fish course was removed and les croquettes à la milanaise was set before them. While the others gobbled their food, Louise pushed hers around the plate. If Mama wouldn't allow Leopold to spend a few days in Woolwich with Arthur, she wasn't about to send Louise to South Kensington for weekly lessons. Mama held the purse strings and the permission.

Thankfully, Mama decided to retire early after dinner. The sigh of relief from the ladies-in-waiting and General Grey was almost audible above the crackle of the grudgingly lit fire in the drawing room. Once they were free, Louise wound her way through the hallways and passages to the smoking room in the distant reaches of Windsor Castle. The masculine room was free of Mama's beloved knickknacks, and was one of the few places Louise could enjoy a clandestine cigarette.

The scent hanging in the air near the room tonight wasn't Prince Christian's cigars but the spicy aroma of Turkish tobacco.

"Bertie! I didn't expect to see you." Louise rushed into the room and threw her arms around her eldest brother. "Does Mama know you're here?"

"She asked to see Alix, so I left my wife to her after paying my respects." Bertie stepped out of her embrace, the cigarette perched between his thin lips trailing smoke over his dark blond head. He was thick in the middle and stocky, with a short beard along the line of his soft jaw. "Probably wants to lecture her about not enjoying life if she's with child again. Heaven forbid the old bat let that go. My boy is fine."

Mama still blamed Bertie and Alix for their first son's premature birth, convinced it was their high living that'd brought Alix to bed at only seven months.

"Once an idea takes hold in Mama's mind it's difficult to dislodge, it's why she insists she's weak and sick and simply waiting to die." Louise tucked a cigarette between her lips and accepted a light from her brother. She sighed at the first heady taste of the spicy smoke.

Bertie snapped the cigarette case shut and left it and the matches on the corner of the table for her. "You'd think a woman as resourceful as you could find a private corner in this mausoleum to exercise her lungs."

"The footmen smoke near the stables and are kind enough to allow me to join them, but it's too cold tonight."

"Don't let Lenchen discover your airings, or they'll come to an end."

"It's not Lenchen you have to worry about but Beatrice," Leopold warned as he strolled into the room, his light steps a contrast to their eldest brother's heavy ones. "She's far more scheming and overly indulged."

Bertie tapped the ash from his cigarette into a crystal tray. "If someone had explained coitus interruptus to Papa years ago, we might have been spared that little devil."

"Is that how you avoid complications with your mistress?" Louise dared.

"Really, you two!" Leopold's pale cheeks flared bright red, the color deepening the dark circles beneath his eyes.

"Someday you'll thank me for that bit of wisdom." Bertie's watch chain rubbed against the billiards table as he leaned over and cracked the cue ball with his stick, sending it sailing into the red striker ball.

"I thank you for the most ruinous conversation I've enjoyed in ages." Leopold rubbed his hands together in delight. "I'm not the prude or innocent Mama believes."

"Neither is our dear sister." Bertie handed the cue stick to Leopold, encouraging him to take a turn. "She probably knows more than you do."

"I doubt that."

Bertie and Louise exchanged dubious looks, silently deciding not to shock their younger brother. When every kiss and stolen moment with Walter had been fraught with the danger of discovery, she'd turned to Bertie for advice. She'd been too afraid to write to Alice, the sister she was closest to, who lived in Hesse, and risk Mama seeing the correspondence. It'd fallen to Bertie to comfort her, and ease her guilt after

Walter had been sacked. It'd been a foolish, girlish fling and the most wonderful summer of her life.

Leopold whiffed the cue ball, making it limp down the table.

Bertie chuckled. "Your playing has improved."

"Hard to develop any athletic ability when Mama treats me like a china doll." Leopold passed the cue stick to Louise, then dropped onto the brown leather sofa, settling the walking stick beside him, the motion pulling his trousers tight and revealing the bandaged knee beneath. "She's stifling me."

"You'll find a way out of this nunnery. Both of you will." Bertie looked at Louise, his mischievous blue eyes serious for once. "You aren't like Lenchen or Beatrice. You have too much spirit to remain under her thumb."

"I'm too sick to do it." Leopold sighed. "But there's nothing stopping Loosy from escaping."

"Except Mama," Louise said. "She clings to us tighter than Thames mud."

"She's surprisingly lenient with you." Bertie chalked the end of his cue stick. "As if she has a soft spot for your headstrong impishness."

"You've indulged in too many of these if you think so." Louise inhaled her cigarette.

"He's right, we're always amazed at what you can get away with," Leopold agreed. "After opening Parliament, I wouldn't be surprised if you have another plan in mind, something she'd never allow any of us to do."

"Marriage, perhaps?" Bertie arched one eyebrow at Louise.

"Heaven forbid." As curious as she was to enjoy more

of what she'd indulged in with Walter three years ago, she wasn't ready for the altar yet. "You of all people know marriage doesn't mean freedom." Bertie and Alix had their own household at Marlborough House, where they held balls and parties Louise wasn't allowed to attend, but their lives were still at the mercy of Mama's temper and whims.

Leopold leaned forward, elbows on his knees. "Then what is it, Loosy?"

She took a long inhale of her cigarette, debating whether or not to say anything, but if anyone could help her, it was them, and she'd need every ally she could cultivate if she hoped to succeed.

While Bertie and Leopold listened, Louise explained about the National Art Training School.

"A royal attending a public school has never been done," Leopold observed.

Bertie leaned against the table. "A bit plebeian, going to the masses, when you could have any tutor you want summoned here."

"To this mausoleum, where ideas wither for lack of life?" Louise crushed her cigarette in the crystal ashtray. "I want new techniques and energy, to make friends with people my age who understand art isn't a hobby but something I must do or I'll run mad."

Bertie shrugged, returning to his game. "I don't understand going about it that way, but I sympathize with needing to escape the old gal. I'll do what I can to help."

Louise selected another cigarette from his case. "I knew you would."

"How will you convince her?" Leopold asked. "She was

positively indignant about me visiting Arthur. She'll balk at you going to London to sit with the riffraff."

"I don't know." Louise lit the cigarette, then waved out the match. "How does one tell a queen, a woman ordained and anointed by God, what to do?"

"By convincing her it's her idea," Bertie suggested.

"I'm not that talented in flattering Mama."

He leveled his cue stick at her, as serious tonight as when he'd advised her not to tell Leopold about her relationship with Walter. "Then find someone who is."

Chapter Three

I have too much anxiety, too much worry and work, and
I miss Lenchen terribly as I can't speak *à coeur ouvert* to
Louise (though she does her best) as she is not discreet,
and is very apt to always take things in a different light
to me.

—QUEEN VICTORIA TO HER DAUGHTER
THE CROWN PRINCESS OF PRUSSIA

Windsor Castle, March 1868

Louise, Mama, and Lenchen worked quietly in Mama's
study. The cold breeze coming in through the open windows rustled the gold tassels on the red brocade curtains,
giving the room the chill of the grave. Lenchen struggled
through stiff fingers to grip the tiny brass key and unlock the
red-lacquered dispatch box on Mama's desk. It didn't matter
that they could see their breath, Mama refused to close the
sash or light the fire, relishing the cold. How the wicks in the
candles didn't freeze, Louise didn't know, but she thanked
heaven for the many layers of clothes protecting her from Mama's rabid need for bracing air.

They'd worked all morning on Mama's correspondence and official papers, Louise diligently doing her duty in the hope of currying Mama's favor. It'd been a week since her last lesson with Mary and there'd been no word about attending school and she hadn't dared broach the subject, she couldn't until she secured a few more allies and a touch more certainty about Mama's opinion, but she must hurry. The spring term began in April.

"I wish to give Lady Lyttelton a wedding gift," Mama announced, adjusting the spectacles perched on her nose. "A diamond broach, and a hundred pounds."

"But she's only been with you for six months," Lenchen protested.

"She is a flighty young woman, but she has served me well. Also, Bill the groom's mother is sick."

"The drunkard groom?" Lenchen asked.

"He is not a drunkard. The whiskey is merely for medicinal purposes. I have instructed Dr. Jenner to visit his mother at my expense. Please see he has everything he needs to treat her."

"Yes, Mama," Lenchen answered before opening a letter. "Lady Stanley has invited us to a tea party at the Westminster Abbey Deanery. She wishes to introduce us to a number of eminent writers and artists, including Mr. Thomas Carlyle, the historian, and Mr. Edgar Boehm, the sculptor."

Louise perked up. Mr. Boehm was one of the sculptors Mary had mentioned and whose work Louise had spent the last week studying. "How grand to meet such eminent men, and think what you can accomplish with a little effort and a great deal of reward. A ride in the royal carriage between

Paddington Station and the Deanery of Westminster will silence Mr. Rearden about you not being seen in London," Louise gently suggested. Mama had dismissed the failed abdication petition in the Commons, but others hadn't. Vicky had dashed off urgent letters to Louise on the necessity of urging Mama to appear in public. It was like forcing a mule down a rocky path it did not wish to travel, but she must try. "Instead of a strenuous public appearance, it's only a pleasant visit with an old friend."

"I suppose it is," Mama mused, pausing in writing her letter. "It has been too long since I enjoyed a chat with Lady Stanley. Why, at forty-one, she chose to leave my service and marry Dean Stanley, I will never understand. Lenchen, send our acceptance."

"Yes, Mama."

Thank heavens. Louise could write to Vicky that she'd successfully convinced Mama to appear in London. Then Vicky might stop pestering her about doing more to encourage her, as if Mama not going out were somehow her fault. One would think, with her husband's country to help manage, Vicky wouldn't have time to meddle in English affairs, but she did.

The clock on the mantel delicately chimed the hour. "Mama, it's time for your weekly meeting with Mr. Disraeli."

"Splendid." Mama removed her spectacles and laid them on the blotter, then rose. Sharp jumped to his feet from his place on the rug, ready to follow her. "If it hadn't taken Lord Darby so long to resign, I might have enjoyed Mr. Disraeli's company a great deal sooner, but some people cling to their positions with no thought for those coming up from behind. Louise, escort Mr. Disraeli to dear Papa's study."

Mama's inability to see she was doing the same to Bertie astounded Louise, but she held her tongue and left to fetch the new Prime Minister. She walked down the Grand Corridor, passing under the large skylight. The sunlight glinted off the gilded frames of the portraits and landscapes Papa had arranged on the walls, Louise and her siblings' works displayed beside those of Van Dyck and Sir Edwin Landseer.

"Your Royal Highness." Mr. Disraeli bowed when Louise entered the Crimson Room, with its red damask wallpaper and red curtains, and immediately noticed the butterfly pin affixed to her bodice. "It's an honor to see my humble gift adorning your radiance."

"I wear it every day as a reminder of your generosity and encouragement." He'd believed her capable of more than servitude, having joined Mama's ministers in convincing Mama to allow Louise to open Parliament. Hopefully, he'd come to her aid again.

He laid a hand over his heart, crushing his black velvet coat lapel. "I do everything I can to assist my friends in all matters."

"Good, for I'm in need of your help." She motioned him into a walk down the Grand Corridor, her heart racing with nervous trepidation. It was one thing to encourage Mama to do something she secretly wished to do. It was quite another to convince her to do something she was against. Mr. Disraeli understood the art of gentle persuasion better than most courtiers, and if anyone could convince Mama an idea was hers, it was him. "As you know, I am a sculptress."

"I've seen the pieces you've done for your family. They are impressive."

"They'd be more so if I could pursue additional studies at the National Art Training School." With each step they were growing painfully close to Papa's study. There was no time to beat about the bush.

He nodded sagely, his true thoughts, whatever they were, skillfully disguised. "A Royal Highness attending a public school is a unique, almost revolutionary idea."

"I was born in a revolutionary year."

"Perhaps this will be another."

"It will be if Mr. Rearden and his ilk have their way. My enrollment will demonstrate Her Majesty's high regard for her subjects and their institutions and disprove Mr. Rearden's accusations that she has scant regard for those she rules."

They stopped outside the closed door to Papa's study and Mr. Disraeli turned to her, considering the idea with all the seriousness he'd displayed while listening to her in the House of Lords. "A brilliant idea, Your Royal Highness, and at a time when we must safeguard Her Majesty's position. Rest assured, I will do everything I can to support you in this endeavor."

"I'll be forever grateful for your assistance." She led him from the bright light of the Grand Corridor to the somber shadows of what had once been Papa's study. A large marble mantel topped with a massive looking glass dominated the room, as did Mary's white bust of Papa resting on a pedestal between the door and the unlit fireplace. Louise rang the bell to announce their presence and Mama entered, her black dress swathing her full form, the lace of her white widow's cap fluttering slightly about her temples with her steady gait.

Lenchen walked the required few steps behind Mama and

remained at her left hand, stopping when Mama did in the center of the room beside Papa's bust.

"Lenchen, leave us." Mama rested one hand on the pedestal to remind Mr. Disraeli of who still held the reins of power. "Louise, you will stay."

Lenchen scowled at Louise as she left. She'd never been granted the privilege of attending a weekly meeting with the Prime Minister. Far from being honored, Louise felt her stomach tighten as she stood beneath Mr. Winterhalter's portrait of Vicky in her wedding dress. Mama probably had some penance in mind for Louise for her remark in the Robing Room.

"Your Majesty. I am your humble servant." Mr. Disraeli dropped to one knee, amazingly lithe for a sixty-three-year-old man. He clasped Mama's outstretched right hand, making her large rings clink together. "I hope to be as successful as you, especially in influencing the lives of your subjects. Your *Leaves from the Journal of Our Life in the Highlands* touched the heart of your people in a way that I, as a fellow author, can only dream of doing."

Mama's regal haughtiness faded into pleased flattery while Louise struggled not to roll her eyes. The family had been horrified when her Highland servant, Mr. John Brown, had convinced her to publish that ridiculous book about Scotland. Since then, they'd endured many nights of Lenchen reading aloud the glowing reviews, Mama's subjects gobbling up the tome with as much enthusiasm as Mama did her pudding.

"Her Royal Highness must have inherited her artistic talent from Your Majesty, who is as accomplished an artist as she is an author." He rose, motioning to Mama's oil painting of Balmoral on the far wall.

Mr. Disraeli's flattery lit Mama up like a Roman candle. "My dear Albert and I were both accomplished artists. Had we not been royalty, we would have excelled in one medium or another."

"Her Royal Highness, if given the opportunity, could excel in a manner to make Prince Albert proud, especially in a more public setting, a school perhaps where the talent first nurtured by the Prince Consort might truly shine and serve as an inspiration to others, especially naysayers in the Commons who think you have no care for your subjects or their institutions."

Mama glanced at Papa's bust. "Mrs. Thornycroft suggested enrolling Louise in the National Art Training School."

"An excellent choice of schools, Your Majesty, one I never would have considered, but I do not possess your superior insight into the matter. Her Royal Highness carrying on Prince Albert's dedication to the arts by honoring the very school he founded is perfect. His belief that art should lift up the common man and help improve his life was forward-thinking. Her Royal Highness could demonstrate to all the superiority of Prince Albert's beliefs while encouraging future artists through royal example."

Mama said nothing, studying Papa's marble face for some direction on what to think. Left without an answer, she did what she always did when something made her uncomfortable. She ignored it. "Mr. Disraeli, shall we proceed with affairs of state?"

"It would be a pleasure." Mr. Disraeli slid Louise an assured smile before resuming his flattery of Mama. He acted as if the matter had been settled, although it hadn't, it'd merely been presented, but Louise had caught the flash of pride in Mama's eyes when Mr. Disraeli had cleverly suggested the choice of schools was hers. He'd set the wheels in motion. Whether or not they continued to roll or fell off the cart remained to be seen.

> *Drove with Louise . . . to the Deanery at Westminster, where Augusta and the Dean met us . . . Went into the Deanery for tea, where, as last year, were assembled some celebrities . . .*
> —*Queen Victoria's Journal*

THE LUSH GRASS of the Westminster Abbey Deanery garden was crowded with Reverend Arthur Stanley's eclectic mix of guests. The lichen-pocked arches of the cloisters surrounded them, the walls dark from weathering and the choking London soot. It was a sunny day, but the usual haze muddied the sky. It was the single advantage to wearing mourning colors. The dreary fabric didn't easily speck in the city's ashy air.

Mama did not deign to mingle with the guests, but stood by a statue of Cupid in a niche in the Deanery wall while Lady Augusta Stanley brought people to her. Lenchen was content with the arrangement, but Louise wore the grass thin beneath her wide skirt from shifting on her feet. She wished to be off to meet the many interesting people, including quite possibly Mr. Boehm, assembled in the garden.

"The poet Mr. Robert Browning," Lady Augusta introduced, but the white-haired gentleman needed no introduction. Mama adored poetry and had insisted her children read it in the schoolroom. Louise, Arthur, and Leopold had preferred novels, secreting many, including Mr. Disraeli's *Venetia*, inside the pages of works like Mr. Browning's until Lenchen had caught them and told Mama.

"Your Majesty, a true pleasure." Mr. Browning bowed, his pointed beard nearly covering his cravat. Mama congratulated him on his newest poem, *The Ring and the Book,* and he returned the favor by offering effusive praise for *Leaves from the Journal of Our Life in the Highlands*.

While they puffed up one another, Lady Stanley joined Louise. "I have someone you must meet."

"What about Mama?"

"Mr. Browning will keep Her Majesty entranced for some time. Come with me."

Lady Stanley guided her toward the gentleman near the fountain who answered her motion to join them by closing the distance with a sturdy stride. He was tall and solid, his fine figure enhanced by a well-tailored suit of cream linen with a subtle brown stripe. His dark curling hair, parted to one side, was tamed but not forced into submission by pomade. A full chevron mustache graced his lips beneath his long straight nose turned slightly down at the end. He was a striking man of about thirty-three who walked tall and erect, his shoulders straight and head high. She wished she had her drawing paper and pencil box so she might sketch the cut line of his jaw and his wide shoulders. Instead, she delighted in watching him approach, trying to commit every detail of him to memory for sketching later.

"Your Royal Highness, may I present the sculptor Mr. Joseph Edgar Boehm?" Lady Stanley introduced.

"Mr. Boehm." Louise extended her hand, ignoring Lady Augusta's surprise at the bold gesture, especially with a gentleman. Louise didn't care. This professor of the National Art Training School must see her as a person, an artist, not a princess in need of something to do.

"Your Royal Highness." He took her hand, bowed, then straightened, the calluses on his palm rough against her kid gloves. He didn't fawn over her as Mr. Browning did with Mama, but stood easy and sure in her presence. "Mrs. Thornycroft told me of your desire to enroll in the National Art Training School. She was kind enough to show me your work. You have natural talent but you lack spontaneity and true insight into your subjects."

Louise pulled her hand back while Lady Stanley stifled an amused laugh.

"Should I thank or curse you for so frank an assessment?" No one outside the family had ever been quite this blunt with her, not even Mary.

"I wasn't lying when I said you have natural talent." He let out a long breath, the warm caress of it gracing her cheek and soothing her indignation. "My pupils and compatriots expect honesty, especially within the safety of the classroom where students learn to gracefully accept praise and criticism. You aren't likely to encounter it anywhere else, especially since your rank will increase praise and dampen criticism until you're uncertain if it's sincere. That uncertainty will make you doubt your work and success, and doubt will rob you of passion and dedication faster than anything I, a student, or a critic might say."

"I may not encounter it at all, as I have yet to receive permission to attend."

"That's why I'm here. Lady Stanley is a friend of mine. I asked her to invite me so we could speak."

Louise looked to Lady Stanley, who admitted her guilt with an unashamed tilt of her head. This excited Louise more than his candor had bemused her or his striking good looks intrigued her. "Assuming you believe me ready for the rigors of school."

"Any young lady who can stand before Parliament and risk their ridicule can handle the opinions of professors and fellow students."

She hadn't considered the other pupils and how they might take her. She was attempting to enter a world she knew very little about, and if the students were anything like their professor, it would keep her on her toes. "Her Majesty won't be so easily convinced."

"Perhaps an esteemed artist who can speak to the benefits of an advanced education might influence her." His plotting, scoundrel-like expression made her heart flutter and she gave as good as she got, peering up at him from beneath her full lashes.

"Then let's see what we can accomplish."

He held out his arm to her and she took it, tucking her hand in the crook of his elbow. He walked confidently beside her, the faint smell of his sandalwood shaving soap carrying over the sweet scent of the sun-warmed grass. It slid through her like the spicy smoke of a Turkish cigarette, and the night she'd first kissed Walter behind the Osborne House mews flashed through her mind. She opened and closed her fingers on his firm arm, shaking off the old memory. Mr. Boehm was nothing like Walter.

When they neared Mama, Lady Stanley hurried forward to escort Mr. Browning away, leaving the path open for Louise to introduce Mr. Boehm.

"Your Majesty, may I introduce the sculptor Mr. Boehm? He executed the excellent statue of Mr. William Thackeray you so admired."

Mama, still basking in the glow of her favorite poet, didn't notice Louise's hand on Mr. Boehm's arm, but Lenchen did. Louise yanked it back, immediately missing the solid feel of him.

"Your Majesty." He executed the required bow with the elegance of Mr. Disraeli, and the slight raise of Mama's eyebrows indicated she was impressed.

"Your homage to the great poet was moving, God rest his soul."

"*Er war ein guter Mann.*"

"*Sind Sie aus Deutschland?*"

"*Nein*, I was born in Hungary but raised in Vienna," Mr. Boehm answered in his perfect English. "My father was the Court Medalist at the Imperial Mint. I began my studies with him before I moved to London to attend Leigh's art school. I teach sculpture and modeling at the National Art Training School. It's a privilege to be accepted into the program, especially for lady artists. I understand Her Royal Highness is a sculptor. It would be an honor to nurture the talent of Prince Albert's daughter and an excellent chance to thank him for everything he did for the school."

"It touches the heart to know my dear Angel is so well remembered." Mama caressed the cameo of Papa pinned to the high collar of her black dress. "He had such grand plans for the school. If only he had lived longer, he could have accomplished so much more."

"Mr. Boehm's statuette of Countess Spencer has made equestrian statues very popular," Louise quickly mentioned, determined to keep the conversation on art and not Mama's endless grief.

"I'm flooded with requests for commissions," Mr. Boehm stated, far more subtle in his obsequiousness than Mr. Browning.

"I adore equestrian statues. Send samples of your work to Windsor Castle. Perhaps I will offer you a commission." Mama raised her hand for him to kiss, ending the meeting.

"It's an honor to be considered." Mr. Boehm bowed over her hand, then took the required steps backward and strolled away. Nothing more was said about the school or Louise's attending, and there was no time to discuss it as Lady Stanley brought Mr. Thomas Carlyle forward.

Louise watched Mr. Boehm make for the arched cloister. He paused, offering her a nod before disappearing into the cloister's long shadows.

"You should be flattered," Lady Stanley said once the eminent historian was entertaining Mama. "Mr. Boehm rarely interrupts his workday to attend a social event. He must have seen something in your art to have made an exception for you."

"He saw a chance to curry royal favor." There'd been no missing the interest in his stunning blue eyes when Mama had offered to consider him, and how quickly the conversation had changed from Louise's art career to his. "He won't give me a second thought after he sends Mama his work."

"He isn't so callous, and there's no harm in pursuing his interests along with yours, especially if it keeps the school fresh in Her Majesty's mind."

Louise hoped Lady Stanley was right.

MAMA'S INTEREST IN the tea party waned long before the sun. Everyone bowed as she walked through the garden escorted by Lady Stanley and followed by Lenchen and Louise. In the forecourt, a detachment of the Third Hussars in their deep blue-and-gold-braided coats waited with the royal coach to escort them to Paddington Station for the return train to Windsor. Lenchen and Louise held back as a footman handed Mama into the carriage.

"You shouldn't have been so familiar with Mr. Boehm," Lenchen hissed, taking a quick sip from a small brown glass bottle.

"You shouldn't drink so much laudanum. It isn't good for you."

"It's for my nerves, which wouldn't be strained if you did more work instead of foolishly trying to attend school, which Mama won't allow." She jammed the cork in the bottle and stuffed it back into her drab gray skirt pocket. "She said so after Mrs. Thornycroft first mentioned it, and she won't change her mind, no matter who presses the matter."

Lenchen took the footman's hand and climbed into the carriage, leaving Louise to step over the crater her comment had left behind. The effort to sit across from Lenchen and Mama and pretend all was well during the ride to Paddington Station was as overpowering as the London stench. Mama didn't notice Louise's taciturn stiffness. She was too busy avoiding being seen by the many people staring in disbelief at the royal carriage deigning to grace the streets or calling for smelling salts or a tonic to soothe her rattled nerves.

After a jostling journey, they entered the cavernous glass and iron of Paddington Station and walked to Mama's private railcar, passing the many people in other trains whose schedules had been delayed by the Queen's.

They boarded the royal saloon, Lenchen sitting on the velvet sofa by the window to sort Mama's papers while Mama sat behind her desk to resume her correspondence. Louise sat in a chair at the far end, perched her sketchbook on her lap, and furiously drew the Deanery garden and its guests, especially Mr. Boehm. He'd come to see her, but it hadn't mattered, nothing ever did unless Mama decreed it should. Tears of frustration and hopelessness blurred her eyes, but she blinked them back. She refused to cry in front of Mama or Lenchen.

"Mr. Boehm was a charming gentleman." Mama doused a letter with blotting powder and blew it off, the tart scent mixing with the locomotive's acrid coal one as it pulled out of the station.

Louise paused in drawing the sculptor's full mustache, surprised by the remark.

"If only he weren't so fanciful. Imagine, Louise attending school." Lenchen laid a plump hand on her bodice in mock astonishment. "A royal spending time with who knows what kind of people is hardly a fitting homage to Papa."

"It's very fitting. Papa always encouraged us to do common things, from cooking at the Swiss Cottage to growing vegetables. He didn't want us to be spoiled or to think too highly of ourselves." The gall of Lenchen to finally assert herself simply to undermine Louise.

"It would bring down the tone of our family and the monarchy."

"It will raise our standing and the school's, ensuring students flock to it and keep it alive, far beyond anything Papa could have ever imagined for it."

"Yes, it would." Mama caressed the cameo of Papa pinned to her high collar, having remained surprisingly quiet during this tête-à-tête. "Of course, Louise will not attend the National Art Training School."

The dictate given, Mama settled into her writing, too engrossed in her work to notice the passing countryside or Louise crumbling inside. Louise wanted to scream like the shrill train whistle, but she couldn't. All she could do was sit still, ignoring Lenchen's smug look, while the light of the tea party and Lady Stanley and Mr. Boehm's hope and encouragement wafted out of the carriage. Not even cheerful waves from the people they passed at each station were enough to lift Louise's spirit. She'd tried to escape the mourning and sameness of her life, and failed. There was nothing left for her but this endless, tedious boredom.

Chapter Four

Today is dear Louise's 20th birthday. She is (and who
would some years ago have thought it?) a clever, dear
girl, with a fine, strong character, and a very marked
character—unselfish, affectionate, a good daughter and
with a wonderful talent for art. She is now doing a bust
of me, quite by herself, which will be extremely good.

—QUEEN VICTORIA TO HER DAUGHTER
THE CROWN PRINCESS OF PRUSSIA

Windsor Castle, March 1868

What do you have in mind for your next piece?" Mary
stood with Louise in the cold, bright studio, the fresh
clay from London lumped on the turntable in front of them.

"I don't know." Louise stared at the shapeless mass, the
irritation, disappointment, and hopelessness of the last few
days since the Deanery tea dampening everything. It didn't
matter what she did next, or ever. She'd never be more than
Mama's servant, all her hopes and wishes trampled by the
royal heel.

"Enough moping about," Mary insisted. "You've faced a setback, every artist does. I refuse to allow you to give up before you've even begun."

"I haven't given up." She had, but she wasn't about to admit it to her esteemed tutor, who'd faced worse in pursuing her career and hadn't quit. Louise couldn't either, even if she couldn't see how this might end in her favor.

"Good. Then tell me what you intend for your next piece. You must keep going, and get used to working without me. We haven't much time left together."

"I don't want to think about that." Mary had agreed to tutor Louise until the beginning of April, when Louise would either start classes or be forced to carry on alone.

"Then think about your work instead."

Louise cleared her mind and focused on the clay, waiting for it to reveal the shape hiding inside, the one she'd reveal with her tools. Mr. Boehm had said equestrian statues were popular. Perhaps she could do one of her horse, Andrew, but she couldn't imagine shaping the clay into haunches and withers. A long minute passed as she tilted her head this way and that, waiting for inspiration to strike. When it finally did, it nearly knocked her off her feet.

"Mama. I'll do a bust of Mama." It was the last subject she wished to pursue, but the wisdom of modeling it came to her as strongly as the image. Louise could model Mama from life, study her every day if she wished, a privilege not even the greatest court painters or sculptors enjoyed, and she could use it to her advantage. "She likes nothing more than a flattering likeness, and I'll give her one. It'll keep the subject and my skills foremost in her mind and that might be enough to change it."

"YOU'VE REALLY CAPTURED the majesty of the old gal, Loosy." Leopold turned the clay-covered table around, and what little daylight remained mixed with the orange lamplight to give life and warmth to Mama's bust. "Except about the nose and jaw. They aren't right."

"They never are for me, but it doesn't matter this time. It can't be too perfect or she won't think I need more lessons." Louise had spent every free moment of the last week working on the sculpture. A sense of urgency drove her as much as the need to lose herself in her work. The spring term would begin in a few weeks and she must be there.

"When will you show it to her?"

"I don't know. It has to be the right moment or this is all for nothing." A noise outside the studio door made them jump. "Someone's coming. Quick, help me cover it."

Louise wasn't about to have whoever was sneaking about see it and ruin the surprise.

They grabbed the edges of a drop cloth and flung it over the bust, then hurried to the windows to pretend they were admiring the garden. A sheen of sweat spread across Leopold's forehead as he settled on the window seat, this slight exertion nearly too much for him. She handed him a handkerchief and he dabbed his forehead, stuffing the damp linen in his coat pocket as Beatrice stepped through the door.

"What are you two up to?" she demanded, Mama's imperious tone in her small voice.

"We're studying the garden for a sketch," Louise answered.

"Leopold isn't supposed to be exerting himself, especially with you. Mama said so, and I can tell you haven't been sketching, you have no pads and pencils."

"We said we're studying the garden, not drawing it," Leopold snapped. "What do you want?"

Beatrice peered about for evidence of an artistic bacchanalia or something salacious to tattle to Mama about. Louise didn't glance at the draped bust, unwilling to inadvertently draw attention to it. Beatrice paid it no mind, having spent enough time in art studios to think nothing of a covered work. Seeing little of interest, she crossed her arms in a huff. "You should be dressing for dinner."

"So should you." Leopold whipped up his walking stick and pointed it at the door. "Now get out before I summon Nanny and see you put to bed with no supper."

Beatrice stuck her tongue out at him and rushed back to wherever she'd come from.

Louise let out a relieved breath. "Why must she be so nasty?"

"She's too young to understand, but someday she will." Leopold trilled his fingers on the cane handle. "She'll want something Mama won't give her, probably a husband, and when we don't rush to support her, she'll regret having been so mean. I certainly won't help her, assuming I'm still here."

Louise didn't assure him he'd live to a ripe old age. Platitudes would cheapen the cruel reality he faced every time he hurt himself and the doctors couldn't stop the bleeding.

Leopold limped to the bust and slid off the cover. "In the meantime, I have an idea about when to show this to Mama."

"Do you intend to tell me?"

"All in good time." He twirled his walking stick, then strolled toward the door.

"Now who's the imp?" Louise yelled after him, receiving a laugh in reply.

"BEATRICE SAID YOU were dallying in Louise's studio instead of resting as you were instructed to do," Mama reprimanded Leopold as the footmen set the first course before them. It was a small group tonight, with only Mama, Beatrice, Lady Ely, and Lady Churchill seated with them. General Grey dined with his wife in their private apartments in the Windsor Tower. Lenchen and Prince Christian didn't join them either, Mama having granted them a rare evening at their home at nearby Cumberland Lodge. "You are not to visit Louise's studio again."

"I'm forbidden from sitting with my own sister," Leopold gasped.

"Sit with her somewhere else." Mama handed Sharp a bit of bread.

"Difficult to do, since she's only ever in her studio when she's not with you," Beatrice piped up. "Who knows what she's really doing up there?"

Louise wanted to jab her fork into the back of her sister's hand.

"She's working on a bust of Mama," Leopold announced, nearly earning a taste of the tines for ruining her surprise. Louise gaped at him in disbelief, but a subtle raise of his hand beside his plate urged her to trust him.

"A bust of me?" Mama set down her spoon, more interested

in the sculpture than in her soup. The pause allowed Lady Ely and Lady Churchill to savor a few spoonfuls instead of devouring them.

"It's a cracking piece. She meant it to be a surprise, but Beatrice ruined it."

"She did. Naughty Baby." Mama wagged a scolding finger at Beatrice, whose shoulders slumped at being reprimanded instead of praised for her effort to stir up trouble. Mama didn't care, her sour mood lifted by the flattery of the bust. "You will show it to me immediately after dinner."

"WHAT A SPLENDID surprise." Mama stood face-to-face with the clay image of herself. "Mrs. Thornycroft said you had advanced but I had not realized how far."

"I've done my best with your likeness, but it's still lacking. If you posed for me, I could perfect every detail, at least as much as my meager skills allow." Louise let the implication of how further studies might benefit Mama's edification hang in the air with the scent of old paints.

Mama touched one finger to her full chin, examining the gray features made warm by the bright lamplight. "A marvelous idea."

"WITH YOUR WORKS of Baby, Arthur, and me, you are becoming a regular Mr. Winterhalter," Mama mused as she sat for Louise, the late afternoon sunlight softening the lines around her mouth and jowls and bringing out the faint ruche and checked pattern of her black dress.

"Perhaps I'll convince your maids of honor to pose for me

and execute a work like his *Florinda.*" Louise leaned out from behind the bust, offering Mama a wry smile.

"You will do no such thing until you are a married woman." Mama laughed, imagining like Louise her maids of honor posed bare-breasted in the garden in imitation of the Winterhalter painting hanging in Mama and Papa's office at Osborne House. Mama's laughter faded as she relaxed deeper into her chair, a whimsical expression spreading across her face. "I adored sitting for Mr. Winterhalter, it was as natural with him as it is with you."

Louise paused in smoothing the arch of Mama's cheek, enjoying this rare tenderness. Their posing sessions over the last week had been a pleasure. The brief daily respite from her duties relaxed Mama and softened her acerbic tongue. They'd discussed watercolors and oil paints and where they might sketch during their walks at Balmoral this fall. "You posed so many times for him you were accustomed to him."

"No, it was something else, an ethereal quality not all artists possess, and I have sat for enough to know." She trilled her fingers on her stomach. "It is why I chose him for the secret picture."

"The one with your hair down in Papa's writing room?"

"Yes. We had to be secretive so Papa would not find out and spoil the surprise, but he did not suspect a thing. He was so accustomed to Mr. Winterhalter painting me, he thought nothing of us cloistered together. You should have seen his face when I unveiled it on his birthday. He always said it was his favorite portrait of me." There were no tears or wailing or black-edged handkerchiefs but the warmth of happy memories. It brought a light to Mama's expression and changed the shape of her features. Louise worked quickly to capture it and the long-forgotten youth it lent to Mama's face. This was the Mama she remembered from her childhood, the one who'd smiled and enjoyed life, the mother who'd risen from an uncertain and lonely childhood dominated by Grandmama and Sir John Conroy to inherit a throne and the adoration and responsibilities of the world. This was the woman Louise would commit to stone. "Papa's face used to light up as yours does when you are engrossed in your art. You have a passion for it none of the others do. Oh, they enjoy it and have their talents, but it seizes you the way it used to Papa, as if you must do it as one must breathe."

"I must," Louise admitted with cautious honesty. "I can't live without it, as you can't live without your letters and journals."

Mama nodded. "May I see it?"

"Of course." Louise set down her tools and Mama came to stand beside her.

She studied the bust for some time, and Louise picked at the clay beneath her nails, awaiting and dreading her reaction.

"It has been a long time since I have seen that face," Mama said at last. "If dear Papa were here, he would say talent should be properly cultivated. You have a great deal of it, but Mrs. Thornycroft is right, you need more training." Mama turned to Louise, not as a queen giving a dictate but as the mother who used to delight in sharing her art with Louise. "I will instruct General Grey to enroll you in the National Art Training School. I cannot spare you for more than one day a week, and you will not stay overnight in London. You will return to Windsor after your lessons."

"Oh, Mama, thank you!" Louise threw her arms around her, careful to keep her dirty hands from leaving marks on Mama's black dress.

Mama patted her on the back, then stepped out of the embrace. "There will be rules, of course. When you are in London, Lady St. Albans will chaperone you to and from Paddington Station, and your lessons must not interfere with your official duties to me and the country. Despite your disappointment as a personal secretary, I need you when Lenchen is unavailable, especially since Baby is still too young for such things."

"I'll do everything required of me, I promise. You won't regret sending me to school."

Mama eyed her up and down. "We shall see."

Chapter Five

To you, dearest child, who have a husband and who have many relations your own age (I have none or only those who are useless) this feeling of dreadful loneliness can never arise as it does with me, who see even my own children one after the other have divided interests which make me no longer the chief object of their existence . . .

—QUEEN VICTORIA TO HER DAUGHTER
THE CROWN PRINCESS OF PRUSSIA

National Art Training School, South Kensington, London, April 1868

Mary escorted Louise up the wide, airy National Art Training School Ceramic Staircase. The colorful tiles lining the overhead arches and walls lent the staircase its name and promoted the works of the school's ceramics department. Light from the high windows illuminated the many men and few women coming and going from lessons on the first floor or the South Kensington Art Gallery and refreshment rooms on the ground floor. Some stopped and gaped at

Louise as she passed, while others tilted into awkward bows. They'd read the announcement of her enrollment in the Court Circular but they were as amazed as Louise that it was real.

She was here, at last.

Louise returned each disbelieving stare with a wide smile and nod, further shocking everyone. "I wish they'd forget I'm a princess and simply treat me as one of them."

"They won't, but with time and diligent work they'll come to view you as a fellow student and artist," Mary assured her.

"Not if the faculty insists on fawning over me." The last hour had been more tedious than exciting. The headmaster, Mr. Richard Burchett, and a number of senior professors, including Mr. John Everett Millais, had gathered in Mr. Burchett's office to welcome her. They'd presented her with a leather art satchel embossed with her initials and a number of welcome speeches. Mr. Boehm hadn't been there, but she'd see him soon enough. His was the first of the two classes on Fridays she'd enrolled in. The other was Mr. Burchett's afternoon drawing class, chosen more for convenience and to honor the headmaster by allowing him to teach royalty than for instruction, but Louise hadn't argued. No doubt, like many eminent artists, Mr. Burchett hoped to acquire a title from Mama in exchange for his loyal service. Louise didn't care and hoped he received what he wanted. She was thankful to simply be here.

"This is the room." Mary stopped before a frosted glass and wood door and faced Louise as her tutor for the last time. "There's a new world waiting for you inside."

"How can I ever thank you for everything you've done for me?"

"By achieving great things." Mary rested her hand on the doorknob. "Are you ready?"

"I am." She adjusted the stiff leather case strap where it bit into her shoulder, feeling as if she were leaving a piece of the past behind with Mary.

"Good luck." Mary opened the door and Louise entered the classroom alone.

All conversation ended the moment she stepped over the threshold. Men of various heights and weights sitting at easels arranged in a crescent around the front of the room rose to their feet at the arrival of a woman. The same ominous silence she'd faced in the House of Lords greeted her again, as did curious looks and outright disdain from at least two of the gentlemen. Clearly, not everyone was thrilled by her presence. How these people would ever see her as more than a royal interloper, she didn't know.

A lone woman in a russet-colored frock at the front of the room stood out among the somberly suited and mustached gentlemen, her presence as jarring as it was welcome. Louise wouldn't be the only female in class, but her rank had forced the woman to rise, widening the already substantial gulf between them.

Louise made for the open seat beside the young woman, set down her supplies, and held out her hand. "I'm Her Royal Highness Princess Louise. It's a pleasure to meet you."

The woman's dark brown eyes went wide, as did those of the others around them. The woman wasn't much older than Louise and wore her dark hair in a tight braid at the back with soft curls brushing her temples, her square face softened by full cheeks and the fall of black bangs across her forehead.

She studied Louise with more kindness than the gentleman in the ill-fitting brown suit occupying the seat on Louise's other side. He glared at Louise with a chill more cutting than the April cold permeating the stone room.

Louise's hand hung awkwardly in the air while everyone watched and waited for the woman to set the tone for their treatment of Louise. Louise waited too, willing her palm not to sweat and nearly heaving a sigh of relief when the woman finally grasped Louise's fingers with a firm shake. "Miss Henrietta Montalba. Welcome, we're glad to have you here."

A snort from the male student on Louise's other side informed her not everyone shared Miss Montalba's sentiment.

"Not Mr. Anthony Montalba's daughter?" Louise asked, ignoring the man.

She let go of Louise's hand, astonishment lighting up her eyes. "The very one."

"I'm familiar with his work." Louise arranged her supplies on the easel the same way Miss Montalba had arranged hers, then took her seat. "I read his *Fairy Tales from All Nations*. It's an insightful book."

The sucking sound of shock from everyone nearly curled the end of Louise's drawing paper. If they were stunned by her reading scholarly books, they'd be a great deal more shocked when they saw her truly work.

Louise was about to say more when the door opened and Mr. Boehm walked in. The students rose in respect and Louise joined them, drawing more curious glances from those amazed by someone of her rank paying homage to a commoner. It was another stark reminder of her position and theirs, one she must bridge if she hoped to make friends.

Mr. Boehm strode to the front of the room, a commanding presence in a navy-blue suit that deepened the blue of his eyes. They were hooded but straight, and quite serious, with no hint of the shine they'd held at the Deanery. He studied his pupils as one might a piece of jewelry before purchasing it, businesslike, serious, especially when he stopped between Louise and Miss Montalba.

"Your Royal Highness," he greeted with a bow, nothing of the spritely humor he'd exchanged with her at the Deanery in his manners today.

"Miss Saxe-Coburg-Gotha, if you please," she politely corrected. "I wish to be treated like any other student."

"So you shall be." He took his place at the front of the room beside a cloth-draped bust, his curtness jolting but not surprising. He certainly hadn't been shy with his opinions at the Deanery. "Good morning, I'm Professor Boehm and this term I'll instruct you on sculpting in clay, marble, and terra-cotta, which is popular in Paris and most likely foreign to most of you. We'll begin by studying various pieces from the South Kensington Museum's art collection. Let's see who they've loaned us today." Professor Boehm flicked off the cloth to reveal a marble bust. "Pope Clement XII by Edmé Bouchardon. Sketch."

A chorus of rustling papers filled the room before fading into the quiet scratch of pencils against paper. Louise followed the other students' lead and drew the bust.

"Monsieur Bouchardon has captured the drape and fold of Pope Clement's skin as well as his mozzetta, giving the stone life and personality." Professor Boehm spoke in a clear, strong voice that carried through the high-ceilinged room as he moved from easel to easel inspecting each student's work. "Realism is in the details of both the clothes and the human form. Focus more on the muscles and structure of his face, Mr. Waterhouse."

"Yes, sir," the handsome young man with the light brown hair and full cheeks near the back of the room answered.

"Sculptors must have intimate knowledge of sinew and muscle and how it shapes the skin, body, and appearance."

Louise studied the drop and swag of the skin under the cardinal's eyes, struggling to replicate it faithfully the way her former art tutor William Leitch had taught her. He'd drilled her on technique until she could draw a landscape exactly as she saw it. He was so unlike Edward Corbould, who'd encouraged flights of fancy with portraits and vistas.

"A faithful reproduction, Miss Saxe-Coburg-Gotha," Professor Boehm noted from behind her.

"Thank you." She sat up straight, basking in the compliment and the earthy scent of sandalwood that mingled with the lingering tang of linseed oil hanging in the air.

"But it lacks life, unlike Miss Montalba's portrait." He nodded at Miss Montalba's sketch, and she humbly sat back to offer Louise a better view.

"Her understanding of how muscle and sinew give a face its form is clear, as is your deficiency in the subject. I recommend you study anatomy books, German ones are the best. They'll help fill the gaps in your education."

"Yes, Professor Boehm."

He moved on and Louise frowned at her sketch, finally understanding why she'd failed to correctly sculpt Mama's cheeks or Arthur's nose. She'd enjoyed the best art tutors but none of them had dared to offer more earthy training, no doubt at Mama's insistence. It'd be a struggle to secure anatomy books without Mama discovering it, but she must.

"All of you should study anatomy, even if you believe you already have a firm grasp of it," Professor Boehm announced. "When we draw from life in a few weeks, it will be invaluable in correctly rendering the naked human form."

Nearly everyone's pencils stilled, including Louise's.

"Certainly you don't mean for us to study from life in a mixed class," gasped the mustached man near the back who'd sneered at Louise when she'd first entered.

"I do, Mr. Allen. You can't miss this important aspect of your training because you're squeamish. For those of you with sterner constitutions, let's discuss the hollow of the cardinal's cheeks."

Louise struggled to concentrate on Professor Boehm's instructions, more worried about Mama's reaction to drawing nudes than correctly capturing the shadows giving the marble face its features. If Mama learned of it, she'd yank Louise from school faster than Beatrice from a marriage conversation. Mama's spies were spread about the household and one could hardly receive a letter without Mama hearing of it. Hopefully, no one here had been recruited to report on her. Even if they had been, she would enjoy this for as long as she could.

"Practice, study, and work to master your skills, cultivate the deep desire for art that comes from your soul so when accolades prove elusive, you have the strength and purpose to continue," Professor Boehm directed near the end of class when every easel held a near-complete drawing of the cardinal. "More artists give up for want of success than lack of natural talent, which all of you possess, but an artist who doesn't cultivate them or the necessary work ethic will see those with lesser gifts and more determination outpace them. The better you become, the more opportunities you'll have, including a chance to exhibit at next year's Royal Academy Exhibition. Do you intend to submit a piece for consideration, Mr. Morgan?"

"I do, sir," the stocky, blond young man seated beside Mr. Waterhouse replied.

"And you, Mr. Harbutt?"

"Yes, sir," the man beside Louise answered with great determination.

"And you, Miss Saxe-Coburg-Gotha?"

"Yes, Professor Boehm."

"Good." The slight rise of the corner of his lip beneath his mustache said more than that single word.

"Royal advantage helps," Mr. Harbutt grumbled loud enough for most of the class and Louise to hear.

Everyone looked at Louise as if expecting her to yell "Off with his head." She'd done nothing to earn Mr. Harbutt's ire, but she'd gain nothing by answering him back. She left the disciplining to Professor Boehm.

"The privilege of royalty will not carry one to success, it will merely blunt the critics who aren't as brave as Mr. Harbutt in offering an unvarnished opinion of royal aspirations," Professor Boehm responded.

Now she very much wished for a head to roll, but she drew on years of royal training to hide her silent simmering. What was he about, encouraging her at the Deanery, then allowing Mr. Harbutt to mock her in class? If Professor Boehm didn't treat her well, then the others wouldn't either, and all hope of making friends would end before it'd even begun. She would tell him so after class.

Outside, the many London church bells began to ring the noon hour.

"That is all for today," Professor Boehm announced. "We will resume our discussion of draping and body structure next week." Professor Boehm strode out of the classroom, not sparing anyone, not even Louise, a second glance.

So much for speaking with him.

The students gathered up their things and filed quietly in twos and threes out of the room.

Mr. Harbutt pelted her with more glares while he packed his worn supplies into a tattered art case before joining Mr. Allen. "I heard Mrs. Thornycroft convinced Mr. Burchett to waive the prerequisites."

"I wish I had such influence, but we aren't all so fortunate," Mr. Allen added before they slipped out the door.

Louise pretended not to hear them as she slid her new pencils and crisp drawing paper into the art case from Mr. Burchett. She'd bring her battered old case next week, along with her chipped and smudged sketchbooks and pencils. She needn't rub her rank in her classmates' faces.

"Ignore them. They're jealous of you," Miss Montalba encouraged.

"It's true. The entry requirements were waived."

"You aren't the first student to be granted an exception. You won't be the last."

"Apparently Professor Boehm shares Mr. Harbutt's opinions."

"I'm sure he had a good reason for not rebuking Mr. Harbutt's rudeness. Professor Boehm can be curt, but he isn't cruel."

"Simply honest."

"To a fault." Miss Montalba laughed, and Louise couldn't help but smile. "It's his way of weeding the serious students from the hobbyists. Those who can't take his criticism or learn from it don't last long."

"I see. Thank you for the encouragement, and the advice."

"Of course. Lady students must stand together. I mean, well . . ." Miss Montalba adjusted her high lace collar, flustered like many others who'd met Louise and treated her as they would anyone else before remembering their place and hers.

"Yes, we must. I look forward to our next class."

"Until then." Miss Montalba dipped a curtsey, then hurried off, falling into step with Mr. Waterhouse and Mr. Morgan, the easy rapport between them obvious and enviable.

The door closed behind them and Louise sat on her stool, thankful for and hating the quiet. For all the morning welcome, no one, including her, had given a thought to what she might do between classes. Mary was gone, Mr. Burchett's class was not for another hour and a half, and Sybil wouldn't arrive to ferry her to Paddington Station until after it was over. She could go downstairs and sketch in a gallery or eat at one of the museum's three refreshment rooms, but she didn't relish sitting alone and pretending the other students didn't notice and whisper about her. She could invite Mr. Burchett to join her, but it'd encourage his fawning and only prove to people such as Mr. Harbutt she was here because of who she was instead of what she could do.

"I don't need to eat, not when I can work," she announced to the cardinal, unpacking her things and attaching another piece of drawing paper to her easel. Discipline at the dining table had staved off the Hanoverian stoutness that stalked her family. It would help her prove to everyone she deserved her place here.

Chapter Six

You will find that as children grow up that as a rule children are a bitter disappointment—their greatest object being to do precisely what their parents do not wish and have anxiously tried to prevent . . . Most extraordinary it is to see that the more care has been taken in everyway the less they often succeed! And when children have been less watched and less taken care of—the better they turn out!! This is inexplicable and very annoying.

—QUEEN VICTORIA TO HER DAUGHTER
THE CROWN PRINCESS OF PRUSSIA

London, May 1868

I've been reading anatomy as you suggested, Professor Boehm," Louise said while he studied her half-finished statuette of the young female model sitting at the front of the class. During the last four weeks, Dr. Ellison, the most discreet and liberal-minded of Mama's physicians, had lent Louise his anatomy books and given her a few clandestine lessons. He'd promised more thorough instruction once Mama left for her spring holiday in Switzerland at the beginning of June.

"You've progressed, but you still have a long way to go." His faint praise given, Professor Boehm moved on to inspect Mr. Waterhouse's work.

Louise wanted to stomp her foot in irritation the way she did after one of Mama's backhanded comments, but she settled into sculpting instead, shaping the terra-cotta on its wire frame and enjoying how quickly it molded into the fall of the model's dress. The model had the fresh look of the country about her instead of the pallor of the city, and she was, thankfully, fully clothed.

"Have you studied nude models before?" Louise whispered to Miss Montalba. Over the last four classes, they'd moved from sketching to modeling, but today was the first time the model was alive. As Professor Boehm had informed them, it would not be the last. Louise wasn't quite ready for the shock of a naked model.

"I have, and in mixed company," Miss Montalba whispered back. "The trick is to act as if nothing is out of sorts, as if the person you're sketching is little more than a Greek statue. Show any hint of discomfort, and others will seize on it and make things worse."

"You mean . . ." Louise inclined her head toward Mr. Harbutt, who studied the sagging terra-cotta on his frame, perplexed and frustrated by its refusal to mold to his will.

Henrietta nodded with a wicked smile, then returned to her work, leaving Louise to hers until the London church bells rang the noon hour.

"Dismissed." Professor Boehm hung his smock on a peg by the door, then left as he always did. Louise had long abandoned the idea of speaking with him about Mr. Harbutt and

Mr. Allen, who'd been no more welcoming after four weeks than they'd been the first day. It made some classes as much an exercise in patience as in sculpting. What the others thought of her she didn't know. No one besides Henrietta ever spoke to her.

"Is Professor Boehm always in such a hurry?" Louise fidgeted with her tools, the opportunity to sculpt between classes uninterrupted by Mama or official demands a welcome blessing. It took the sting out of having no one to meet and nowhere else to go.

"Professor Boehm keeps to an exact schedule. It's why he's so prolific. No dillydallying for him like Mr. Whistler and others. Do you intend to stay behind and work again this week?"

Louise rolled a lump of wet terra-cotta between her hands, feeling a fool for being caught out. "I do."

"May I join you? Professor Boehm said you might appreciate the company and some tutoring in applying anatomy to your works, or we could simply, as he said, enjoy a nice female chat."

"So he does have a sense of humor and a care for his students."

"More than most professors, especially those set against female education." Miss Montalba sat on her stool and waited until they were alone in the room to speak freely. "Artists can be such a jealous lot, especially men when it's a woman or someone from an artistic family succeeding. It's why Mr. Harbutt is so surly with you. You and I have connections to future patrons. He doesn't, and it's hard going for him. It always will be."

"Mrs. Thornycroft never warned me of this." She'd rarely spoken of her career, outside of the high points.

"Perhaps she didn't wish to discourage you. She's had it worse than most, with her success eclipsing her husband's and gaining royal favor, but she has the support of her family, which, like ours, have encouraged her."

"Mama isn't as enthralled with my attending school as you believe." She shouldn't admit this, but something about Miss Montalba's easy manner inspired the intimacy.

"You're in good company, then. Many ladies' families see no benefit in their education, even those enrolled in the female teaching school, Miss Saxe-Coburg-Gotha."

"Louise, please."

Her brown eyes, so dark one could not see the difference between the pupil and the color, widened and then settled into a cheerfulness that reminded her of Sybil. "Then you must call me Henrietta. While we work, I'll tell you what happened at Mr. Whistler's last Show Sunday."

"Show Sunday?"

"Artists open their studios on the Sunday before a show to preview their works to friends and patrons. People attend for the gossip as much as the art."

"I'd love to hear about it." There was more than anatomy Louise needed to learn, but a whole world she'd caught glimpses of and longed to enjoy.

They worked for the next hour and a half before leaving their pieces to dry into half-finished faces and hair. Tonight, the students who worked to help pay their tuition would throw them out, and next week they'd begin again.

"Thank you for joining me, and all the grand stories."

"It was my pleasure." Henrietta slipped her leather art case over her shoulder and encouraged Louise into a walk as students for the next class began to file in. They split into two rows lining the center aisle. Louise smiled to the gentlemen who made clumsy, awestruck bows to her.

"Have you seen the Royal Academy Exhibition?" Henrietta asked once they were in the hallway.

"I have not."

"You must. This is the last year it'll be at Trafalgar Square. Take special note of Mr. Leighton's *Ariadne Abandoned by Theseus*. It's breathtakingly poetic."

"I'll do all I can to see it, but I'm expected in Woolwich this week. Mama has donated my bust of Prince Arthur to the Military Academy."

"How exciting to have them accept it. I have yet to have a work displayed."

"With Her Majesty offering, they didn't have a choice."

The Cadets possess a splendid library, consisting of two large and handsome reading-rooms, stocked with books . . . On the walls hang several fine portraits, among them those of the Queen and the late Prince Consort, presented by Her Majesty. In a niche, prettily arranged among the book-shelves, stands the well-executed bust of H.R.H. the Duke of Connaught. What makes this work of art still more dear and interesting to the present and future generations of Cadets is the circumstance that it is almost entirely due to the clever chisel of the Prince's lovely, amiable, and high-gifted sister, the Princess Louise.

—*The Graphic*

"THE ROYAL MILITARY Academy is honored to receive this bust of Prince Arthur, newly commissioned lieutenant of the Royal Engineers," General Sir David Wood, commandant of the Royal Military Academy, Woolwich, announced to a polite round of applause. After watching Arthur graduate and put his fellow cadets through their maneuvers, Mama, Louise, Leopold, Lenchen, Arthur, and a select number of dignitaries had withdrawn to the school library for this small unveiling.

"A splendid piece from a fine sculptress whose talents rival those of Donatello or Bernini," General Sir George Pollock complimented Louise once the official event ended and the guests had splintered into small groups in the library and the adjoining reading rooms.

"You are far too generous." *And absurd to suggest I'm on par with Italian Renaissance masters.*

"It was my idea to donate the piece to the school," Mama announced, drawing all attention away from Louise and back to her. "I felt it a fitting memorial to my beloved Prince Arthur's time here."

"Quite right, Your Majesty." The generals fell over themselves to further ingratiate themselves to Mama, quite forgetting Louise.

"Smile, sister, you're a success," Arthur congratulated when she slipped away to join her brothers. Arthur was dashing in his blue uniform with the red stripes and gold epaulets, a sword and scabbard at his hip. "Everyone is singing your praises."

"They're praising my rank, not my work." The first flush of excitement when the marble had been revealed to applause had faded along with her pride in her accomplishment, exactly as Professor Boehm had predicted at the Deanery. "How do you do it, Arthur? How do you prove to everyone, including yourself, you've earned your honors, not had them handed to you?"

"I don't. You'll never silence their doubts, only yours, and you do it by working harder and longer than everyone so you know, deep down, you've earned every accolade."

"You sound like my sculpting professor."

"He's a wise man."

"A vexing one too, ready to toss me to the wolves in class one moment and encouraging Miss Montalba to help me the next. I can't tell if he likes or loathes me. Heaven knows what the rest of them think." No one else had joined her and Henrietta to sculpt after class and fewer still said more than two words to her. "The treat me like a curiosity instead of a fellow student."

"They're afraid to approach you. They think you're above them, sitting around in court dress and jewels, eating off gold plates, and looking down on them," Leopold said with a bitter snort. "They don't realize our chains are gold, not our plates."

"Chin up, old man," Arthur encouraged. "You'll get your turn with Oxford, then you can agonize like Loosy over your fellow classmates."

"If they're anything like this crowd, it'll be dreadful." Leopold spat with the unvarnished opinion of a younger sibling. Since their arrival, Leopold had been forced to mingle with the cadets and senior officers, the gap between them obvious. They were students, MPs, and military men who enjoyed life in a way Leopold had yet to do.

Mama motioned for Arthur to join her and General Sir David Wood. "Excuse me, I'm being summoned."

"Can't even talk to our brother without Mama stepping in," Leopold grumbled when Arthur left. "Everything depends on her whims, and those change as fast as the breeze. So, you plan to continue lessons despite everyone not fawning over you?"

"A bad day there is preferable to most here, and it's the first time in a long time I've had something real and grand to look forward to instead of endless days of boredom."

"At least one of us has the chance. I wouldn't place too much store in those classes, if I were you. They won't last."

"You're quite the sour grapes today."

"Because I love nothing more than watching my brother and sister get the things I want while I get nothing." He tapped the end of his walking stick against his shoe, and Louise couldn't fault him for being angry. It was the truth. "I've had a letter from Walter."

Louise remembered her onetime love and how besotted she'd been with him. She hadn't thought of him for some time, too focused on her studies to think of much else. However, it didn't ease the guilt making her stays beneath her gray brocade dress embroidered with roses grow quite tight. "How is he?"

"Holidaying in Scotland. I don't know what he sees in the dreadful country."

"He loves it." He'd been the only bright spot that summer at Balmoral, a respite from grief as he'd whispered to her behind the mews of how clever and talented she was.

"I still can't understand why Mama dismissed him, especially since she still pays him."

"Who told you that?"

"Walter, although he never said why."

"You know how generous Mama is with servants, even the ones who displease her." Or she was purchasing his silence with a stipend, meaning she knew about her and him, but Louise wasn't certain and she wasn't about to ask. "She's more generous with them than us."

"Especially the ones who please her. Look how she fawns over that brute Mr. Brown."

He motioned to the tall Highlander standing in his gray kilt at attention near Mama, her favor for him the only reason a man of his low station who always reeked of whiskey was allowed to remain in her employ. "Yes, she does, and too much."

Her devotion to Mr. Brown had sparked disgusting rumors of him being the Queen's stallion. Without repeating the stories, for no one was brave enough to tell them to Mama, Bertie and Alice had tried to warn Mama about the dangers of favoring Mr. Brown. She'd refused to listen, flying into a fit instead and wailing about Mr. Brown being the only person devoted to her happiness. What Mr. Brown was devoted to was gaining everything he could by coddling and fawning over Mama. His service to her, whatever it comprised, had raised him to great heights and foisted him on all of them. However, if the ugly gossip was true, it meant Louise wasn't unique in seeking pleasure and freedom in the arms of a commoner. Of course, Mama would never see it that way, as she never saw Mr. Brown wavering on his feet from too much whiskey or how rude and nasty he was to everyone. She only ever saw what she wanted.

* * *

"On Friday, Your Majesty and the Prince of Wales, are scheduled to visit the H.M.S. *Galatea*. The Friday after, you both will review the troops of Aldershot, and the Friday after is the laying of the foundation stone for St. Thomas's Hospital," General Grey read from his diary. He, Mama, Louise, Lenchen, and Leopold sat in the saloon car, using the train ride from Woolwich to Windsor to review their schedules. General Grey sat on the velvet sofa, back stiff with the regal bearing of a military man, his mustache short and well groomed, with a splash of white where it curved down to meet his short beard.

"Alix is too ill to join us. Louise will accompany us in her place," Mama decreed.

Louise jerked up her head from where she bent over her diary. "Fridays are my art lessons. I can't miss three weeks of classes."

"I can attend in Louise's place," Leopold offered.

"Certainly not. It is too exerting on your delicate system." Mama rolled her rocker blotter with the pink blotting paper over her fresh entry.

"Perhaps Princess Beatrice or Princess Christian may take Princess Louise's place so as not to interfere with Her Royal Highness's schooling," General Grey gently suggested. He was one of the few who dared to gently push back against Mama. If more people did that, they'd all be a great deal better off.

"No. Since Louise constantly insists I appear in public, she can assist me at the events."

"Might I visit the Royal Academy Exhibition to make up for my absence from class?" Louise asked.

"No, there is too much to arrange for my trip to Switzerland to spare anyone to organize a formal visit."

"If you didn't insist on an entourage of sixty people and packing your desk and bed, there might be less to arrange."

"You are very impertinent today. Be thankful I am leaving you in England instead of insisting you do your duty as my companion. General Grey, Lenchen, let us review the dispatch box."

With a sympathetic glance to Louise, General Grey joined Mama and Lenchen in attending to the official papers.

Louise huffed to the back of the saloon to join Leopold where he sat with his leg resting on a stool. His knee had swelled after a morning on his feet. She fell into the chair beside his, flipped open her drawing pad, and furiously sketched a picture of Arthur on the parade ground.

"I told you she'd ruin your classes," Leopold whispered. "This time it's for no other reason than spite. Who knows why she'll do it next time?"

"I won't let her take this from me." She touched the butterfly pin on her bodice. "If she insists on my attending Friday events, then I shall, and I'll make sure she doesn't ask me again."

Princess Louise may be styled the beauty of the Royal Family. She has regular features, an agreeable expression, a fair skin . . . and an elegant figure, which shows none of the Guelph tendency to "spread out." Her smile may be said to light up her face. The disposition of Princess Louise is serious, but her manner is not grave, and

she keenly relishes fun, wit, or humour . . . the Princess
has distinct individuality of character.

—*Fifeshire Advertiser*

LOUISE STEPPED OUT from behind the curtains, and the
massive crowd in the large pavilion housing the St. Thomas's
Hospital foundation stone burst into wild applause. She followed the crimson carpet to the canopy of state where Mama,
Bertie, Lenchen, and Prince Christian stood waiting for her.
She had to focus on every step and not falter, barely able to
hear the people over her beating heart. They'd warmly welcomed the others, but there was no mistaking the heightened
cheers for Louise in her green moiré gown with the silver
edging, its soft emerald sheen shining even in the diffused
light. Louise risked Mama's fury by showing her up like this,
but she had no choice. She couldn't allow Mama to interfere
with her schooling more than she already had over the past
two weeks. After today, Mama wasn't likely to force her to attend another Friday event for quite some time.

Louise climbed the three small steps to the dais and took
her place in front of her gilt chair, a veritable bird of para-
dise beside Mama in her black crepe and Lenchen in her
deep mauve. All Mama's complaints about the crowd straining her delicate nerves vanished as she glared, healthy and
quite composed, at Louise. Louise had contrived to leave for
the ceremony from Marlborough House with Bertie, prevent-
ing Mama from seeing her dress until this moment. The coal
hardness of her eyes told Louise she was angry.

Instead of shuffling, chastened, to her place, Louise held

her head high, raising thunderous applause each time she waved at the crowd.

"Well done," Bertie whispered when Mama joined the president of the hospital at the foundation stone. The president addressed the crowd with the usual formalities while Mama stood beside him like a silent crow. "You'll catch hell for this."

"Not this time, or she'd have to admit they're cheering for me and not her. She might even end half mourning to dismiss my dress. Whatever she does, she won't include me in many upcoming events for fear of it happening again." For the moment, she was safe from Mama's interruptions.

Chapter Seven

I envy you having been to Naples, such a beautiful place,
I should give anything to see it. We have such dreadful
cold weather here again . . . it must be charming weather
with you now.

—PRINCESS LOUISE TO PRINCE ARTHUR

London, June 1868

Heaven knows how they'll take me after missing the last
three classes," Louise worried as Sybil's carriage carried them from Paddington Station to South Kensington. For
all her triumph in the Pavilion, and the many nasty stingers
she'd received afterward, she'd been right. Mama hadn't as-
signed any more Friday appearances for Louise before leaving for Switzerland. While Mama was on holiday, Louise
would enjoy six weeks of freedom. Mama had even allowed
the servants to discard their black mourning armbands and
for Louise and her sisters to abandon half mourning. Louise
had visited her ladies' tailor at once, ordering a slew of new
dresses in dusty rose and sapphire-blue, and a host of practical frocks and aprons for the messy work of sculpting. How-

ever, the new dresses couldn't shield her from Mr. Harbutt's or Mr. Allen's venom. They were sure to gnash their teeth at her return and she didn't expect Professor Boehm to silence them.

"Miss Montalba will be pleased," Sybil assured her as the carriage rolled to a stop in front of the school. "It can't be easy being the only female."

"I hope so, or I'm back to sitting by myself between classes."

"Before you go, here are the cigarettes you asked to have my man purchase for you." Sybil removed a tin from her reticule and handed it to Louise, who tucked it in her art bag.

"Whatever would I do without you?"

"Endure Lady Ely as a chaperone."

"Heaven forbid." Louise took the footman's hand and stepped out of the carriage.

The warmer June weather had taken the chill off the school hallways, but not Mr. Harbutt and Mr. Allen's faces when she entered the classroom.

"Welcome back," Henrietta greeted when Louise reached her seat. "I thought you'd given up on us."

"If it weren't for my official duties, I'd never miss a class." Louise set her things beside the table with the turning wheel and clay.

"Students who consistently miss classes aren't usually allowed to return," Mr. Harbutt reminded, brave enough to state what many others were probably thinking. "They take places more dedicated students might enjoy."

"Then I must work harder to catch up."

Mr. Harbutt snorted in disbelief, then returned to setting out his tools.

Louise, determined to ignore him, slid on her smock, arranged her things, then perched on her stool to study the model seated on the dais at the front of the class. The dark-haired man with a strong face wore a flowing Naples-yellow dressing gown secured by a sash. The antimony color highlighted the rich olive tone of his skin, and the silk draped his crossed legs, ending at his bare feet and skimming his thin toes. Dark, curling hair framed his long face and sharp cheekbones, giving him the appearance of Leonardo da Vinci's *St. John the Baptist*. Louise imagined sculpting him with a shepherd's crook in a rough sheepskin garment.

"Good morning, students." Professor Boehm's voice rang out from the back of class. "Allow me to introduce our model, Mr. Antonio Corsi."

Mr. Corsi rose and performed a theatrical bow as Professor Boehm came to stand beside him.

"Some of you see Mr. Corsi and think him a saint or shepherd. Don't. Never mistake a sitter's initial pose for a true likeness. It's a façade they adopt for their benefit and yours. Wait for them to relax into their true self. Hone your portraiture skills so when the revelation comes you're quick to capture it." Professor Boehm turned to Mr. Corsi. "Take your position."

"Yes, Mr. Boehm." Mr. Corsi rose and tossed aside his robe with the flourish of a Covent Garden actor.

He was stark-naked beneath.

Louise sat rigid in her chair, forcing her cheeks not to flush and her hands to remain in her lap and not rise to shield her eyes. He slid one foot in front of the other, then twisted his torso, curving his arms out like a discus thrower on an ancient Greek vase. The light from the windows highlighted the ripples of his stomach, the smooth expanse of chest, and his taut thighs and arms. Louise immediately understood why he'd been chosen for today. His form was exquisite, so much so she could barely breathe.

He could have warned me. She hazarded a glance at Professor Boehm, who didn't spare her a look. Perhaps it was for the best he hadn't sent word to her and risked Mama or Lady Ely finding out and spoiling everything.

Beside her, Henrietta sat as outwardly composed as the other students, all of whom must have known about today. Louise would've too if she hadn't missed so many classes, but she had and it no longer mattered. There was nothing to do but face it; after all, it wasn't the first time she'd seen a man in such a state. Except she and Walter had been alone in the Osborne House outbuilding, the thrill of his chest beneath her fingers as exhilarating as the risk of being caught. She hadn't been sitting in a room full of gentlemen.

"Sculpt," Professor Boehm commanded, and the clink of tools drifted through the room.

Louise took up her metal spatula and, willing her fingers to stop trembling, began shaping the rough outline of Mr. Corsi's body. She worked the clay into curves, her first shapes rough and awkward, but with each movement of her hands and the tools, she drifted deeper into the place where nothing existed except the model and her emerging statue. The hour ticked by, the squeak of turntables and the occasional clearing of a throat mixing with the faint noise of London. Not even the familiar fall of Professor Boehme's shoes on the floor, his subtle voice as he offered students advice, disturbed the steady progress of her sculpting.

She regularly studied Mr. Corsi against her likeness of him and corrected where needed. He was an excellent model, so steady in his pose that nothing about him changed until nearly an hour into class. The shift was so slight she thought she'd imagined it, but he was no longer the Greek discus thrower but a young man saved from poverty by the unique set of his features and his talent for remaining still. The muscles of his legs stiffened a touch and his tobacco-stained fingertips trembled ever so slightly.

Without thinking, Louise removed the tin of cigarettes from her bag. She set a cigarette between her lips and lit it, the sulfur flash making everyone pause. She walked up to the dais, took the cigarette out of her mouth, and placed it in Mr. Corsi's, holding it so he could inhale. At once the muscles in his thighs relaxed and his fingers stilled. She offered and withdrew the cigarette as Mr. Corsi needed, ignoring how close she stood to the nude man and tapping off the ash until there was little left. She stubbed it out on a nearby piece of marble.

"Thank you, Your Royal Highness." A faint Italian accent colored Mr. Corsi's words.

"My pleasure. I know how hard it is to hold a pose for so long. I've done it many times."

Louise turned to resume her work and stopped at the gape-mouthed shock of her classmates.

She traced the embossed tobacco leaf on the tin, inwardly kicking herself for publicly revealing her shocking habit in the most scandalous way imaginable. She hadn't intended to blatantly flounce convention, simply to offer Mr. Corsi much needed relief.

She squared her shoulders, ready to take on whatever criticism Mr. Harbutt or Professor Boehm tossed at her when she saw the faint flicker of respect flash through Mr. Morgan and Mr. Waterhouse's eyes. Even Mr. Harbutt betrayed his silent and grudging respect before he hid it behind his usual sneering disdain.

Louise strode to her seat, tucked away the cigarettes, and took up her tools, unwilling to further distract the class. Professor Boehm came up behind her and watched her work, his presence making her more nervous than how close she'd stood to the nude Mr. Corsi. At the faint inhale of breath before he spoke, Louise's neck muscles tightened and she braced herself for a rebuke. Mama was right, she was too impertinent for her own good.

"You've seen the man beneath the pose, Miss Saxe-Coburg-Gotha. Well done."

He moved off to review Mr. Harbutt's work and Louise smiled in coy triumph.

"YOU MADE QUITE an impression on everyone today." Henrietta took a deep inhale of her cigarette and slowly exhaled the smoke. They sat beneath a tree in the far corner of the school and museum garden, enjoying the fine weather before Mr. Burchett's drawing class. The headmaster was always late, giving them no reason to hurry. Louise needed the calming smoke to get through the rest of the day as much as Mr. Corsi had needed it to hold his pose.

"I hope they're impressed enough not to mention it to the papers." Her enrollment and what little freedom she enjoyed would vanish if they did.

"They won't rat you out and risk missing another stunning story. Artists are a gossipy lot; they love a tale as much as a new movement. But they're also discreet. If they weren't, half of them wouldn't be able to live the way they do."

Louise was about to ask how some of them lived when Mr. Morgan poked his head around the tree. "There you are."

"We've been looking for you." Mr. Waterhouse dropped on the grass beside Louise, who tucked the cigarette tin beneath the wide hem of her blue skirt. He slid her a wicked smile. "You aren't fooling anyone, not after that show in class, but don't worry, I won't breathe a word about it to anyone."

"None of us will," Mr. Morgan assured her.

Henrietta flashed an *I told you* so look as Mr. Waterhouse fished a pack of cigarettes out of his pocket and offered her one.

"You're contributing to the corruption of a princess, Mr. Waterhouse," Louise said.

"Nino, please, it's what all my friends call me. I do hope we can be friends."

"Most assuredly." She leaned forward to light her cigarette on his match, rewarding his boldness with a glance from beneath her lashes and raising a slight flush along the line of his high cheekbones. He was her age, with brown hair, a high forehead, and a full pointed beard. He wore a camel-colored suit with a matching waistcoat and trousers. She sat back, drawing her lips into an O to exhale the smoke. Walter had said this made her already full lips even more alluring.

The appreciative look in Nino's dark eyes told her Walter was right.

"You can call me Mr. Morgan. It doesn't seem right to be so informal with a princess."

"As you wish, Mr. Morgan," Louise teased, raising a blush along his hairline at even this informality.

Nino flicked out the match. "Professor Prinsep has invited a few of us around to Mr. Whistler's studio this afternoon. They studied together in Paris and are quite chummy. We promised to bring you along."

"What about Mr. Burchett's class?" Louise ended the flirting. There could never be more than friendship between her and any of these gentlemen and she should never suggest otherwise, either to them or herself. There was nothing but heartache down that path, as she'd discovered with Walter.

"Skip it. You'll learn more from Mr. Whistler."

She shouldn't, but she couldn't miss the chance to see the artist's studio as a student without the protocol of a formal visit, and Mama was too far away to stop her today. "It sounds grand."

THEY FOLLOWED PROFESSOR Prinsep and some other students through South Kensington to Mr. Whistler's No. 7 Lindsay Row house and studio. Louise walked with Henrietta, Nino, and Mr. Morgan. A great deal of gentle dissuasion had convinced Professor Prinsep not to dance attendance on her during their stroll.

"Mr. Whistler is unconventional, but there's no mistaking the Paris influence in his art," Henrietta observed from beside Louise. "But he understands our need to develop a native style."

"Odd for an American to be concerned about British style," Nino replied.

"He's been here so long I think he considers himself British," Mr. Morgan said.

A wife in a smart bonnet cocked a curious head at Louise as she passed, certain she recognized her but dismissing her because of the humble company. Louise did nothing to encourage a second look, enjoying the anonymity.

"Miss Montalba, grand to finally see you again." A young man in a slate-gray suit jogged up beside Henrietta, breathing heavily from his rush to catch them. He leaned across her to examine Louise, and she stood up taller, enjoying the attention and giving him a great deal more to admire. "Introduce me to your friend."

"Your Royal Highness Princess Louise, may I introduce Mr. Mark Rogers?"

"Blimey." The young man nearly tripped as he tilted into a bow before Henrietta's firm hand on his arm stopped him. "While she's in school she is simply Miss Saxe-Coburg-Gotha, which you'd know if you hadn't missed Professor Boehm's class. Where have you been?"

"In Middlesex with my brother. He needed help finishing a commission and Professor Boehm thought I'd learn more with him."

"Mr. Rogers's brother is a sculptor and his father a woodcarver," Henrietta explained.

"Then you have the advantage of natural talent, Mr. Rogers," Louise complimented.

"So do you, Miss Saxe-Coburg-Gotha," Nino complimented. "I've never seen a student handle a model like you
did Mr. Corsi. You even impressed Mr. Harbutt. It'll give him
something to think about when he's cleaning classrooms tonight."

"Poor dear." Louise was genuinely sorry for him.

"Suffering improves one's art," Mr. Morgan added in his
thick northern accent.

"So does consumption, but no one wants that," Mr. Rogers
said.

"Mr. Morgan, are you a sculptor?" Louise asked, eager to
encourage more of this easy rapport with her fellow students.
It was the first time they'd treated her as one of them.

"I'm a medalist, and Professor Boehm is one of the premier
men to learn medaling from. Like you, I want as much of Professor Boehm's blunt and insightful criticism as I can get."

"He does lay it on thick, doesn't he, Miss Saxe-Coburg-
Gotha, especially with you?" Nino sympathized.

"I've been assured it's a necessary part of my studies."

"Here we are," Professor Prinsep announced as he led them
through the wrought-iron gate and front garden of the stately
three-story house. It wasn't at all the garret studio she'd expected, but the house of a gentleman.

"Prinsep, you've brought me guests." Mr. Whistler, a monocle tucked into his right eye, rose from his easel, tugged off
his smock, and tossed it over the chair. He worked before a
white sheet draped on the far wall above a white fur carpet. A
woman in a long, shapeless white frock stood in front of it, her
deep red hair bright against the pale background.

"Your Royal Highness, may I present Mr. James McNeill

Whistler?" Professor Prinsep introduced. At the mention of Louise's name, the model fled into an adjoining room.

"I'm honored to welcome you to my humble studio." The young American with his harsh r's and dark, curling hair, the blackness of it marred by a small tuft of white above his forehead, bowed to Louise with all the lack of reserve of his fellow countrymen. He was short, only an inch or two taller than she and at least a head smaller than the other gentlemen but his personality filled the room.

The other students waited patiently for their turn with the noted artist, one or two of them crossing their arms in indignation at being overlooked in favor of royalty, but there was nothing Louise could do except return the greeting. There were few places for them to sit while they waited, with more packing crates and boxes than chairs and settees strewn about the room.

"Thank you so much for allowing me to come and view your breathtaking art." She motioned to the painting of a woman at a piano, her young daughter resting her arms on it, her white dress a contrast to the severity of the black instrument.

"The talk of the 1860 Royal Academy Exhibition. 'A fresh breath of color in an otherwise dreary exhibition year,' Mr. Millais called it, but it's an old work. These are my most recent ones." Mr. Whistler escorted her to a set of paintings of a bay with boats and docks hanging on the far wall. They were done in muted colors and lines, the images painted as if seen through a heavy fog, a representation of the images rather than a true likeness. "I painted these while I was in Valparaiso."

"Was the air as poor there as it is in London?"

"It was perfectly clear. It's a new style I'm experimenting with. We'll see what the critics, especially that scalawag William Rossetti, think of it."

"He won't like it, Mac." Professor Boehm's deep voice carried over Louise's shoulder, raising an unexpected chill along the back of her neck as he walked into the studio. "He can't stand the new styles."

"None of them can, the dodgy old fogeys. But I'll make them see there's more to art than Greek gods and old wars. Art for art's sake, I say. No need to shove meaning or a history lesson into every canvas."

"Perhaps the others would enjoy hearing of it too." Louise motioned to those quite forgotten by their host. They uncrossed their arms, surprised Louise had spared them a thought.

"You're right, how rude of me. If you'll excuse me. I leave you in Spuch's capable hands."

Louise arched an eyebrow at Professor Boehm. "Spuch?"

"A nickname from our time at the École des Beaux-Arts. Mac said it's the sound of wet terra-cotta hitting the floor."

"I'll drop some next week and see if he's right, assuming you don't have another surprise in store for me. You should've warned me about today's lesson."

"That was the lesson. You entered cold and conducted yourself with exceptional professionalism, and compassion. *Gratulation.*"

"*Ich danke ihnen.*" She continued their conversation in German, glancing about to see if anyone understood them, but they didn't. Most here spoke French, but German offered

them a touch of privacy. "And Mr. Harbutt's constant belittling, which you never stop?"

He shrugged, far from chastened. "Insults are part of every
artist's life. The more accustomed you become to them in the
safety of class, the less they'll sting when you enter the larger
art world, where backstabbing and petty quarrels are practically their own movement."

"It appears I have a great deal more than technique to
learn." She peered up at him through her lashes, but far from
raising a boyish blush, it increased the unyielding intensity of
his gaze, tempered by amusement.

"Everyone does."

"I suppose it becomes easier with time."

"No. It simply becomes different, quite possibly harder, but
it's as necessary as studying the old masters in Italy."

"An experience I have yet to enjoy. I want to go, but I can't
visit anywhere without Her Majesty's permission, and she refuses to holiday in Italy. She says the air isn't good for her
frail constitution. She's as healthy as the horses you model.
I'm sorry, I shouldn't have said that. Mama tells me I'm impertinent. Sometimes she's right."

"You aren't impertinent but honest, and don't apologize
for wanting independence, everyone does. My father was the
Court Medalist at the Imperial Mint in Vienna. He expected
me to follow in his footsteps. If he hadn't been such a tyrant,
I might have worked with him, but I couldn't bear him ruling
my life."

"There's no escaping a queen."

"We all have our rulers, especially artists who bow and
scrape to patrons and create what the market demands or

starve. My portraiture is on the verge of dominating my trade; until then, equestrian statues are a must."

"I saw the pieces you sent Mama for review, they're exquisite."

"They aren't my first passion, as I'm sure opening factories and attending the Queen's Drawing Room aren't yours."

"No, they're not."

"You'll find your freedom someday, Miss Saxe-Coburg-Gotha. I'm certain of it." He brushed a dried fleck of clay off the sleeve of her royal-blue peplum over the straight skirt. His featherlike touch was barely perceptible through the layers of cotton, but she felt it. His callused fingers with their clean nails lingered on the sleeve, the skin white against the dark fabric before he lowered his hand. "Perhaps it won't be in sculpting, but sketching or painting."

"Those don't settle me the way sculpting does. I crave the activity."

"There's meditation in the physical work, a kind of letting go of one's cares and troubles and being free for that few hours of work that no other art offers."

"Yes," she breathed. Not even Mary had understood this ephemeral aspect of her art. Work for Mary was a necessity, not a means to escape, she was too happy with her life to want to run from it, but Professor Boehm knew. It was there in his deep blue eyes as he listened and silently encouraged her to continue. "Everyone thinks my life is nothing but balls and palaces. They don't see the restrictions and loneliness, the endless days of nothing. This is the first time I've been around people my age who share my passions and treat me like a person instead of a princess."

"It's because you treat them like equals, not subjects. Mr. Corsi couldn't stop talking about your kindness. He didn't expect it from you; most don't."

"Did you?"

"I did, and I look forward to seeing the great things you'll achieve once you learn to use your advantages instead of seeing them as a hindrance."

"If only it were so easy."

"Time, maturity, and patience will help."

"Has it helped you?"

"Time and patience have helped, but I'm still waiting for maturity."

Louise laughed, drawing the attention of many others in the room, including Mr. Whistler, who hurried to them.

"Spuch, you've had Her Royal Highness to yourself for long enough." Mr. Whistler held out his arm to Louise. "May I escort you in to lunch?"

She was reluctant to relinquish Mr. Boehm's company, especially with the charming gentleman she'd met at the Deanery replacing the stoic professor. She longed to experience more of this gentleman, but Mr. Whistler was her host and she couldn't be rude.

She tucked her hand in the crook of Mr. Whistler's arm and allowed him to lead her to the dining room. "You're as bold as your signature."

She pointed to the painted butterfly in the corner of a large portrait of the redheaded model hanging outside the dining room door.

"We are all butterflies with our art." He motioned to the

butterfly pin on her dress. "We begin as ungainly, chubby caterpillars and eventually blossom."

"We do."

The dining room, with its large table in the center and mismatched chairs, was as much a studio as the rest of the house, with canvases in various stages of completion resting against the walls. Louise sat beside Mr. Whistler at the head of the table, Henrietta at her other side, and Mr. Boehm at the far end. She relished the vigorous conversation over cold meats, buckwheat pancakes, and cheap wine, doing her best to keep up with the conversation. Their talk of artists and movements enthralled her, but she listened more than she spoke, too unsure of her opinions to express them.

When the conversation turned to Mr. Whistler's time in Paris, she roared with laughter at his tales. Mr. Boehm joined in the gaiety, laughing as heartily as the others when Mr. Whistler told of eating his French landlady's goldfish because she'd served too many fish dinners. If Louise hadn't seen so much of the stern professor in class, she never would've believed this Mr. Boehm the same man.

One person who remained elusive during the lunch was the redheaded model.

"Where's the woman who was here when we arrived?" Louise quietly asked Henrietta. "Mr. Whistler doesn't seem the kind to ostracize his models."

Henrietta plucked her napkin from her lap, then laid it back down, smoothing out the wrinkles. "Miss Hiffernan resides with Mr. Whistler, but they're not married."

"I see." She glanced at Professor Boehm. He rested his elbows on the table, his fingers laced beneath his chin, studying her as a man does a woman and not an artist his subject. There was danger in his rich blue eyes, not the kind to crush a woman but to sweep her away. She turned back to Mr. Whistler, laughing at his story about his failure as a West Point cadet, but always aware of Mr. Boehm. She didn't dare acknowledge him again. He was her professor, not a superior specimen of a man, and if she thought otherwise it might undo everything she'd worked so hard to achieve. There could never be anything more than a professional relationship between them.

Chapter Eight

E. Boehm . . . did more for modern art, than any one of
the day. If you remember . . . it was dull heavy and bad
classic, he was the first almost to introduce life and ac-
tion into his work, also it . . . should be shown by you, the
Queen, what you thought . . . I feel sure you will wish all
done to show and honor . . . E. Boehm . . . and his great
talent as much as you appreciated his works . . .

—PRINCESS LOUISE TO QUEEN VICTORIA

National Art Training School, July 1869

To Professor Boehm, and another successful term." Nino
raised his glass.

"To Professor Boehm." Everyone saluted Professor Boehm,
who sat at the head of the table of students enjoying the Grill
Room's weak wine.

After the visit to Mr. Whistler's studio last year, and the
many times they'd returned since, Henrietta, Nino, Mr. Rogers, Mr. Morgan, and Louise had become quite chummy. Every Friday they came down from the school to the Grill Room
to enjoy the tradesmen's lunch of poached eggs, spinach, and

a bun, Mr. Wilson, the maître d', reserving their usual corner table for them beneath the stained-glass windows depicting the great heroines of classical Greece. Today, Louise treated them to roast beef in honor of the end of a successful year. She would've held a dinner for them somewhere more elegant, but Mama still refused to allow her to remain in London after classes. Over the last year, she'd used the lunches, and a number of absences from Mr. Burchett's class, to cultivate friends and visit as many artists' studios as possible. Henrietta had been right. None of them had ratted her out to the press or Mama, preferring her company and acquaintance to a newspaper story.

"Thank you, Mr. Waterhouse, for the gracious compliment." Professor Boehm leaned back in his chair, his suit jacket unbuttoned to reveal the waistcoat cut tight to his slender waist. "I regret the end of another term, especially since you've decided to abandon sculpting for painting."

"Nino, you didn't tell us. How naughty of you," Louise scolded.

"Alas, the canvas calls to me more than the stone, but don't worry, my dear Miss Saxe-Coburg-Gotha, you won't be rid of me so easily." He winked at her, still the lothario. She would miss him.

"Good, for I'm in need of a model for an imp."

They broke into hearty laughter and students at surrounding tables paused in the middle of hand gestures or sentences to look at them before returning to their conversations. Their disinterest in her was a far cry from those awkward first few weeks a year ago.

"I'll miss this at Balmoral," Louise said to Henrietta, breathing in the lively atmosphere as deeply as the scent of chops from the plate-warming room. Blue and white majolica tiles decorated the bottom half of the walls and rimmed the dark wood fireplace. The tiles had been painted by the National Art Training School female students, who'd been honored to have their work so prominently featured. The craftsmanship was remarkable, and when Louise finally had a home of her own someday, she'd commission tiles from those women. "I wish I could stay in London or take you all with me. It's so dreary in Scotland."

"Don't worry, I'll keep you informed of everyone and everything they're doing and saying." Henrietta regularly wrote to Louise with the gossip when Louise was absent at Mama's command. Mama had been a great deal less interfering since St. Thomas's, but she still stepped in from time to time to remind Louise of who was in charge. "We'll be waiting for you when you return; until then, you must join me at the unveiling of my statue of Mr. Burchett." Henrietta had been chosen to sculpt the perpetually tardy professor and headmaster, an honor for a student, especially a female one.

"I wouldn't miss it."

"And my exhibition at the Berners Street Gallery," Nino called down the table. "We need a royal to pull in the punters."

"You can meet Sir Coutts Lindsay and Lady Blanche Lindsay," Mr. Morgan said. "They're quite keen on finding new talent, and plan to build a gallery to showcase artists rebuffed by the Royal Academy."

"Speaking of galleries, I must regretfully draw our lunch to a close." Professor Boehm rose, bringing the others to their feet. "I'm expected at my studio. Thank you very much for a splendid meal and another interesting term."

In a flurry of conversation and laughter, they left the Grill Room, bidding one another goodbye as they set off to their next class or appointment, the gentlemen heading for Mr. John Marshall's lecture on the human form at University College Hospital and Henrietta to Mr. Millais's office to discuss her commission.

Louise watched her friends leave with a heavy heart. She'd correspond with them while in Scotland, but it wouldn't be the same easy rapport, wit, and laughter as they enjoyed when together.

"Will you return next term?" Professor Boehm asked, lingering behind.

"I don't know. It's never entirely up to me." Mama's grumbling about Louise's lessons interfering with her work and the need to finally choose a husband had reached a near-fever pitch lately. After dinner last night, Mama had presented yet another list of potential suitors Louise had refused. Marriage was one of the few things expected of a royal daughter and a duty she couldn't shirk forever.

"I'm certain you'll succeed in convincing Her Majesty to allow you to return."

"You're an optimist, Professor Boehm."

"An artist must be to survive. May I be so optimistic as to hope you'll accept an invitation to visit my studio? I'm working on a memorial statue of Lord Holland for Holland Park.

The piece could benefit from your unique perspective of aristocratic subjects."

"Are you sure you wish to hear my real views? You might find them quite shocking."

"Or scintillating." He arched one eyebrow, his scoundrel-like expression making her heart flutter as much as his eagerness for her opinion. After their brief conversation at Mr. Whistler's last year, they'd been nothing but professional in one another's presence, so much so she sometimes wondered if the intimacy they'd shared had really happened or if she'd imagined it along with the many stolen glances she'd caught from him across the classroom and various galleries. She'd ignored every one, refusing to allow her fancy to lead her down another reckless path like her attraction to Walter had done.

Seeing Professor Boehm now, she realized she hadn't imagined it. It was as clear as the subtle shift in Mr. Corsi before she'd offered him the cigarette. "I'd be happy to visit, but it must be this afternoon or there won't be another chance for some time. We leave for Balmoral soon."

"I see clients between three and six, but I'll clear my appointments for you today." For the first time since the first class, he bowed to her before turning on one heel and striding away.

Another person I used to call on as a small boy was the great sculptor . . . Joseph Boehm at his Studio in The Avenue, Fulham Row. I used to like this studio because it was full of stone statues of people and horses and it was very interesting to see . . . On one occasion a very grand lady accompanied with another visited the studio. A lot

of animated conversation occurred but I cannot recollect
a word of it but it seemed that the lady was greatly in-
terested in some special sculpture . . . Joseph presented
me to the Princess Louise who gave me some very fine
sweeties and who was greatly amused that I should of my
own free will like to visit the studio by myself.
—Memoires of Charles James Whistler Hanson, James
McNeill Whistler's son

"I'M QUITE JEALOUS. None of the studios in any of the royal residences are as well appointed as this one." Louise took in the high-ceilinged room in this portion of a large building near Sydney Close where she and Sybil had ventured after class. The Avenue, as it was called, stood a mere mile from the school, and Professor Boehm's studio in it was filled with bronze horses with or without riders, maquettes for larger works, and numerous tripods with busts and statuettes in various mediums and in different stages of completion. Heavy Italianate carved furniture stood against the walls besides bookcases crammed with books in French, English, and German on various artworks and artists, some with their spines out and organized, others shoved haphazardly on top. Large gilded mirrors hung on the walls, amplifying the natural light from the row of north-facing windows, making the white human skull on the desk even brighter. "Do you live here?"

"None of us do, and there are twenty of us, including Mr. Pointer and Mr. Dicey, but their studios aren't as large as mine." He opened a door to a well-appointed sitting room with a separate entrance from the main hallway. "My higher-ranking commissions prefer private accommodation for sittings or discussing contracts. I've made a great deal of progress in portraiture over the last year, so much so, I can pick and choose which, if any, equestrian statuettes to do."

"You haven't abandoned them?"

"Sometimes I can express my moods or thoughts better through a familiar old subject instead of a new one."

"I know, landscapes do the same for me at times." She studied him in this moment of familiarity, his stern features softening and making him even more handsome.

He didn't flinch from her gaze, teasing her with a steady look. He didn't flirt like Nino, but pinned her with a striking stare to make her go weak in the knees. He was the devil with admirable self-control.

Sybil cleared her throat, breaking their quiet interlude.

"Might I take advantage of your sitting room and rest?" Sybil asked, offering them a touch of privacy while still upholding her chaperone duties.

"Of course." Professor Boehm settled her on the sofa, then closed the door behind him. "Allow me to show you the room Mr. Sargent, the new chap down the hall, calls my holy of holies."

He pushed open a second odor and ushered Louise into a room filled with uncovered marble and bronze statues waiting to be perfected before they were properly draped. "This is where I store statues of aristocratic clients who don't want their half-finished forms seen."

"Your dedication to them and your work is impressive."

"I don't work. I labor. Come, I'll show you Lord Holland." He guided her back to the main studio, walking so close beside her the cuff of his pants legs brushed the hem of her skirt. "I've done it in plaster to be cast in bronze."

They stopped before the statue of the august statesman seated in a chair, one hand on his knee, the other grasping the end of a walking stick. His clothes were as wrinkled as his bald head was smooth. There was a liveliness Professor Boehm had captured in the subtle smile that gave life to the full cheeks and deep-set eyes. "He's quite charming."

"I'm not sure he's dignified enough. I only had old portraits to work from, and they weren't particularly detailed. I'm concerned about what the family will think. A great deal depends on getting this commission right."

The pragmatic professor was gone, replaced by a vulnerable artist doubting his piece as she'd done her bust of Arthur. She felt sure if she condemned it, he'd smash it and start over.

"He's perfect." Without thinking, she took his hand, his faith in her opinion touching her. "He's so lifelike, I feel as if I know him the way Mama did when he served in her cabinet. She speaks fondly of him and everything he did for her and Papa. That's what people will see, it's who you've captured. Manor houses are teeming with aloof ancestors. The Hollands will feel as if you've re-created the man they loved, not some untouchable patriarch."

"Thank you for your honesty." He covered her hand with his and raised it to his chest, drawing her closer to him.

She should let go, resist the temptation in his voice and touch, but she couldn't. "You're very welcome, Professor Boehm."

"Edgar, please."

"Edgar." The sound of his name on her lips was as tender

as his fingers against hers. She gazed up at him, the faint flicker of his pulse in his neck just visible above the crisp line of his white collar. He stared down at her, the intensity in his expression nearly taking her breath away. She yearned to slide into his arms, lay her head on his chest, and feel more of the vulnerable man beneath the confident professor. No man had ever laid himself this bare to her, not even Walter.

The click of a doorknob and the subtle squeak of hinges forced Edgar to release her. They stepped apart, placing a respectable distance between them.

"I'm sorry to interrupt, Your Royal Highness, but we must be on our way if you're to make the train to Windsor," Sybil announced.

"Of course. Thank you, Professor Boehm, for a stimulating afternoon." Louise returned with some difficulty to her formal airs. "I look forward to seeing the piece when it's complete."

"It'll be my pleasure to show you." Neither of them wished to part, but they must. "Until we meet again."

He bowed, his eyes never leaving hers until she reluctantly turned and made for the door.

Each step that carried her past the other studios and out the main entrance pulled down the lightness she'd experienced with Edgar. With him, there was passion, and art. Ahead of her was mourning and stultifying boredom. She wanted to run back to him, throw herself in his arms, and forget for a while her position and life, but she continued forward, leaving the cool shadows of the building for the light of the front walk and the muffled confines of the carriage.

"Mr. Boehm is a very charming man," Sybil hazarded as the carriage rocked into motion.

"He is." She stared out the window, her fingers still humming from his touch, before Sybil's voice brought Louise back to the grime and stone of London.

"I've seen that look on your face before. I know what you're up to, and it isn't entirely art."

"There's nothing between us, there can't be." She wasn't a woman to be courted by an artist no matter what his manners or rank, but every feeling about him she'd denied for the last year had washed over her when he'd stood with her. She must be strong and resist his allure. Such weakness could undermine and undo everything she'd worked so hard to achieve.

Chapter Nine

Mr. Boehm . . . is a young Hungarian . . . full of talent, who does beautiful statuettes and groups of animals etc and busts . . . he is going to come to Balmoral in the autumn to do (what dear Papa always wished) statuettes of . . . me, which I think will be very pretty.

—QUEEN VICTORIA TO HER DAUGHTER
THE CROWN PRINCESS OF PRUSSIA

Balmoral Castle, Scotland, September 1869

"Prince Christian must find something to do besides gad about." Mama scowled out the study window at Prince Christian, who stood smoking by the bushes. It was a rare clear day and he was taking advantage of it to air his lungs, much to Louise's envy. She was forced to remain inside assisting Lenchen with Mama's business, marooned in the wilds of Scotland. "He knows I detest the smell of cigarette smoke."

"If you gave Prince Christian something more to do than eliminating the frogs at Frogmore, he might not stand about," Lenchen mumbled, her dark vermilion velvet dress still straining at the seams from the weight of her second son, born months ago—in February.

"If he were resourceful, he would find something to do." With quick, irritated flicks of her pen, Mama began another letter to her ministers.

"He raises our children because I'm here with you instead of with them."

"You should be thankful for it. Babies are disgusting creatures and quite uninteresting until they reach two years old, especially if they are ugly."

Lenchen banged the royal seal into the wax but said nothing. Louise didn't dare dip her oar into this pond. This was Lenchen's battle to fight and if she chose to surrender, Louise couldn't help her, but she felt her frustration. The last few letters from Henrietta had been filled with news of her friends, Mr. Whistler and Edgar. She didn't dare write to Henrietta about how much she treasured each sentence about Edgar or to ask for more. She couldn't correspond with him either. All she could do was send apologies for missing Henrietta's unveiling and Nino's showing at the Berners Street Gallery, all the while resenting her exile at Balmoral.

"I would ask Prince Christian to engage a sculptor for me, but he has no artistic ability." Mama removed an envelope from her desk and began laying the photographs from inside it on the blotter. "Louise, you may help me choose which one to engage. I will have a statuette of me done to present to Mr. Disraeli in thanks for his work as Prime Minister. That he should have been ousted so soon by that awful Mr. Gladstone still makes me shudder."

Louise stood behind Mama at her desk and studied the

photographs of statues from over Mama's shoulders. Edgar's funerary monument to Lord Cardigan immediately caught Louise's notice. If Mama intended to sit for a sculptor, it would be him. "Mr. Boehm's likeness of Lord Cardigan for St. Peter's Church is divine. Look at how beautifully Mr. Boehm has captured his eternal repose."

"Yes, he has." Mama picked up the picture, her morbid fascination with anything mourning drawing her to study the peaceful face of Lord Cardigan resting on a marble pillow, his uniformed chest covered with the honors he'd received during the Crimean War, including the one Mama and Papa had presented to him after the Battle of Balaclava.

"I'm sure his being Louise's sculpting professor has nothing to do with her praise of him," Lenchen sneered.

"Then Louise knows better than either of us his true talents. Louise, write to him at once about a commission. Anyone who can render the deceased with such tenderness can execute a work on my behalf."

"Yes, Mama." Louise sat at the writing desk by the window and began a formal letter to Edgar, careful to conceal the excitement making her fingers tremble. Once ensconced in Scotland for her fall holiday, Mama rarely deigned to leave Balmoral until they ventured to Osborne House for Christmas. It meant Edgar would have to come here. She lifted the nib from the paper, hesitant to write the next words. Her life in London had been so different from her one with Mama, and bringing Edgar here meant sharing him and a part of that existence with her. She wished to keep it for herself, but she couldn't deny Edgar the opportunity to secure royal patronage. It'd propelled Mary's career to grand heights. It might do the same for his, allowing him to follow his artistic desires, and perhaps more earthy ones.

She chewed the wooden end of the pen and watched the clouds pass over the hills outside the window. Their shades of gray reflected in the moving water of the River Dee flowing down from the Grampian Mountains and through the Royal Deeside where Papa had chosen to build Balmoral. The rolling hills stippled with yellow-green shrubs and deep green pines were grand today, or the thought of Edgar coming here made her think they were. She shouldn't sit here dreaming like an overwrought heroine in a novel, but Edgar had ignited in her something only ever inflamed by her art, and she might soon be near him again.

"MEETING WITH CLIENTS of standing is always a delicate business but nothing like this." Edgar adjusted his cravat for the third time since he and Louise had left the medieval entrance hall beneath the mounted stag heads and started along the lower corridor toward Mama's Drawing Room. He was somberly dressed, his usual light linen suit replaced with a dove-gray wool one that offered some protection from the Scottish cold.

"Is this what you meant by things becoming different and not easier?" Louise asked. With the servants packed off to his room with his things, they were released from the stilted greetings and mundane questions about his journey that'd dominated the half hour since his arrival.

"This is precisely what I meant."

They stopped before Mama's closed study door and Louise brushed the flecks of train ash off of his shoulders. She shouldn't be so familiar with him, especially with Lenchen or Beatrice skulking about, but she'd endured the dreariness of the last three weeks to reach this moment and he was finally here. She didn't dare say aloud how glad she was to see him, but gripped the cold brass doorknob and ushered Edgar into Mama's sitting room.

Mama stopped treadling her spinning wheel, her newly spun singles wound on the large bobbin. She worked before the wide window, the large draping curtains embroidered with Scottish thistles drawn open to reveal the countryside. Sharp lay at her feet on the red-, black-, yellow-, and blue-striped tartan carpet designed by Papa. His tartan design filled every inch of Balmoral, and was detested by Arthur, Leopold, and Bertie, especially when they were forced to wear the patterned kilts to the Ghillies Ball or during walks along the frigid moors.

Mr. John Brown never minded the cold, his legs always visible beneath his gray kilt and jacket no matter what the weather. He stood behind Mama like a suit of armor, glaring at Louise. "Ye should knock first."

"You should remember your place, and address me as Your Royal Highness."

"Now, now, you two, we have a guest," Mama soothed, far more tolerant of Mr. Brown's insolence than anyone else's. "Welcome, Mr. Boehm, to my humble country house."

"It's magnificent, Your Majesty. The landscape is inspiring."

"I'm never happier than when I sit quietly here with my watercolors or spinning wheel. I owe this sanctuary to my dear Albert's foresight."

"He was a man of remarkable tastes."

"Indeed he was." She let go of the wool fibers and shifted to face Edgar. "As you know, I brought you here to execute a statuette of me for Mr. Disraeli. What pose do you have in mind?"

"I had a number of suggestions drawn up, but seeing you here has given me another idea." Edgar tilted his head from side to side, studying Mama as he might a model or a student's work. "I imagine sculpting you as you are now, seated before your spinning wheel, the mother of a people, the adviser to ministers, all of whom are as loyal to you as the dog at your feet. A humble portrait will stir people's hearts with memories of hearth and home and deepen their love for you."

Sharp raised his head from where it rested beside Mama's feet and Mama reached down and scratched behind his floppy ears. "A splendid idea."

"Daft to sculpt a queen as a crofter's wife," Mr. Brown muttered.

"I will have him portray you the same way," Mama teased, so enraptured by the image Edgar described, Papa could have spoken against it and it would've sparked one of their old rows.

"Sartenly not, wammen. Won't waste me time lolling about for Mr. Bum and his fancy bit of clay, not when there's Your Majesty to be tending to."

"I am sure Mr. Boehm is capable of rendering you from a few sketches, you old sourpuss." Mama laughed, and Louise stood mortified at their banter. For a woman who never allowed anyone to forget she was Queen, she certainly enjoyed a lack of decorum with this nasty servant. "Can you sketch this rascal quickly, Mr. Boehm?"

"I can, Your Majesty."

"Good, then you will execute what studies you can of my irascible Mr. Brown and I will pose for you as needed. We will each have our portrait statues done, Princess Louise too, perhaps with her horse Andrew. Would you like that, Louise?"

"Very much." She didn't dare look at Edgar, afraid to give too much away, especially under Mr. Brown's scrutinizing glare. "I'd also like to continue my studies by assisting him. After everything Mr. Disraeli has done for you, the statuette must be perfect."

"It must be. You will work with Mr. Boehm and see to it he has everything he needs. This will be your project as much as it is his. I look forward to seeing what you both create."

"YOU HOLD YOUR pose as well as a model," Edgar complimented from where he sat on a bale of hay, one ankle resting on his knee and the sketchbook perched on his leg. The quick scrape of charcoal over the paper mingled with the horses' neighs and the grooms' distant laughter. Edgar flicked quick looks at her between lines, the curls above his forehead falling down across his eyebrows when he bent over his paper. He sketched faster than anyone she'd ever seen before, and with amazing precision.

The unbuttoned sides of his coat hung open, the heat of the stables bringing a flush to his skin along his hairline as he executed studies of Louise and her horse Andrew. She stood before the stall, holding Andrew's bridle and stroking the Thoroughbred's long nose to keep him calm. The stable was one of the few warm places at Balmoral, Mama offering her beloved horses a comfort she rarely extended to humans.

"I've had years of practice remaining still." It was all Louise had done since his arrival despite wanting to spend every moment with him, but she'd learned the hard way with Walter about indulging girlish impulses. Edgar was here to work, cultivate royal patronage, and instruct her, not dally with her and risk losing it all.

"I was surprised when that Brown fellow delivered Her Majesty's note begging off. She's been generous with her sittings." It'd been a week since Edgar's arrival, and Mama had occupied most of his time. Today was their first proper moment together alone.

"Mama is at the crofters' cottage with that brute." Andrew jerked back his head and Louise tightened her grip on the leather, cooing softly to settle him. "She says she gossips with the crofters' wives, but who knows what they're really up to?"

"Given the things I overheard when Sir Edwin Landseer exhibited his painting of Mr. Brown holding Her Majesty's horse, I can imagine."

"You should hear the gossip whispered here."

He glanced up from under his full straight eyebrows at her. "I have."

Louise winced at the thought of people believing the ugly rumor of Mr. Brown and Mama being secretly married and her allowing him conjugal privileges. The possibility it might be true nearly made her sick.

"Don't think about it," he encouraged. "You're frowning and ruining the line of your face."

"Then tell me something to make me forget it. Tell me about Vienna and your father." She'd spent a year under his tutelage and knew little about his personal life and past. He never discussed himself during class and she'd only caught glimpses of the more private Edgar during their brief discussions, ones she'd thought about too many times over the last few boring weeks before his arrival.

Edgar shrugged, rubbed out a line, then continued sketching. "He had one of the most impressive private art collections, gathering everything from Egyptian papyrus to a Van Dyke he acquired from a friend. Mother said it was the best education I and my brothers could've had and it'd serve us better than any other."

"What does she think of your career, and you sculpting for the Queen?"

"If she were here, she'd be proud. She died when I was ten." He stilled his pencil above the paper. "Losing her changed everything."

"I know what you mean. It was the same after I lost Papa." Louise stroked Andrew's long nose, his calm wide eyes reflecting the image of Edgar, everything death had stolen from them as heavy in the air as the scent of horses and hay. "Is your father proud?"

"No." Edgar resumed sketching, but the pencil moved more slowly. "He was never the same after my mother died. Nasty, bitter, quick with criticism, short with praise. When my older brother set off for London, Father said he'd never amount to anything without his help. He was twice as nasty when I followed. Every letter I've received since has been nothing but suggestions on how I might improve this piece or that. It's taken years for me to be able to be honest with people about my work, and myself."

"At least you can be honest with others." Louise rubbed the snaffle joint on the bridle with her gloved thumb, making the metal shine. "A princess must always be semi-divine to everyone she encounters, but I'm not. Far from it."

"I know." He turned the sketch around to show her, and she gasped. It wasn't the staid, regal, or overtly innocent picture every photographer and royal painter insisted on foisting on her image. Instead, she appeared as a woman with a horse, the hint of a smile tugging up the side of her mouth and brightening her eyes. He'd caught her profile, not downcast or demure but boldly looking forward into a future she was determined to claim.

She let go of Andrew and crossed the hay-strewn floor to take the sketchbook, the paper still warm from where he'd held it. "You do see me."

"From the moment you appeared with Her Majesty at the tea, the sun sparkling in your hair. You remind me of Millais's *Mariana*, isolated in grief but pining for life."

"'My *life is dreary, he cometh not,' she said; she said, 'I am aweary, aweary.'*" She recited the line from the Tennyson poem that'd inspired Mr. Millais's painting, one she'd read many times after Mr. Tennyson's visits from his estate near Osborne House. "I've experienced more real life in the last year in your class than I've ever known before, felt more possibility than anywhere else, and I don't want it to end."

She brushed the falling curls off his forehead, caressing the line of his temple and the edge of his cheek with the backs of her fingers. He covered her hand with his and turned to press his lips against her palm, his warm breath cutting through her leather glove and clouding her mind until she could think of nothing, not Mama, the sketch, or the risk of discovery. Nothing mattered except Edgar. If she slid her hand behind his neck and leaned down, she might press her lips to his and catch something of the passion illuminating his cerulean-blue eyes and echoing in her chest, but she didn't move. She couldn't lose him the way she'd lost Walter.

"You're scowling again," he whispered, drawing her away from her fears and back to the pressure of his fingers entwined with hers.

"It won't happen again." She withdrew her hand and stepped back.

"Your Majesty, Your Majesty," the muffled voices of the grooms outside greeting Mama and her usual soft reply carried in through the stable door.

Louise handed the book to Edgar and hurried back to Andrew, while Edgar returned to his sketch. He wasn't at it long before Mama appeared in her black wool dress, the hem damp with mist. Sharp trotted at her side and Mr. Brown lumbered in behind her.

"Good afternoon, Mr. Boehm. Are you getting on with your studies of Louise?"

"I am, Your Majesty." He stood, handed her his sketchbook, and petted Sharp, who rested his paws on Edgar's legs.

Mama scrutinized the sketches while Mr. Brown scrutinized Louise and Edgar like an agitated Highland bull. It was a wonder he didn't sniff the air for the faint scent of passion. The earthiness of the stables wasn't pungent enough to cover it, and he frowned at Louise, who didn't dare flinch at his scowl. She would not be bullied by this insolent drunk any more than she had been by Lady Ely, nor would she feel guilty. She and Edgar had done nothing more than talk and touch, and it would remain that way.

"Your eye for horseflesh is as keen as for people," Mama complimented, returning the sketchbook to Edgar. "I look forward to your finished pieces, especially Mr. Brown's. I want to see what you make of him in the end. I think a full-sized statue for the garden will do, don't you, Mr. Brown?"

"Don't need to be honored like some pagan idol," Mr. Brown mumbled.

"You old sourpuss." Mama swiped a playful hand at Mr. Brown, her fingers catching his kilt and making it flutter up a touch to reveal the very solid and naked thigh beneath. "Come along, Mr. Brown."

With a rare lightness of step, Mama made for the house, Mr. Brown trotting behind her as faithfully as Sharp.

Louise and Edgar exchanged nervous looks, as uneasy about the near-indiscretion as about Mama flirting with Mr. Brown.

Chapter Ten

... I hope to see a whole collection of your works of art
when I return. I must give you a sitting for a bust for the
last was far from successful ...

P.S. No sign of a husband yet???

—PRINCE ALFRED TO HIS SISTER, LOUISE

Balmoral Castle, Scotland, October 1869

Your growing grasp of anatomy is showing." Edgar brushed
the slivers of marble off Louise's work. "It's given your
pieces more realism."

"If only the sitter could've been different," Louise lamented.
Mama had insisted Louise complete another bust of her, feeling it most beneficial for Louise to work on the same subject
as Edgar. Louise sculpted beside him nearly every day, peppering him with questions and listening attentively to his directions and instructions. He hadn't resented her presence or
her constant questions, patient with her, especially when it
had come time to carve the white marble blocks. He'd helped

her sketch Mama on the marble, then guided her in the first strikes with the point chisel to reduce the block of stone to a rough form. He'd urged her to be deliberate as she'd worked with the tooth chisel to slowly refine the image, guiding her through every step of the process.

Here, he wasn't the handsome man in the stables but the professor in the classroom, and she'd been careful to remain his student despite the desire torturing her every time he stood close beside her, the sweat and heat of him as powerful as her need to sculpt. "At least Mama didn't insist on my doing a bust of Mr. Brown. I'm certain I couldn't do it without adding devil horns."

"He deserves it." Edgar slapped the dust off his coat sleeves, raising a cloud of the fine white marble powder that covered nearly every surface in the room. "What is that dreadful noise?"

He cocked his head toward the sound of a bagpiper missing more notes than he played.

"Mama's usual Highland entertainer is deep in his cups again."

"She doesn't notice?" He winced at another off note.

"She only ever sees what she wishes, and she refuses to see drunk servants or to dismiss them. She says they have a hard lot and must cope with it as well as they can."

"I admire Her Majesty sympathizing with the plight of her servants. It's a rare quality in a monarch."

"One you've captured well." She turned Edgar's clay statuette of Mama seated at her spinning wheel around on its turntable. It would soon be packed up and returned to Edgar's studio with the afternoon messenger so it could be delivered to Mr. Young's Pimlico foundry to be cast in bronze. "She appears regal and plain all at once."

Edgar had smoothed Mama's face, rounded her fuller cheeks and jowls, and softened the fall of her heavy black dress, adding as much detail to the drape of the fabric as he did to the Sovereign and Sharp at her feet. In her simple widow's cap, her fingers gripping the wool and working it into thread, she was the Mama Louise remembered from childhood, the one who used to show Louise how to work the fibers during the tranquil evenings with Papa at Osborne House, the ones that'd died with him.

"Is it as bad as that?" Edgar wiped away the single tear that slipped down her cheek, his rough fingers gentle against her skin.

"It reminds me of another, happier time." She stepped around him and picked up the rasp, setting it against her marble and rubbing it quickly back and forth to smooth the chisel marks from Mama's cheek. The curve of the stone made the rasp slip, threatening to ruin her hard work.

"Let me show you." Edgar reached around her and grasped both of her hands in his over the wood handle. With a firm but light grip, he slid the metal back and forth over the marble cheek, smoothing and softening the stone, the gentle rock of his chest against her back, his arms around her, calming her. She followed his fluid movements until he let go and she guided the tool with the practiced precision of an experienced sculptor. "That's how you do it."

He remained close behind her, and when she paused, he leaned over her shoulder to blow the dust off and reveal the smooth stone beneath. He turned to look at her and his breath whispered across the hollow of her neck. His lips were tantalizingly close to hers, the yearning ache of her body as strong as the one in her fingers from clasping the rasp. He didn't move and neither did she, the two of them so close and yet as far apart as two creags across a great gleann. "The stone yields under your skill."

"As I do yours." She buried her fingers in his thick hair and rose up on her toes to kiss him, but he stood up tall, chin raised in defiance of her passion, and his.

She let go and tossed down the rasp with her other hand, the metal and wood clattering against the table. "How long are we to do this dance, pretending there's nothing between us?"

"As long as necessary." He walked to the window with a view of the River Dee, the same frustration coursing through her making his neck and shoulders stiff. "If you weren't who you are, I'd kiss you, but you're a princess, and I'm a lowly sculptor."

She laid her hands on his shoulders and rested her cheek against his back, the tight muscles easing beneath her touch. Everything he said was true, but she rebelled against it as she did every dictate and restriction Mama foisted on her. "I'm a woman who wants you as much as you want me, and I'll accept you on whatever terms I can have you."

"Not if it means both of our ruin." He covered her hands with his, his chest rising and falling with a deep sigh. "There are so many things keeping us apart."

"Only if we let them." From this high in the castle, only the kestrels winging over the hills searching for prey could see them. They were free for a few moments to be nothing more than a man and a woman. "Don't push me away, then tell me you care for me as much as I care for you. We understand each other as no one else does, and no one might ever again. I won't lose that. Say you want it too, tell me, and we'll find a way to be together."

He whirled to face her, clasping her arms. "I want you, I have from the first, and every moment we've been together since. I don't want to lose you."

He drew her into a kiss and she sank into him, the thrill of his lips against hers as potent as the danger of anyone, from Lady Ely to General Grey, happening in on them. General Grey would say nothing, but Lady Ely would burn the castle down in order to tell Mama, and it'd pull Edgar's chances for royal patronage down with it. Still, they remained in one another's arms, reveling in the intimacy and the danger.

They broke from the kiss, and Louise laid her head on his chest, his heart beneath beating as fast as hers. He rested his chin on the top of her head, the pressure of it threatening to dislodge the combs holding her curls in place. She'd fix them before they parted. Nothing must be out of sorts or suggest anything untoward had taken place in the tower studio. "We must be careful, or we'll never enjoy a moment's peace together."

He breathed a deep sigh she felt reverberate through her chest. "If I were here longer, we could, but I'm leaving tomorrow."

She jerked back to face him. "What?"

"I wanted to tell you sooner, but you've been so happy, I didn't wish to ruin it. The statue of Her Majesty is complete and the one of you and Mr. Brown will be done in London. My new assistant Mr. Gilbert and I must also attend to my other clients."

"When will I see you again?" She shouldn't wish for their next meeting, but be thankful for the distance he was placing between them.

"I don't know." He took her left hand in his, and rubbed one callused thumb over the back of it, pausing at her bare ring finger to trace the curve of it. He turned her palm up, reached into his pocket, and took out a medal the size of a pound coin and pressed it into her hand.

She examined the medal. His profile was on one side and hers on the other, both expertly and tenderly rendered in gold. "It's beautiful."

"There are two copies." He laid his hand on his chest. "I have the other."

She closed her fingers over the medallion, the metal warming in her palm. She didn't beg him to stay or rail against the unfairness of their separation. Like him, she understood their positions and what they meant to both of them, but he cared for her, deeply, and she would hold on to that until they could be together again. "It'll be so dark here without you."

He tucked a curl that'd slipped out of her hair ribbon behind her ear, his fingers lingering near the nape of her neck. "Then look for the light, everywhere you can. Don't let the shadows dominate you, but allow them to draw your attention to the most beautiful aspects of the composition, and know that even when I'm not with you, I think about you every day."

"As I do you."

He traced the line of her jaw with one finger, studying her, committing her to memory, as she memorized his expression in this moment, filling her soul with his essence so it might carry her until their next meeting. She would keep it with her as she did the medal and look to it when things seemed dark.

Went to see poor Leopold, who was lying flat on his back, very quiet, very pale, and looking very sad. It upset me much to see him like that.
—*Queen Victoria's Journal*

"YOU TWO NEVER tell me anything," Beatrice whined to her sisters, as they turned the corner of the castle, the wind striking them face-on and fluttering the bottoms of their thick tartan skirts. "You both tell Leopold everything, or you write to Alice about all sorts of interesting things, but you won't say two words to me."

"I don't tell Leopold anything," Lenchen gasped through heavy breaths, struggling to keep up with Louise's quick stride.

"Louise does," Beatrice insisted, dancing around them like an overeager spaniel. "Why won't you tell me?"

"Because you aren't allowed to hear anything, so there's no point, and you'd simply tattle to Mama if you did hear anything interesting, and get us in trouble," Louise spat, irritated at having her exercise curtailed. She'd nearly walked her feet to the bones after Edgar left last week, her frustration eased with each step over the craggy rocks and paths of the hills surrounding the castle. Today, she was forced to stick to the grounds so Lenchen wouldn't collapse from overexertion.

"Your Royal Highnesses." Reverend Robinson Duckworth,

Leopold's tutor, hurried toward them, the long hem of his frock coat flapping about his thighs. "I don't wish to alarm you, but Prince Leopold has had an epileptic attack."

"Is he all right?" Louise demanded.

"As well as can be expected, but Mr. Brown has taken up sentry at his door and won't allow anyone except Dr. Jenner to enter. I tried to have a word with Dr. Jenner when he came out, but Her Majesty commanded his attention and insists His Royal Highness rest in isolation."

"I'll see Leopold at once. That old goat won't dare block me from his room." Louise grabbed her thick wool skirt and made for the castle.

"Mama doesn't want you to disturb him," Lenchen called after her, unable to keep up.

"Or I could comfort and soothe him and make things better."

"That's my hope," Reverend Duckworth said, falling in step beside Louise as they entered the castle and made for Leopold's room. Behind them, Beatrice urged Lenchen to walk faster, but Lenchen insisted she couldn't. So Louise left them both behind to struggle up the staircase.

"This illness will make your brother's dark moods worse," Reverend Duckworth worried, stroking the blond mutton-chops along the side of his square jaw. Out of earshot of Lenchen and Beatrice, he resumed his usual informality with her. "A man in his delicate health must keep his spirit up or he will fail."

"I know." Louise felt awful. She should've spent less time mooning about the moors over Edgar, and more time with Leopold. Ever since Arthur had left for Canada to take up his appointment with the Rifle Brigade, Leopold had been moody and withdrawn, ruminating over everything their brother had that he didn't. Instead of distracting him, she'd left it to Reverend Duckworth to entertain him with stories of his eminent Oxford friends. "We'll find a way to bolster his spirit. We must."

They approached Leopold's bedroom, where Mr. Brown stood before the door, arms crossed, his stern stance matched by the tight set of his pale-whiskered jaw. "Her Majesty ordered no one to come in."

"I will not be told by a servant what to do. Stand aside." Louise waved a dismissive hand at him.

"Louise, stop, you're making a scene," Beatrice insisted from behind her, having left Lenchen struggling up the stairs on her own. "Mama won't like it."

"Ye best listen to your sister."

"You best listen to me, Mr. Brown." Louise stood toe-to-toe with him, forced to look up at him. "You will step aside at once or I'll see to it Mama hears every ugly rumor circulating through London and Scotland concerning her fondness for you. I know Mr. Ponsonby and General Grey have done all they can to shield her from it, but I won't. I'll tell her everything, and I'll show her the newspaper articles too."

She'd burned them years ago after reading them, afraid back then of being caught reading something so salacious, but he needn't know that.

"You'll tell them what?" Beatrice demanded, clinging to Louise's arm. "What are people saying?"

"Ask Mr. Brown."

Mr. Brown lowered his arms, sobering in the face of her

threat. "Ye wouldn't be upsetting Her Majesty like that or polluting Baby's mind with twaddle?"

Beatrice stomped her foot. "I'm not a baby."

"I very much would," Louise promised, chin set against the man's hard glare.

"Louise, let it be," Lenchen, who had finally caught up to them, wheezed, grabbing Louise's other arm and trying to pull her away.

Louise shook out of her grasp, her eyes never leaving Mr. Brown's. "Let me in."

She'd be damned if she'd back down.

Mr. Brown studied her, his whiskey-sodden breath as overpowering as his obstinacy. He ignored Lenchen and Beatrice, while Reverend Duckworth waited behind them for the standoff to end. Moments passed, and she thought they might stand here all night when she caught the faint glimmer of respect ripple across Mr. Brown's face. It vanished as fast as it'd come, hidden by his spite at having been routed. He stepped aside and pushed the door open with one large hand.

"Ye can go in, but not t'others."

Louise slipped past him, and he slammed the door closed behind her, blocking out Beatrice and Lenchen's protests.

"Loosy, how did you get past that brute?" Leopold turned his head against the large pillows, the white linen emphasizing the dark circle under his eyes. Worry gripped Louise, but she hid it behind a bright smile. He looked so frail and weak, and she shuddered at how this attack could've stolen him from her. Any of them could.

"I gave as good as I got." She closed the open sash, blocking out the chill wind making the room like ice.

"Mama won't like that," Leopold weakly teased.

"Good." She perched on the bed beside him and took his hand in hers, warming the cold skin. "What are you doing, giving us all a fright?"

"My demanding and rigorous schedule has left me exhausted. Arthur never gets tired or sick. He sees the world while I lie here and rot." His fingers tightened around hers with surprising strength. "I don't want to linger, Loosy. When the end comes, I want it to be quick. I'll miss you, but I won't miss this body of mine torturing me. I'll enjoy the freedom. It'll be the first I've ever known." He turned his face away, and the fire behind them crackled and popped as it tried to consume the meager amount of wood placed on it. Louise added another log to the fire, then took the poker from the stand and prodded it, encouraging the flames to rise.

Leopold finally turned back to Louise. "Why are you here listening to me moan instead of in your studio daydreaming about your sculptor?"

"He isn't my sculptor, he's Mama's."

"You can lie to her, Lenchen, and Beatrice, but not me. When that Boehm fellow was here, it was as if this dreary place were draped in sunshine and spring flowers for you. You don't love it here, no one does except Mama."

He yawned, his slender chest beneath his white nightshirt rising and falling with the effort.

"You should rest."

"That's all Mama is going to make me do after this. I'll be forced to sit here alone pondering my end."

"Not if I have anything to say about it. I won't let her or that swine Brown stop me from visiting you or let them keep you a prisoner in your room. We'll sit together and plot something delightful for us to do when you're better."

"Stay, please, until I fall asleep."

"Of course." She settled beside him on the bed and tucked the coverlet in tight around him, but he grabbed her hand.

"Promise me something, Loosy."

"Anything."

"Promise me you'll find happiness, for both of us."

"I will, and I'll help you find your happiness too."

* * *

Some days later, Louise met with Bertie in the billiard room, one of the few places they could have any privacy. She cracked the striker ball so hard with the cue stick, it skipped over the other balls, hit the edge, and bounced across the floor.

"If you don't resolve things with that sculptor of yours very soon, you'll turn into quite the shrew." Bertie bent over and picked up the ball, tossing it in the air twice before setting it back on the near-frozen felt. The bone-chilling Scottish cold permeated everything, even the heavy billiard table.

Louise didn't care if the whole castle was covered in icicles. The frost stiffening her fingers helped ease the pain in her heart. Dr. Jenner was sure Leopold would recover, this time, as the attack had been mild, and after a few days of rest the color had already returned to his cheeks. So that was settled, at least for now.

The issue of Edgar was another matter.

"There's nothing to resolve." She'd told him everything, needing to speak with someone, and he'd listened with as much sympathy as when they'd discussed Walter.

"So I see." He took her cue stick as if afraid she might impale him with it. "I admire his honorable nature. Most men I know wouldn't display his resolve. It's commendable but foolish. It won't douse the flames but make them worse."

"I don't suppose you'd be willing to tell him that."

"Good gracious, Loosy, I'm the Prince of Wales, not your procurer. I can't wantonly hand you off to a willing but stubborn gentleman." He motioned for her to step aside so he could take his shot. The Balmoral billiard room was small and made more cramped by the large bookcases on either side. One had to leave the room simply to change their mind. "Settle the matter on your own."

"How? We aren't free and I can't ruin him." She dropped on the sofa crammed in the corner beneath hunting paintings and across from the closed door. "I'm already worried our mostly innocuous indiscretions are already known and Mama is simply waiting to pounce."

"If Mama paid attention to anyone besides Mr. Brown she might notice something peculiar, but she doesn't, so you're most likely safe."

"What about the servants? They aren't shy with whispers about Mama and Mr. Brown and are apt to say anything when they're in their cups. Any whiff of scandal could destroy Edgar."

"As Mama pretends not to notice the inebriated messengers, charwomen, and bloody near everyone else in this wasteland, she isn't likely to hear what they say about anyone, assuming one can understand them through the slurs. As for your sculptor, given what you've told me about that Whistler fellow and his arrangement, maybe Mr. Boehm wants a bit of scandal. It might increase his fame among those artist types."

"He isn't that kind of gentleman." Mr. Whistler's efforts to hide Miss Hiffernan from his widowed American mother who'd come to live with him had filled Henrietta's letters. She'd read them all to Leopold and Bertie, much to their amusement.

"Then there's only one thing for it. Remove the taint of scandal."

"How?"

"Get married."

"That isn't a solution, just more trouble."

"Stop acting like a rebellious child and became a grown woman." Bertie crossed his arms over his chest and eyed her as if she were a simpleton. "Given our unique positions, the limited choices we have in selecting a spouse, and our inability to divorce or separate, discreet arrangements are our only option. A married woman, assuming she's done her duty by her husband and produced an heir, enjoys a certain amount of freedom an unmarried woman will never have."

"I won't marry some penniless and droll foreign prince."

"Nor should you. An Englishman will understand the way of things better than a German prince. So long as you're discreet, no one will openly comment on what might be common knowledge, nor remark on the likeness of a child to the father. Choose a gentleman liberal enough to look the other way and tolerable enough to make marital relations a pleasure instead of a drudgery."

She curled her lip in disgust. "I'm not so much selecting a husband as a stud mare."

"Any port in a storm." Bertie shrugged, coming around the table to face her. "If you wish to follow your natural inclinations, you'll be safer married than unmarried, so stop this mock-prudishness and do what must be done or rot away as a spinster with Mama."

A knock at the billiard room door startled them both.

"Who is it?" Bertie thundered.

Lady Ely crept in like a scared mouse, more cautious of Bertie than she'd ever been of Louise. She carried a black-edged stinger and held it out to Louise. "For you."

"Her Royal Highness," Bertie corrected, and the woman flinched.

"For Your Royal Highness." She laid it on the corner of the billiard table, then fled the room.

Louise eyed the stinger, afraid of what it might say.

LOUISE STOPPED AT the entrance to the garden and stuffed the stinger in her pocket. Mama sat alone on a garden bench, no attendant in sight. Mr. Brown had probably nipped around the corner to take a pull off a whiskey bottle. Sharp sniffed among the hedges and the unplanted beds, digging in the dark soil.

"You summoned me, Mama?"

"You have been very rude to Mr. Brown this past week," Mama scolded from where she sat on the cold stone bench sketching the mist-covered hills.

"He's been rude to me. He should know his place." She sat beside Mama, who handed her a clean sheet of paper and a spare pencil from her box. Louise began sketching the same view, thankful to have something to do, otherwise she'd worry the buttons off her coat.

"His place is by my side, assisting me."

"It's undignified for a queen to have such a servant." She didn't dare mention the rumors. It was the one thing she could hold over Mr. Brown's head and, if ever need be, Mama's.

"Mr. Brown, like all Scotsmen, is an unspoiled and unreserved child of nature who brings me joy, something I have not experienced since the moment dear Papa breathed his last. Given my heavy responsibilities, I deserve the attention of the single person most devoted to me. You will not be so difficult with him in the future."

"Yes, Mama." That Mama's happiness came from a drunk and not her children stung. Louise scratched out a line of bushes in the distance, too agitated to draw details. She wasn't about to show that awful man anything more than the contempt he deserved, but she was in no mood for a row.

Mama took a deep breath of the bracing air, as pleased with herself as with the misty view. "I never have the same clarity anywhere else as I do when I am here. The quiet of Scotland allows me to think and ponder. Here, I am away from everything, and the solitude brings me peace. I wish you had such a place."

"I do, in my studio, when I work." Louise stopped sketching to study the view. "There's a tranquility there I can't find anywhere else, except when sitting outside with my paint box and easel or sketchbook."

She felt vulnerable telling Mama this. Mama didn't belittle it but nodded. "It is most settling to sit and draw."

She patted Louise's hand, holding it a moment before returning to her sketch. The two of them sat quietly together drawing, the rush of the River Dee faint in the distance, the wind rippling through the trees and grass and hills the only conversation.

After some time, Mama glanced over at Louise's sketch. "Very well done." She closed her sketchbook and turned on the bench to face Louise. "During my walk the other day, I came to a number of decisions. Given your instruction with Mr. Boehm this last month, you will not return to the National Art Training School in the spring. You have progressed as far as necessary and there is no point in continuing, since there is little you can do with it."

"There's a great deal I can do with it. I can submit my new statue of you to the Royal Academy Exhibition."

"A princess has no business competing with commoners. We are above such things, we must always be."

"I wouldn't be competing, but honoring them with the privilege of displaying your image. If my piece sells, I'll donate the proceeds to the home for war widows, the same as Vicky does when she sells her art in Prussian charity exhibitions. If it's good enough for the Crown Princess of Prussia, it's good enough for me."

Mama studied her a moment, her face unreadable before responding. "You may submit the piece to the Royal Academy, but do not think of it as anything more than charity. You have had your instruction, your freedom to work. It is time for such frivolity to end. You are nearly twenty-two and should be married."

"I won't marry a foreign prince."

"On this we are in agreement. The English people will not see another princess and her settlement shipped off to some foreign land. I explained this to Vicky, but she refused to see reason. However, Mr. Gladstone had been much more sensible about it and is diligently drawing up a list of potential English suitors."

"You discussed this with Vicky and the Prime Minister before you discussed it with me?" She was tired of Mama, her government, the press, and the people having more say in her choice of husband, and at times her life, than she did.

"The marriage of a princess, even one as far down in the succession as you, is a matter of state," Mama said without shame. "You will review the list and choose those you wish to meet, and I will arrange for them to dine with us at Windsor. I must tell you, my preference is for Lord Lorne. His grandmother, the Duchess of Sutherland, God bless her soul, was my Mistress of the Robes. I very much like the thought of my dear old friend's grandson being my son-in-law."

She didn't share Mama's enthusiasm, too caught up in dreams of Edgar to consider anyone else, but not childish enough to believe she could become his wife. Her union must have the blessing of Mama and her government and the people. They'd never give it to a mere artist, no matter what his talent. Bertie was right, this was the only way. And in that moment, Louise knew she was sealing her fate. She'd just have to make the best of it. "All right. Parade him and the others in front of me and we'll see which one will do."

Chapter Eleven

> I quite agree about the difficulties of the unmarried la-
> dies. Their position is a very false and bad one—and re-
> ally untenable. You can't make a young unmarried girl
> quite independent. Think what it would have been, if it
> had been so with my Maids of Honour?
>
> —QUEEN VICTORIA TO HER DAUGHTER
>   THE CROWN PRINCESS OF PRUSSIA

London, January 1870

I'm barely let out of Windsor to dine at Marlborough House but Mama practically flings me at Mr. Gladstone in the hopes I might trip over some eligible suitor," Louise grumbled as the carriage rolled to a stop in front of Mr. Gladstone's 11 Carlton House Terrace home. The white wedding-cake front with its columns and square tiers rose up over the street corner, bright lights illuminating the windows. "I'm sure to die of boredom before the evening is over."

"Think of the joy your funeral would bring Her Majesty," Sybil joked with an edge of truth.

"For that reason, I intend to remain alive." She took the

footman's hand and alighted from the carriage, Sybil following her.

They crossed the long entrance hall and under the transom-cased openings to the reception room. Mrs. Gladstone left her place beside one of the four large black marble columns and came forward to greet them.

"Your Royal Highness, you honor our humble home." Mrs. Gladstone's face glowed with excitement, her pale skin made more delicate by the dark hair framing her face. She wore a wide-skirted dress of midnight-blue silk with matching ruffles and a lace shawl.

"I'm honored to be here." Louise accompanied her up the double staircase with its curving wrought-iron-flowered banister to the sitting room at the top. The low conversation between the dark-suited guests and the wide-skirted women stopped when Louise appeared. She recognized Viscount Sydney and his wife, Lord Chamberlain, Viscount Halifax, Earl Granville, and a mixture of other men and their wives who'd been given the honor of dining with her and the Gladstones. It wasn't the people she knew who caught her attention but the multitude of young men making this not only a dinner party but also a stud farm.

Mrs. Gladstone made the introductions and Louise gave each person the required attention before being left to stand with Sybil by the black marble fireplace. All the gentlemen faded away after their initial greeting, eyeing her as a curiosity instead of a woman, too shy to say more than two words to her and quietly removing themselves from the running for her hand. What a shame. If it weren't for the trip to London, it'd be a wasted evening. Mr. Whistler was hosting a party tonight and she and Sybil had decided to attend no matter how late it might be. Edgar would be there. They hadn't spoken since Balmoral, and she wouldn't miss the chance to see him.

"Perhaps I should simply choose one and put us all out of our misery." Louise opened her fan and waved it before her face, trying to cool the rush of excitement at the thought of seeing Edgar. She wasn't here for him but these gentlemen who were as dull as dishwater.

"Would anyone bat an eye if you did?"

"They wouldn't, but if I'm to share a bed with a gentleman I feel no rapture for, he must at least pique my interest and have the strength of character to approach me." They stifled giggles behind gloved hands. Louise's matched her dress of shell-pink silk over a white satin skirt trimmed with bows and tulle. At the start of husband hunting, she'd summoned her favorite ladies' tailor, Doré, and ordered a host of new gowns in colors that made Mama nearly balk.

Mama would've refused the dresses if Bertie's wife, Alix, hadn't convinced her they were the ideal for catching a potential husband's eye. So was being seen in society. Mama had finally realized what every matron already knew. Locking daughters away in the country did not further their marriage prospects.

"Your Royal Highness, may I introduce Lord Lorne, son of the Duke of Argyll?" Mrs. Gladstone escorted a square-jawed man of good height to Louise.

"Lord Lorne, I remember you. How is your family?" The Argylls' ancestral home wasn't far from Balmoral, and she'd attended many children's teas and dances there with her siblings as a child.

"They're quite well." He spoke with the same accent as Louise instead of Mr. Brown's brogue, but his voice was high and nasally from a broken nose Louise vaguely remembered Mama mentioning. His slightly off-center nose didn't detract from his square chin and tapered jaw and a forehead made to appear wider by his thick blond hair.

"I read your books about your travels." Mama had insisted on it after his mother, the Duchess of Argyll, had sent her copies. Much to her surprise, they'd been quite good. "Your time in Rome during General Garibaldi's failed invasion was gripping, I can't imagine visiting there at the height of the danger."

"I couldn't resist, and since I was already in Vienna, it was easy to abandon Bucharest for Rome. Quite by chance, my chum Gerald Talbot and I were on the same train as Garibaldi during his escape from Italy. He was most congenial when we introduced ourselves, regaling us with stories of the war and his hopes for Italy. Gerald and I were almost arrested when the Italians stopped the train and came for Garibaldi. If we hadn't made a jump for it when the soldiers weren't looking, who knows where we might've ended up?"

"Quite the adventure." With his pale blond hair and blue eyes, he didn't seem the type to rush in where angels fear to tread, and yet he had. Most intriguing.

"I'd love to hear more about your travels." Louise nodded to Sybil, who politely excused herself to speak with Mrs. Gladstone about ensuring Lorne was seated next to Louise at dinner. Their hostess was most obliging, and while they ate, Lorne regaled Louise with his stories of touring America and meeting General Lee and General Grant at the end of the

American Civil War. He described the beauty of Jamaica and the islands, creating a vivid picture of the white sand beaches and the vast wildness of Canada. She was impressed. It was unusual for a duke's eldest son to want to see something of the world.

"Arthur has written to me of how beautiful and wild Canada is. He also told me all about Italy after his visit there. I so desperately want to see Rome and Venice. I long to study the old masters," Louise said as the footmen laid cups of sweet ices before them.

"When the situation in Italy allows, I hope you get the chance to tour the grand galleries and masterpieces." He raised his wineglass to her and she returned the gesture, allowing her ice to melt as he described his experiences in Rome. He spoke to her as Leopold or Arthur might, charming in a way that reminded her of Mr. Whistler but much less ostentatious and self-important. Of course, one could hardly stand on great formality when he'd seen her in a short skirt and pigtails and she remembered him in knee britches.

She was, to her surprise, disappointed when dinner ended, but pleased he chose to remain beside her discussing art and Italy until Mr. and Mrs. Gladstone drew the evening to a close.

"Thank you for a very pleasant evening, Your Royal Highness." Lord Lorne handed her into the carriage.

"Thanks to you, it exceeded my expectations."

"It was my pleasure." He stepped back and the footman closed the door behind them and they set off.

"A charming man," Sybil said.

"He's the best of the lot so far." But nothing could compare to the thrill of seeing Edgar. Louise unpinned the mesh modesty panel Mama had insisted be inserted in the gown and stuffed it in her reticule. Without it, the square-cut bodice displayed the swell of her bosom to its full advantage, and the gold chain holding the medal of her and Edgar underneath draped down to nestle between her breasts.

They arrived at Mr. Whistler's, the outside of the house as staid as 11 Carlton House Terrace but the gathering inside as exhilarating as a quick-moving train. There was no more real furniture than before, and women in full evening gowns sat on packing crates beside those in the loose, corsetless gowns favored by the artists' models and wives. A half-painted yellow wall abutted the white one she'd first seen with Miss Hiffernan posed against it, the dripping paint cans and still-wet brushes left on the floor in front of it. In chipped and mismatched vases throughout the room, headily scented flowers perfumed the air, their scent blending with the more earthy ones of Mr. Whistler's favorite buckwheat pancakes and cornbread, the food of his native country.

"Art should be independent of claptrap," Mr. Whistler announced from where he stood on a sagging cane chair, arms out wide, his usual duck suit exchanged for a dapper evening one paired with high-polished patent-leather shoes. A bright red handkerchief poked out from his coat pocket, as much a contrast to his impeccable black suit as the yellow paint stains on his fingers. "It should stand alone, and appeal to the artistic senses, not play on emotions such as pity, love, and the like."

"Here, here," the cheers went up from around the room.

Louise stood on the threshold unnoticed by the guests, having instructed the butler not to announce her. She enjoyed the brief moment of anonymity and the chance to breathe in Mr. Whistler's energy and excitement.

"I enjoy Mr. Whistler, but sometimes I feel sorry for him," Sybil said from beside her as they watched him continue his oration.

"Whatever do you mean? He's commanding the room."

"It's commanding him. He's so determined to put on a show for everyone, he has no chance of ever being himself with any of them, not even Miss Hiffernan."

"Are any of us allowed to be who we truly wish to be?"

"No, but we can be as honest with others and ourselves as our positions allow. A lesson Mr. Whistler must learn if he wants to be happy or remain with Miss Hiffernan."

Louise studied Miss Hiffernan where she stood beside Mr. Whistler, one hand on his thigh, the other on the back of the chair, quite unnoticed by him as she worked to keep him upright. The lines at the corners of her full lips were more drawn than before, Mr. Whistler's grandiose speech not nearly as inspiring to her as to everyone else.

"My dear Princess, you have arrived." Mr. Whistler hopped off the chair and, taking Miss Hiffernan by the hand, approached Louise.

"How could I miss this?"

"If you'll excuse me." Miss Hiffernan tried to pull out of his grip, but he held her tight.

"Please, don't leave on my account," Louise insisted. "I'd very much like it if you stayed."

The worry in her wide brown eyes eased and a small smile spread across her face. She exchanged a look with Mr. Whistler, who stood quite sure of himself, but Louise had no time to speak to her, as Mr. Whistler motioned to a slender man with a pointed beard passing nearby.

"Sir Coutts, I have an artist you must meet."

"No introduction is necessary. I know of Her Royal Highness, her reputation as a sculptress precedes her."

"You flatter me, Sir Coutts."

"But he doesn't lie," Mr. Whistler insisted. The two of them shared the current fashion of full mustaches, but Sir Coutts was fair-haired and paler.

"You must honor me with one of your works once my new gallery is built. A talent such as yours shouldn't remain hidden," Sir Coutts insisted.

"I'd be honored."

"Coutts will help us show those stuffy Royal Academy men they aren't the arbiters of taste or style," Mr. Whistler said. "But I will dominate your time no more, Miss Saxe-Coburg-Gotha." Sir Coutts gaped at the informality, and Mr. Whistler ignored him and pointed toward the dining room. "Your friends are in there and quite eager to see you."

"You're a devil, Mr. Whistler."

"I know, and it'd be a pleasure for this devil to make the introductions for Lady St. Albans." He offered Sybil his arm and she took it, allowing him to lead her into the mess of packing crates and guests.

There were more canvases along the dining room walls than before, and the guests stepped around them to reach the table and choose slices of apple pie and pieces of cornbread from the American fare laid out on an old drop cloth.

Edgar, Nino, Henrietta, and Mr. Morgan stood at the far end of the room beneath three Japanese scrolls of mountains and white cranes hung on the wall and a shelf decorated with blue and white Chinese bowls and vases. This was the first time she'd seen Edgar since Scotland, and he nearly took her breath away in his black evening coat, the darkness of it widening his shoulders and deepening the rich chestnut color of his hair.

"I need someone to make the die from my wax model of the medallion for the London Annual International Exhibition. Mr. Morgan, are up to the challenge?" Edgar asked.

Mr. Morgan nearly choked on his apple pie. "It would be an honor, sir. Thank you so much for considering me."

"I enjoy giving friendly young talent a leg up. If Mr. Rogers hadn't returned to Birmingham, I'd have work for him too. I'll inform the committee of your agreement and send the necessary contract."

"It's very kind of you to share you work and honors with others," Louise complimented, joining the group to a round of surprised welcomes.

"Such sweet praise makes me almost wish I'd continued sculpting." Nino stepped around Mr. Morgan to bow over Louise's hand. "Congratulations are in order for you, my dear Miss Saxe-Coburg-Gotha. The Royal Academy selection committee was beside themselves when you entered your bust of Her Majesty for the Exhibition."

Edgar watched her from over Nino's shoulder, too confident in himself and their affection to be threatened by the young swell.

"I heard, when the school's Board of Governors learned of it, they discussed renaming the female school in your honor," Henrietta said. "They thought it might encourage women from aristocratic families to attend and pay fees, but cooler heads prevailed."

"Thank heavens. I prefer my patronage to be more tangible." She caressed the fall of the gold chain down her chest to where it disappeared beneath her bodice, drawing Edgar's gaze to the swell of her breasts before he raised it.

"Come, gentlemen, I hear Mr. Whistler waxing poetic about Valparaiso and I wish to hear it." Henrietta, sensing a change in the air, drew the others away. She must have guessed there was something between Edgar and Louise. Most likely they all had, but, as they did with Miss Hiffernan and Mr. Whistler, they turned a blind eye to it.

Despite their leaving, other guests still drifted through the room, and there wasn't a private corner or balcony to be found. Louise and Edgar managed a small space for themselves in front of a large half-finished canvas of an elderly woman in profile wearing a long black dress. A white widow's cap covered the back of her hair, the ends of it draping down her thin shoulders.

"She reminds me of Mama." Except the severity of her age was softened by a hint of color on the apples of her cheeks and the affection in her focused gaze.

"She's Mac's mother."

"I must meet her."

"Come here often enough and you will, but I advise against it. Mac isn't a rascal you want to get entangled with."

"Jealous?"

"Of course." He winked at her, and she longed to lose herself in his arms, to meld against him as tightly as her corset against her body. If they were alone, she might press her lips to his and make the long months of loneliness since she'd last seen him disappear, but this tepid closeness was the most they could enjoy.

"My *Her Majesty at Her Spinning Wheel* is going to be exhibited at the Royal Academy near yours. It's already caused quite a stir, and for all the right reasons."

"You've stirred me in ways I never thought possible," she whispered, the other guests out of earshot. "I haven't sculpted or drawn the same since you came to Scotland. Even after you left, once I was done moping, I couldn't stop working."

"Nor I since leaving you, my hunger to do larger works is insatiable." He leaned in to allow his breath to brush the curls beside her ears before straightening when yet another couple promenaded past. "Mac is writing to General Robert E. Lee's son on my behalf to suggest a large bronze of him in Virginia. I also submitted proposals for a Prince of Wales statue in Bombay and one in Melbourne. His Royal Highness has become as grand a patron as Her Majesty."

"He's quite impressed with you." A couple drifted by, forcing them into silence until they'd passed.

"I'm sure you had no small hand in shaping his opinion."

"I might have had some influence with him."

Another couple approached the painting, stopping to admire it before moving on.

"The newspapers are abuzz with rumors of your possible engagement to Prince William of Denmark," Edgar said, sending a jolt of worry through Louise.

She had no idea what Edgar thought of the very real possibility she might marry another man. She hoped he was as liberal-minded as Mr. Whistler and the others when it came to domestic arrangements. There was no way to know until it was decided, and at the present she was as far from becoming engaged as when she'd begun the search. In everything she was doing to gain him, she might lose him. "They're only rumors. Stories about me sell newspapers, so every man I speak with becomes the subject of one."

"Except me."

"Never you. I cherish you too much to expose you to such slander."

"When can I see you alone again?" The need in his voice matched the desire coiling deep inside of her.

"Send word through Sybil when you're free at your studio. I'll do what I can to visit you there. I can't endure another minute without you." She would surrender everything to him the next time they were alone, if he would have her.

"Nor I you." He craved her touch as much as she did his, it was there in his invitation and the fire in his eyes. He wouldn't refuse her here as he had at Balmoral, and her heart caught in her chest in both yearning and worry.

She hoped he wanted her this much when she was another man's wife.

It seemed so strange being amongst so many, yet feeling so alone, without my beloved husband! Everything so like former great functions, and yet so unlike! I felt much moved, and nearly broke down when I saw the dear name and the following inscriptions—"Honour to the memory of Albert the Good . . ."
—Queen Victoria's Journal

Windsor Castle, February 1870

"You will not dine in London again, not at Marlborough House or anywhere without me," Mama announced from across the open carriage where she sat beside Lady Ely. Mama's full figure rocked in time to the steady gait of the horses pulling them through Frogmore to Papa's mausoleum. Today was their wedding anniversary, and the end of yet another year without him. Her usual white veil was replaced with a black one and even Louise had been forced to eschew her new dresses for an old black frock.

"How do you expect me to meet gentlemen if I don't regularly venture to London?"

"I will invite suitable young men here to dine."

"And scare them off with a glimpse of their future if they marry me?" she mumbled into her shoulder.

"What did you say?"

"Nothing, Mama."

"Good, it is about time you learned to hold your tongue. I know you visit artists' studios without my permission."

"They're my friends." Besides seeing Edgar, she'd spent time with Henrietta and Nino, and had made more forays to Mr. Whistler's every time she stayed with Bertie in London. She couldn't show Edgar's studio too much favor or Mama would become even more suspicious than she already was. Thankfully, Sybil always accompanied her, helping silence potential gossip.

"You are not to be on such familiar terms with those people. They are too bohemian and licentious for a princess in your unmarried state, and it was wrong of Lady St. Albans to allow it. By being so intimate with Lady St. Albans, you have encouraged her to forsake her duties. In the future, Lady Ely will chaperone you in London."

Horror at her new assignment twisted Lady Ely's face before she hid it behind her parasol.

"I blame Bertie and that awful Marlborough House Set of his. He is a bad influence on you." Mama continued turning over the subject like the wheels of the carriage. "Do not emulate him. You cannot risk becoming a spinster by being so lax with your behavior, and a princess must marry."

"Beatrice will take comfort in that decree." Everyone in the family knew Mama planned to keep her youngest unmarried and by her side for good.

"Baby's future is not your concern." Mama banged her fist on the side of the carriage, making the horses toss their heads so the carriage driver had to click to settle them. Mr. Brown sat beside the driver pretending not to listen, but Louise knew he heard every word. "You will limit your activities and acquaintances to people and events I approve of."

Louise crossed her arms, fuming in silence. She touched the Edgar medal where it was pinned inside her corset, and the worry that she'd been caught out by one of Mama's spies tightened her stomach. Edgar might be cut off from the royal patronage at any moment, hobbling his career and seeing him banished from her life as fast as Walter had been. Once again, it would be her fault, her affection ruining his happiness and hers. It wasn't fair, when all she wanted was his heart and success.

"Your Majesty, we're nearly there." Mr. Brown motioned to the patina copper roof of Papa's mausoleum coming into view through the trees.

Mama clutched her prayer book to her chest, the sudden shift from anger to grief nearly overturning the carriage. She stared at the Portland stone building as if Papa were waiting inside to greet her.

Lady Ely handed Mama a black-edged handkerchief and Mama pressed it to her cheeks, wiping away the fat tears sliding down them. If Louise weren't so angry, she might grasp Mama's hand in sympathy, but she didn't move. It didn't matter how much Louise might be suffering in her grief and troubles, she'd never receive the same courtesy in return from her mother.

No one did, not even Alice, who'd written to Mama in grief at losing her poor little son Frittie, only to be told the death of a husband was far worse than the loss of a child. Louise, acting as secretary, saw her mother's callous words. She would rather have burned the letter than send it, but she hadn't been able to, any more than she could step out of this carriage and walk back to Windsor.

They rolled to a stop at the base of the mausoleum entrance and Mr. Brown stepped off the box and offered Mama his arm. She leaned heavily on him as they climbed the stone steps, Louise and Lady Ely following them.

"Look at the trouble you've caused for both of us," Lady Ely hissed at Louise as they passed the two large guardian angels standing watch at the Romanesque entrance, as indifferent to Louise's plight as Mama.

All pretense to the ancient world ended the moment they

crossed the threshold, the plain light-cream-and-gray exterior giving way to vibrant Renaissance colors inside. Gilded frescoes of saints, cherubs, and angels covered the walls, and the stained-glass windows in the dome washed the marble philosophers in their niches in multicolored light. Everything whispered of Papa's love of Renaissance art, especially Raphael.

Mama, leaning hard on John Brown's arm, stood in front of Papa's massive sarcophagus, the dark Aberdeen granite a contrast to the white marble effigy of Papa in repose. He was carved with his face turned slightly toward the empty space on his left, waiting for the day when Mama's effigy would be there to gaze back at him.

"He was so perfect. He was not meant for this cruel world, and he was never truly happy or at peace in it either," Mama said to Mr. Brown, her voice whispering among the angels looking down on them from the high ceiling. "Without him, I have nothing to look forward to except my eternal rest beside him. I welcome the day, and I am certain my dear Albert longs for it too."

No, he's doesn't, Louise wanted to scream at Mama; but she wouldn't listen, any more than the stone figures could hear. *He was happy with us and never would've chosen death over us for any reason. He wanted us to live, as he wanted to live. He simply wasn't strong enough.*

Tears blurred her vision of the fresco behind Papa's effigy of Jesus emerging from the tomb. There was one similar to it in Ludwig Gruner's book on Italian frescoes, the one Papa and Louise had spent hours studying when Papa had been designing the Palace Garden, drawing on their inspiration to inspire his. He'd been enchanted by the life and energy infused in the works of Raphael and the old masters. He would've recoiled at them being used to glorify his death, and would've railed at Mama for wrapping herself in mourning. Louise had overheard their rows a few months after Grandmamma's death, when Papa's patience at Mama's prolonged mourning for her mother and her refusal to face her ministers and duties had worn thin. He never would've allowed Mama to wallow in grief or surround herself with people who encouraged and indulged her morbid fascination.

You shouldn't have left us. You know how much we needed you. Everything would be so different if you'd stayed. She could see the life she, Leopold, and her other brothers and sisters would've enjoyed if Papa had lived. The joy and love of planting vegetables in the Osborne House garden or decorating the large Christmas tree at Windsor with him would've accompanied them as they'd grown up. Instead, they faced nothing but the perpetual gloom of Mama's ceaseless mourning.

Louise wiped away the tears dampening her cheeks, the darkness and pain that'd hollowed her during those first awful weeks after Papa's passing settling over her again. She sniffed back tears and Mama turned at the sound.

"Oh, my poor dear." She grasped Louise's hands, looking at her with all the care and concern she'd shown when Louise had been deathly ill with scarlet fever at fourteen. "You feel it too? As though there is nothing without his light and support."

Louise nodded, surprised. Perhaps Mama understood her better than she realized, and if she told her everything in her

heart, her desire for freedom, the need for art and a life beyond the duties of a personal secretary, she might understand.

"Do not worry, someday we will be happy and together
again in heaven." Mama entwined her arm in Louise's and
brought her to stand before Papa's sarcophagus. "Draw hope
from that."

Louise wanted to wrench away and yell at her to stop, to let
Papa go and live. She wanted to scream until her cries made
the walls crumble and the copper roof cave in. Instead, she
stood silently beside Mama, helpless to make her want to live,
to stop her from reaching for someone she could no longer
touch, or to understand why she herself wanted more than
meaninglessness and mourning.

Find the light. Edgar's words whispered in the quiet, and
Louise gazed up at the gilded ceiling, with its stars and rows
of carved angels standing foot-to-head and rising up to the
center. Their bodies glittered against the cobalt-blue star-
bursts encircling the center, the sunlight catching every brilliant gold fleck lovingly applied to the red Portuguese marble.
Every detail filled her with the same awe the portraits in Herr
Gruner's book had inspired in Papa all those year ago. Papa
was dead to Mama and beyond her reach, but he was here
with Louise in every angel's face, the fall and curves of the
marble scholars in their niches encouraging her in their silence to crave, do, and learn more.

Art for art's sake, she said silently to herself. It was here
to speak to her not of the lessons of history or philosophy but
what she needed most at this moment, the love, encouragement, and strength Papa had once given her.

Chapter Twelve

Princess Louise was charming last night, and won the hearts of everybody. H.R.H. had Lord Ilchester on her side and Lord Rosebery opposite . . . Lord Dalrymple (pleasing but young) never took his eyes off the Princess but he was too shy to speak. So was Mr. Compton and Mr. Robartes . . . Lord Granville does not think much progress was made last night, but it will not be without use for the future, in encouraging young men to approach the Princess.

—LORD GRANVILLE TO QUEEN VICTORIA

London, March 1870

"If you want the torture to end, then make your selection," Bertie scolded, the two of them enjoying a rare moment alone in the carriage ferrying them back to Marlborough House from the Deptford Dockyard after their christening of the H.M.S. *Druid*. Bertie had ordered Lady Ely to ride in the carriage behind them and she'd obeyed. The day had been a jostle of brief glimpses of the blue sky through the thick clouds. Driving sleet forced spectators to crouch in doorways and under the slim eaves of the brown brick buildings lining the streets along the carriage route. "You've been at this for months and we're all tired of it."

"I don't see why any of you are concerned with my decision at all." There'd been a flurry of letters between Mama and Vicky over Louise's decision to marry a subject instead of a foreign prince. While Alice counseled patience and acceptance, Vicky railed against it, worried Louise's decision might lower her standing in the eyes of her husband's imperial family. "Besides, I have yet to meet a gentleman worth his salt. There must be another way."

"Not unless you want to become a pariah. Papa's mother was cast out of her country and sons' lives because she chose love over duty. The same will happen to you if you do something so foolish. You'd never see me, Leopold, Arthur, or England ever again."

"You three wouldn't be so heartless."

"Mama would be, and so would her subjects." He motioned to the people crowding the narrow Deptford roads to cheer and wave them on. The faint tang of champagne from droplets blown back on her purple velvet skirt after she'd broken the bottle against the hull mingled with the scent of Bertie's Turkish cigarettes. "You're royal, not human, and if you ruin their illusions, they'll crush you."

"I know." It wasn't simply Vicky intruding on her affairs but the entire nation.

"There's another, more practical matter to consider if you're thinking of an ill-advised route." He took off his top hat and set it on the seat beside him, running his fingers through his hair to straighten it. "I had tea with Lady Walden yesterday.

On my recommendation, she commissioned your sculptor to do a statue of Lord Walden's favorite horse. The woman she met with to discuss the contract and payment details was Mrs. Boehm, Mr. Boehm's wife."

The carriage bottom could've fallen out and dropped Louise on the pavement and she wouldn't have felt it.

"He's married?" She wanted to throw up and at the same time take a chisel to every piece Edgar had executed at Balmoral. "He can't be. In all our time together he's never mentioned a wife."

"Have you been forthcoming with him about your marriage prospects?"

She shifted on the squab. "Not entirely. I didn't think it necessary until something was decided."

"Then stop playing the innocent. Someone must have told you."

"My friends never mentioned it, not even Mr. Whistler." Although she realized he wasn't the most reliable gentleman when it came to domestic arrangements. He and Miss Hiffernan had recently parted ways after he'd confessed to siring a child with the parlor maid.

"You must have suspected, or at least assumed."

"I didn't." She touched the medal beneath her bodice, not sure if she should grasp it or toss it in the nearest fountain.

"Because you didn't want to. You wanted him, consequences be damned."

Bertie was right. Like Mama, she'd seen what she'd wished to see. She'd rushed into Edgar's arms and bed with the same girlish enthusiasm and carelessness as with Walter, but the clues had been there in Edgar's well-managed money, his clean tailored clothes, the studio not attached to a house where, as she well knew, family often interrupted work. "Are there children?"

"Three girls and a boy, all of whom are a consequence, and you must either carry on or end things."

"I can't ruin a marriage." She'd listened to Alix fret over Bertie's infidelities enough times to not be glib about what continuing with Edgar meant. She wondered if Edgar's wife knew. She must. No wife could be that blind.

"You don't know what kind of marriage it is. Mrs. Boehm might appreciate her husband finding comfort elsewhere. A few discreet inquiries into her character and the nature of their relationship will give you an idea of how best to manage her and the affair."

"Don't say it like that."

"Use whatever pretty words you like, but it is what it is, and you'll manage it a great deal better as a married woman with the protection of a husband's name." He slid a gold watch from his waistcoat pocket and checked the hour. "Whatever you decide, be quick about it. The best of the lot will be snapped up by younger girls without overbearing queens for mamas if you don't decide soon."

"You're a hard one." She swiped at him and the watch, but he dodged her strike, closing the case and sliding it in his pocket.

"I'm a realist, and despite this current fancy, so are you. Even if you break off with your sculptor, you're better off married in a home of your own than with Mama."

It was a bitter truth she'd avoided for as long as possible, attending dinners and meeting gentlemen because it was required but never taking them or the situation seriously. She tried to consider the young men she'd met, but all she could think about was Edgar and the next time they'd be alone together. Even after everything she'd learned, to her shame she still wanted him. Every intimacy they'd shared in his studio, exploring one another's bodies in the precious hours they could steal together, and each conversation afterward had been more real to her than anything in any drawing room with anyone else. However, Bertie was right: There were choices to make. She knew how much his infidelities cut Alix, and she was doing the same to another woman. She shouldn't, but Edgar understood her as no one else did, saw the woman beneath the Princess, and encouraged her to strive and live. She couldn't lose that. "You've met some of the scions thrown at me. Who do you think will pass muster?"

"The one accommodating enough to be practical about the situation." Bertie removed his cigarette case from his coat pocket and held it out to her. She selected one, then drew the window curtain. They were out of Deptford and the rain had driven the few curious onlookers along the road inside, allowing her a clandestine smoke.

"How does one even broach the topic with a gentleman? I've barely been able to discuss more than horses with most of them, much less something this indelicate."

"You're a clever girl. You'll sort it out."

Louise drew in a deep breath, then slowly let out the smoke. "Will Edgar have me on these terms?"

"If he doesn't, there are others." He inhaled his cigarette and let the smoke out slowly to block his face before it drifted away.

Louise barely tasted the spicy tobacco. It wasn't right, what she was doing. Edgar was married, but she knew vows were no guarantee of love. Certainly no one in her family had married under such conditions. Affection might come later, but it'd never been there from the start. If it existed with Edgar, if he wasn't a cad she'd been foolish enough to believe, then she would do what must be done to be with him.

"I'll need your help managing things." No one else sympathized with her delicate situation like Bertie did. "The first will be a meeting with Edgar."

Bertie is returned greatly pleased to have been to Mr. Boehm's today and saw the two monuments to our beloved friends—the two Deans. They are beautiful and so like.

*—Queen Victoria to her daughter
the Crown Princess of Prussia*

"MR. BOEHM, HOW good of you to see me on such short notice," Bertie greeted Edgar in his Marlborough House study. Bertie had conjured up an excuse to keep Louise in London with him and Alix another night.

Louise listened from behind a painted screen of French ladies at Versailles. Through the crack between the hinged panels, she could see the back of Edgar's head where he stood beneath the portrait of her brother in his naval uniform. She wanted to rush out from behind the screen and demand to know where they stood and what future, if any, they might enjoy, but she waited for Bertie's cue to reveal herself, both anticipating and dreading it. Despite her sweating palms, she had to face him. She wasn't a coward, but she felt like one today, as well as a lovesick ninny.

"I'm happy to accommodate your Royal Highness's request, especially in regards to the Bombay bronze. You own an impressive sculpture collection." Edgar motioned to the group of statuettes and busts under the stained-glass window beside the fireplace, including a copy of Louise's bust of Arthur. "I recognize a number of accomplished artists, especially this one."

"Studying beneath you has been one of my sister's greatest pleasures. She's thrived under your instruction, in more ways than one."

Edgar's silence greeted Bertie's none-too-subtle innuendo, the heaviness of it broken by the crack and pop of the burning logs in the fireplace.

"I'm sorry if I've offended Your Royal Highness." A slight nervousness marked Edgar's words, and if Louise hadn't been listening so intently, she might have missed it. "Artists are passionate individuals, not always to our benefit."

"I'm not offended, but it isn't my forgiveness you need." Bertie reached his hand behind the screen and Louise took it, allowing him to escort her out like a princess, not a wronged lover.

Edgar beamed at Louise, before the stern look on her face made his smile drop.

"You two have a great deal to discuss, but do it quickly. I can only occupy Lady Ely for so long. She's not an engaging woman." Bertie made for the door, pausing before leaving.

"Don't fret about the Bombay piece, Mr. Boehm, the work will continue no matter what you both decide. You're too talented a sculptor to lose."

His ominous announcement made, he closed the door behind him, offering them a few precious minutes of privacy. Louise wished she could squander it in his arms, but she must be clear on where they stood, and what the future held for them.

"I'm told you're married."

He straightened his silver cuff link. "I thought you knew."

"People don't enjoy telling princesses unpleasant things."

"Then I'm sorry I didn't inform you myself. I didn't think it necessary. I'd promised to always be honest with you. I've failed in that regard."

After a lifetime of sycophantic courtiers, tutors, and servants, she'd learned long ago to recognize falsehood and shallow flattery. It was why she and Sybil were so close, and why Edgar had captured her heart, until this moment. She wasn't sure what to think of him. "I won't be made to look like a fool simply because I lost my head."

Edgar ran his fingers over the top of the bronze statuette of a horse and rider on the table beside Bertie's rolltop desk. "Fanny and I met when we were very young. Her brother and mine raised objections to the match, ones time has proven to be well founded. Our personalities are too different. Fanny is a woman of solid things with little imagination or passion."

"Yet you remain with her." It was a story too similar to the ones Bertie had heard from his mistresses.

"She's the mother of my children, and stood beside me during the lean years before I found success. I won't deprive her of the standing and respect owed a wife by abandoning her in my profitable years, especially since she's partly responsible for them." It was like Bertie and Alix. Bertie was always respectful to his wife and her position as the Princess of Wales, but it didn't stop him from wandering. Despite his infidelity, Alix was certain he'd always return to her, and he did, in his own way. "Fanny has a way with money and clients and I rely on her to manage the children and household so I may work. It's a suitable arrangement for both of us."

Louise admired his determination to stand beside his wife, to give her every honor a companion and helpmate deserved, except his full affection. "Are there others besides me?"

"There have been, and I was as discreet with them as I've been with you. I won't publicly insult her or you."

"Does she know about us?"

"I'm sure she does, but beyond my tutoring you, it's a subject we don't discuss, and she's as discreet as I am in all matters. A requirement for dealing with our varied clients."

She wanted to believe him, to fall in his arms and allow his kisses to wipe away the doubt draping her like a drop cloth, but she couldn't. It all sounded too neat and tidy, as if he were telling her what she wanted to hear instead of the truth. It was time to be honest with him and see if that decided the matter. "You understand, given my position, I won't remain without a husband for much longer."

He opened his arms, palms up in resignation. "We both know what's expected of us."

"You don't care that I'll be another man's wife?"

"Of course I care, but I'm a mere subject, a man who might touch the stars but never the moon." He marched up on her, passion and agony flaring in his eyes. "Every day I curse our positions for keeping us apart. Each time I read you might be betrothed, I imagine you sharing his name, his life, his bed, and I want to break everything in sight. If I could make you entirely mine I would, but I can't."

She clasped his forearms, the muscle strong and taut beneath his suit. He wanted her as much as she wanted him, the deep frustration of their separation flowing through him as it did through her. She raised her hand and laid it aside his cheek, the slight edge in his jaw muscles easing beneath her touch. "What are we going to do?"

Behind her, the doorknob clicked and they stepped apart for the sake of appearances. Bertie entered, closing the door behind him and saying nothing about their blushes and avoiding glances.

"Lady Ely is proving most difficult to distract. I fear if Mr. Boehm doesn't take his leave while Alix is amusing her, this will all be for nothing."

"Yes, Your Royal Highness. Thank you again for your kindness and consideration." Edgar bowed to Bertie, then took Louise's hand in his, tilting over it and glancing up at her through his thick brow. "If you ask me to fight every day for us to steal what happiness we can, I will. You have only to ask."

Words failed her. Every step they took down this road meant more danger, deceptions, and risks, and it all might be for nothing if he was a lying cad.

At her silence, he squeezed her fingers before releasing them and making for the door.

"My man will show you the safe way out." Bertie handed

Edgar off to his valet, who held far more dangerous and demeaning secrets than this one.

Edgar tossed one last glance back at Louise. "I await your answer."

He strode out of the room.

"Everything settled, then?" Bertie asked, as if they'd merely been discussing a contract.

"No." She wanted Edgar as much as she'd wanted a place at the National Art Training School, but she wasn't a complete simpleton. She'd make discreet inquiries about Mrs. Boehm and discover if everything Edgar had told her about the nature of their marriage was true, then decide if there was a place for him in her life, even if it was outside the bounds of a church service and vows.

Chapter Thirteen

Her Majesty, has ever manifested a warm interest in the prosperity of the arts, of which she has on this occasion given a substantial proof by permitting her accomplished daughter, Her Royal Highness Princess Louise, to send to the exhibition a marble bust executed . . . by her own hand a faithful likeness of her own mother . . . the princess has produced a likeness of our beloved Queen in which truth is happily combined with art and taste . . . every artist and lover of the arts throughout this kingdom will appreciate this honor conferred on the arts . . . the Queen has signified her intention of honoring the exhibition and inspecting our new galleries.

—Speech by the Royal Academy president at the Royal Academy Exhibition Opening Banquet

London, April 1870

Let me be the first to tell Your Majesty how glad I and the Royal Academy are to hear His Royal Highness, Prince Alfred, was not mortally wounded by that awful Fenian in Australia. A rebel trying to assassinate the Prince while he was visiting a hospital is beyond contempt," Sir Francis Grant, president of the Royal Academy of Arts, offered Mama as he led her, Bertie, Louise, Sybil, Lady Churchill, and various attendants through the crowded galleries of Burlington House and the annual art exhibition.

"We appreciate your gratitude," Mama said, deigning for once to make a public appearance, much to Vicky's glee. She hadn't been shy in writing to congratulate Louise on bringing it about.

The people parted at the royal approach, turning their backs on the massive number of paintings covering every inch of wall to bow and curtsey to Mama. Louise could hardly see the wall colors through the gilded frames hung cheek-by-jowl up to the curved ceilings.

"The Royal Academy is certainly taking advantage of the extra exhibition space." Louise wondered how anyone but the most renowned artists could hope to gain notice in the muddle. If she weren't a royal, her piece would probably be collecting dust in the attic where Nino told her every rejected entry went to die.

"The move to Burlington House was one of our best decisions," Sir Francis Grant said in his Scottish brogue, his square face framed by large muttonchops that still held a touch of black. He'd painted Mama many times, his ability to add grandeur to subjects, as much as his Scots roots, winning her favor and a title for himself. "The former premises were too cramped and dark, but here the selected works have a place to shine and be seen. None more so than Your Royal Highness's."

He led them to a plinth enjoying pride of place in the center of the Octagon Room where the sculptures were displayed. On top rested Louise's marble bust of Mama that she'd completed with Edgar at Balmoral. Around it was a frenzy of tables, plinths, socles, and shelves cluttered with men, women, horses, and various other figures. The skylight did all it could to allow in the sun struggling to shine through yet another thick fog, robbing the marble of its crystalline glitter and the dark bronzes of their subtle shine.

"I knew I was right to encourage Her Royal Highness to pursue additional studies." Mama basked in her image, while Louise nearly choked on the hypocrisy. She wished she could rewrite the past as easily as her mother often did. "She has such natural talent and an eye for the regal tempered with the familiar."

"Her piece is as elegant in its presentation of Your Majesty as Mr. Boehm's is timeless. We've heard nothing but praise for his work from both members and viewers. The critics are in awe of it too." Sir Francis led them to the far end of the room, where Edgar's marble statuette of *Her Majesty at the Spinning Wheel* stood. "The brilliance of portraying Your Majesty in a pastoral manner so even the lowliest of your subjects may contemplate your maternal care for them is brilliant."

"Mr. Boehm's skills are to be marveled at and I am pleased beyond measure to have discovered him. He completed a most fitting tribute to my Highland servant Mr. Brown with a full-sized statue and a number of busts. No artist has ever captured Mr. Brown's stoic character as well as Mr. Boehm," Mama proclaimed to awkward smiles and glances, the memory of Sir Edwin Landseer's portrait of Mama on horseback with John Brown holding the reins and the rumors it'd sparked still fresh in their minds. Mama didn't notice the sudden unease around her, so pleased with Sir Edwin's portrait that she'd ennobled him for the painting that'd scandalized so many.

"Is Mr. Boehm here today?" Louise asked with as much nonchalance as she could muster. "I wish to congratulate him on his success."

"He is. I asked him to be present when I showed Her Majesty his statue, but, as is his habit, he shied away from anything smacking of an unveiling."

"Mr. Boehm is as humble as he is talented." Mama appreciated his desire to avoid the limelight.

"He's far more talented than some I see displayed here," Bertie observed, raising the tip of his walking stick to a bronze head of a woman captured in surprise.

"Ah, Monsieur Rodin. He has a *unique* style," Sir Francis mused, sharing Bertie's lack of admiration for the artist and his submission.

Louise found it fascinating, the young woman's amazed expression so lifelike one almost didn't notice her rough-sculpted hair or shoulders, the dark bronze adding to the realism of her natural pose.

"Careful what you say about other sculptors' works, Bertie," Louise warned with a smile. "Or a disgruntled artist might try and assassinate you."

"Heaven forbid." Sir Grant clasped his hand to his heart, not sharing the royal sense of humor. He continued to lead them through the galleries, but Louise barely heard anything he said about the pencil drawings and landscapes, too busy searching for Edgar in every face. They hadn't seen each other or spoken since the meeting at Marlborough House when so much had been left unfinished. She had no idea how he would take her today, and wished they didn't have to meet in a public venue, but there was no choice. At least Sybil was accompanying her today and not Lady Ely, who was laid up at Windsor with a nasty cold.

The group progressed into the Landscape Room and Louise fell farther and farther behind, loitering at the back with Sybil.

"This is your chance to sneak off," Bertie whispered to Louise, sensing her eagerness to explore the galleries on her own. "I'll keep Mama and this lot amused for as long as I can."

"Thank you." She and Sybil ventured to the second sculpting room. Henrietta had a small piece on exhibit there, the face of a child done in terra-cotta, and Louise expected her and the rest of her friends to be there. Not seeing them, they returned to the Octagon Room, admiring the bust of Empress Eugénie tactfully placed far from Mama's to avoid drawing unfair comparison between Her Majesty and the elegant French empress. Louise noticed a small crowd collected around her piece.

"Let's sneak over behind them. I want to hear what they think of it."

It might be her only opportunity to overhear an unfettered opinion. She didn't have to wait long.

"Her Royal Highness should've submitted it under a pseudonym," a lanky man with a thick head of wispy brown hair said to the woman beside him. "I believe more is said in deference to her rank than her skill."

"You are mistaken." The elderly woman beside him raised a silver handheld monocle to one eye to better examine the royal image. "It is competently done."

"See the flaws of flesh about the neck and the slight jowls. It indicates the lack of an experienced hand." He scribbled his thoughts in his notebook before tucking it and his pencil in his pocket. "Let's see how Mr. Boehm's version of Her Majesty compares."

"Who was that?" Sybil asked once they were gone.

"Mr. William Rossetti, the art critic." Tomorrow he'd print his impressions of the exhibition and single out artists for praise or scorn. What he decided to write about her work would influence how people viewed it and her. She wondered if others shared his opinion.

"He's the worst of an already bad lot." Mr. Whistler slid in between them, reverent enough not to take their arms but irreverent enough to stand so close. "If I could drown every art critic in the Thames, I would, especially him. Imagine, allowing one man's opinion to control everyone else's. Who appointed him the ultimate arbiter of taste?"

"He's self-anointed, and widely read," Louise commiserated, startled by this first brush with true criticism. Edgar had been right. It was easier to digest after enduring many frank opinions from her classmates and friends.

"One of these days, I'll knock him off his self-made throne," Mr. Whistler vowed.

"If anyone can accomplish such a feat, it's you. Where is your piece?"

"Sir Francis has packed the exhibition with portraiture, as much to aggrandize himself and his genre. Landscapes have been given scant attention, and as my works are studies of the docks complete with the fog I so love to paint, they didn't find favor with this year's jury."

"Perhaps if you didn't paint the fog."

"No, I must include it in every study of the Thames."

His exaggerated insistence made Louise forget Mr. Rossetti, and she was about to tease him for his love of hazy landscapes when the sight across the room silenced her.

Edgar entered with a woman on his arm, the ring on her left finger announcing her position as much as the courtesy with which he escorted her to *Her Majesty at the Spinning Wheel*. Mrs. Boehm was not stout but not thin, four children having widened her figure a touch from what Louise guessed was once a trim one capable of turning Edgar's head. She held his full attention today while Louise stood here gaping at him.

"Your Royal Highness, might I escort you to the portrait gallery?" Mr. Whistler asked, noting their entrance and Louise's pallor.

"Please."

They walked out the opposite door before Edgar could see her, eager to avoid any uncomfortable encounters. She tried to admire the exhibition, but all she could think about was Edgar's wife on his arm, a place she could never occupy. He'd said they were more business partners than man and wife, but they'd appeared happy and content. If they'd groused at one another with thinly veiled barbs, she'd readily agree to Edgar's proposal and take comfort in what he'd told her, but their domestic harmony made it so difficult to accept.

"You were aware of her but didn't expect to see her here,"

Mr. Whistler ventured, astute enough to guess what'd sobered Louise.

"Are there others I should be aware of, so I'm not surprised again?"

"Lady Cardigan a number of years ago, and a model here and there, presently leaning on some inferior artist's arm, but no one since he met you." A boyish smile spread across his face, his thrill at discovering she wasn't squeamish about the realities of life greatly amusing him.

"He's quite open with you about his affairs," she observed.

"What else is there to do but chat while we work?" He lowered his voice, discreet for once. "Spuch has been miserable since your last meeting. His inability to speak with or see you tortures him. I told him suffering is good for one's art, but he didn't appreciate it."

"Leopold said the same thing and I threatened to whip him."

"Then discover where you stand, with all parties involved, so both of you can move forward in whatever way you choose and stop torturing yourselves and us."

"You mean speak with Mrs. Boehm?" Her heart raced like an Ascot thoroughbred at the thought of speaking to a wife about her husband's infidelity. Despite Bertie's assurance that it was necessary for her to delve into the nature of the Boehms' marriage, it felt like a bridge too far.

"Exactly. Shall I make the introduction?"

"What would I say to her?"

"The truth, and ask for the same in return."

"I'm not sure I wish to hear what she has to say to me." It might be a string of words to make even the crude Mr. Brown blush.

"It might surprise you, but act quickly. You may not have another chance."

She didn't like the idea at all, but he was the second person to suggest she fully understand the lay of the land before proceeding. Bertie had said she was clever enough to sort out what to say when it was time to speak frankly about indelicate matters, but heaven help her if nothing came to her at present. "All right, arrange it."

"I'm at your service." He bowed, then jerked up quickly, flicking his head back to fling his dark hair off his face, and left to make the arrangements.

"You're braver than I am," Sybil said, adept at appearing as if she'd heard nothing while overhearing everything.

"Or more foolish."

"Your Royal Highness." The nasally voice forced Louise to turn and come face-to-face with the Marquess of Lorne.

"What a pleasant surprise. I hadn't expected you to be here today," Louise greeted, thankful for the brief distraction. "Are you as great an art lover as you are a world traveler?"

"I'm here with Lord Gower, who's quite the art lover and a sculptor."

"I've seen your uncle's works and read his books on the past masters," she teased, as amused as everyone by the two young men who were the same age, and as thick as thieves, being uncle and nephew. Lord Gower was the late-life child of Lorne's great-uncle, the Duke of Sutherland. "His artistic and scholarly pieces are quite impressive."

"So is your bust of Her Majesty in the sculpture room. Very well done, it puts Mr. Story's work to shame, but I'd never say so directly to him." He winked at her and she laughed.

"You know Mr. Story?"

"Monsignor Stonor, the Papal Legate, introduced me to the Story family when I was in Rome. I had the privilege of visiting their studios. They have quite the English artistic community there."

"The Storys also have enough talent and family members to found their own movement."

"The Barnes School, I've heard of it. If you and your brothers and sisters had been free to develop your artistic gifts to the fullest, you could've founded one too."

"You and your eleven siblings could do the same if you were so inclined."

"Artistic talent doesn't run in my immediate family the way it does yours, and, as you know, there are limits to our freedom." The weight and responsibilities of his station settled over him the way they often did her, easing the width of his smile. She and her siblings were constrained by their standings as princes and princesses. He was confined by his position as the eldest son of a duke. He might have more freedom to travel and dabble in writing, but like her he could never fully wade into the deeper waters of those ponds.

"We have a great deal in common, Lord Lorne. I hope to see more of you when we venture to Balmoral."

"It's my wish as well. Congratulations again on your success." He bowed and took his leave, joining the lanky Lord Gower with his well-trimmed Verdi beard and mustache to continue through the exhibition.

"A charming young man. Well traveled and educated. A rare find." Sybil flashed a supercilious smile Louise tried to ignore but couldn't.

"He is quite intriguing." But enough so she could stand to look at him across the breakfast table every morning? She didn't know, but she intended to find out. She must make a decision, and soon, especially with Mr. Whistler returning as if he had arranged the grandest coup since Cromwell overthrew King Charles I.

"Mr. Whistler, I find the excitement of today fatiguing. Is there somewhere in Burlington House where I may rest?" Louise asked loud enough for everyone around to hear, playing the game, as she always must, to keep up the thousand pretenses demanded by her position.

"If you'll follow me, I'll show you to one of the private sitting rooms upstairs."

"Thank you." She and Sybil followed Mr. Whistler to the main staircase and up to the first floor, through a few more galleries, and to a small room near the back of the building. He showed her and Sybil inside, where Mrs. Boehm stood waiting. If the sight of Louise was a shock to the woman she didn't reveal it, as poised in Louise's presence as Mama used to be in public before Papa died.

The sinking feeling that this was not the first time Mrs. Boehm had faced one of her husband's paramours almost made Louise abandon the plan, but she'd come this far in her sins. She could hardly avoid confession now.

"Your Royal Highness, may I introduce Mrs. Joseph Edgar Boehm?" Mr. Whistler said, returning, like Louise, to the required formalities.

The woman curtseyed, her manners impeccable. Given Edgar's aristocratic clients, Louise wasn't surprised.

"It's a pleasure to meet you, Mrs. Boehm. Congratulations

on your husband's great success. Her Majesty and the Prince of Wales are admirers of his work."

"My husband speaks highly of your talents too." There was no mockery or double entendre in the compliment.

"If you ladies will excuse me." Mr. Whistler bowed out of the room and Sybil took up an unobtrusive place by the window, offering as much privacy as she could under the circumstances. If her presence troubled Mrs. Boehm she gave no sign of it, more than likely accustomed to lady chaperones.

"Thank you, Your Royal Highness, for everything you've done for Mr. Boehm's career. Her Majesty's patronage and yours has meant a great deal to him and our family."

"It's my pleasure to promote him. I care a great deal about Mr. Boehm."

"I know."

Oh dear. How Bertie managed this many times over, she didn't know, but she couldn't very well back out now. After all, she was a princess, the Queen's daughter. If she could face Mama or Parliament, she could face a situation of her own making. "May we speak plainly, Mrs. Boehm, about the true reason for this interview?"

"If you wish." Mrs. Boehm glanced at Sybil.

"You needn't worry about Lady St. Albans. She's as discreet as the grave."

"Then may I be so bold as to explain the matter as it stands?"

"Please." Louise might not know what to say until it was time to speak, but she was tired of all this dancing about.

"Mr. Boehm explained to me the nature of things between you. I feel it my duty to explain the nature of things between us. We were very young and impulsive when we married, I had not the dowry or connections to secure a good match and was in danger of being left on the shelf. Edgar was a foreigner and quite without a suitable income. My brother, who'd done little to help me secure a husband through his poor business dealings in Liverpool, was against the match, but I brought him grudgingly around. He had no idea what it was like to be looked down on and overlooked, to see his chances for a future, children, and home of his own fading year after year, and how wonderful it was when Edgar noticed me. It was as if everything I'd despaired of having was laid at my feet, and it was. While we've been happy in our own way, the initial passion did not last. I gave him four children, much to the detriment of my health, and the doctors recommended I have no more. While I find the arrangement satisfactory, Mr. Boehm, as a man, has natural needs and I've encouraged him to attend to them where he sees fit. I never thought he would reach so high in his interests, but I'm glad he has. Since securing Her Majesty and the Prince of Wales' patronage, and Your Royal Highness's friendship, my position among my friends and acquaintances, especially in my brother's eyes and my old circle in Liverpool, has risen higher than anything I could've ever imagined. I'm not a heartless or scheming woman, Your Royal Highness, but I crave success as much as Edgar, and in this manner I've achieved it. My husband is a sculptor to royalty, and perhaps one day his talents, with your assistance, will earn him a title."

Over Mrs. Boehm's shoulder, Louise caught Sybil's wide-eyed astonishment, her ability to pretend she wasn't listening vanishing at Mrs. Boehm's plain confession and none-too-subtle suggestion. Louise did everything she could not to mirror her friend's expression but to remain placid. She hadn't known what to expect, but it hadn't been this. "I assure you, Her Majesty is very pleased with his works, and I expect more and better things for him, and you. A baronetcy, perhaps, and a position as Sculptor in Ordinary are not beyond consideration, especially with my and the Prince of Wales' encouragement. It would be my pleasure to promote the appointment of Mr. Boehm to such a high estate."

The woman's eyes sparkled with possibility and Louise could almost see her standing before her brother and reveling in him calling her Lady Boehm.

"I'm glad we had the chance to come to an agreement, Mrs. Boehm, and I wish you and your husband great success."

"Thank you, Your Royal Highness." She executed a curtsey worthy of any peer's daughter and backed out of the room, closing the door the behind her.

Sybil shook her head in amazement. "If I hadn't been here to hear it, and you'd told me about this interview, I'd think you'd made it up."

"So would I."

"No wonder she does so well with Mr. Boehm's contracts. Such a force, and never once rude or disrespectful."

"Or subtle. I admire her boldness. It's earned her the respect and success she craves." The same things Louise had been fighting for. She hoped, when the situation called for it, she would be as courageous in pursuing her ambitions as Mrs. Boehm.

"We should return before we're missed."

They made their way back downstairs, taking their time in the portrait gallery for Louise to settle herself before she was finally forced to rejoin the royal party. She stood before Professor Prinsep's *The Death of Cleopatra*, the vivid oranges, reds, and blues of the Queen and her attendants' togas bright against the faint hieroglyphics. Her despair at her defeat was palpable in the slouch of her body on the throne as she slipped from life, her dead serving woman sprawled at her feet. Louise never wanted to give up like that, to believe all hope was lost and there was no reason to carry on in the face of failure.

"Prinsep outdid himself this year," Edgar said from beside her.

Her body vibrated from the nearness of him and the faint scent of sandalwood hanging in the air between them. She longed to slip her hand in his, to feel his sturdy grip, to lean her head on his chest and hear again the thudding of his heart, to enjoy his strong arms around her, but they must remain politely apart. "It's perfect."

"Nothing we create is, it can't be or we'd never stop working on one piece instead of starting others. The curse of our craft is accepting imperfection."

"We must find what happiness we can in our imperfections and restrictions." She tilted her head to view him from the side, too afraid to face him and give away the passion making her skin flush. "It's the most we can hope to achieve in our positions."

He laced his hands behind his back and nodded, catching the meaning in her words, and like her unable to say what he truly wanted. "There's danger in accepting them too, that our work won't live up to other's expectations."

"All we can do is fight to glean from it what happiness we can, to steal from the imperfection whatever joy it offers. It's a challenge I'm willing to accept if you are."

His glance said more than any words could. "I am."

Chapter Fourteen

Lord Lorne was only thought of amongst others—and I always wished for him . . . Louise however wanted to judge for herself, and very properly said she could not and would not marry anyone she did not really like. And so I asked him to come here for a few days (I had had several other visitors here before) . . . And the more Louise saw of him the more she likes him. His devotion to her is quite touching . . . I doubt not, whatever your feelings at first may be, that you will rejoice at the prospect of dear Louise's happiness—which I think is very great . . .

—QUEEN VICTORIA TO HER DAUGHTER
THE CROWN PRINCESS OF PRUSSIA

Balmoral Castle, October 1870

Louise and Lorne climbed to the top of Craig Lurachain. Louise, invigorated by the climb, waited for Lorne to catch up. He joined her, slightly winded but in good spirits, his cheeks ruddy from the sharp wind. At the top stood Papa's pyramid-shaped cairn, the granite stones covered in white lichen and green moss, the commemorative plaque dark with weathering.

Weeks of wrangling between Mama and Mr. Gladstone, of Mama negotiating with the Duke and Duchess of Argyll, all the while fending off Vicky's indignant letters, had led Lorne and Louise to this ridge overlooking the valley. The last few months had been more dinners, dull rides through Windsor Great Park, broken by what brief afternoons she could steal with Edgar at his studio while she stayed with Bertie at Marlborough House. They were painfully few and precious, each one driving Louise's need to finally choose a husband and be free of Mama.

Mama had ordered the household out for an afternoon picnic with the express order that Louise and Lorne could wander off on their own with no one, especially Lady Ely, following. While the others ate, they'd set off through the woods and up the hill to the cairn.

"Did Mama tell you how to propose?" Louise admired the view of the Royal Lochnagar Distillery nestled in the valley below. The mist had cleared since this morning, the sun dimmed, then revealed, by a multitude of full, passing clouds. In the distance, a small rainbow hung over the Cairngorms Mountains.

"She made a few suggestions." He wore a tweed suit with a waistcoat of the Argyll tartan, as indifferent to the cold as Mama.

"Feel free to discard them, it'll be one of the rare times you can if you commit to this."

"Why wouldn't I ask for your hand?"

"Why would you?" It was the one question she hadn't asked him in the few times they'd been together since the Royal Academy. Dinners and Drawing Rooms were difficult places for intimate and scandalous conversations. Edgar could read her moods and feelings with a mere look or comment. With Lorne she must be blunt. "Once you become a member of this family, which you'll never truly be, as I'm sure the letters between Mama and your father have made you acutely aware, whatever life you had before will vanish."

"Good. There isn't much of it since I returned to England." He scraped a bit of lichen off the cairn with one fingernail and flicked it to the ground. "Shall I bend down on one knee, or did you have something else in mind?"

"Do as you like, but we must talk first. Neither of us is here because of our rapture for one another, no matter what everyone might believe."

"Nothing wrong with a little acting to make the masses happy. Pleased people do not overthrow monarchs." Napoleon III had been deposed in September and forced to flee with Empress Eugénie and their son, Louis-Napoléon, the Prince Imperial, to England. Mama had taken to her bed for a week with nerves over the dreadful affair, afraid it might happen to her. With her crown sitting uneasily on her head, she needed happy, distracted subjects. "I saw firsthand the destruction civil war wrought in America and Italy. I refuse to see it or revolution happen here."

"Our union isn't grand enough to change the course of anything."

"It's enough to renew the people's love for the royal family, and distract them from their troubles, but you're right, it's not built on passion. We have our similarities, and in matches such as this, it's the most we can ask for."

"It will be if I have the luxury of my own household, the ability to travel, and to visit what theaters and galleries I wish."

"Including gentlemen artists' studios?"

"What do you mean?" She knew exactly what he implied but wanted him to say it plainly.

"A friend of mine, aware I'm being considered as a suitor, felt compelled to mention your friendship to Mr. Whistler and others to me."

"Lord Gower?"

Lorne nodded.

It made the need to marry even more necessary. Not even Mama with her network of spies suspected Louise's visits to studios might have a different reason behind them, but her friendship with artists was common enough knowledge to become gossip. That Lorne hadn't specifically mentioned Edgar was a relief. It meant some secrets were still being kept. "My acquaintances are not as salacious as you suggest, but I have no intention of giving them up."

"I have no intention of abandoning my interests either. I only ask for the public respect due a husband."

"Of course." She was relieved, having expected him to stalk off in indignation, clutching his morals as he did his Tam o'Shanter.

"I also wish to reap the benefits of joining an unusual family. I want a real position and responsibility, one more notable than the Liberal MP for Argyllshire. Perhaps Foreign

Secretary or some other cabinet position, one only obtained through an intimate connection to Her Majesty."

She admired his ambition. It was yet another thing besides art and a desire to travel they had in common. However, there was more to a marriage than trips abroad.

"Speaking of intimacies." Louise toed a small stone with her boot, not relishing this aspect of the conversation but needing to discuss it.

"It will be required. There must be an heir." He didn't seem any more thrilled by the idea than she did, but he understood their duty.

"If there aren't any?" She didn't have the courage to tell him what the doctors had said about the scarlet fever and her chances of having a child. She assumed Mama had broached the subject with the Duke of Argyll in one of her many letters and he'd spoken to his son.

"I have five brothers. There's no worry of the line dying out."

"Then I'll assist you in gaining your desired post and we'll both agree to leave one another to our private pursuits while publicly playing the happy couple."

"Good. Then we understand one another." He pushed away from the cairn, took her hand, and dropped on one knee. "My dear Louise, will you marry me?"

"Yes, Lord Lorne, I will."

"YOU'RE MAD, ALL of you." Vicky clasped the long strand of pearls hanging around her neck. Louise thought she might tear them off and toss them on the drawing room floor. "To congratulate Louise on this humiliating engagement is beyond the pale."

"That isn't very kind, Vicky," Alice gently chided from her seat on the sofa beside Lenchen. Both Alice and Vicky and their husbands and children were at Balmoral for a holiday, as was Arthur, who'd recently returned from Canada. They'd be together through November before Alice and Vicky returned to their countries and the rest of them journeyed to Osborne House for Christmas. Alfred had the good fortune to avoid this family gathering by sailing for India on a diplomatic tour a few months ago. Leopold had begged to be allowed to accompany him, but Mama had refused. Beatrice was upstairs with Mama, who still did all she could to shield her youngest daughter's delicate ears from any talk of marriage.

"Allowing Louise to debase herself and our family by marrying a commoner when she might have had the Crown Prince of Denmark is insulting," Vicky pronounced in her someday-to-be-empress-of-Germany arrogance. "He doesn't even have the money to properly maintain her."

"Lord Lorne isn't a fishmonger but the son of a duke, and will be a duke one day," Louise reminded through gritted teeth.

"But he isn't one now and is quite without the income that comes with the title, assuming there's any money left once he does inherit. The Duke of Argyll is careless with his finances."

"Even if he isn't a wealthy prince, what does it matter to you? He isn't going to be your husband and you don't live in England anymore," Louise challenged. She was certain this was the right decision, but Vicky's objections caused the doubt to slide in like moisture through a stone wall.

"The Emperor and Empress already sneer at me because

I'm English. They and the rest of Fritz's family will lord this over me and make no end of difficulties about it."

The reality Louise faced if she and Edgar had dared to defy convention was in every wrinkle of disgust on Vicky's face, reminding her why she was in this position. "I think they don't care for you for a far different reason than because you're English."

Arthur and Leopold snorted in laughter from where they sat hunched over a chessboard in front of the bow window beneath the heavy Scottish-thistle-embroidered curtains.

"This is very serious." Vicky nearly stamped her foot on the red and gray tartan carpet.

"Louise is right, it isn't your concern, and it doesn't matter because it's already done," Bertie proclaimed from where he sat smoking a cigar and watching the spectacle from the thistle-embroidered wing chair beside the fireplace. "Mama wrote to the Duke and Duchess of Argyll, and once they reply, the engagement will be announced in the newspapers and settled. Louise will always be a princess no matter who she marries."

"But Lord Lorne will never be a prince. Louise will always take precedence over him, and he will be subservient to her, especially in public when he's forced to walk behind her. What self-respecting gentleman can endure that?"

"Papa managed if for over twenty years and succeeded," Bertie reminded Vicky.

"Lord Lorne is hardly his equal."

Louise exchanged an exasperated glance with Bertie. She took a deep breath, determined to be mature and levelheaded in this discussion so Vicky couldn't accuse her of acting like a child. "Lord Lorne and I have discussed the more practical matters of our future and I assure you he is quite satisfied with the arrangement."

"Then he's either a liar or a fool." Vicky wagged one stubby finger at Louise. "Mark my words, he will mind very much when he must always play second fiddle to you, and there is nothing worse than a petulant husband overshadowed by his wife."

"Enough of this," Alice insisted, stepping in as always to make the peace. "We should all celebrate Louise's happy news, not trod on it, and if we can't, we should hold our tongues. This is the first time so many of us have been together in ages. Let's not spoil it with fighting."

"Here, here," Arthur piped up from the chess table.

"That isn't helpful, Arthur, neither is Alice's interfering when it isn't asked for," Vicky said with Mama's petulant sneer. She'd been Papa's favorite, but she resembled Mama with her full round face and perpetual self-righteousness. With her slender nose and chin, Alice resembled their father more.

Alice narrowed her eyes at Vicky. "Instead of pestering Louise, you should put your obviously superior diplomacy skills to use with Emperor Wilhelm and stop him from causing trouble with Hesse."

"It isn't my fault your husband didn't properly prepare his military or finances so your country was so easily invaded by mine. I've heard you regularly beg Mama for money for your houses and children."

"Enough of this bickering," Bertie bellowed.

"Finally, he acts the king," Vicky mocked.

"At least I will rule."

"Only because you're a man. I was firstborn and far more intelligent, and if there were any justice in this world, I'd sit on the throne."

Bertie tugged the bottom of his waistcoat straight. "Careful, dear, your jealousy is showing."

Leopold and Arthur burst out laughing, knocking over their pieces in their glee. Lenchen took a subtle sip from her brown bottle while Alice covered a laugh with the back of her hand. Louise didn't move a muscle, refusing to catch more of Vicky's ire. She'd never seen her so riled. Vicky could be a joy to be around, sketching with Louise or doing watercolors with Lenchen whenever she visited, but she was haughty and nasty today. Her superiority of opinion made it difficult to remember her better qualities, such as her love for her children and husband, and Louise wondered if such displays of arrogance were what had soured the Emperor and Empress on her. Vicky threw back her shoulders and, holding her head high, swept out of the room.

"That wasn't very nice, Bertie," Alice gently scolded.

"She deserved it," Leopold said, righting the chess pieces.

"She did," Bertie agreed.

"Well, now that's settled, it's time to dress for dinner." Alice rose, bringing them all to their feet. She approached Louise, clasped her by the shoulders, and laid a gentle kiss on her forehead. Louise missed Alice. She'd been a rock during Papa's illness, nursing him and seeing to Mama. She also treated Louise like a grown woman instead of a child, offering practical, and sometimes intimate, advice whenever she could. "Congratulations. I'm very happy for you and excited to help with your trousseau while I'm here. You're in desperate need of guidance."

She looked up and down the front of Louise's frock. It lacked a corset and crinoline, falling in the more flowing, bohemian lines of Henrietta and so many other female artists' and muses' dresses.

"I like this dress," Louise protested.

"It's fine for family but nowhere else. People demand elegance from royalty. It's why you're so popular and others aren't." Alice slid a glance at Lenchen, then wrapped her arm around Louise's shoulder and guided her to the door, the two of them barely noticing Lenchen slipping past them and down the gallery toward the stairs. "Your engagement will make you more so. Mama and many others are already calling it a love match. When the newspapers seize on it, you'll have quite the role to play. I have no doubt you're up to it."

Alice gave Louise a little squeeze, then slid her arm from around her and left her at the door to go to her room and dress for dinner.

"A lot of tosh, that love match nonsense," Leopold teased.

"Lord Lorne was breathing and available. That was his greatest recommendation," Arthur added.

"Shut your mouths, you rascals." Louise plucked a pillow from the chair beside her and lobbed it at her brothers, who were laughing too hard to dodge it.

"Alice is right. It'll be sold as a love match, and heaven help you if you don't give a proper performance," Bertie agreed.

"She'll act so well, she'll put Sarah Bernhardt to shame," Leopold said, laughing.

Bertie dropped the end of his finished cigar in the weak

flames of the fireplace before offering Louise his arm. "Walk with me. We have a few things to discuss."

"Such as how far down the salt her husband will sit." Arthur hooted.

"Or if Lorne will hold her train instead of the pages," Leopold added.

Louise stuck her tongue out at her brothers, making them laugh harder, their jokes following her and Bertie out into the long gallery.

"Don't let them bother you. They're simply taking the piss because they know you can handle it."

"They don't trouble me at all, especially since they're right. I chose Lorne because he was the best option out of many awful ones. It certainly wasn't for love, no matter what Alice or Mama or the newspapers say."

"Only a besotted fool in need of fantasy would believe otherwise. What does your sculptor think of it?"

"I haven't told him, but he must have guessed." The Court Circular reported on every movement made by her and her family. It was sure to have been reported that Lorne was here and speculated on why.

"He still needs to hear it from you."

"I'll write to Sybil and ask her to break the news. It's not ideal, but it's the only way." She was stuck in this godforsaken wilderness for at least another month. By then the entire nation would know.

"Brace yourself for a less-than-pleasant response."

"We discussed the eventuality that I'd be married, and everything is settled." As well as it could be, given their situations.

"What a man can tolerate in the abstract is quite different than what he'll tolerate in reality. Be prepared, his reaction may not be what you expect."

"Nothing in this strange situation is."

"You'll also need to place some distance between the two of you for a while. Alice is right. The people will eat you alive it they think they've been lied to after your settlement is granted by their MPs and the wedding paid for by their taxes."

"How long?"

"A year, possibly two, or until a child is born."

"Is this the grand freedom you said marriage would give me?"

"Be patient, Louise. You'll get what you want, but not if you botch it by rushing things. It isn't in your nature to live like a nun, any more than I'm willing to live like a priest. After a year or so with Lorne, you'll need your sculptor."

"What do you mean?"

He fingered his watch chain, making it clink against his waistcoat buttons, as if he were embarrassed. It wasn't possible, not with all the public scandals he'd endured over his short life. "Whatever agreement you've come to with Lorne, I'm sure it'll suit you, but as a husband, he isn't likely to keep you happy in the conjugal manner. From what I've heard spoken about in the clubs, it isn't up to his tastes."

"I . . . see." Not an unusual trait among artists, and it made a few things they'd discussed on their betrothal walk clear. "Yet another detail to manage, but not impossible."

"An optimistic view, one I hope circumstances allow you

to keep. Congratulations, my dear." He gave her a kiss on the cheek, then left her at her room.

She sat at her writing desk, slid a sheet of paper out of the drawer, and, taking up her pen, wrote in the vaguest terms possible instructions for Sybil to speak with Edgar about the engagement. She hated to leave it to her friend, who'd already done and risked so much to help her, but she had no choice. He must hear of it before Mama's government made the official announcement. She hoped Edgar understood. She didn't want to lose him.

I yesterday gave my consent in Council to her marriage which has called forth a great burst of delight. People call this "The most popular act of my reign." . . . the popularity of this step and this marriage all over the empire, including Ireland, is quite marvelous. And, when the Royal Family is so large . . . to connect some few of them with the great families of the land—is an immense strength to the monarchy and a great link between the Royal Family and the country.

—Queen Victoria to her daughter
the Crown Princess of Prussia

London, February 1871

"Lady St. Albans visited my studio about doing a cast of her son's hands. She was kind enough to share the news of your engagement with me before it was reported in the newspapers." Edgar stood in his studio, chisel in one hand, hammer in the other, a leather apron covering his trousers. The shirt beneath was unbuttoned near the neck, revealing the V of chest beneath and the sheen of perspiration dampening his skin. "She's a very kind woman. Please give her my condolences on the passing of General Grey."

"Thank you. Her heartache is eased by the joy of being with child. The baby is expected in July." Louise twisted her reticule string around her fingers. General Grey's sudden death from a stroke last month had been a shock to everyone. Louise had done a bust of him and presented it to Sybil, holding and comforting her in her grief as Sybil had done so many times for Louise.

"Then offer her my congratulations as well."

They stood in silence a moment, the noise of the street muffled by the closed windows.

"I suppose congratulations are in order for you too." Edgar struck the chisel with the hammer and specks of marble flew off to join the litter of stone around his feet.

The sinking feeling that Bertie might be right about Edgar's reaction settled in the pit of her stomach. She and Edgar hadn't spoken since her engagement, a wounded knee having kept her at Balmoral for an extra month to recover and denying her the chance to return to Windsor, and London, before the family had retired to Osborne House. Since then there'd been nothing but wedding preparations. They consumed nearly every moment of her day, making even this brief visit to Edgar's difficult to arrange. "The wedding is set for the twenty-first of March."

"So soon?"

"Mama is eager for it to take place. I think she's afraid I'll change my mind."

"You won't."

"I can't." As Alice and Bertie had predicted, the public had gone wild at her marrying a commoner. There were newspaper articles about every aspect of her wedding preparations, plates and teacups with her image and Lorne's adorning shop windows. Special dances and musical numbers had been composed, all of it to celebrate the grand love match between Her Majesty's daughter and the Marquess of Lorne.

He whacked the chisel again and a small piece of marble flew off to hit Louise's boot. She kicked it away, nothing about today going as she'd imagined. She'd pictured him taking her in his arms, covering her lips with his kisses, the two of them looking forward to a future that, if not strange, was at least theirs. Instead, she could feel a growing distance between them, one more troublesome than the differences in their ranks.

"I'm sorry."

"I'm the one who should apologize. It wasn't right to draw you in, to make promises and commitments I couldn't keep, to take liberties with you I had no right to. I'm older and should've known better." He emphasized every word with the strike of his chisel, his cuts sloppy and uneven.

"Don't, you'll ruin it." She laid a steadying hand on his arm. "I don't blame you for anything, not after everything you've given me."

"Ruin?"

"Real life, encouragement, affection, the strength to carry

on during difficulties, and the bravery to display my talents and risk criticism and praise. My life is so much fuller because of you, and it will always be so."

He lowered the chisel and hammer and faced her, the resignation on his face making her heart stop in fear. "It can't be this way."

"What do you mean?"

A knock at the door forced them apart. A moment later, Mr. Gilbert, Edgar's assistant, entered. "Lady Cardigan has arrived to discuss the bust of Dowager Lady Cardigan."

"Show her into the sitting room and offer her some refreshments. I'll be with her shortly."

"Yes, sir." Mr. Gilbert left to see to Edgar's patron, her arrival increasing the knot in Louise's stomach as much as Edgar's aloofness.

"I've thought a great deal about it since Lady St. Alban's call, and we can't carry on as we thought." He delivered the blow as swiftly as if he'd hit her with a chisel and hammer.

"Is it because of Lady Cardigan? Mr. Whistler told me about her and you."

"That was a brief dalliance that ended years ago."

"Yet she's here and you're sending me away."

"For your protection and no other reason." Edgar dropped his tools on the table with a clatter that made Louise flinch. He stepped up close to her and lowered his voice. "If my hours for welcoming clients weren't so strict and well established, someone might've stumbled in on us last spring, and then where would you be? Where would I be? We both have responsibilities, you to Her Highness and I to my wife and children. Neither of us can afford to ruin our reputations. I love you, Louise, more than I've ever loved anyone before. I don't want to give you up, but I must."

She touched her chest and the medal, not expecting to hear those words, especially like this. "If you truly loved me you wouldn't let me go."

"Because I love you I must, I won't see you pilloried." He brushed her face with his rough hands, the fine dust marking them and her delicate skin. "If we're discovered, you'll be judged harder than if Lord Lorne did the same. Mrs. Millais has endured years of social scorn because her marriage to Mr. Ruskin was annulled. That rotter wouldn't consummate the marriage and she had every right to leave him, but she still suffers for something that wasn't her fault. Not even Millais's success has fully redeemed her. Imagine what'll happen if you stray from your marriage vows with me. You'll be treated like a pariah, a harlot. No one will risk displaying your work or seek your patronage, and who knows how Her Majesty will punish you? We've taken too great a risk already. What if I had gotten you with child?"

"I told you what the doctors said."

"Those quacks aren't always right, and I won't be the cause of your downfall or misery."

She let go of Edgar, everything in her rebelling against his words and the unfairness of it all. She hadn't asked to be born royal or forced into marriage with a man merely because he was compatible. She wanted to remain in Edgar's studio, his arms around her as he encouraged and nurtured her in a way no one had ever done before, but, for everything he'd given her, he was right. She could pretend at being the art student, the artist, the lover, but in the end she was still the princess and bound to everything it meant. "It's over, then, isn't it?"

He opened and closed his hands at his sides. "It has to be, and you know it too."

"I do." And she hated it. "Will I see you ever again?"

"We're sure to encounter one another in the future. Perhaps when you're a marchioness, mother, and mistress of your own home, it won't hurt as much."

"Never." She laid her hand on the side of his face, the faint stubble along his cheeks pricking her palm the way the tears did her eyes. Sacrifice, it was always sacrifice, and yet everyone outside the palace thought she had everything. "I'd give it all up to stay with you."

"You'll always be with me." He touched his lips to hers, the longing and disappointment coursing through her filling him too, their hearts beating against the invisible boundaries forcing them apart.

He broke from the kiss at Mr. Gilbert's knock.

"Come in."

Mr. Gilbert entered, pretending he didn't feel the tension or notice their pained faces. "Lady Cardigan is waiting for you."

"Please escort Miss Saxe-Coburg-Gotha out the other way."

"Yes, sir."

With one last longing look at Louise, Edgar turned, took off his smock, and slid on his clean coat, keeping his back to her so he couldn't see her leave.

She followed Mr. Gilbert out the other entrance and down the deserted hallway. She climbed into her carriage, holding back the tears until she was safely inside and had closed the curtains. She'd feared something would arise to steal him from her and end their time together. She'd never guessed it'd be Edgar who'd quietly draw it to a close.

Chapter Fifteen

The engagement of the Princess and Marquis aroused the enthusiasm of the country.

The nation hailed with unfeigned pleasure the news that a Princess of the Blood Royal was about to wed a commoner, and that this was to be no mere State Alliance, but a "love match." . . . The Esteem in which her Royal Highness is held has been evinced by the expression of goodwill and respect which have found daily utterance; and if any evidence were wanted of the national love which is felt for the Princess who to-day begins a new era in her life, that would be easily found in the countless tributes of regard which have come in during a period extending over several weeks . . .

—*Morning Post*, March 22, 1871

Windsor Castle, March 21, 1871

Louise stood in her wedding dress in her dressing room at Windsor Castle. Outside, bunting hung between the buildings of Eton and across every shop window. Crowds filled the streets, cheering each carriage that passed ferrying its regal guests to St. George's Chapel.

"Who's that?" Louise asked when an especially large cheer went up.

Sybil raised her lorgnette and peered through the window. "Emperor Napoleon, Empress Eugénie, and Louis-Napoléon."

The dressers, maids, hairstylist, and royal jeweler had been dismissed after they'd finished, leaving Sybil and Louise a rare moment alone. The last few days had been a whirlwind of dinners, receiving guests in the sitting rooms, and meeting royalty and relatives. In a few minutes Louise would join Mama in the carriage to ride down the hill from the castle to St. George's Chapel. Mama had insisted on joining Bertie in escorting Louise up the aisle to Lorne, who waited with his family in the Bray Chapel, to make Louise his wife.

Louise touched the blue-sapphire-and-diamond pendant Lorne had given her as a wedding gift. The stone's hue matched the church ribbons, the bridesmaids' dresses, and Lorne's Colonel of the Argyllshire Volunteer Artillery uniform.

"No backing out now," Sybil teased, adjusting the two daisy-shaped diamond pins, a gift from Leopold, Arthur, and Beatrice, holding the Honiton lace veil to Louise's orange-blossom-and-myrtle wreath. The Devon lace makers hired to weave the veil had perfectly followed Louise's design and carefully embroidered delicate sprigs of heather and myrtle and orange blossoms along the edges.

"I don't want to." This marriage meant freedom. Already she had a treasure trove of dresses and jewels to wear whenever and wherever she chose. Mama had promised her an annual stipend in addition to her settlement from Parliament, and apartments at Kensington Palace and the funds to redecorate them. She'd build the art studio she'd always dreamed of in the garden, and none of it would be possible if it weren't for today.

"Good, because yesterday, in the High Street, I saw an advertisement for a Princess Louise perfume. I wonder what the people think you smell like."

"Today it's orange blossoms and myrtle." They were part of her wreath, train, and dress, the sweet fragrance having settled since the first overpowering waft when the dresser had attached the flowers to her bodice and hem. Everything about her dress, from the Irish poplin woven in Dublin, to the veil and flowers, was from Britain. Craftspeople and fabric makers from all over the Isles had been employed to dress the English Princess who was marrying an English subject.

"It can't be any worse than all the songs written for us."

Leopold had insisted on ordering every new book of arrangements advertised and having them played after dinner. They consisted of old Scottish reels and folk songs and a few atrocious new ballads Arthur eagerly warbled. Even now, Louise could hear the faint strains of Mr. Godfrey's specially written wedding waltz played by the Grenadier Guards in St. George's Hall, where Louise and Lorne and their guests would enjoy the wedding supper. The music joined the mass of saucers, plates, novels, and pamphlets with Louise and Lorne's portraits adorning them. She was sick of looking at her face whenever she rode through London or Eton, and it was the single benefit of not being allowed to Town more often, that and being in no danger of seeing Edgar.

She ran her hands over the bodice, unconsciously searching for his medal, but it wasn't there. She couldn't wear it today and hope to conceal it from everyone, including the man about to become her husband. Her thoughts should be on Lorne, but all she could think of was Edgar and the last time she'd seen him in his studio. She touched her lips, remembering the feel of his against hers, a tender moment they'd both wished to expand into forever but couldn't.

Outside, another wave of cheers went up from the crowd lining the way from the castle to the chapel.

"Leopold, Arthur, and Beatrice's carriage is driving down," Sybil said from the window, one hand holding the lorgnette, the other resting on her slightly rounded belly. The seamstress had hidden her condition beneath artfully arranged panels and bows, allowing her to take part in today's celebration before she retired from society until after the baby's birth. "The crowds will go hoarse when you finally appear. Oh, Louise, I can't wait until next Season when we can dine together at dinners. We'll be the toast of the London social whirl, the Duchess St. Albans and the Princess Louise, Marchioness of Lorne, hostesses of distinction."

"No more Lady Ely scowling at me or telling me who I can or cannot talk to or dance with. No one deciding what invitations I may or may not accept. I'll attend art gallery openings and Show Sunday luncheons." Louise grabbed the sides of her dress and twirled, making the lace and poplin spin about her legs.

"Until then, don't ruin your dress." Sybil stopped her, adjusting the pins and flowers before stepping back to admire her. "When you have a child, our children will play together."

"I hope so." Louise wanted children very much, but whether she could have them remained to be seen.

The door opened without a knock, the maids and footmen quite forgetting protocol in the merriment of the day. Mr. Disraeli swept in on a cloud of cologne, dressed in a gray morning suit, a top hat tucked under one arm. His usual curl was waxed down on his forehead, which seemed more wrinkled and aged since the last time she'd seen him.

"Your Royal Highness, you are a stunning bride." He tipped into a bow, quite beside himself at having received an invitation to the social event of the year. He was bold to expect a private audience with her, but she didn't mind. He was too charming, and had done too much to help her, to refuse. "Your marriage to a subject has silenced the wagging republican tongues. The people are proud of the Princess who decided to remain in England and the Queen who encouraged it. Well played."

"Thank you, Mr. Disraeli, your friendship and support have always meant a great deal to me." She motioned to where the gold butterfly had been pinned in the center of a cluster of orange blossoms.

"You honor me." Tears filled his eyes, as did a humbleness she'd never seen in him before.

A footman entered carrying a long black box tied with blue ribbon. "This arrived for you, Your Royal Highness."

"Another set of jewels to adorn your natural radiance?" Mr. Disraeli asked.

"Odd they should arrive so late." Her wedding presents were laid out in the Rubens Room, the jewels, plate, and china sent from royalty, and English cities and organizations displayed on tables for visitors to admire. She thought it odd someone should risk missing the chance to showcase their generosity by leaving it so late, until she read the note of congratulations written in Edgar's strong hand. It said nothing more than the expected words, no sentiment beyond the formality expected, but it meant more to her than all the jewels and plate downstairs. She looked up, locking eyes with Sybil, the first genuine flush of excitement in months making her heart race.

"It must be from your fiancé, to bring such radiance to your cheeks." Mr. Disraeli chuckled, and Louise cursed her impulsiveness.

Sybil, ever the conscious courtier, twined her arm in Mr. Disraeli's and guided him to the door. "Come, Mr. Disraeli, let's give the bride-to-be a moment alone. It may be her last for quite some time."

"I'm sure it will be. Her Majesty intends to visit the newlyweds tomorrow morning before they set sail for Italy. I cautioned her that a new couple needs time alone, but Her Majesty will have her way."

The closing door cut off the rest of Mr. Disraeli's comments. Louise, with shaking fingers, untied the ribbon securing the box. She lifted off the slender lid to reveal a bronze statuette of two horses galloping together, the lines of their muscles evident in the dark metal. One horse nuzzled his neck over the other, their manes fluttering behind them. On the base was a brass plate affixed with two rivets and *Together in Spirit* engraved in black letters.

She clasped it to her chest, the cold metal warming beneath her hands. He hadn't forgotten or stopped loving her. Tears filled her eyes, but she didn't dare allow them to fall. Her performance wasn't over yet, but her heart, so heavy with the weight of her responsibilities, soared. The statuette was Edgar's promise to not forget her and what they'd meant to one another, and she never would. He'd given her so much to strive for, helped her achieve and experience things she'd never thought possible before, including what it was like to love. If she could change everything and bring them to be together again, she would, but for today the memory of their time together was enough.

The day was brilliant, and never had the glorious old chapel of St. George looked to greater advantage . . . The stalls of the knights of the Garter and the seats below them were filled with ministers, their wives, and other high dignitaries; and the whole place was a blaze of uniforms, jewels, gala dresses, and magnificence . . . the bride, accompanied by the Queen, the Prince of Wales, and her uncle the Duke of Saxe-Coburg appeared at the grand entrance and slowly walked up towards the altar. Lorne went through the ordeal with admirable self-possession. The bride very pale, but handsome. The whole scene was superb, full of pomp, music, pageantry, and sunshine . . . At four the newly-wedded pair left the castle . . . under a shower of rice, satin shoes, and a new broom that John Brown, in Highland fashion, threw after their carriage as it left the quadrangle for the station.
—*Lord Ronald Gower's Diary*

Rome, April 1871

Louise sat on the remains of a marble pillar, her sketchbook balanced on her lap, drawing the magnificent ancient forum. The warm breeze ruffled the corners of the pages and made the ribbons of her bonnet flutter. Below her, people wandered through the weathered ruins of the once-grand city, stopping to stand in the shadow of the Arch of Titus or the arches of the Basilica of Maxentius. Others, like her, sat with their paints or charcoals to study the work of the long-dead artisans who'd crafted the Eternal City.

Below them, Lorne and Lord Paget, the British Ambassador, explored the Curia. Lorne looked up at Louise, shielding his eyes with one hand while raising his other in greeting. She waved in response, then looked past him to the Renaissance buildings cluttering the city, the sight inspiring her as much as those of Florence had done days before. There'd been no one to stand beside her as she and Lorne had viewed Michelangelo's David, no Mama to tut in disapproval of the naked figure or shoo them through the Galleria dell'Accademia di Firenze for fear the giant David might arouse Beatrice's interest. "It's all so grand."

"Having lived here so long, I sometimes forget its effects on the newly arrived," Lady Paget, the ambassador's wife and Louise's Roman lady companion, said from where she sat in the shade of a nearby tree. "It's the same with newly married couples. I love Lord Paget, but it's from the fondness of years, not the first flush of a new marriage as with you and Lord Lorne."

Lady Paget paused, clearly expecting Louise to agree and

swoon over her husband, playing the part of smitten bride, but she was more enchanted by the view of the city than of Lorne. Everything from the warm weather to the pillars of the Temple of Romulus, preserved because the pagan temple had found new life as a church, was so different from anything in England or anywhere Mama had dragged them to in Germany or Switzerland. The warm weather made the charcoal pliable against the paper, and soothed the muscles of her hands and back. What she wouldn't give to live in this balmy climate instead of the fog and bitter cold of England.

"Perhaps we should return to the gentlemen. Lord Lorne must be eager to be with his bride," Lady Paget suggested, ready to retreat to the comfort of a hotel or café where they could sip cool lemonade, but Louise wasn't about to leave. This afternoon was her time to explore the city before she must dress for a dinner hosted by the British Legate. Afterward, there was a dance hosted by Lady Paget where Louise and Lorne would be introduced to every British subject abroad who'd wrangled an invitation to the royal reception. Louise wouldn't have a moment alone until she retired for bed in the wee hours of the morning.

"I think the gentlemen are fine without us. Even in the first flush of marriage, a little absence creates a great deal more longing, wouldn't you say?"

Lady Paget frowned more from this than from the potent Roman sun. She was constantly encouraging Louise into Lorne's company, and heaven knows why. They were married, that was enough. They needn't spend every moment together. Bertie would caution her to do better at appearing more taken with Lorne, but in Italy, away from all but Lady

Paget's appraising eye, she didn't need to act or pretend.

Edgar would encourage it too.

Stop it. Edgar was her past, his bronze gift a memorial to what had been between them and not a promise of what would be. For all her lackluster feelings for Lorne, he was her future and a tolerable traveling companion. He'd eagerly shown her the wonders of Florence, but as they'd stood on the Ponte Vecchio and watched the River Arno flow through the heart of the Renaissance city, it wasn't Lorne she'd yearned for but Edgar. They couldn't be together but she couldn't stop thinking about and wanting him.

"I understand Lord Lorne is escorting you to Mr. Story's studio tomorrow," Lady Paget noted, never able to remain quiet for more than a few moments. If Mama hadn't insisted the woman follow her about in Rome, Louise would've abandoned her to explore the city herself. However, with Sybil in London preparing for her confinement, she had no choice but to tolerate Lady Paget.

"I wrote to Mr. Story asking to see his statue of Cleopatra. After reading about it in *The Marble Faun*, I'm curious to see if Mr. Hawthorne's description of the piece is accurate."

"You won't be disappointed."

IT WASN'T *CLEOPATRA* who left Louise speechless, but the grieving angel draped over the headstone of Mrs. Emelyn Story in the center of Mr. Story's studio in the Palazzo Barberini. The marble angel's despair was so potent it could move stone to tears.

"It's beautiful." Louise traced the line of the marble angel's arm as if to ease her unfathomable pain.

"Since my dear Emelyn's passing, I've found more comfort in this work than anything I've ever done before. She's
the voice of my pain at being left behind, of Emelyn traveling far beyond my touch or voice." Mr. Story fiddled with
the pince-nez hanging by a cord from the top button of his
waistcoat. He was slender, but not frail, years of hard work
with large stone pieces making him hearty for a man of his
advanced years.

"I understand." Louise circled the angel in the austere studio. The Renaissance palace with its classical front was decorated with large tapestries, baroque wallpaper, and gilded
furniture that flowed from one connected room to another. "I
once did a painting of Mama and Papa together in Mama's
dream, the only place they could reunite once he was gone.
Nothing I've done since has conveyed such despair as this
poor angel. I don't even have to name the feeling to know it's
one I've experienced."

"Great pain flowing into one's work makes it transcend
language."

*As the artist combines material with thought without the in-
tervention of any other medium, his creation would be perfect,
if life could also be breathed into his work.* Papa had written
those words to her once, praising sculpture and encouraging her pursuit of it. It was the lesson she had yet to learn.
She could capture the real Mama or Arthur, but she couldn't
sculpt into the stone the many emotions she brought to her
studio.

"Teach me how to do this. I want to give my sculpture this
depth of feeling." To pour into the statue everything words
could never express. "Mr. Boehm taught me to capture a sit-

ter's true character and likeness. He didn't teach me to embed the hardest and deepest feelings as you've done."

"He's a master at revealing subjects. I envy his talent for it. It's a rare gift." He set his pince-nez on his nose and straightened the wide edges of his mustache. "I'll teach you what I can, but I warn you, it won't be easy."

"It never is, but I still wish to learn."

LOUISE SPENT THE rest of their time in Rome with Mr. Story, learning his techniques and applying them to her own. Lorne came with her in the mornings, wandering about the warren-like rooms of the palazzo or selecting a book from the vast library and sitting quietly in the corner to read while Louise and Mr. Story worked. When they were not deep in lessons, he showed her his other pieces, including the life-sized statue of the Assyrian Queen Semiramis.

"She reigned on her son's behalf after her husband died, a remarkable feat for a woman at the time," Mr. Story explained.

"One worthy of being memorialized in marble. You've captured her regal air, and the steely intent she used to hold the throne when so much was against her."

"She will be a great deal more regal when I complete the drape of her tunic. I sometimes wish I did more contemporary sitters so I could render modern clothes, as you and Mr. Boehm do, but I'm partial to classical subjects and, at my age, unwilling to change."

"A man of your talent shouldn't have to."

"I'm honored, Your Royal Highness. Ours is a lonely work. We never know until it's revealed how it will be received.

Even then we must wait for writings and pamphlets. Compliments are music to an artist's ear."

LOUISE, WITH GREAT regret, said goodbye to Mr. Story and Rome, the marble crucifix with the angel lovingly arched over the cross, arms outstretched to support the dying Christ that she'd begun with him carefully packed in straw in a crate. There wouldn't be time to finish it during their travels. Louise must wait until they returned to England to better perfect the angel's gentle face and the care in her expression for the dying savior.

"Thank you for introducing me to Mr. Story. He was magnificent," she said to Lorne as they waited in their railcar for the train to set off for Venice. The quiet of Mr. Story's studio had been replaced by a cheering crowd gathered at the station to see them off. Louise had begged Mama to allow them to travel incognito, but she'd refused, sending telegrams to each of their destinations to announce their arrival and draw the people curious to see the English Princess and her commoner husband.

"Venice will be even grander. I'll introduce you to the art colony at the Palazzo Vendramin Calergi. You'll enjoy them, especially Mr. Passini, assuming the crowds allow us through." He waved awkwardly at the people, uncomfortable with the rush of attention and admiration. "Do you think people will ever tire of staring at us?"

"No." Louise waved to them as she would any of Mama's subjects, offering a charming smile to the peasant women in their full skirts, their colorful shawls draped over their shoulders and tied at the front of their plain white blouses. "This is what you wanted. You'll have to get used to it."

"I don't think I ever shall." Lorne nodded to a group of young women in loose-cut peasant blouses who called seductively to him. The tips of his pale ears under his hat turned a faint red.

"You'll have to better attend to your wardrobe too, especially once we're home, or the press and public will be merciless in their comments." She'd attributed his shabby way of dressing to the hustle of travel and the time spent among dusty ruins, but his continued wearing of the same worn traveling suit made her wonder.

"They must think well of me and respect me." He picked at a loose thread on the knee of his pants. "I understand the Viceroyalty of Ireland will soon be available."

"You're aiming very high." There'd been talk of appointing Bertie to the position, finally giving him a chance to train for his future as king, but Mama had balked at the suggestion, still not trusting him to do more than fritter about London.

"It's as good a position as any to set my cap at. Close to home but not too far from our families, and think of the influence we'd have there, not only on the government and people, but the arts."

"It does have that advantage." She'd promised to help find Lorne a position of esteem in Mama's government and she would, but not one so far from England. She refused to be banished from London, Leopold, and her friends just when she'd gained the privilege of a married woman to move freely among them.

. . . *this makes me answer you rather tardily about Alice. I would rather you had not met her so soon, for I know her* curiosity *and what is* worse *and what I hardly like to say of my own daughter,—I know her* indelicacy *and coarseness—and therefore if you go I wish* you *and Lorne (painful as it is to me to say it—as she was as nice and refined as any of you and has learnt all this from the family there) to be on your guard. When she came over in '69 and saw Lenchen again she asked her* such things, *that Christian was shocked—and Mary Tek . . . told me* she never *was* so shocked *as she had been at the things Alice had* said to her!

—*Queen Victoria to Princess Louise*

Darmstadt, June 1871

"Look at you, a wife at last." Alice held Louise at arm's length, appraising her as a mother might a daughter just returned from holiday. They stood together in the private waiting room in the Darmstadt train station, these brief two hours the most they'd spend together before Louise and Lorne's train left for France and the newlyweds continued home to England. "Sit, eat, I want to hear all about your married life."

Alice ushered Louise to the table laid with meats, cheese, and bread. The train station's private waiting room was cheerful, with copper tiles, leather seats, a large woodstove, and thick windows of green frosted glass to shield the Princess and the Grand Duchess of Hesse from curious eyes. They chatted for some time, Louise telling Alice of the wedding, the two of them laughing at the story of how Louise and Lorne had barely had time to compose themselves the next morning before Mama had insisted on visiting. Alice told Louise of her children and her nursing work with the Princess Alice Women's Guild.

"You've become quite the Florence Nightingale," Louise congratulated.

"I do what I can to assist women and relieve the suffering of many."

"You always excelled at that." It'd been Alice who'd nursed Papa during his last dreadful illness, then managed Mama's ministers and officials when Mama had been too grief-stricken to rise from her bed and speak to them. She'd come to England again last October when the nasty abscess on Mama's arm had led to an infection. For all Mama's complaints about Alice's medical interests, she didn't balk at using them when the occasion called for it.

"Enough about me." Alice poured more tea from the silver service. "I want to hear about your married life. Does Lord Lorne conduct his marital duties to your satisfaction?"

"He manages them well enough, and Mama would be scandalized if she found out I was discussing it with you. She thinks your interest in female matters is disgusting." Louise appreciated Alice's openness and willingness to broach intimate subjects, ones Louise couldn't even discuss with Bertie. Alice had a strange fascination with female concerns, shocking a number of women in the family, including Mama, by inquiring into the particulars of their situations and health.

"I know. Mama already wrote imploring me not to speak to you about the more intimate aspects of your marriage, but I wish to know if you're happy and content. If not, I hope I can help."

"I might need your assistance." Louise snapped out the napkin over the cotton skirt of her brown traveling dress. Lorne did his husbandly duty with adequate diligence, but he didn't have Edgar's enthusiasm or appetite. Given what Bertie had said about Lorne's interests, she wasn't entirely surprised, but she was a touch disappointed. But, as Bertie had said, any port in a storm. Without Edgar, late at night could be a tempest for Louise, and Lorne was good enough. "Nothing has come of our time together."

"It's too soon to be certain."

"Dr. Sieveking said the severity of the scarlet fever meant I might never have children." The weight of it fell as heavy on her today, as it had when he'd made the diagnosis.

"I've spent enough time with the sick and wounded to know doctors are more often wrong than right."

"But Mr. Stirling and Mr. Boehm," Louise hazarded in a low voice. There were no servants to overhear, they'd been dismissed, but to admit to her elder sister she hadn't been innocent on her wedding day still made her voice quaver.

"I see." Alice sat back and sagely clasped her hands in her lap.

"You aren't scandalized?"

"I am, but understanding your temperament and how similar it is to Bertie's, I'm not surprised. He also told me of you and Mr. Stirling. Were the gentlemen careful?"

Dear Alice, practical as ever. "Yes, especially Edgar, I mean Mr. Boehm."

Alice straightened the silver knife next to her plate, considering the matter. "If in a year there's still nothing, write to me and I'll send you what advice I can. Perhaps, when you're in

England and settled in a home of your own, you'll be blessed. In the meantime, attend to your marriage and see it succeeds. Its failure will make you miserable."

Alice sighed, and Louise at last noticed that her sister seemed more tired and drawn than she had ever been before.

"Is something wrong between you and Louis?" she asked.

Alice and the Grand Duke of Hesse had been married for ten years and Louise always thought them affectionate and well matched. The death of their poor little Frittie seven years ago had broken Alice's heart, but Louis had been so caring and supportive. Clearly, something had changed.

"The differences between us seemed so minor when we were first married, but they've since created a chasm we can't bridge. Louis has no desire to learn and grow beyond what he already knows, and he detests my charity work, despite everything it's done to help the women of Hesse. I know the arrangement between you and Lorne is not a love match, but you have many things in common. Build and strengthen those, don't allow those bonds to wilt, as you search elsewhere for happiness."

"There's no longer anyone else."

Alice tilted her head in disbelief, Edgar's name lingering in the silence between them. "Wherever your heart lies, don't neglect Lorne. Look at Bertie and Alix; they have a bond they've formed out of respect and affection, even if it is not love. Better to keep your husband as your friend than your enemy. You don't want him working against you. It could cost you a great deal more than you realize."

The warning in Alice's words made Louise's tea go cold in her mouth. If she and Lorne abided by the terms of their agreement, they'd get on well, but they'd never be close. She could already feel the lack of effort between them, the growing disinterest beneath their polite cordiality.

A knock at the door, and Alice's lady attendant entered. "It's time, Your Highness."

"If only I could keep you here longer." Alice clasped Louise in a hug, holding on to her for a long moment before letting go. "We'll talk again at Osborne at Christmas."

Alice escorted her out onto the platform, pausing with Louise before she boarded the train. "Be happy. You deserve it, and continue with your art lessons. You always were so talented."

Chapter Sixteen

Darling Loosy, I am all impatience to hear how you get on in your new home, for it will be stranger to you than *anything else* yet. Pray *don't rush* about in London, as you always used to do! Visiting and going to exhibitions, shops, and studios, without ever getting fresh air and exercise which you know always ended in making you *quite* ill. Pray be prudent and reasonable. And don't ever go out (when Lorne is not there) without *some* lady *or other*.

—QUEEN VICTORIA TO PRINCESS LOUISE

. . . Princess Louise showed me a monument she is working at . . . a crucifixion, with the Angel of the Resurrection supporting the head of the Savior's—an ambitious work, and a very original idea.
—*Lord Ronald Gower's Diary*

1 Grosvenor Crescent, London, July 1871

Louise worked to shape the wings of the little cherub, carefully adding each detail of the feathers. The Kensington

Palace apartments Mama had promised them were in dire need of repairs, so she and Lorne were settling into a rented house in Grosvenor Crescent until the apartments were made habitable.

Louise had turned one of the sitting rooms with a north-facing window into a studio, and she'd spent the last few days here diligently working on the cherub. While Louise and Lorne had been exploring Italy in April, Alix had given birth to her son, Prince John. The poor babe had lived for a single day, passing away in Alix's arms. Her heartache and Bertie's had been beyond words. Louise, drawing on her lessons with Mr. Story, hoped this small figure gave Alix some comfort. It wasn't enough, it couldn't be, but she must do this, channeling so much into the angel's curls and cheeks. She didn't know what little Prince John had looked like, but she sculpted him with Alix's eyes and pointed chin and Bertie's nose and full cheeks. A tear slipped down her face and she wiped it away with her wrist, her hands too dirty from the clay.

She stepped back and studied the cherub, the angle of the neck where it tilted its head to look up at the viewer well done, but the chubby raised arm wasn't right. She wished Edgar were here to help her. She hadn't seen him since returning to London, but the shadow of him lingered in every conversation with Mr. Whistler, Nino, and Henrietta.

As much as she longed to visit him, she'd stayed away, just as he'd asked her to do. She'd also taken to heart Alice's advice to strengthen her relationship with Lorne, but it required more effort than she'd anticipated. Lorne was pleasant enough to sit with at tea, and to dally with at night, but their conversations didn't flow the way hers and Edgar's had.

Lorne's interests were in many ways similar to hers, and yet they were so different. She couldn't speak with him about her hopes and dreams the way she had with Edgar, but they could discuss her designs for new sculptures or various new movements from Paris. Lord Gower, his constant companion, had encouraged Lorne's interests in the arts and increased Louise's circle of artist acquaintances, but he was also the only friend she and Lorne shared.

She didn't speak to Lorne about her fears over the lack of a child either. It was difficult enough disappointing Mama, who sent hopeful letters every time Louise had so much as a headache. To continue having to admit her courses still appeared each month and her stomach remained flat was an agony she could not escape. She caressed the full cheek of the cherub with the backs of her fingers, longing for a child and afraid it might never happen.

She picked up her tools and scraped them through the clay to create the curve of delicate hair and ringlets. The work soothed her pain and worry until she forgot everything except the feel of the spatula in her hands, the pliability of the clay, and the image taking shape before her.

She remained busy with the sculpture for some time until a knock at the door forced her to straighten. She opened and closed her tight fingers and rubbed the ache in the small of her back. "Come in."

Lorne entered, coming around the table to admire the cherub. "It's beautiful."

"It isn't enough. I can't imagine their grief."

"Their loss is an all-too-sad occurrence. At least Princess Alix survived. So many mothers do not." He ran his thumb and forefinger over the edge of the letter he carried, then held it out to her, the stricken look on his face making her stomach sink. "Louise, before you read this, you must be strong. I fear you must be brave and prepare yourself for a horrible shock."

She took the letter. It was from Mrs. Grey, Sybil's mother. A few days before, Sybil had given birth to a son. All seemed well, but suddenly, last night, Sybil had taken ill and succumbed to childbed fever early this morning.

"No, it can't be." Louise read the letter again and again, struggling to take in the news. Her dearest friend was gone, snuffed out like a candle at the end of the evening. "I saw her just yesterday. She was tired, as one would expect after such an ordeal, but she was fine, the baby was fine."

Lorne stared at his shoes. "I'm very sorry, Louise. She was such a lovely person, and this is an awful tragedy. She will be missed by many."

"She was my dearest friend, and if you understood anything of my life in court, you'd know how much she meant to me."

He frowned. "Since we've returned, I'm coming to understand what you tried to explain to me before. It is a hard life to comprehend, that is, until you live it."

She lowered the letter and looked around the studio. It was all the same, the fire, Lorne's patience, the dustcloths draping the furniture and covering the rugs, and yet everything had changed.

"Shall we go to the sitting room, perhaps find something to eat or rest?" Lorne asked, picking at a small lump of wet clay, at a loss for what to say or do to comfort her.

"No, I want to work." If she didn't, the grief would crush

her. "Please write to Mama on my behalf and let her know. I don't have the strength to do it right now."

"I will." He took her hand and kissed it, holding on for a moment, sincerity filling his blue eyes before he let go and quietly left.

Louise scooped more clay out of the box where it was kept moist for her use and set it on an empty tripod. She had no idea what she might model, but it would be something for Mrs. Grey, for Lord St. Albans, and the baby, something worthy of Sybil and the years of friendship. Louise worked until late into the night, oblivious to the footmen coming in to light the lamps and fire, not touching the plate of food Lorne sent to her, too frustrated by her inability to properly shape the clay into Sybil's hands, hair, or face. She could picture her dear friend as clear as day, but nothing she did made her image take shape before her. In frustration, she crushed the sad figure beneath her palms, then fell into a chair to weep, too tired and heartsick to continue.

"LOUISE?" EDGAR LOOKED up from the sketches on his table, as astonished to see her as if one of his statues had come to life. "You shouldn't be here. We agreed."

"I know." She glanced around his studio, words failing her. Everything was the same as it'd been the last time she'd seen it before the wedding, only the faces on the busts had changed, and the number of them. There were more, with larger statues mixed in among them. "I shouldn't have risked coming here, but I had to see you."

"Why? What's wrong? What's happened?"

"Sybil's dead."

He came around the table and enfolded her in his arms. She clung to him, the months without him vanishing. She'd believed his reasons for them to part. She gave them no weight today, reveling in the life and vitality coursing through him, the things Sybil no longer enjoyed.

"I saw her that afternoon. We were laughing together, and her son was so beautiful in her arms. By the morning, she was gone." Louise wept. "It isn't fair. She was good and kind and had her entire life to enjoy. She should be here with us, her child and me, not in the churchyard."

He gently rocked her, offering no empty platitudes about God's will or fate or any of the other silly things people had told her after Papa's death. He simply listened and held her and, when the tears finally subsided, settled them both on the sofa next to the fire, the sky darker outside the windows, the sun covered by London's endless fog.

"I tried to sculpt her, to create something for me and her family to remember her by, but I couldn't. No matter how hard I tried, I couldn't sculpt her," she whispered.

"The grief is too fresh. When the initial shock passes, you'll find the right way to honor her."

"Help me, please, I'm not ready to let her go." Despite every rational thought telling her to abandon him, to find another tutor, another friend to lean on, she couldn't.

"You never will." He pressed his lips tenderly to hers, the comfort in his kiss spreading through her to push back the desolation snapping at her soul. He touched his forehead to hers, his breath whispering across her cheeks. "I'll teach you portrait medaling, we'll work together to create something you and her family can hold."

"I'll come here every day to work."

He sat back, arm still draped about her shoulder, but something of the practical professor sliding in beneath the comforting lover. "You can't or there'll be talk."

"I don't care. I've spent too long away from you because of fear and other people's expectations. I won't have you stolen from me as Sybil was. She should've had her whole life to enjoy, but it's gone. I don't want the same thing to happen to me, and us." She despised death and grief and everything it'd ever ripped from her, but she was alive. She would live in his arms, as often as she could. "When I was in Italy, each vista I saw, every statue I sketched, I imagined you seeing it before me and wondered what you might say and think about it. I had a taste of the world you used to describe and I want more of it. I won't be shoved back into the royal box where life and passion are forbidden. You told me to search for light, and I will, because it's here, with you."

She slid her hand behind his neck, the scent of marble and sweat permeating his skin filling her senses as she drew him into a kiss. He didn't resist or pull away, falling into her embrace as deeply as she did his. The passion carried them along and swept away every objection either of them had ever raised. He still loved her as much as she loved him, and nothing would ever separate them again.

They lay on the large settee in the sitting room, the door locked against visitors, a velvet coverlet draping them. Louise rested her head on Edgar's chest, running her fingers through the hair on his chest and listening to him breathe in the semidarkness. Outside, rain slid down the windowpanes, muffling the sounds of the passing carts in the street. Edgar gently stroked the back of her arm with his fingers, watching the shadows from the firelight dance across the plaster medallion.

"A beautiful evening," Louise murmured, the heat of his body shielding her from the chill.

Edgar pressed a kiss to her forehead. "How long before you have to leave?"

"Lorne is at the House of Commons and won't be home until quite late. The entire evening is mine." She rolled on her back and stretched like a cat before settling beside him.

He turned on his side and propped his head up on one hand. "Arthur Sullivan is having a party tonight. Would you like to accompany me?"

She sat up, gathering the coverlet about her chest. "Is it safe for me to attend?"

"Arthur and his guests would be thrilled to have you and aren't foolish enough to ruin a chance to have you back again."

"YOUR ROYAL HIGHNESS, I can't tell you what an honor it is to welcome you to my home." Arthur Sullivan, the composer, met them at the door to his Bolwell Terrace house in Lambeth, a simple brick building in a part of London unlikely to be visited by royalty except when opening an almshouse. Louise had certainly never been here, but the narrow street of brick buildings difficult to discern in the dark offered a touch more anonymity for tonight's adventure.

"I couldn't fail to meet the composer who's done for comic opera what Mr. Whistler and Mr. Boehm have done for art, freeing it from the rigidity of classics to bring it splendidly into the present."

Mr. Sullivan nearly melted into a puddle at her compliment, and it took all Edgar's diplomatic skill to pry Louise away from the composer.

"Your Royal Highness." Sir Coutts approached without ceremony, a champagne glass in one hand, a cigarette in the other. "Don't think I've forgotten your promise to provide my new gallery with a piece when it opens."

"I won't disappoint you. Send word when you're ready and I'll gladly make something available to you."

After a few more pleasantries, Sir Coutts drifted away and a parade of other luminaries from the theater and art world came before Louise. After their initial shock at her deigning to grace their gathering, when they realized she wouldn't lord her status over them and expect them to bow and scrape to her, they left her to mingle as if she were any other guest.

"Art must temper the ugliness of factories and workhouses," Madeline Wyndham insisted from beside her husband, the Honorable Percy Wyndham. They were a stunning couple, both with dark hair, but while Percy was reserved, his wife was gregarious, and they were keen collectors of art and artist friends. "It must give everyone, including the common man, something beautiful to view and aspire to."

She and her husband continued in this vein while Louise listened, enraptured by their ideas. The two of them made her think of Papa's desire to help the poor improve their lives through art, but she didn't say so, afraid to parrot Papa in front of these clever people instead of expressing an original thought of her own.

"You didn't say much to Mrs. Wyndham," Edgar observed after the Wyndhams had moved on to chat with other guests.

"I felt an utter simpleton in their presence and didn't wish to open my mouth and prove it."

"Don't allow let them to intimidate you. They're an intelligent couple, but not as much as you or they think. Come, I have someone less arrogant with her intellect you must meet."

He guided her to an elderly woman with a long face and wide, round eyes framed by large waves of dark hair. "May I introduce Madame Amantine Dupin, or as you know her, George Sand?"

"Mrs. Sand, I'm familiar with your novels." And the many scandals surrounding her. Like Miss Hiffernan and Mr. Whistler, Mrs. Sand lived openly with her married lover whose wife was involved with another man. If Mrs. Sand walked easily among this crowd Louise had nothing to fear about anyone here tattling on her. Louise thrust out a hand to the elderly woman. "It's a pleasure."

If Mrs. Sand was shocked by a member of the royal family greeting someone who'd written favorably about the deposers of Emperor Napoleon III, she didn't show it, her serene countenance never changing as she explained her views on the Second French Republic.

"THAT WAS QUITE an evening, far more than you'd promised me." Louise stood with Edgar in Mr. Sullivan's doorway, her carriage waiting outside. They'd arrived separately and they'd leave separately, her heavenly night ending too soon.

"You took it in like a starving man at a banquet."

"Until this year, I was, and you've whetted my appetite for more." If they were alone she might kiss him and rile in him the fires licking at her, but, as accepting as these guests were, she knew better than to tempt fate. They were very permitting, but she didn't dare discover where their open-mindedness ended.

"Good. There's a showing next week at Georges Petit's gallery, French paintings of a new style he's very enthusiastic about. There's a place for you there if you care to join me."

"I do, and anywhere else you believe I might flourish. When may I visit your studio again?"

"I'll send word."

"Make it soon. I won't stay away from you so long ever again."

Chapter Seventeen

THE PRINCESS LOUISE AT BRIGHTON. OPENING OF
A SCHOOL OF SCIENCE AND ART. Her Royal Highness
the Princess Louise (Marchioness of Lorne) gave another
evidence of her active interest in matters calculated to
advance the pursuit of artistic studies by specially visiting Brighton yesterday for the purpose of opening a new
School of Science and Art. Her Royal Highness . . . was
accompanied by the Marquis of Lorne . . .

—*Daily News*

Windsor Castle, February 1872

Since the tragic loss of Lady St. Albans, you have been quite
without a proper Lady of the Bedchamber. I very much
miss Lady St. Albans, she and General Grey were a light to
us both." Mama touched the corner of her eye with her handkerchief, and Louise didn't deny the sincerity of the gesture.
Even if Mama didn't really understand how much Sybil had
meant to Louise, she'd genuinely admired General Grey and
Sybil and grieved them both. "She was a good friend to you

and is sorely missed. However, despite our feelings, there are more practical matters to address."

Mama set the handkerchief beside her plate, a subtle tremble in her hand. They sat across from one another in the Oak Dining Room at Windsor Castle, Louise summoned from London for an afternoon tea and a motherly chat, their first since Mama had returned from Balmoral.

"What matters?" She'd missed a meeting with Edgar for this but didn't dare reveal an ounce of irritation. Mama had been much less demanding since her wedding, allowing Louise to avoid journeying to Scotland for the fall for the first time so she could establish her household.

"You venture out a great deal in London alone. It is not seemly for you to travel about without the company of a lady or your husband. You should be with Lord Lorne, doing things together instead of spending so much time apart."

Louise took a sip of her tea, irritated by Mama's concern. Lorne was quite happy to do whatever it was he did when he wasn't with Louise, and when they were together in public, they still maintained the happy-couple ruse. Mama should be thrilled, not irritated. The marriage was, at present, a success. "We have different interests."

"Papa and I were always as one. We never kept such separate schedules." She picked at the tart on her plate, hardly eating it. She must be quite distressed, to have lost her appetite.

"Lorne and I have many common interests. Our work with the Girls' Public Day School Company and the provincial art schools." In the spirit of Papa, who'd been a great champion of education, Louise had pursued this new interest. She'd been surprised when Lorne had decided to join her, especially to committee meetings and the opening of new schools. It, and attending art showings with Lord Gower, were nearly the only things they did together.

"A wasted endeavor, if you ask me," Mama sniffed. "As for you and Lord Lorne, in private you may have all the separate interests you like. In public, his pursuits must be yours, and everywhere you go must be with him or a proper lady's companion. You must be vigilant in guarding yourself from untoward criticism."

Louise set down the teacup, the familiar grief descending over her and smothering the desire to fight. She missed Sybil's laughter, and her willingness to assist Louise with any scheme. If Mama knew how much Sybil had helped Louise undermine her, she might not speak so well of her, but Louise would never allow that. Sybil had been there for Louise in the lonely years after Papa's death, she'd seen the desolation of Louise' life and done all she could to try and ease it. Louise missed her every day.

"I have a list of suitable married women who might serve as your Lady of the Bedchamber." Mama produced a sheet of paper from the chair beside her and laid it on the table.

Louise left it where it lay, not even glancing at it, the dampened will to fight suddenly reignited inside her. "I will choose my own companions."

"For your dinner table, not your official duties."

"For my household, myself, and all manner of occasions." The last thing she needed was a dour old widow following her about and sending word back to Mama. She'd never be able to see Edgar again, and she wasn't about to let him go. "I also won't be joining you at Osborne House in December. Lorne and I intend to visit the South of France. We find English winters intolerable."

Mama sat back in a huff. "Neither of you may leave England without my permission, and I will not grant it."

"You ask me to spend more time with my husband, and when I inform you of my plans to do so, you refuse."

"We always go to Osborne House for Christmas. Lenchen's and Bertie's marriages have not altered those plans, and neither will yours. I allowed you to take leave from Balmoral. That is enough. You will go to Osborne House."

"I will not." Mama needed to know she couldn't make Louise dance to her tune the way she did Lenchen.

"Why must you torture me with disobedience when my nerves are already strained and I feel weak?" She pressed the back of her hand to her forehead, the paleness of her cheeks made more pronounced by the black silk, but it didn't trouble Louise. Mama could go pale as quickly as she could produce tears.

Louise stirred more sugar into her tea, quite bored. "I'm sure you'll recover from this episode, as you have from every one before."

That brought the color back to her cheeks. "Why have I been cursed with such children?"

"Why can you never see the good but only the bad? I do everything asked of me, opening factories, schools, taking your place at the Queen's Drawing Room."

"As you should. The people granted you a settlement and demand a return on their investment. I pay you a yearly stipend and require continued obedience as thanks, especially if you expect me to pay for your Kensington Palace apartments refurbishments. They will be quite expensive and you cannot afford them on Lorne's paltry allowance from Lord Argyll."

Louise turned her teacup in the saucer, aware she was standing on thin ice. As Vicky had feared, Lorne did not have the money to properly maintain Louise, and they relied on Louise's marriage settlement and her yearly stipend to meet their expenses. It was time for a dignified retreat.

"If you won't allow us to travel to France, will you consider a place for Lord Lorne in your government?" She said nothing about Osborne House, neither agreeing nor refusing to go.

"As you will not entertain my candidates, I will not entertain yours. You may go." Mama snatched up the silver bell from beside her and shook it with a fury.

Louise, with the required curtsey, took her leave. Mama had retreated on the matter of her Lady of the Bedchamber, but the issue of Osborne House still remained. It was a shallow victory.

"GOOD FOR YOU, telling her what's what and how things will be in your household," Leopold congratulated as Louise pushed him in the wheeled chair over the Windsor Garden paths. A recent bleeding attack had left him unable to walk, deepening the dark circles beneath his eyes. "I wish I could do the same. I wrote a letter to her about attending Oxford and how Reverend Duckworth is eager to help arrange it. I composed it in the most tepid terms possible."

"Quite a feat for you."

"To hear her talk, you'd think I'd written it in blood. All

she could do was complain of how I'd spoken to others about it before her. The daft cow. I can't count how many times I've mentioned it to her over the last three years. She said she'd consider it but I couldn't speak with anyone about it while she did. You're the only person I've dared mention it to."

"Her willingness to consider it is promising. It's how my attending art school began."

She rolled the chair farther along the path, past the fountain, the grass brown with the frost. Leopold sat wrapped in blankets, the two of them careful to keep out of sight of the windows for fear Mama would see he was bundled up against the cold instead of suffering in it.

"You have no idea how lonely and dour it is without you here," Leopold said, sighing. "Lenchen hasn't been well. I suspect too much laudanum but I don't say anything. With her often indisposed and you not being here, Mama's work falls to me and Beatrice. Baby's thrilled to finally be treated like a grown-up. I'm bored stiff with Mama's correspondence and watching her and that awful Mr. Brown tittering and laughing like a courting couple."

"Dreadful man, but with Beatrice doing more, Mama will want less from you and me."

"Mama suggested Beatrice preside over next season's Drawing Rooms instead of her. Imagine those poor debutantes putting all that work into their gowns and curtseys, only to be presented to a child. Have you heard of anything more ridiculous? At least she'll get to do something. All I ever do is rot here."

"You could join her at the Drawing Room, inspect the new crop, as one might say."

"How very wicked of you, Loosy. I hadn't thought of that." He rubbed his chin like a rake before slapping the arm of his wheelchair. "What's the point? None of those girls would want me for fear of tainting the bloodline with my weakness. Even if one did, Mama will never allow me to marry, any more than she'll allow Beatrice. I'll be stuck here forever until some attack or other does me in."

"I'm sorry I haven't been here for you more. It's selfish of me to forget you." He deserved a career and life as Alfred and Arthur enjoyed, instead of being tied to Mama's apron strings. If only Mama could see it.

"I don't expect a deliriously happy newlywed to remember her younger brother," Leopold said with a cynical tilt of his head to look back at her.

"The honeymoon is over."

"Did it ever really begin?"

"No." Louise stopped the chair and came around to face Leopold. "When you're well, I'll have you to London for the Season."

"Mama won't let me go."

"I'll speak with Bertie and we'll find a way to arrange it. I'll introduce you to all the young ladies and artists I know. It'll make waiting for Mama to decide about Oxford a little less tedious. It'll be grand, I promise."

She wouldn't forget him or leave him behind to suffer from Mama's constant demands, but find a way to help him live and experience the world.

Chapter Eighteen

. . . I hope that Wednesday or Thursday will be equally convenient to Your Royal Highness to honour me with a call in the afternoon and to give me your valuable advice on the design I am just preparing . . . I have the honour to be Your Royal Highness's ever faithful servant J. E. Boehm.

—Joseph Edgar Boehm to Princess Louise

London, May 1872

It needs a great deal of work, Your Royal Highness," Mr. Edward Godwin, the architect, mused, picking at the crumbling sitting room plasterwork with his fingers. The Kensington Palace apartments Mama had granted Louise and Lorne were filled with moldering curtains and faded wallpaper installed in King George III's reign and quite forgotten since. Difficulties with the drains and bickering between Major Henry Ponsonby, Mama's new private secretary, and the plumbers had held up the renovations.

"You needn't worry about the apartments. Mr. Aitchison

is drawing up plans for those. I asked you here to design my studio. Mr. Whistler and Mr. Boehm said there's no better gentleman for the task." She opened the French doors and escorted him into the bright sunlit garden. "It'll be primarily for sculpture and some painting, but I especially need privacy, so the studio will be in the most secluded part of the garden."

"I'll speak with Mr. Boehm and other sculptors I know about requirements for a sculpting studio and base my designs on their suggestions."

"A perfect plan."

He toured the far end of the garden near the high wall protecting the palace from the streets beyond. Mr. Godwin studied the light and placement, discussing her needs while making notes in a small leather notebook, his long black beard touching the buttons of his shirt as he looked down to write. The studio took shape as they spoke, a place where she could work in peace or seclusion with Edgar. It would be magnificent.

After their meeting, Louise returned to 1 Grosvenor Crescent to change. Edgar had arranged for her to meet Dr. Elizabeth Garrett, England's first female physician. She was eager to discuss Dr. Garrett's work with medicine for women and her place on the London School Board. If anyone might have more suggestions on improving women's education, it was her. Afterward, she and Edgar would return to his studio for a more languid afternoon discussion.

She smiled wickedly as she descended the stairs, the skirt of her flowing bohemian-style dress in one hand, her wide-brimmed hat in the other. The flowing silhouette of the frock with the draping Watteau-like back instead of a bustle meant fewer laces and tapes and made dressing and undressing at Edgar's studio far more pleasant.

She straightened the large silver cross hanging around her neck, the one she'd designed in November to commemorate Mama's recovery from the horrible infection. During Louise's last contentious tea at Windsor with Mama, she'd thought Mama had been playing at being weak and out of sorts. So had everyone else, until she'd grown feverish and Dr. Jenner had diagnosed a blood infection. While Mama lay gravely ill at Windsor, Louise had channeled her guilt over their harsh parting into the cross, hammering out the silver into the fine angles, each hammer strike evident in the polished metal. Mama's slow recovery had softened her irascible nature, her directions coming now as requests instead of demands, making them a great deal easier to ignore.

In the end, she and Lorne had spent Christmas with the family at Windsor, Mama too ill to travel to Osborne, so the argument's point had become moot. It'd been their first family Christmas in the castle since Papa's passing, and a gloomy, trying season as typhoid had once again gripped their family, this time threatening Bertie. They'd spent the dreaded December 14, the anniversary of Papa's passing, crowded around Bertie's bed, sure he was going to die. He'd miraculously recovered. Afterward the people and Mama had found a new love for the heir to the throne while Louise had thanked God for sparing her brother. She'd be lost without his help and advice.

She tugged on her gloves in the entryway, the carriage waiting outside to ferry her to Edgar's Fulham Road studio, when Lorne stepped out of his study.

"Going out again?" He leaned against the arched library doorway, wearing a maroon velvet dressing gown in need of a good wash. His fingers were stained black from writing ink and his hair was disheveled. Lorne had many pleasant traits; cleanliness was not one of them. It was an odd habit she and Lord Gower had done their best to change, but for reasons known only to Lorne, he refused to take better care of himself.

"Mr. Boehm is refining my technique with medal modeling. I wish to produce small prizes to give the students of our charity schools for their academic awards."

"He's very generous with his time and willingness to tutor you. I hope it isn't to the detriment of his other clients."

The skepticism coloring his words made her leery, but she fitted her hat over her hair in the mirror, determined to appear as if nothing were amiss. "Mr. Boehm knows best how to manage his time and clients."

"Do you?" Lorne picked dirt from beneath his nails and rubbed it on his already stained dressing gown.

She carefully slid the hatpin in above the wide brim. "Whatever do you mean?"

"It isn't right for you to go about London visiting gentlemen artists' studios without a lady present. You don't want people to get the wrong idea."

"I see Mama has written to you again. One would think with a country to run she wouldn't have time to meddle in her married children's affairs."

"This does concern her country. We must appear together in public more, or people will talk. It's a love match, after all."

"We're going to the opera tomorrow night with Alix and Bertie. They can see us then."

As irritating as Lorne was on the matter, he was right. Since returning to London, she'd been reckless in spending so much time with Edgar. She could dismiss Mama's concerns. She'd fret whether Louise spent every night at the theater or beside the fireplace dying of boredom, but if Lorne felt the need to comment, the situation was more serious than she'd realized.

"I'll engage a Lady of the Bedchamber. That should stop tongues from wagging." The thought of making inquiries made her sick. Replacing Sybil felt like burying her all over again, but she needed a proper companion. She couldn't spend every moment with Edgar, or even Henrietta, and without someone to talk to and plot with, the loneliness of her house and marriage was sometimes difficult to bear.

"Have you spoken to Her Majesty about a position for me? I've heard nothing about anything, and I refuse to be compared to Prince Christian."

"You have your poems, and when they're done you'll have the arduous task of finding a publisher. That's something."

"I want more." He banged his fist on the table beside him, making the vase with the roses on top rattle. He never spoke with such force and she wished he'd do it more. He'd be a great deal more tolerable if he insisted like a man instead of whining like a child. "You promised me more."

"I spoke to her, but she was quite stubborn on the matter. I'll think of someone I can discuss it with who can better influence her. Until then, continue with your poems. It's good to have something of one's own that no one else can take away."

With a curt nod, he returned to his study and closed the door behind him.

"YOUR ROYAL HIGHNESS, I'd be happy to speak with Her Majesty about a position for Lord Lorne," Mr. Disraeli offered from beside Louise in his box at the Royal Italian Opera, Covent Garden. She sat directly beside him, close to the railing so the entire theater could see him honored by royalty deigning to visit his box instead of him being summoned to hers. It'd made him nearly flutter out of his seat in excitement, especially when he'd noticed her wearing the gold butterfly pin.

"I knew I could count on you. Thank you again for all you've done for me." She rose, waving to Bertie from across the theater to ensure everyone in the orchestra seats not already watching noticed her. All of London society was here to see Madame Pauline Lucca and the Royal Italian Opera in the opening night of *Fra Diavolo*. Louise was less interested in the story of the impoverished innkeeper's daughter and her poor soldier than she was the social dances around her.

She left the box, making her way along the opulently appointed hallways and grand, sweeping staircases with their marble banisters and red velvet rugs. The flickering of the gas lights in their crystal sconces deepened the rich purple silk and gold lace trim of her dress and sparkled in the facets of her diamond parure wedding gift. At Alix's suggestion, Louise had visited the House of Worth in Paris on her and Lorne's return from Italy last year. Her sister-in-law's praise of the dress designer's talents had not been exaggerated, and Louise had ordered evening gowns and afternoon dresses with full bustled skirts, fitted bodices and jackets, and no modesty panels. The diamonds she was free to wear would be the only thing to cover the swell of her full breasts above a slender waist.

Despite the outlay, she'd been careful to guard her marriage settlement and annual income and not squander it. Without it, she'd have to go begging to Mama, who already chafed under Alice's constant requests for funds. Prussia had leveled heavy fines on Hesse for siding with losing Austria in the Austro-Prussian War and the payment had depleted what little remained of Alice's dowry.

The footman opened the door to Bertie's box and Louise swept inside. She stepped up to the railing and waved across the theater to Lady Lyttelton, now Lady Cavendish, drawing more of the audience's attention. Louise glowed as much under their notice as she did in the footlights. The only dullness was not having Edgar by her side.

"What was all that with Mr. Disraeli about?" Bertie asked when she finally took her seat between him and Lorne. Alix remained at Marlborough House, ill with what many suspected might be another pregnancy. She and Bertie were spending a great deal more time together since his bout of typhoid in December. He sat at the front of his box watching the performance onstage, as well as Louise's, and basking in the public's newfound love for him.

"I spoke to him about a position for Lorne in Mama's government." Louise wished she were home with the sickness of early pregnancy, but more months had passed and there was still nothing. She touched the medal of Sybil she kept pinned in her corset beside the one of Edgar, missing her dear friend more than ever.

"Thank you, my dear, it's most appreciated." Lorne raised her gloved hand to his lips and loud applause rose from the audience. Even the performers onstage paused to pay their respects to the royal couple. When the occasion called for it, Lorne could perform as well as Louise, although his black evening suit was not nearly as crisp in its lines and tailoring as Bertie's. At least he wasn't wearing his dressing gown and he genuinely did appreciate her speaking to Mr. Disraeli; it was there in his wide smile and the pride with which he waved to the audience before they and the performers returned their attention to the stage.

"House of Commons not scintillating enough for you, Lorne?" Bertie raised his lorgnette to scan the other boxes.

Lorne released her hand, ignoring Bertie's dig. "Lord Gower is seated across the way. Do you mind if I speak to him?"

"Not at all."

With all the respect due to a wife, and exaggerated so those in the orchestra seats could see, Lorne took his leave.

"Your performance is better than the one onstage." Bertie beckoned to someone across the theater that Louise couldn't see.

"We're all players, are we not?" She hoped the people lost interest in them before the cracks in their performance and marriage grew too large for anyone outside the family to ignore.

"We are."

The footman moved aside the curtain and showed a woman into the box. She was only a few years older than Louise, her fresh face tempered with an air of worldliness with a curved but short, full nose, a well-defined chin, and cheeks made fuller by a wide, open smile framed by dark blond ringlets.

Bertie rose, and, taking her hand, brought her forward. "Lady Sophia Macnamara, how kind of you to join us."

"It's a pleasure." Lady Macnamara bowed with grace tinged with a subtle humor that removed all solemnity from the formal introduction.

Louise wondered what Bertie was about, bringing this woman here. She couldn't be one of his lovers. He'd never been overly clandestine with his affairs, but he'd never been blatant enough to publicly invite them into his box with his sister.

He scowled at her as if to say it wasn't what she was thinking. "Lady Macnamara's father, Lord Listowel, is one of Her Majesty's Lords in Waiting. I think she'd do very well as your Lady of the Bedchamber."

"Are you sure you wish to be considered, Lady Macnamara? Royal service can be quite dull."

"If it keeps me away from my sod of a husband, I'd become your scullery maid."

Louise exchanged an amused look with Bertie. The woman was certainly intriguing. Whether she was suitable to act as Louise's companion remained to be seen. Bertie might think her acceptable, but he'd been a poor judge of character in Lady Randolph Churchill. He might have greatly misjudged this woman, who, if she was as lax in keeping secrets as she was with her opinion of her husband, wouldn't do at all.

Louise motioned to Lorne's empty seat. "Join me, Lady Macnamara, so we might become better acquainted."

"Please, call me Smack. All my friends do."

"You have a great many friends?"

"Not as many as I'd like. My husband has a talent for driving them away, but he'd be positively afraid of you, and tickled pink his wife has risen so high. It'll keep him on his estate in Ireland, where he can continue to rile his tenants. I keep hoping he'll irritate one enough to shoot him, or that perhaps he'll drink himself to death, but no such luck."

Louise wondered if she'd ever think of Lorne in such harsh terms. "You're very frank."

"I can be very discreet when necessary; if I weren't, my husband would never be accepted in a respectable household again. I assure you, secrets are safe with me. Wouldn't you agree, Your Royal Highness?"

"Most definitely."

Neither of them elaborated on how Bertie knew, but Louise trusted he did.

"His Royal Highness has told me about your art. I think it marvelous for a married woman to have *personal* interests to occupy her, especially in times of difficulty."

"My work is a great comfort." *She knows.* How much she knew, Louise couldn't say. Nothing about her expression had changed to reveal anything except her admiration of Louise and her continued desire for the position. Both traits, supported by Bertie's recommendation, swung Louise in her favor. Louise extended her hand to Smack, who took it with a firm grip. "Welcome to my household, Lady Macnamara. I think we shall be grand friends."

Chapter Nineteen

Madam—I cannot tell you how charmed and delighted
I am to know that you are coming tomorrow . . . I shall
be at the gallery in Suffolk Street to receive Your Royal
Highness at four o'clock. I hope also that perhaps Mr.
Boehm may be able to come at about half past four—and
he would be far better able to point out the pictures than
I should unaided!

—James McNeill Whistler to Princess Louise

London, March 1874

Ironic the Crown Princess of Prussia should donate art to
an exhibition for orphans and widows of German soldiers,"
Henrietta observed as she, Louise, and Smack stopped to
view Vicky's contribution to the charity art show at the New
British Institution. These were the first pieces Vicky had exhibited in Britain, but Louise's works had been shown many
times at the Royal Academy, the Fine Arts Society, and the
Berners Street Gallery over the last two years. It'd allowed
her to hold Show Sundays of her own and repay the kindness

of many artists by inviting them to her finally redecorated Kensington Palace apartments.

"I think it fitting, since Emperor Wilhelm's soldiers created so many widows and orphans," Smack said.

"Her Royal Highness has a talent for depicting women and infants." Henrietta admired Vicky's oil painting of a mother and child in a sunny courtyard.

"Babies are a special subject for her." Louise avoided them in her work, the reminder she still didn't have one of her own too painful. And the numerous letters from Vicky asking when she might welcome another niece or nephew didn't help.

Dinners with Mama were no more comforting or encouraging, with Mama always kind enough to mention how Lenchen had given birth to her third child since Louise's marriage. Only Alice's letters on the subject didn't make the back of Louise's neck tighten, her advice and suggestions more practical and tender than anything else she'd received. But even following Alice's advice had not yielded any results.

"I think her watercolors are much better." Smack drew their attention to the two studies of German interiors. "The Crown Princess doesn't have Your Royal Highness's eye for detail or your ability to reveal a sitter's true personality. Her woman and child could be anyone in a crowd. I don't feel as if they're special or known to her."

"Well done, Smack," Louise praised her friend, who'd increased her knowledge of art in the last two years. "You sound like Mr. Ruskin."

"Don't say so too loud or he might hear you and write

dreadful things about your pieces." Henrietta tilted her head to where Mr. Ruskin stood examining Louise's bust of Leopold and her niece Princess Victoria, Alice's eldest daughter.

Mr. Whistler came up behind Louise, his white cotton duck suit crisp against his suntanned skin. "Mr. Ruskin is worse than Mr. Rossetti or Mr. Henry James in their puffed-up arrogance of opinion."

"True, but tonight I'm in need of his assistance. Would you bring him to me?"

"Only because you're a princess. Otherwise, I'd take him outside and give him a good thrashing." Mr. Whistler strolled off to collect the critic.

"Louise, I'm in desperate need of Miss Montalba's assistance." Leopold, a rakish smile gracing his lips beneath his thin mustache, said, hurrying back to them. At Bertie and Louise's urging, Mama had allowed him to visit them in London more during the Season, so long as they kept him to a strict schedule of sedate carriage rides in Rotten Row and one or two dinners with carefully selected and boring old men. Louise, Bertie, and Leopold had immediately discarded those instructions, filling his diary with invitations to society events. Bertie employed his influence with reporters to keep all mention of Leopold's attendance out of the newspapers. Society had done Leopold a world of good, bringing the color to his cheeks and returning life to his blue eyes, especially when speaking with a pretty young lady such as Henrietta. Louise had introduced them his first day in London, and the easy and friendly informality she enjoyed with Henrietta had expanded to encompass Leopold. "I must know if she's familiar with that gorgeous creature standing with Mr. Millais?"

He leveled his walking stick at a statuesque woman in a simple black velvet dress. She was tall, with a shapely form and rich auburn hair gathered in a loose chignon at the nape of her curved neck, the sides left loose to brush her defined cheeks and chin. Mr. Millais stared at her with a rapture Louise noticed from across the room.

"Her name is Mrs. Langtry. She's from Jersey. Mr. Millais and others call her the Jersey Lillie. She's fast becoming their favorite model."

"She's a stunning creature. Might I impose upon you to introduce me?" He offered her his elbow.

"It would be my pleasure." Henrietta escorted Leopold across the room to make the introduction.

"I wonder who he's more interested in, Mrs. Langtry or Henrietta?" Smack mused, having been on the receiving end of Leopold's gallantry more than once.

"Perhaps she'll gain a royal patron."

"It would be good for them both if she did."

Mr. Whistler returned with Mr. Ruskin, his tight smile conveying he was tolerating the man for her benefit and no other reason.

"Mr. Ruskin, what a pleasure to see you again." Louise extended her hand for him to bow over. "Prince Leopold is a great admirer of your writings and hopes to attend Oxford. Perhaps, with your assistance, we can secure his enrollment."

Mama still resisted Leopold's request to attend Oxford, but lately there'd been signs of her relenting. It was time to apply more persuasion, and a man such as Mr. Ruskin, don of art at Oxford whose views on art aligned so closely with Papa's, might help sway Mama in Leopold's favor.

The critic's face lit up at the prospect of a royal protégé. "It would be my pleasure to aid His Royal Highness in whatever way possible."

Mr. Whistler rolled his eyes behind Mr. Ruskin, and Louise had to focus on the art critic's striped suit to keep from laughing. "Mr. Whistler, might I impose upon you to make the introduction?"

"The things I do for those I adore." With less enthusiasm than Henrietta, Mr. Whistler led Mr. Ruskin to Leopold, interrupting her brother's fawning over Mrs. Langtry.

"Congratulations on making Mac endure Mr. Ruskin for more than five minutes without a row." Edgar's strong voice drifted over Louise's shoulder.

She turned to face Edgar, willing her cheeks not to flush and give away her excitement. "He'd do well to court him instead of tweaking his nose."

"It isn't Mac's style."

"I didn't think you'd be here tonight."

"I couldn't stay away." Dark circles sat heavy beneath his eyes and a new gauntness shadowed his face that even his charm couldn't hide.

"You look exhausted. You're working too hard."

"I have very demanding clients."

"Perhaps they shouldn't disturb you so often."

"Nonsense, my patrons are my greatest priority." He motioned her to walk with him through the gallery. She fell in step beside him, Smack trailing behind them, as diligent and accommodating a companion as Sybil had once been. Louise wanted to take his arm and lean on him as she had when they'd walked the hills around Balmoral so long ago, but propriety demanded they remain apart. They passed another plinth where a copy of his *Her Majesty at the Spinning Wheel* rested for people to admire and bid on. Copies of the statuette had been a great success with both Mama, who presented them to royal favorites, and the public, who purchased whatever copies Edgar made available with patriotic zeal.

"Mac says your studio is finally complete? I'd love to see it. Tonight, perhaps, before I'm forced to leave for Woburn. The Duke of Bedford has commissioned a memorial statue for Woburn Abbey. I'm to consult with him and complete the preliminary sketches and designs. I'll be gone for some time."

She shouldn't leave with him, but with Leopold entranced by Mr. Ruskin, and Mac and Henrietta engaged in a thorough dissection of each submitted work, Louise could dismiss Smack, and she and Edgar could slip away to the quiet of her studio and no one would notice. It might be their only time together for who knows how long. "Yes."

"IT'S A WORK of art in itself." Edgar, hands on his hips to draw back the edges of his coat, stood in the middle of Louise's Kensington Palace garden studio and leaned back to take in the high mansard roof. Along the north side of it was a bank of windows, and beneath them whitewashed plaster walls to help reflect the light. A large fireplace and chimney occupied the south wall, the mantel framed by majolica tiles from the female tile makers at the National Art Training School. The center of the studio was wide open, with space enough for multiple works. A small hallway along the front led to a sitting room and large closets for Louise's supplies. "Mr. Godwin has outdone himself."

"It's wonderful to have the space and privacy to sculpt. I can work when I want, how I want, and there's no one to bother me."

"You could execute larger pieces in here, really stretch your wings and discover what you're capable of."

"I've never done anything large." She strolled behind him, trailing her fingers along the width of his shoulders. "I'd need a great deal of help."

"It'd be my pleasure to assist you." He entwined her in his arms and kissed her, bending her around him and backward like in Monsieur Rodin's *The Kiss*, which had caused such a flurry in Paris. She relished his touch, craving him as she did the heady thrill of displaying her work.

At last she broke from him, sliding her hand down his arm to grasp his fingers and lead him to her sitting room. "Allow me to show you my holy of holies."

Afterward, they lay together on the large sofa in the sitting room, entwined in the velvet coverlet, the smoke from their cigarettes rising to form a gray mist in the cool air.

"I want you to teach me to sculpt larger pieces when you return from Woburn."

"You'll hate me for doing so." He tucked one arm behind his head. "The bigger the work, the more you see every fault in your execution, where the chisel slipped, where you failed to smooth or shape things properly, every mistake immovable, unfixable, until you want to pull it down and recast it until it's perfect. It's a curse you don't want."

"It isn't the only curse I don't wish to have."

He caressed her cheek with his fingers, tucking her loose hair behind her ear. "Still nothing?"

"No." She sat up, pulling her knees to her chest. "Alice isn't even encouraging anymore. At least she doesn't pester me about it the way Vicky and Mama do. Their comments are like spears to my heart."

He sat up beside her, stroking her back. "I'm sure they don't mean to be cruel."

"They don't, but it hurts because I know the fault is with me. You have children." She wiped the tears off her face. "The wanting and the failure each month is awful, and there's nothing I can do to make it go away. I still grieve for Sybil and Papa, but time has made their losses easier to bear. Every month, it's as if my hopes die all over again and there'll never be an end to this grief. I've spent years struggling for the things I want, and despite Mama and my position, I've achieved them in ways I never thought possible, but I can't force a child." She gathered the coverlet around her and walked to the window with a view of the garden. The large trees and bushes shielded the windows from Kensington Palace. The dark, moonless night would hide Edgar when it was time for him to slip out through the side gate. "Why am I denied a child while Mama and Vicky, who barely wanted children, were given so many?"

He came up behind her and wrapped his arms around her. "There's no rhyme or reason to it, and you'll torture yourself searching for one. It's what every artist who doesn't find success says about those who do. The bitterness churns their insides until they can't think of anything else. Don't let it happen to you."

"How can I avoid it?" She leaned into him, allowing him to help her carry this grief as he had so many others. "No wonder Lenchen takes solace in laudanum. I would too if I thought it would ease the pain, but it wouldn't. It'd simply make things worse."

He turned her to face to him and laid his hands on either side of her face. "That's what I love about you: no matter how dark things are, you can see the sensible and face it. Keep being strong. Strength won't stop it from hurting, but it'll help you bear it."

"I don't want to bear it."

"I wish you didn't have to, but you do. Weather the storms as you always have and never give up."

Madam and dear Princess, A cygnet for your Royal Highness's gracious acceptance. It is good for princesses, but should be tasted in the banqueting chamber of some moonlit Isle, surrounded by swans in melodious chorus! Alas! I cannot offer your Royal Highness the Isle which you deserve, but deign to accept the humble tribute of your faithful servant . . .

—Benjamin Disraeli to Princess Louise

44 Belgrave Square, London, June 1874

"If the poor are unhealthy, they can't be expected to appreciate the beauty of art amidst the ugliness of poverty and machines, or be raised up by it. We must attend to their bodies as well as their spirits," Louise said to Madeline Wyndham, who nodded thoughtfully.

"I hadn't considered the matter from that perspective, but

you're right. I'd like to assist your efforts with your infirmaries and women's hospitals. It is important."

"I'll arrange it at once." They discussed the matter a while before Mrs. Wyndham moved on to speak with Mr. Burne-Jones.

"You held your own against Lady Wyndham tonight," Mr. Disraeli complimented, coming to join her in front of the stunning portrait of Madeline Wyndham by George Frederic Watts. The subject stood facing the viewer, her skin smooth with the pearly glow preferred by the Pre-Raphaelites, luminous against her dark dress and background. "I haven't seen a debate with such passion since the last House of Commons session. You've truly come into your own."

"I've been fortifying my education in preparation for this for some time." Including taking in every detail of this sitting room, determined to make her Kensington Palace one as grand a showplace for art and taste as this one, where portraits and paintings from Mr. Burne-Jones and even Mr. Whistler decorated the walls.

"Good. Nurture your mind with great thoughts, for you will never go any higher than you think, and you've climbed quite high with your sculpture."

"I have you to thank for helping me find this path." She twisted the pearls from Papa's mother around one finger, the creamy orbs clinking delicately against the butterfly pin attached to the silk soutache trim of her burgundy gown.

"Never waver from it or allow anyone to drive you off it."

"My feet aren't the only ones in need of a route. Prince Leopold is aching to attend Oxford. He also needs the chance to come into his own."

"Her Majesty is against it?"

"Yes. And perhaps the man whose return to the premiership has so delighted Her Majesty and whom she intends to ennoble as First Earl of Beaconsfield could convince her. You have a way with Her Majesty."

"As Your Royal Highness has with me." With a modest tilt of his head, his curly hair, now more gray than black, fell forward. He'd aged a great deal since his first premiership, prior illnesses having thinned his face and slowed his once-nimble gait. "Together, we'll set Prince Leopold on his path and see what he makes of himself."

On Wednesday morning I . . . went through the ceremony of "matriculation." In the evening the Vice-Chancellor, Dean of Christchurch, and Dr. Acland dined with me. On Thursday I went to my first lecture, which was one delivered by Professor Ruskin on the art of engraving, it was most interesting . . . In the afternoon I went to the Deanery and heard the charming Miss Liddells play and sing, they are very pretty indeed, and very nice.

—Prince Leopold to Princess Louise

Guildhall, London, October 1876

Louise rose to her feet with the crowd to applaud Leopold at the end of his speech to the Corporation of London and seven hundred distinguished guests. The Lord Mayor had conferred on him the freedom of the City, and his time before the aldermen reminded Louise of her opening of Parliament. Louise hoped this would be the start of a new and better life for him, as her debut in the Commons had been for her.

"Where is Lord Lorne today?" The Lord Mayor in his long ermine-trimmed crimson velvet robe asked Louise, shifting all the attention from Leopold to her during the reception afterward.

"He's on a tour of Ireland."

"How grand of him to take on official duties. I'm sure the people of Ireland will be disappointed at not seeing his beautiful wife."

She didn't correct his mistaken belief that Lorne's trip was something more than a tour with Lord Gower. The less anyone outside the family knew about her and Lorne's strained relationship, the better.

"I couldn't miss the opportunity to watch Leopold speak. He was magnificent." Louise's compliment shifted the conversation back to congratulations for Leopold. She stepped aside to allow Leopold to fully enjoy his triumph, and Major Henry Ponsonby, Leopold's assistant for today, approached her.

"Her Majesty is unhappy you didn't accompany Lord Lorne to Ireland," he said quietly so the others couldn't hear, his fingers laced behind his slender back, stately in his frock coat and waistcoat, his watch chain visible. "She's concerned too many people have noticed the distance between you, as the Lord Mayor made quite clear."

"Then she shouldn't have granted him leave to go."

"I did point this out to Her Majesty, but she didn't appreciate the reminder." Major Ponsonby wasn't shy in pushing back against Mama, and while he was often more cunning and successful than General Grey had been, Mama was still as difficult as a donkey to lead. "I suggest Your Royal Highness recall Lord Lorne before Her Majesty does, and amicably settle the matter."

"Thank you for your sensible advice, Major Ponsonby. I'll see to it at once." She had no desire to spend time with Lorne, but if a public show kept Mama at bay, she'd write to him immediately.

I cannot deny that the tone of your answer to my observations has surprised and pained me. I think you forget in speaking to me of people not knowing what married happiness was if they could wish to be a single day apart, that for 22 years there were no two people more united and happier than my dear Husband and I were, and that to us separation was always a trial . . . I am the first to disapprove the style of the present day when wives go out to amusements alone, the husbands going to their clubs etc. and think that their lives should be as much in common as possible . . .

—*Queen Victoria to Lord Lorne*

London, November 1876

"Your patronage and support have done so much for us, Your Royal Highness," Dr. Garrett said as thanks to Louise as she led her and Lorne on a tour of the New Hospital for Women. "The expense of running the hospital is so great, we could never hope to remain open if it weren't for your help. There isn't another institution in England where women seeking medical advice from women or eager to be trained in medicine can come. Perhaps one day Your Royal Highness will be in need of our services," Dr. Garrett suggested with a lilt in her voice, escorting Louise into the maternity wing of the hospital.

"One can hope." Louise's heart dropped but not her smile, as Dr. Garrett escorted her and Lorne past the beds of mothers and their newly delivered babies. Some slept with their swaddled babes in their arms, others quietly nursed them as Louise passed, her heart breaking. "These mothers are fortunate to have you and the hospital."

"We also help foundlings by placing them in suitable homes in the country, then arranging for their education in a trade when they're older."

Louise steeled herself against the unfairness of life. She longed for a child and had none, while some mothers willingly gave their babies away. And others were faced with what might be a terrible and difficult decision.

Dr. Garrett escorted them to the surgical theater, with its viewing gallery for female students. They visited the dispensary, with its shelves of glass bottles filled with medicines to serve the needs of charity patients. In each ward, women of various ages tended the sick, oversaw administrative duties, and compounded medicines. It was like no hospital Louise had ever visited before, and she plied Dr. Garrett with questions about the new surgical techniques and procedures, eager to write to Alice about everything she'd learned. Alice was one of the few who knew of this visit. Louise had kept it a secret from Mama, who was not

enamored of the female doctor, thinking her an abomina-
tion instead of a necessity.

Lorne trailed behind Louise, ignored by everyone, including the all-female staff who gathered in doorways and along
the railings to catch sight of Louise. She didn't disappoint
them, readily approaching the nervous and blushing nurses
to ask them questions about their work or patients. Thanks to
her anatomy training, she understood many answers better
than expected.

At the end of the visit, Louise collapsed against the carriage squabs, the strain of so many discussions, and appearing as if all were well in the maternity ward, leaving her
exhausted. She touched her bodice and the medal of Edgar.
He'd told her to be strong and she had been, but she hated it,
wanting to lay down this burden, but she couldn't. She must
always pretend she wasn't crumbling inside at the reminders
of her barrenness, and play the part of the perfectly poised
and polite Princess.

"I don't know why you summoned me from Ireland to tour
a women's hospital," Lorne grumbled. "It's bad enough when
I have to trail behind you at railroad openings and military
reviews and I'm all but ignored by the press and the crowds,
but a women's hospital where there is absolutely nothing for
me is pointless."

"I told you, we have to keep up appearances or people will
talk."

"What they should be talking about is my appointment to a
post of importance and the things I'm accomplishing there."

"I secured you a place on Mama's Privy Council." It'd
been the only position Mr. Disraeli had been able to convince

Mama to give him. "What you choose to do or not do with it is up to you."

"There's nothing to be done with it. It's a token gesture where I'm expected to sit and stay silent. Whenever I do speak up, the other counselors are vicious in reminding me my opinion is not needed or wanted."

"What more do you want?"

"For you to uphold your end of the bargain, as I've upheld mine. I say nothing about those artist friends of yours and whatever liberties you allow them."

"You should be happy someone is stepping in to do your duty, otherwise there might never be a child."

"I don't care what they do with you. Nothing will come of it anyway."

For the first time, Louise felt as Smack did about her husband, wishing someone might rise up and rid her of him, but if they did, and God saw fit to finally grant her a child, she still needed the protection of this marriage and his name or it'd be a scandal not even she could overcome.

Chapter Twenty

Beware of incurring debt (as Alice has to a very serious extent) so I shall not be able to help you—I *cannot* with the help I have been *asked* and maybe *obliged* to give your other sisters. As I give you £2000 a year I *have* a right to see that the money is not improperly or at least improvidently and unnecessarily spent . . .

—QUEEN VICTORIA TO PRINCESS LOUISE

Windsor Castle, April 1877

Y ou must stop your visits and public support for Mrs. Garrett at once," Mama said to Louise from across her desk. "It is not seemingly for you to patronize a woman engaged in such inappropriate activities. A woman doctor. Lenchen, have you heard of anything so ridiculous?"

"I have not, Mama."

"Alice is a great admirer of Dr. Garrett and her work on behalf of women. Many poor or destitute mothers have found solace in her care." Louise rubbed the end of the beaten silver cross around her neck so hard the pads of her fingers polished it.

"Alice's interests are indecent. It is unseeingly for you to follow in her footsteps. Patronize the School for Cookery or something of that sort. You see how Lenchen is much admired as the president of the Royal School of Art-Needlework."

"I'm sure she is," Louise replied dryly, certain she'd die of boredom at any of their committee meetings.

"Their work isn't political either, and in many ways Mrs. Garrett's is," Lenchen observed from where she sat by the windows sorting Mama's correspondence. "It isn't our place to show favor to any political cause. We're supposed to rise above and be separate from it all."

"Especially when it is my money you are using to support that woman. It is as if I am supporting her too and it cannot be had, especially now that I am Empress of India as well as Queen of England." She rubbed Sharp's head, the dog resting its chin on Mama's lap. Mr. Disraeli's greatest achievement on Mama's behalf had been to raise her to the elevated rank, one she didn't shy from lording over everyone, especially Vicky, who had yet to become an empress. "You will not speak or engage with Mrs. Garrett again."

Louise silently fumed, irritated at having her yearly stipend held over her head to make her obey. If she had the freedom to sculpt and sell her pieces, she might earn enough to do without Mama's money and control, but Mama would balk at Louise entering into commerce more than she did Louise supporting Mrs. Garrett.

"You are also not to continue hosting Leopold in London. You and Bertie have taken advantage of my generosity in allowing him to travel by escorting him to dances and dinners not sanctioned by me. I will not have Bertie encouraging his corruption or you stoking his insolence. I refuse to have him led astray by those bohemian artist friends of yours. He is a guileless and innocent boy."

"He is twenty-four years old, he hardly needs permission to dine with his sister or attend social events."

"He is my son, and he and you will do as I say." Mama tapped the ink off her pen as if the matter were settled. It might be, in her mind, but not in Louise's. Leopold deserved some semblance of a life outside the palace walls.

"May I take my leave?" She didn't want to have this row again.

"No, you may assist Lenchen with my correspondence."

"I will not. My place is beside my husband, not here."

Mama slammed down her pen. "You are never beside your husband."

"That is not true. He accompanies me to art school openings and charity bazaars to benefit women's infirmaries, and will be at a number of future events." She and Lorne, through Smack and Major Francis de Winton, Lorne's private secretary, had arranged a renewed schedule of appearances to keep up the pretense of a happy marriage while ensuring they didn't spend too much time together.

"You should accompany him to his interests, sit in Parliament when he is there, and help make him a better politician." Mama rose and came around the desk, clasping Louise's hands in hers, a sincere concern filling her eyes. "All I want is your happiness. It is all I have ever wanted for my children. You would be so much more content and not need to flitter about London if you had someone as devoted to you and your well-being as I have Mr. Brown to attend to mine. Lord

Lorne could be such a person for you if you but nurtured him and made his interests yours."

Edgar was for Louise just as she suspected Mr. Brown was for Mama, but Louise dared not ever admit it. "Lorne and I have as much in common as can be expected of a man and wife, and we live together as best we can. He isn't my drunken servant like Mr. Brown is yours, and I am not his monarch."

Mama let go of Louise's hands and marched back to her desk. "You are not his helpmate either, nor are you mine. Instead of settling my well-meaning and heartfelt concerns, you do nothing but irritate me by ignoring the most sensible advice and insulting my dear friend Mr. Brown. You are dismissed."

Louise left Mama's office, irked at having been sent out like a servant but relieved to not have to review dispatches. She had things to do in London, and needed to hurry to make the train. She was so involved in her thoughts about tonight and Edgar and dinner at Sir Coutts's she nearly tripped over Beatrice.

"Louise, may I speak with you?" Beatrice's face had gained a soft roundness that made her look younger than twenty. Her swan-white dress had a wider skirt and more lace and fripperies than the current fashion preferred, and it added to her youthful demeanor. But her tight-pressed lips spoke of more adult difficulties.

"A request. How refreshing an approach." Louise kept walking, ignoring her youngest sister. She'd had enough of Mama and Lenchen and wasn't in the mood for more irritation from any of her siblings, especially from Beatrice and her tattletale ways.

"Please, I need your help." She stopped in front of Louise, forcing her to halt in the hallway. "I know I've been perfectly dreadful in the past, but you have no idea how lonely it is here."

"I think I do know."

"No, you don't. You always had Lenchen, Arthur, and Leopold to play or study with. And Bertie's always been on your side. I've had no one, no siblings or friends my age, nothing but Mama, who is so demanding. She smothers me like she does Leopold."

Louise softened her hard stance, seeing Beatrice in a new light. She was so much younger than the rest of them and Mama kept her as close as Sharp. If Louise thought she'd had few outside friends as a child, Beatrice was a near-recluse. It wasn't difficult to see her childhood sourness had been due to bitterness and loneliness, emotions Louise knew too well. "What do you want?"

"To attend the State Ball in July. The Prince Imperial will be there and he promised to dance with me." She held out the sides of her skirt and twirled down the hall and then back again. "He's handsome and ever so sweet to me when Mama and I visit him and Empress Eugénie at Camden Place."

"I'm surprised Mama allows you to speak with him at all."

"We speak when she and the Empress are busy and she doesn't notice. Oh please, Louise, you have a gift for talking Mama into things, what with your schooling and Leopold's going to Oxford. She listens to you in a way she doesn't do with the rest of us."

It struck Louise that Bertie had said something similar once. Hearing the comment on Beatrice's lips made it more perplexing. Mama never indulged her, and everything she had she'd gained through fights and struggles and alliances with Mr. Disraeli and others.

Her siblings always made it sound as if she simply asked and was granted her requests. "I'll do what I can, but she isn't apt to listen to me at present. I'll broach the subject when she's in a better mood, and I'll speak with Bertie and see if he can help."

If Beatrice was this entranced by the handsome young man, it might be the undoing of all Mama's plans to make Beatrice her unmarried old-age companion. Ruining their mother's intentions, more than anything else, might convince Bertie to help her.

"Oh thank you, thank you. You don't know what this means to me." She flung her arms around Louise and squeezed her tight before skipping off down the hallway, her head clearly filled with dreams of waltzing with the Prince Imperial.

Mama railed when any of them defied her. It would be an absolute tempest if Beatrice decided to do the same by demanding a husband, and Louise hoped she was here to see the day it happened. She prayed that when the time came, Beatrice had the strength to fight for a life of her own.

H.R.H. the Princess Louise went to Sir Edgar Boehm's studio by appointment and unattended by lady or gentleman. She discussed some of the sculptor's latest work with him . . .

—EASTERN DAILY PRESS

London, May 1877

"What is this?" Louise leveled her fan at the nude statue of Skittles, Bertie's current paramour, her hands thrown back, her robe gathered around her enviable hips in the manner of the Venus de Milo. Except this statue had a face and supple arms and an eroticism the one in the Louvre could never match.

"A commission from the Prince of Wales."

"She's a stunning woman, with an enviable figure."

"Not nearly as grand as yours." Edgar slid an arm around her waist and pulled her to him, covering her lips with a kiss. He wore a steel-gray suit, the two of them ready to venture to Sir Coutts's long-awaited Grosvenor Gallery opening.

"Flattery from a man who's had his hands on the marble body of another woman."

"She means nothing to me, simply a commission for the Prince of Wales, and His Royal Highness Prince Leopold."

"Leopold?"

Edgar slid a letter off his worktable and held it up to Louise. She recognized the letterhead and Leopold's hand. "He asked me to commission a painted copy of a dimension appropriate for hanging above his bed."

Louise took the letter, her cheeks burning at so earthy a consideration being written by Leopold. But, she reminded herself, he *was* a man, with all the same desires and cravings as Bertie, no matter how much Mama tried to deny it. Half his letters to Louise from Oxford had been about pretty young women, especially Alice Liddell, the Dean of Christchurch's daughter and Lewis Carroll's inspiration for *Alice in Wonderland*. He'd kept whatever relationship they'd enjoyed a secret, even from her, but Louise had her suspicions. "Dear me, Oxford certainly broadened his horizons. Imagine what a dukedom, a living, and a house of his own might do if Mama ever grants it." Recently, Mama had made Arthur Duke of Connaught and Strathearn and given him the use of Clarence House. Leopold had been positively livid at not receiving the same consideration—a title in addition to prince, and a household of his own.

"He'll get one. He has your persistence when it comes to pressing matters with Her Majesty."

She leaned across the table and touched her lips to his, his mustache tickling her skin. "My persistence has paid off."

"Indeed it has."

Sir Coutts Lindsay, the proprietor and director of the Grosvenor Gallery, has adopted May-day as the fittest period for admitting to view his collection those who make a point of being amongst the first to "do" any new exhibition of pictures. His patrons, therefore, this year have four clear days' start of the Academy for inspecting an exhibition of art-work which is full of variety and interest, and in many respects singularly unique . . . while in the space devoted to sculpture are examples by the Princess Louise, Count Gleichen, Professor Kopft, Mr. Boehm, Professor Encke, etc.

—Week's News

THE CATHEDRAL CEILING of the Grosvenor Gallery in Bond Street brought a reverence to the inaugural exhibition, and the toast of society and the arts mingled beneath the grand skylights to view the pictures on the high walls. They moved from the West Gallery to the East Gallery, and the Sculpture Gallery at the far end, where Louise's equestrian statue *Geraint and Enid* stood on display beside Edgar's terra-cotta bust of the artist Edward Armitage.

"You've made me proud, Your Royal Highness," Mary Thornycroft congratulated Louise.

"I owe my success to you for starting me on this path."

"I couldn't allow your natural talent to go to waste." Mary smiled, little about her having changed over the last few years except the gray in her dark hair at the temples and the wrinkles at the corners of her eyes and lips. She was still the serene, proud tutor who'd escorted her into the National Art Training School. "You've accomplished far more than I'd ever dreamed for you."

Mary wrapped her in a hug, the old familiar scent of rosewater perfume enveloping Louise and taking her back to those innocent and uncertain days.

"Would Papa be proud?" Louise whispered.

"He would be."

Mary let go of her, tears glistening in her eyes as much as Louise's.

"Her Royal Highness has flourished since the day you brought her to my classroom," Edgar said. Unlike Louise, he didn't care to stand beside his piece and receive praise.

"Careful, you'll puff up my ego. In humbleness, I'll say I owe my accomplishments to the marvelous studio Mr. Godwin built me."

"Mr. Godwin is a miracle worker," Mr. Whistler announced,

his white cotton duck suit crisp and his monocle polished so it shone in the natural gallery light. "I'll need one if he's ever to finish mine. He's a genius with a revolutionary design and the Metropolitan Board of Works balks at it, thinking a white house with a green slate roof beyond the pale. I refuse to throw up another one of those foreboding Gothic gargoyles already littering Chelsea. I'm an artist, not a Brontë heroine. My new studio will be clean, simple, and free of architectural fripperies. With your endless charm you could persuade them to change their minds and approve the plans."

"They have no reason to take my advice, but Lord Lorne knows someone on the board. He might have some influence there. I'll speak with him about it when he returns from his sailing trip in the South of France."

"If you will excuse me, Your Royal Highness," Mary gently interrupted. "I wish to see Mr. Watts's portrait of Mrs. Wyndham. I've heard so much about it."

"You won't be disappointed."

With the promise they'd meet up again to chat, Mary set off through the gallery designed to resemble an opulent Grosvenor Square home rather than a stuffy and staid museum, with sofas for lounging and chatting among the works and palms in grand pots to soften the hard lines of the columns and plasterwork.

Mr. Whistler remained beside her and Edgar. "Lord Lorne is there and you are here, and never the twain shall meet."

"Some things and people are best savored at a distance," Louise replied without regret.

"Mr. Ruskin is one of them." Mr. Whistler nodded to where the art critic stood taking notes on one of the paintings. "He said I'd thrown a pot of paint in the public's face with my *Falling Rocket* because I dared ask two hundred guineas for it. It's the same price the Honorable Mr. Wyndham paid for my *Nocturne*. Quite the bargain, if you ask me, but Mr. Ruskin didn't before lobbing his debased criticism at me. I should sue him for libel, teach him and his ilk they aren't the sole arbiters of taste or opinion."

"A bad idea, Mac," Edgar warned.

"Lawsuits aren't a pleasant experience, and the scandal and newspaper reports benefit no one," Louise cautioned, having endured enough of Bertie's to know. "Forget what he said and continue doing exactly what you like, as you've always done."

"No, Mr. Ruskin needs a hard lesson." The fire in his eyes suggested he might bring a suit against Mr. Ruskin. For both their sakes, she hoped cooler heads prevailed. "If you'll excuse me, there is Millais. I wish to know how he convinced Mr. Disraeli to pose for him instead of me."

Mr. Whistler stormed off, leaving Edgar and Louise beside her work.

"He won't start a fight here, will he?" The normally spirited and languid Mr. Whistler was more agitated than she'd ever seen him.

"No, but he might get into a scrape with the first gentleman he sees on the way home."

"I worry about him."

"Write to him tomorrow, today enjoy your grand success."

"It's like nothing I've ever experienced before." She lowered her voice. "Except when I'm in your arms."

He winked at her, the subtle exchange the most they could

indulge in before more people came forward to congratulate her on her work. Among the many admirers who praised Louise was the esteemed Mr. Frederic Leighton who also showed in the exhibition. While he admired her submission, she marveled at how far she'd come. She had a home and studio of her own, proudly displaying her pieces alongside such luminaries as Mr. Millais and Mr. Edward Burne-Jones. She never could've imagined any of this during the bleak years at Windsor, when Mary's gentle friendship and tutelage had carried her through many dark and lonely days. Those times were far behind her and she'd never again be the derided Princess under Mama's thumb, hoping and pining for more and afraid she'd never achieve it.

By command of the Queen, a state ball was given yesterday week at Buckingham Palace . . . The Prince and Princess of Wales arrived at the palace from Marlborough House, attended by their suite and escorted by a detachment of the 2nd Life Guards. Princess Louise and the Marquis of Lorne . . . were present . . . Dancing commenced upon entry of the Prince and Princess of Wales with the Imperial and Royal personages into the saloon at a quarter before eleven o'clock . . . Nearly 2000 invitations were issued . . .

—*Illustrated London News*

London, July 1877

Buckingham Palace was alight for the State Ball. The attendance of the Emperor of Russia and his son and heir the

Grand Duke Alexi increased the pageantry and pomp. The bright red uniforms of the Yeomen of the Guard, usually so visible where they stood at attention along the walls, were lost in the sea of satins and silks, uniforms and medals, gold epaulets and brightly painted fans as the guests crowded in the Grand Hall and up the Grand Staircase, stopping on each step to converse, so one could hardly move in the crush.

In the ballroom, massive gaslit pendants and tall brass candelabras illuminated the room. Overhead, the high arched ceiling caught the thousands of voices and mingled them with the notes of the music. The palace glowed with fresh paint and gilding, the statues of *History* and *Fame* holding court above the Canopy of State and Mama's coronation throne. Bertie had refused to host a ball in the Tsar's honor in a neglected and dirty palace. After much wrangling and with Mr. Disraeli's assistance, he had convinced Mama to properly clean and polish the State Rooms so they shone as they had during the last State Ball—which had been held before Papa had died.

In the balcony at the back of the ballroom, in front of the large organ whose pipes glinted with a fresh polish, the Coote and Tinney's Band played quadrilles and waltzes. Mr. Coots waved his baton to instruct the musicians, and couples whirled about the center of the room, the watching guests crowding to the sides or forced into the adjoining galleries and supper rooms. Those not dancing rested on the crimson velvet benches below Papa's beloved Raphael-inspired paintings.

Louise and Lorne moved through the crowd, accepting every welcome extended to them. More than one person complimented her on the success of her Grosvenor Gallery showing, making her glow more than the lights reflecting in her diamonds. Louise wore a cream silk moiré dress with the fitted bodice embroidered with crystals and pearls and a full bustled skirt that whispered when she walked. Lorne had chosen his Prince Charlie kilt with the fitted jacket over the Argyll family tartan. It was the first time they'd been together in weeks, Mama's insistence he be here his only reason for attending.

"I look like a Highland peasant compared to the Russians," Lorne muttered from beside her, having perfected the smile and wave required of him but stiff about the shoulders. He wore the few honors Mama had bestowed on him but they were sorely lacking compared to the Russians, who nearly tipped over from the weight of the medals on their jackets. "If I'd been appointed Viceroy of Ireland, I could hold my head up higher. My chest would certainly be more decorated and I wouldn't appear second-rate."

"I did all I could to progress your cause, but it wasn't up to me, and my influence only extends so far."

"It extends far enough when you're assisting yourself or your artist friends."

She ignored this last dig, deciding this wasn't the time to suggest he assist Mr. Whistler with the Board of Works. Lorne was in a terrible mood and if she hoped to get through this evening without a row, the less said between them the better.

Smack walked behind her and beside Major de Winton, who also attended in Highland dress. Louise and Smack both wore sashes of the Argyll tartan, a complement to their male escorts, Louise's sash attached with a gold-and-diamond

Scottish thistle pin. None of her siblings had worn kilts in the Balmoral tartan, despite Mama's request to do so. They were dressed in the military uniforms of their various volunteer or auxiliary regiments.

Alfred, the wide chest of his Royal Navy uniform covered in ribbons and medals, was present on one of his rare appearances in England. He stood with his new wife, the Grand Duchess Marie Alexandrova. Her chin was raised in haughty disdain, and she looked down on the gathered crowd as if they were part of a country dance and not the highest and most important people on the world's stage gracing the premier palace of Britain. A parure of massive diamonds and rubies hung heavily about her wrists, throat, and ears, the jewels as overdone as her attitude. One would think, from her jewels and stance, she was the Queen of England and not the Tsar's daughter married to the Queen's second son.

"Your Royal Highness, thank you ever so much for the charming bust of Alfred you gave us for the wedding. I have it to look at when he's off with the Royal Navy." The Grand Duchess entwined her arm in Alfred's and looked up at him with a stomach-churning adoration he returned. Louise wasn't surprised, given how hard the two of them had fought against numerous objections on both sides to achieve this marriage. She only hoped the passion didn't burn itself out too soon and that it was far more genuine than anything Louise and Lorne had ever shared. "Such a unique skill for a Royal Princess. Your enjoyment of such *common* pleasures is very interesting. As is Lord Lorne's talent at writing. I don't think I've ever read anything quite so interesting as his book of poems."

Louise gripped her fan tight to keep from rapping the insolent chit on the forehead. Beside her, Lorne radiated with anger hidden by a practiced smile, one she'd come to simultaneously appreciate and loathe at every public event they attended when he was forced, as he was tonight, to walk behind her in deference to her rank and endure similar cutting slights.

"We are helping Britain lead the world in art and literature, while Russia leads the world in arrogance and famine," Louise said with a cutting smile.

The Grand Duchess's jaw dropped open and Alfred went red about the temples. "Come, my dear, there are Prince and Princess Christian."

He escorted his indignant and suddenly speechless wife away, the Grand Duchess's sneering look falling on many people who turned up their noses at her haughty air.

"Society and England are going to be a difficult place for her if she continues sneering at everyone, but that's for her to discover." Louise wasn't about to assist her with friendly advice. She didn't deserve it. What she deserved was a good dressing-down by a very hostile society.

"It doesn't mean what she said isn't true. Your interest in sculpture is unseemly for a wife," Lorne said.

"And you are actually a commoner." Louise narrowed her eyes at Lorne for disparaging her art. It was the one thing she thought he understood about her.

"If I'm not too common to mingle with the guests, might I ask your leave to seek out some refreshments?"

"You needn't ask me as if I were the Queen. I've never lorded my position over you."

"You might as well, everyone else does." He stalked off, leaving her alone in the crowd.

"The Grand Duchess thinks too much of herself, all the Romanovs do, and I can't imagine why," came a woman's voice from beside her, the English softened by an elegant French accent.

Louise bowed to Empress Eugénie. "I'm delighted to see you here, Your Imperial Majesty."

It'd been four years since her husband's death, and Eugénie had adopted half mourning. Her dress, and even her presence, was sure to scandalize Mama, especially when the newspapers reported on it in the morning. She wore a stunning gown of black silk with bright violet silk stripes. It was tasteful to her position but fashionable, emphasizing her still-slender waist. She was square-faced, the tall peaks of her diamond tiara giving it more length and adding to the luster of her still-dark hair peppered with gray. She was an empress, a mother, and a widow but unlike Mama, there was nothing matronly about her.

"My husband is gone, *mon petite cher*, but I am alive and must live. Where is Her Majesty?"

"Mama never attends balls. If she could decree it, no widow ever would."

"This is where my grand friend and I differ. I miss France and my old life, but I am not dead, and do not look forward to death. I have the generosity of my friends who support me so I may live safely in England, and I have my dear Louis-Napoléon. His bright future helps me savor the delights of the present." She leveled her impressive fan at her handsome son, the twenty-one-year-old Prince Imperial, who danced with Beatrice. He was tall, thin, and distinguished with dark hair parted and smoothed in the middle and a full chevron mustache, well maintained with crisp edges. Beatrice, her head and eyes usually cast down in shyness, stared radiantly up at the handsome and lithe young man. There was no mistaking their mutual interest.

"Perhaps they'll make a grand love match, as you have done," Empress Eugénie suggested.

"I hope not." Across the room, Lorne chatted with Lord Gower with more animation and exuberance than he'd ever shown her. "I'd never wish such *happiness* on anyone. I'm sorry, I shouldn't have been so indiscreet."

Eugénie laughed lightly. "Do not despair, I am a woman of the world who understands these things. If it weren't for the birth of Louis-Napoléon, I would have been forced to endure more of my husband's, shall we say, less-than-flattering charms. I was grateful there were others to amuse him. He was a good man who made me an empress, and I am forever grateful but not arrogant about my situation. I can't be. I have learned from the loss of my throne, country, husband, and fortune how humbling life can be, even for the high-and-mighty. The Grand Duchess will discover it too, or perhaps she already knows and that is why she is so terrible." The arch of one eyebrow hinted at a salacious story.

"Do tell."

"I heard the Grand Duchess once indulged a preference for His Imperial Majesty's aide-de-camp, and that is why the Tsar eventually relented and allowed her to marry Prince Alfred. Of course, it is only a rumor, but one never knows with these sorts of stories." Her smile told Louise she believed this one.

Louise, given her own indiscretions, could hardly fault the

young woman. Louise was many things, but she wasn't a hypocrite. "I see she appreciates the common gentlemen too."

"We do what we must to live and claim happiness. Do it with a smile and delight, Your Royal Highness, and never regret it. The memories will carry you through the most difficult times and give you hope for better days." She unfolded the wide fan painted by Mr. Winterhalter with cameos of her and the late Napoleon III, a memorial of their time in England when the Emperor and Empress had captured the nation's interest with their elegance and grace. Louise had only been seven during their visit and unable to join in the festivities, but Papa had written to her about Eugénie's clothes and activities. She was a glittering, elegant woman. Age had made her more distinguished and dimmed some of her radiance, but not even the loss of her throne, country, and husband had snuffed out her joie de vivre. Death and loss were woven into her life like the mother-of-pearl sticks that were stitched into her fan. It wasn't her entire reason for existing. Louise prayed she could face life's disappointments with the same high spirits.

Chapter Twenty-One

In the first place you *both* know well that I have always only wished you to do what was for your good *physically* and *morally*. But I *certainly* expect that *confidence* and *consideration* which are due to me both as a mother and a Sovereign. You should have told Lorne that *none* of the Royal Family *can* go abroad without the Sovereign's leave and I have even as a *Mother* a *right* to be consulted as to what you think of doing . . . All these observations would have been avoided if you had openly consulted me and it is indeed most painful for me to have been treated with so little confidence. *How you* blamed Lenchen for want of the same, and yet she and Christian would never have dreamt of going abroad without asking my opinion and consent.

—QUEEN VICTORIA TO PRINCESS LOUISE

Balmoral Castle, Scotland, November 1877

It is a fine thing for a budding poet to be the honored consort of a popular princess. His position makes his books sell. Had, for instance, any other man but the Marquis of Lorne written *Guido and Lita*, the Press would've given it tardy and short notices, many of them satirical, and the public would've left a great part of the issue for the trunkmakers. But being the husband of the daughter of the Queen he is at once made famous," Lenchen read aloud from the newspaper with barely hidden glee.

"That's enough, Lenchen, and quite unnecessary." Louise snatched the *Leicester Daily Post* out of Lenchen's chubby fingers, crumpled it between her palms, and threw it in the fire. The flames rose up, giving off a rare heat as they consumed the nasty words before dying down.

"I didn't write it," Lenchen sniffed, rubbing the ink from her fingertips.

"You didn't need to read it either."

"Especially since it isn't true." Lorne stood, yanking straight his stained waistcoat, his fair skin blotchy with anger. Neither Prince Christian nor Bertie rose. Lorne wasn't royal and not owed such respect. "My poems are excellent but the critics begrudge success to anyone who hasn't rotted away from consumption in a garret. When I release my *Book of Psalms*, I'll make them eat their nasty words." He stormed from the room.

Louise and Bertie exchanged weary looks. Neither this book nor Lorne's last had brought him the success he craved. It didn't mean Lenchen needed to rub it in his face.

"Are you proud of yourself, Lenchen?"

"I am." Lenchen rose, staring down her nose at Louise before she left.

"I never thought she'd be more difficult than Beatrice."

"Give it time. Beatrice may yet outdo her." Bertie perched

his feet on the stool in front of his chair. "As for Lorne, perhaps he should write about Scotland, or a biography of Mama or Papa, something the people will eat up."

"I'll be sure to suggest it." It'd be taken about as well as Mama's command that she and Lorne join her at Balmoral. They'd avoided the yearly progress from Windsor to Osborne to Balmoral and back to Windsor by visiting Baden and other spa towns in search of a cure for her barrenness. While Lorne was off amusing himself, Louise, when she wasn't taking the waters, toured the museums and galleries, visited artists, and studied old masters. The wanderlust had grown while her belly remained flat, unquenched. Only art and Edgar ever filled the emptiness, the hours of creativity alone or with him shielding her from the pain.

"Aye, there, what are ye doin' laying about when Her Majesty told ye to dress to join her for a walk on the moors?" Mr. Brown hollered from the doorway.

"Do not dare to speak to us in so curt a manner," Bertie hollered, but Mr. Brown didn't back down. He drew himself up to his full height, storming up to Bertie, who held his ground.

"I'm here on the Queen's orders, by her right I'll be talkin' to ye as I do."

Louise grasped Bertie's fist to keep him from swinging it at Mr. Brown, sure the Highlander would strike back and do more damage to Bertie than he might do to the drunkard.

"She wants to see ye too, missy," Mr. Brown spat at Louise, and Bertie twisted his hand to catch hers and keep it from flying at Mr. Brown's cheek.

"Bastard," Bertie growled once Mr. Brown was gone. "If he lives long enough to see me crowned, I'll destroy him and every likeness of him Mama ever commissioned and banish him."

"Even Edgar's fine statue?" Louise mimicked Mama's opinion of the piece enjoying pride of place in the garden. Bertie sneered every time he passed it.

"Even his." Bertie stalked off to his room and Louise made for Mama's, eager to be finished with whatever unpleasantness she was about to face before returning to her rooms to change and face Lorne. The misery of Balmoral was stretching out to encompass everyone today.

Louise raised her hand to knock on the barely open door to Mama's study but stopped. Mr. Brown and Mama talked softly inside, Mama laughing with girlish delight. Louise peeked around the corner to see Mama sitting near the unlit fire, Mr. Brown beside her.

"Was it here?" Mama asked, pointing to his thigh just above his knee.

"No, ma'am, it was farther up."

"You mean here?" Mama slid her hand up under Mr. Brown's kilt as if caressing his behind. He didn't push her hand away and she didn't blush, staring at him as if she had every right to touch him. Louise choked in surprise, and Mama withdrew her hand, her smile dropping.

"Who is sneaking about?" Mama demanded, her voice tight with embarrassment.

"You summoned me?" Louise entered, staring at Mr. Brown to make clear he knew she'd seen whatever they'd been doing before she'd inadvertently revealed herself.

"I have decided you will not take the waters at Aix-le-Bains this winter but join the family at Osborne." Mama waved a hand of dismissal at Mr. Brown, who left with his usual heavy steps, careful to throw Louise one last cowing look, but she didn't shrink under it. The jumped-up peasant could bully others, but not her.

"The arrangements have already been made." Louise stood before Mama's desk, irked at the looming presence of Mr. Brown's bust sitting on the corner of it. If Edgar hadn't sculpted it, she would positively despise it.

"Then undo them."

"I'm hoping the waters will help me have a child."

"Time with Lord Lorne would do you more good. He will accompany you. Who knows what might come of it?"

"Nothing will come of it. I appreciate your concern, but the situation is beyond hopeless, and we're happy as we are now and you must accept it."

"I must do no such thing, nor will I have my advice and instructions continually ignored. You are a Princess of the Royal Blood, the daughter of the Queen. Everything you do reflects on me and the throne." Mother rose to her feet, dislodging Sharp, who growled at being disturbed. "See to your marriage or I promise you there will be great consequences."

She wrapped her knuckles against the desk, then turned and left, Sharp trotting behind her.

Louise grasped the socle supporting Mr. Brown's bust, ready to slam the terra-cotta to the floor. Mama's inability to see what was plainly in front of her, ignoring the unpleasant and thinking the solution as simple as decreeing a thing must be done, irritated her beyond measure. No amount of royal dictates could make Louise's marriage a happy one.

Louise released her tight grip on the bust, righting it when it wobbled, before she noticed three thin letters tied with a red ribbon hidden beneath the socle. Mama usually bound her correspondence with black ribbon. Louise turned the pack over, wondering what about these had merited such flash, only to see *Mrs. Brown* written on the front envelope in Mr. Brown's twisted handwriting. She slid the top one out from under the ribbon and opened it, immediately regretting her curiosity.

All the rumors ever whispered about Mama by the Balmoral servants, the Osborne grooms, and the foreign press were confirmed by Mr. Brown's badly written verses of adoration and intimacy. His words made Louise retch and blush all at once and she snapped the letter closed, ready to condemn it to the fire, if one had been burning. If she took them to her room and burned them, Mama would notice they were missing, and possibly suspect her, but she wouldn't turn out the castle or Louise's room in search of them. She should set them back where she'd found them, but she couldn't risk someone else finding them either.

Louise tucked the letters in her bodice. She might decry Mama's control, but she wouldn't see Mama, the throne, and the family debased by her conduct. It was one thing for Louise and her siblings to make mistakes, but for Mama to fall from grace, especially in so sordid a manner, would hand the still-grumbling republicans the power and encouragement to rip her from the throne. Louise and her siblings would be cast onto the mercy of generous friends or Alice or Vicky's begrudging families, forced to live on handouts or, worse, executed by revolutionaries as Emperor Maximilian of Mexico had been. She'd seen the devastation wrought on Empress Eugénie and her country and family after the fall of France. She couldn't risk visiting the same destruction on England and her family by allowing Mama's misstep to come to light.

LORNE DIDN'T TURN when Louise entered their shared sitting room, too busy scribbling in his journal at his writing desk. The letters sat hard against Louise's chest as she racked her mind for some place to hide them. She was about to retire to her room when Lorne banged off the excess ink from his pen so hard she thought he might chip the crystal inkwell. "Your family does all they can to belittle me because I'm not royal. I don't need the press doing it too."

"When you publish your work for the world to see, you find everyone has opinions about it, not all of them favorable. Mr. Rossetti once called me an amateur, and Mr. James doesn't shy from criticizing my work for the American press. You'll eventually get used to it and grow a thick skin. You must, or you'll never survive your grand plans for glory."

He tapped his pen against the paper, mulling over what she'd said. "You're right, I need to let barbs bounce off me instead of taking them to heart or I won't succeed. I know I can write. My travel books were well received."

"Bertie suggested you try biographies of Her Majesty or dear Papa. Those would sell like mad and you'd have the advantage I've always enjoyed when I sculpt Mama, ready access to the subject."

"Yes, I would." He touched the tip of the pen to his lips, intrigued by the idea. "Do you think it could be done?"

"I don't see why not, and a biography of Papa would win you nothing but Mama's gratitude and praise. It'd go a long way to helping you achieve your political aims."

"It would." He smiled at her in a rare moment of camaraderie. She didn't hate him. Time had just shown they had so little in common—except ambition. Perhaps Mama was right and if they spent more time together they could develop a friendship to help them navigate the turbulent waters of their marriage, and his position and hers.

"Did you speak with the Board of Works about Mr. Whistler's studio?" Louise asked, hoping to bolster their moment of peace by turning to his expertise. The plans for Mr. Whistler's White House studio had dragged on for over a year, and now with Mr. Whistler embroiled in a nasty and expensive slander case against Mr. Ruskin, if it wasn't approved soon he wouldn't have the money to see it through.

Lorne's face twisted in disgust, the petulant husband she'd walked in on returning. "Even when we're companionable, all you can think about is your artist friends, especially that awful hack Mr. Whistler. He doesn't even have the decency to be discreet, fawning over you in public. It's embarrassing and revolting. I can only imagine the *favors* you've granted him to encourage such devotion. It's more than you've ever done for me."

"I don't care for your insinuation," she snapped, ashamed to think she was grateful he suspected Mr. Whistler as her lover instead of Edgar. "I don't ask you about your acquaintances, don't trouble with mine or complain about your lot. You have more responsibilities than Prince Christian has ever enjoyed."

"Prince Christian has children to attend to. I don't even have that."

"I'm doing all I can to give you one. I want, pray, and beg for it, but I have no more control over that than I have over what the newspapermen print about us or what Mama does."

"So you say, but you'll do anything for your brothers and your artist *friends*. You practically work miracles for them, while I get nothing." He stormed to the closet, pulled the creased leather valise off the shelf, and began shoving shirts, pants, and coats inside.

"What are you doing?"

"I'm going to Inveraray to visit my parents. There's no reason for me to stay here and suffer; after all, I'm not royal."

"Mama hasn't given you permission to leave." As she'd be sure to sternly remind Louise once he left.

"That's never stopped you from doing what you like. Make whatever excuses you wish. I won't return." He snapped the bag closed, gripped the handles, and stormed out of the room, leaving Louise in the chill by herself.

She wandered to her bedroom and sank onto the bed. She'd never married Lorne expecting to be happy, but she hadn't expected the marriage to add to her misery or his. She did everything she could for him and herself, asking Mama and Mr. Disraeli for positions, begging Mama to ease her grip on them and her siblings, and still it was never enough. She did all she could to bring about a child too, but every month her courses still came.

She touched her chest, the warm metal outline of Edgar's medal pressing against the soft skin of her breasts. She wished he were here so she could lay her head on his shoulder and tell him her frustrations. Instead, they remained inside her, unable to even be committed to paper. She couldn't risk Mama or Mr. Brown finding the letters and exposing everything.

Every day she struggled to hold on to what she'd gained, and every day something or someone tried to tear it away from her like the tides of the Thames pulling at an old dock day after day, until bit by bit it gave way. She didn't know how long it would be until something large was ripped from her for good. Who knows what it would be or when?

Chapter Twenty-Two

Dear Lady Ely having been here and acting the part of chaperone to Louise, besides being a dear friend of ours, has been informed of today's *Event* in strict confidence. She can bring any message from you which might under present circumstances be difficult for you to convey to me personally.

—Queen Victoria to Lord Lorne

London, June 1878

Pounding on Edgar's studio door ripped Louise and Edgar from their languid rest in each other's arms.

"What the devil?" Edgar untangled himself from Louise's embrace and tugged on his shirt. "Who's there?"

"Mr. Gilbert," Edgar's assistant whispered through the door. "Her Majesty has arrived to view the Carlyle statue."

"What's she doing here?" Louise jumped from the couch and pulled on her chemise. "She rarely deigns to visit London or an artist's studio. She summons them to her."

"Well, she's here." Edgar grabbed his trousers from where he'd tossed them on the floor. He tugged them on as he crossed the room and cracked open the door. "Where is Her Majesty?"

"Downstairs. Shall I show her up?"

"After you escort Lady Macnamara from the sitting room to the back entrance, show Her Majesty up the stairs as slowly as possible. Take her to the sitting room through the hall entrance and offer her refreshments. Tell her I'm composing myself and will be with her shortly."

"Yes, sir."

Edgar closed the door as Mr. Gilbert hurried to delay Mama's arrival as much as he could. Thankfully, Louise's driver always waited in her plain black carriage a few streets away. She never dared to have him park in front of The Avenue and draw attention to her comings and goings.

Louise helped Edgar with his suit, straightening his cravat and shirt and coat. There was no time for her to dress.

"Remain behind the screen. It's dark in this corner, and if you don't move, she shouldn't notice you're there. I'll do what I can to keep her from lingering." He raked his fingers through his hair to straighten the curls as Louise slipped with her clothes behind the screen, the floor cold against her bare feet.

From her hiding place, she heard Edgar stroll leisurely to the sitting room door, take a deep breath, and pull it open. "Your Majesty, you honor me with your visit."

"Princess Christian told me of the marvelous statue you executed of Mr. Carlyle, did you not, my dear?" Mama's voice carried in through the open door. Louise barely dared to breathe for fear of being discovered.

"I did. It's all anyone can speak of," Lenchen agreed, and

Louise wondered who she considered everyone. If it wasn't Mama's correspondence or a laudanum bottle, Lenchen rarely noticed it.

Cold fear slid through Louise. Had Lenchen discovered something about her and Edgar and deliberately led Mama here? It didn't seem possible, yet here she stood, almost naked behind a screen in her lover's studio, with Mama and Lenchen on the other side.

"I have been informed you have a copy of it here. I should like to see it and judge the quality for myself."

"Of course, Your Majesty. If you'll follow me into the next room, I'd be happy to show it to you."

He led them into the holy of holies and the time dragged on as Mama praised the excellent expression on Mr. Carlyle's face, marveled at how lifelike and real he appeared, and complimented Edgar on perfectly capturing the eminent historian more accurately than Mr. Whistler's dreadful portrait, which had made him appear more like a rumpled pile of clothes than a much-admired luminary.

Louise held her breath from behind the screen, half-dressed in her chemise, clutching her corset and frock to her chest. Her hands, arms, and legs ached from keeping still. She was too afraid to shift a muscle and have Mama or Lenchen notice the sound of fabric rustling and seek out the source. She couldn't dress without Smack or Edgar's assistance, and if Mama or Lenchen discovered her, hell would reign down on her.

Finally, when Louise thought she might cry out in agony with her stiff muscles, they returned from the holy of holies.

"Thank you, Mr. Boehm, you have been most gracious in humoring me without prior announcement. We will go now and leave you to your work."

After an agonizing exchange of pleasantries and good-byes, the door at last clicked closed.

Louise didn't dare step out from behind the screen, afraid Mama or Lenchen might return on some trumped-up pretext. It wasn't until Edgar's voice from the other side of the screen whispered to her that she eased her grip on her clothes.

"They're gone."

She stepped out into the room, shivering as much from nerves as the chill.

"Let's get you dressed."

With hands far steadier than hers, he helped her into her clothes, tying laces and fastening hooks with practiced fingers until she finally appeared as she'd entered two hours before. In the large looking glass over the mantel, she fixed her hair, pinning it back into the simple style she favored, thankful for her more bohemian tastes. Anything more elaborate, and she'd appear as bedraggled as Sharp after a bath. She straightened the front of her jacket, noticing at once something wasn't right. "My butterfly pin is missing."

"You're certain you were wearing it?"

"I am. It must've fallen off." They searched the studio, peering under chairs and tables, but there was no sign of it.

"I'll search for it and instruct Mr. Gilbert and the char-woman to do the same."

A soft knock at the sitting room door made them both freeze. "Louise, it's Smack."

She cautiously opened the door, peering around it to ensure she hadn't walked in on anything indecent before hurrying forward. "If Her Majesty came here, who knows where she might go next? You should return to Kensington Palace at once."

"I agree." With one last longing look at Edgar, neither of them needing to say anything to punctuate the gravity of what'd happened, she and Smack left.

"COME INTO THE sitting room, Louise," Mama commanded from inside the green-trimmed sitting room with the red walls of Louise's Kensington Palace apartments.

Louise exchanged a worried look with Smack as she handed her reticule and hat to the footman. Taking a deep breath to compose herself, she strode in to greet Mama, Smack following behind.

"You are dismissed, Lady Macnamara," Mama ordered.

"Yes, Your Majesty." Smack dipped a very low curtsey and backed out of the room.

"Mama, what a pleasant surprise. I didn't expect to see you in London." She must have ordered the carriage into the mews, for it hadn't been in the drive, giving Louise no warning of this ambush.

"No, I do not suppose you did." She sat on the gilded sofa in the center of the room, out of place beneath walls barely adorned with portraits and landscapes and tables not crowded with knickknacks or clutches of silver-framed photographs. The simplicity of the room's decor was quite a contrast to Mama's love of clutter.

Lenchen stood behind Mama, glaring at Louise as one might a naughty child who'd broken a vase.

"I would've been home sooner to greet you, but I was visiting Miss Montalba's studio." Louise had commanded her carriage driver to take her through Rotten Row numerous times to settle herself and provide some plausible excuse for why she hadn't been here to greet them.

"We know exactly where you were and who you were with." Lenchen laid the butterfly pin on the low table in front of Mama, then stepped back in triumph.

Louise wasn't about to allow her to win or ruin any chance she might ever have of being with Edgar again. She'd been the consummate actress with Lorne during the first year of her marriage. She'd make Covent Garden proud with this next performance. "Wherever did you find that? I lost it some time ago and thought it gone for good, but here it is. Tell me you didn't come all the way to London to give it to me."

"We found it in Mr. Boehm's studio."

"I can't imagine how it got there, as I haven't been to see Mr. Boehm in ages. Mr. Whistler must have given it to him to return to me, he's in Paris at the moment, but I and a few friends visited his studio before he left. It was afterward I noticed the pin was missing. I must have lost it there."

"Do you really expect us to believe this?" Lenchen hissed, not about to be thwarted in her crusade to ruin Louise. "Mrs. Wyndham meets her lover at Mr. Watts's studio. Who were you meeting at Mr. Boehm's?"

"I wasn't at his studio when you were there, was I? No, because I was with Miss Montalba, who will tell you so. Then I drove through Rotten Row. All London can attest to seeing me there. How dare you accuse me of anything else, or turn something as innocent as a lost pin into a slur on my reputation?"

Doubt flickered across Mama's face and Louise prayed her habit of ignoring the unpleasant would win out again. Mama stared at the butterfly pin, her face unreadable, before she looked up at Louise as she used to eye Mr. Gladstone when he disagreed with her. "Leave us, Lenchen."

Lenchen stalked out of the room, closing the door hard behind her, but neither Mama nor Louise winced. They stared at one another, a match of wills as strong as the Rock of Gibraltar. Everything depended on Louise convincing Mama she was innocent.

"Despite whatever Lenchen told you, I've committed no sin beyond patronizing talented artists, with Lady Macnamara always accompanying me, just as you advised."

"Yes, you have been very clever in that regard. I am not certain who the liar is in the situation, but where there is smoke there must be flames. You have been up to no good, and while I am not sure with whom, I assume it is that dreadful Mr. Whistler. Lord Lorne told me you appealed to him to intercede on his behalf for a studio, and he complains bitterly about the attention Mr. Whistler affords you in public. Mr. Whistler's lack of manners, his overt familiarity, and his inability to acknowledge his place and rank make me believe he is scoundrel enough to compromise a married woman and a princess who does not have the wherewithal to think of herself and her position."

"He's an honorable man."

"Your defending him makes me believe I am right, as does

his involvement in that awful slander case against dear Mr. Ruskin, who did so much for Leopold at Oxford."

She wasn't correct, but nothing Louise might say would raise Mr. Whistler's esteem in Mama's eyes, and she couldn't endanger Edgar's livelihood or her freedom by admitting the truth. Mr. Whistler sought no royal favor and, with Mama's opinion of his work, wasn't likely to receive it. To her shame, Louise allowed her to believe Mr. Whistler was her lover. "Mama, be reasonable. Lenchen has always been jealous of me and is trying to poison you against me."

"You think I do not know how you carried on with Walter Stirling?"

She could've knocked Louise over with a feather. Louise had always suspected Mama knew, but she never expected her to announce it so bluntly. "I don't know what you mean."

"You know exactly what I mean, and if Leopold had not been so young and sick, I would have told him the truth about why I dismissed Mr. Stirling, but I did not. I thought you had gotten such childish and foolish notions out of your mind, but I see that is not the case. One can overlook the follies of a stupid young girl, but not a mature woman."

"You aren't being fair."

"I have been more than fair and indulgent with you than anyone else, but no more." Mama rose and walked to the window to view the garden and the roof of the studio visible through the trees. "There is a matter I have been considering for some time, one brought to me by Mr. Disraeli and supported by the Privy Council and a number of ministers. I believed it a bad idea at first, but I have since come to realize it is for the best."

Louise worried the soft gold of the butterfly's body between her thumb and forefinger. Mama couldn't publicly punish her and risk a scandal, but she was more than a mother, she was a queen and empress and even her smallest requests were treated by everyone as commands. Louise might not always obey her, but others did. There was no telling what she'd demand of those around her to punish Louise.

"Lord Lorne has asked for a place in my government, a position of esteem to confer on him the respect and position owed a princess's husband. He wishes to assert his place as the head of your household and no longer be looked upon as little more than your train bearer."

"He knew what he was getting into when he married me, as Papa did when he wed you."

She whirled to face Louise. "Do not bring Papa into this conversation. He would be horrified by your behavior and it would mortally sicken him, as Bertie's indiscretion did. You must be taught a lesson in obedience to the Crown, your position, and your husband. Therefore, after great consideration of the needs of my realm and my family, I have decided to appoint Lord Lorne to the position of Governor General of Canada."

"Canada?" Fear made her fingertips go cold.

"As my direct representative in Canada, Lord Lorne will be treated with the same respect accorded to me and you will stand behind him as a subject and a wife should. It will be announced in this evening's session of Parliament, made public for all to hear, and once it is official, nothing you can do or say will change it. You are a stubborn, insolent woman, but you are not cruel or stupid. You will not do anything to publicly damage the family, and my place, and Bertie's future one on the throne."

The glare she pinned on Louise made her take a step back. *She knows I have Mr. Brown's love letters to her.* And she was right, Louise wouldn't use them against Mama and risk harming Bertie or the monarchy. She would have to find another way out of this predicament. "I won't go. I refuse to be banished to a wilderness thousands of miles away from everything and everyone I care about."

"You will, and you will be in public everything expected of a queen's daughter and the wife of my representative. Your popularity among the people will endear you to them, which will help Lord Lorne in his new position, and you will do everything you can to support him. If you do not, if you think to defy me, I will see Lord Lorne's term extended from five years to ten or have him posted somewhere even further away until you are brought to heel. I have indulged your whims, tolerated your flagrant disregard for respect and convention for too long. You will learn your place as a wife and a daughter and you will accept it or you will never return to England."

Mama swept past her in a rustle of silk taffeta and clinking jet beads, swung open the door, collected Lenchen, and left.

Louise stood in the center of the room, the weight on her chest as heavy as if the entire palace had fallen down on her.

"Louise?" Smack slowly entered the room.

"You heard what she said?"

"I did. The walls between this room and the next aren't very thick."

Louise dropped on the sofa. "She's taking everything from

me. Everything I've wanted and strived and fought for, everything I've achieved, and banishing me to the ends of the earth."

"No, she hasn't taken your spirit." Smack sat down beside her and clasped Louise's trembling hands in hers. "For years I lived in exile with my husband. He did everything he could to break my spirit, but I wouldn't let him. I won't let Her Majesty do the same to you. Go with Lord Lorne and do in Canada what you've done here. Create a life in spite of her. If anyone can do it, it's you."

"And Edgar?"

"You'll find a way there too."

Louise jumped to her feet to pace the room. "How can I, when there'll be an ocean between us? Love can survive death, but not this much distance and time. Five years is an eternity."

"Trust him, Louise. He's stayed with you for this long, understood your position like no other. If he truly loves you, he will again."

"I can't ask this of him, not when I've taken so much of him already."

"You have no choice."

She closed her hand over the butterfly pin, careful not to crush it. "I never do."

Dearest Louise . . . I have heard that Lorne is appointed Governor General of Canada. I hear from Arthur that you are in low spirits about it which you naturally would be having to leave behind your dear country and all your friends and relations. But no doubt when you are more settled down there, you will like it very much as it must be a beautiful country and the people there are very nice.

—*Princess Louise Margaret, Prince Arthur's fiancé, to Princess Louise*

"CANADA?" EDGAR SET down his chisel and hammer. Nothing of what she'd told him about the confrontation with Mama had fallen on him as hard as this last part. The weight of it made his fine, straight back curve in a defeat she felt in her bones. "For five years."

"Longer if I don't play the part of the obedient Governor General's wife and princess."

Edgar rubbed his forehead with his dust-covered fingers, streaking the line of sweat beading at his temple and sliding down his tight jaw. "Does Her Majesty know about us?"

"She thinks I've been carrying on with Mr. Whistler, and I allowed her to believe it. Even if she suspects you, she'll treat you as she does all her servants and ignore the unpleasant. She did the same with Walter, fired him but found him another position and continued to pay him."

"To keep him from talking?"

"Well, he never did talk . . . but she adores your statues and busts of Mr. Brown. Your reputation will be safe, and so will your livelihood. Though I should apologize to Mr. Whistler for making him our scapegoat."

"It'll probably amuse him, and he'll enjoy counting the

Queen among his quickly growing list of enemies," he offered with a listless laugh.

"I wish we had his disdain for decorum."

"We do, we simply aren't as obvious with it. That's why we're in this situation." Edgar dropped down on a stool, more defeated than she'd ever seen him. She picked at the flecks of marble on his worktable, waiting for him to offer his usual sensible advice, but he sat still and stared at his feet.

"I don't want to leave you and everything I've built for who knows how long. I won't even be here for Arthur and Princess Louise Margaret's wedding. There must be some way for me not to go. I simply have to find it."

"There isn't a way. You said it yourself, there's no escaping a queen, an empress."

"You showed me I was wrong."

"Don't, Louise."

"Don't keep fighting at being brave the way you taught me? Don't keep striving and wanting to control my own life instead of always being at the mercy of Mama and my position?"

"Don't torture yourself with what can't be."

She stared into his tired eyes, the disappointment of their coming separation as hard in them as it was in her heart. The honesty of truth filled them too, the reality of her position and his that they'd fought against for so long, tried to pretend didn't exist, resisted and avoided, finally crashing down on them. "I'll go to Canada, and you'll remain here."

She stroked the top of a bronze statuette of a rearing stallion fighting against the blacksmith clutching his lead and trying to bring him under control. The animal's struggle for freedom echoed in the bronze ripple of his muscle, his raised front hooves ready to strike out at his restraints, but he wasn't free, he never would be. The blacksmith gripped the lead tight and the stallion would soon drop back onto all fours, subdued, the fight in him fading.

"You're frowning and ruining the line of your face." Edgar's low, gentle voice broke the quiet as he approached her, cautiously, as if she might bolt like the horse.

"I'm thinking of you."

He settled his dark fingers against her cheek, the skin warm against hers. "I'm honored to inspire such a beautiful woman."

She covered her hand with his, nestling into his palm. "How will we bear it?"

"As we always have, with bravery and acceptance. I'll be here when you return, and with you when you're there, as I always am when we're apart."

Chapter Twenty-Three

The Viceregal party reached Ottawa, their final destination, on the afternoon of the 2nd of December . . . when the special train, with its garland-decked engines, steamed into the depot, the Mayor and other officials were waiting upon the platform, surrounded by a guard of troops, and by crowds of citizens under dripping umbrellas. The Mayor after presenting the Princess Louise with a bouquet, read the address of welcome, to which His Excellency replied, and then the band struck up "The Campbells are Coming," and the Marquis and Marchioness, with their suite, were conducted to . . . Rideau Hall, where they were found refuge for the night. The next day the Marquis went to the Senate Chamber in the Parliament Buildings, and there received a number of deputations from city officials, and societies . . . The streets of the city were profusely decorated, there being many handsome triumphal arches, and much display of bunting; and in the evening there was a grand illumination of the public buildings, to witness which the Princess

and the Marquis rode out in a carriage, escorted by a
torchlight procession . . .

—THE GRAPHIC

Rideau Hall, Ottawa, Canada, December 1878

Cannons boomed through Ottawa, and the assembled dignitaries in the large Tent Room rose to their feet as Judge
Ritchie finished swearing in Lorne. Lorne climbed the dais
to take the throne as Her Majesty's representative, and Louise followed, standing slightly behind him on his left, a place
she'd occupied many times before with Mama during Drawing Rooms and other official events. She never thought she'd
hold it with Lorne.

He sat stoically on the red velvet as a parade of ministers and dignitaries including Lieutenant General Sir Selby
Smyth, Sir Richard Cartwright, and General MacDougall
came forward to kneel before him and pledge their fealty to
the Crown. Even the Honorable Sir Archibald Macdonald,
Lieutenant Governor and acting Viceregal until today, sober
for once since their arrival, succeeded in kneeling.

Lorne looked the part of royalty, his Windsor uniform with
the gold-oak-leaf-embroidered cuffs and collar crisp and
clean. The Order of the Garter and the Order of St. Michael
and St. George glistened on his chest, further signifying his
prominent position as Her Majesty's representative in Canada. Across his chest he'd draped the green riband of the Order of the Thistle, much to the approval of the many Scotsmen
in attendance and in the government.

Louise wore a black silk dress with a white petticoat, the

satin's clear color reflected in the diamond tiara adorning her hair. She'd chosen the austere frock so as not to clash with the red-and-white stripes of the Tent Room and to match her mourning mood, one she'd struggled to endure as much as the seasickness since boarding the steamer in Liverpool. Every day they'd sailed west to their new positions, the life she'd loved had faded farther behind her and she had no idea when she might see it, her friends, or Edgar again.

"His Ex is certainly enjoying the attention," Smack whispered from behind her, drawing a slight scowl from Major Francis de Winton.

"Good." He'd gotten exactly what he'd wanted, and at her expense.

The ball afterward in the robin's-egg-blue-walled ballroom, with its curved and gilded ceiling, tall windows overlooking the woods, and a large portrait of Mama at one end, was as tiring as the ceremony. Louise had been sick the entire voyage to Canada, and since their arrival, there'd been little time to recover. It'd been nothing but receptions and welcoming committees as every city they'd passed through to reach Ottawa had plied them with flowers and welcome speeches. If the schedule Smack had shown her while she'd dressed was any indication, it would be weeks before she might properly rest. There were so many societies and officials to meet with, she might never know a moment's peace or find a chance to draw or sculpt.

Her surroundings did little to bolster her mood. The ballroom was grand enough, but the company was shabby, the dresses and coiffures twenty years out of style, at least for those trying to be fashionable. Those not in military uniform or court dress appeared in their Sunday best, giving half the room the look of a country fair. The difference in dress separated the two groups, at least those not cluttered around the punch bowl, their words growing more slurred by the cupful. The two groups stood across the ballroom from one another, each side eyeing the other with disapproving suspiciousness, reminding Louise yet again of her exile from London and society.

"Rideau Hall is quite shoddy and not at all up to your usual standards," Lady Smyth observed to Louise, sneering into her champagne punch. She was short and thin and wore her hair in outdated loops of braids. She stood with Lady Cartwright, wife of the Finance Minister, who was as frosty and unfashionable as her companion. "You will, of course, wish to refurbish it to better reflect Your Excellencies' exalted station."

"I refuse to spend public money on the hall, not when the economy is so depressed."

"Quite right," Lorne concurred in a rare moment of agreement with his wife. "Lord Dufferin's renovations last fall are sufficient. Why, Rideau Hall has more modern features than half the houses in England, don't you think, my dear?"

"Hmmm," Louise answered, wanting to flinch at the forced affection. She wasn't willing to put so high a polish on the residence, but she wouldn't contradict Lorne in front of a snob like Lady Smyth either. The woman's nose was already bent out of joint because Louise had convinced Lorne to rescind his order requiring court dress for tonight. It'd riled up the part of Canadian high society, such as it was, who hoped the Viceregal couple's arrival would usher in a new refinement in the provincial capital, while irritating the vast majority who feared she and Lorne would be too full of themselves to mix with commoners. "His Excellency and I are quite aware of our station. We need not lord it over anyone."

Lady Smyth clearly didn't agree, pursing her lips in disapproval. "As you wish, Your Royal Highness."

She took her leave, muttering to Lady Cartwright under her breath about there being more tradesmen than gentlemen in attendance tonight. She stood with the other ladies of society, flinging looks at the plainer wives standing across the ballroom. What Louise wouldn't give to retire to her rooms, as messy as they were with her things still not properly arranged, and lie down or sketch, but she couldn't. She had a role to play, as much as Lorne, and she intended to do it as well if not better than him.

"Lorne, we must dance." She drew his attention to the tension rippling beneath the melodious notes of the orchestra. "If we don't give these two groups something to do besides sneer at one another, we might spark a civil war."

It was then Lorne noticed the difference between the guests. He held his hand out to her. "Shall we?"

"Not with each other. You ask Lady Smyth to dance, I'll choose one of the merchants." She instructed Smack and Major de Winton to do the same. Smack readily approached a gentleman with a thick mustache and long wild hair and invited him onto the floor. Major de Winton hesitated until a nod from Lorne forced him to ask for the hand of one of the society daughters, who blushed and giggled while being led out.

Lorne approached Lady Smyth, who was tickled pink to be asked to dance by the Governor General in front of all her friends. Her superior smile dropped when Louise crossed the room to a burly man in fur boots and a thick wool coat.

"Will you do me the honor of dancing, Mr. . . . ?" Louise asked.

"Parker." He led her out to the dance floor, stomping more than striding. Louise took her place with him for the waltz as if he were a foreign prince at a State Ball. "I'm a salmon fisherman, have a hundred men catching fish for me. If you're going to be one of us, you'll have to learn to do it."

"Do what?" Louise admired his dancing skills; he was quite lithe for a man of his size.

"Fish for salmon."

"I'd be delighted to learn, especially if you teach me."

The burly man grew a size larger at the request.

The dancing continued, and the Viceregal party's willingness to draw out people from both sides of the room soon thawed the icy division. When everyone was properly paired and dancing, Louise made her excuses, in need of a rest.

"Well done, Your Royal Highness," Lady Macdonald congratulated. "I hope His Excellency is as successful at bridging the divide in the Parliament."

"We'll see."

"Your Royal Highness, might I be so bold as to request your company in the Little Drawing Room?" Lady Macdonald asked, having been a great deal more helpful than her often-inebriated husband in settling them into their new home. "There's a gift from Lord Dufferin and others you'll wish to see."

"I'd be delighted."

Lady Macdonald led Louise and Smack out of the ballroom. The music and noise of the ball faded as they passed through the narrow, pillared main entrance hall, where footmen helped inebriated guests out the front door and into their waiting sledges.

"I must apologize for that," Lady Macdonald said. "The festivities are too much for those unaccustomed to them."

"I'm happy they've enjoyed themselves." If Mama had taught Louise anything, it was how to ignore drunks.

They made their way through the salmon-colored reception room to a hallway flanked by sitting rooms, including the Consort's Study and the Governor General's Study. There'd been so little time for Louise to explore Rideau Hall since their arrival, and many rooms still awaited her examination. Lady Macdonald led them to a room across from the Consort's Study and ushered them inside. She opened the gas jet on the lamp, rubbed her satin slippers on the carpet, and touched the brass fixture with her fingertips to create a spark to light the gas.

What Louise saw in the orange flicker took her breath away. It was a full studio with everything she needed to paint, draw, and sculpt.

"Lord Dufferin is quite the artist, and when the Prince of Wales informed him of your talent, especially in sculpting, he decided to leave his studio and supplies for your use," Lady Macdonald explained.

"I must thank him for this. It's so much more than I expected. What are these?"

On a long side table were a number of works she knew well, having seen all of them at one time or another in the studios of Mr. Whistler, Nino, Mr. Morgan, Henrietta, and Edgar, each with an accompanying letter.

"Prince Leopold sent these with instructions for how to present them," Lady Macdonald explained. "He said they're to be the first pieces in the art museum you intend to establish for us. I'll leave you to inspect them."

She left, and Louise plucked the note off of Henrietta's painting and tore it open.

Miss Saxe-Coburg-Gotha, I've arranged to travel to Canada next fall to visit you, if you'll have me, and together we can paint the wild vistas, Henrietta wrote.

"Write to her at once and tell her to come." Louise handed the letter to Smack, then opened the next one, leaving Edgar's, the most cherished, for last.

She chose Mr. Whistler's next, a clear view of the Thames at daylight, the ships so evocative one could almost see them bobbing on the tide.

Madame—I feel it incumbent upon myself as your painter—by devotion if not by office—to offer Your Royal Highness, as a tribute of devotion and gratitude, a favorite picture of my own—which has successfully resisted the danger of sale on more than one occasion—and which I send herewith. In it, I would timidly hint that, while I recognise nature's masterly use of fairy fog—I still do love to look at her when she is beautiful without it.

Mr. Whistler's letter made her laugh for the first time since boarding the *Sarmatian* as she imagined him at his easel resisting the urge to add fog to the picture.

The next was a musical composition by Mr. Sullivan.

I am so very, very sorry I missed seeing Your Royal High-
ness again before you left. I have sent to you a poem of
Lord Lorne's about Canada I set to music. I titled it "Do-
minion Hymn," a far grander title than it perhaps de-
serves. I ask leave to visit you when I tour North America
with The Pirates of Penzance *next winter. It will be so*
very long until then. I am, madam, Your Royal High-
ness's ever faithful and devoted servant, Arthur Sullivan.

"Another guest to invite." She handed Smack the letter,
moving at last to Edgar's bust of Bertie beside a marble cast
of Leopold's hand and a similar one of Alice's left hand resting on a piece of cloth. She plucked up his letter and opened
it. She didn't expect Mr. Whistler's or Mr. Sullivan's heartfelt
sentiment. It wasn't Edgar's way and neither of them could
afford the risk, but between each word would be a deeper
meaning to carry her through their long separation. If she
could find a reason to return home, perhaps to Arthur's wedding in March, she would, but at present there was none. This
faint connection between them was all she had, and it, and
his insistence that someday they'd be together again, must
carry her through.

The bust of his Royal Highness the Prince of Wales is for
the people of Canada. The casts of the hands of Princess
Alice and Prince Leopold are for you. The Grand Duch-
ess was kind enough to pose for me when she was last in
London and Leopold came to my studio before you left.

I hope to soon send one of Prince Arthur's hands along with portrait medallions to help you keep those you love, and who love you very much, close while you're so far away. I am ever your humble servant, J. E. Boehm.

She touched her bodice and the medal of Edgar beneath, the pain as strong as the joy. He loved her, but he was miles and years away.

14th Dec.—This terrible day come round again! When I woke in the morning, was not for a moment aware of all our terrible anxiety. And then it burst upon me. I . . . met Brown coming in with two bad telegrams . . . with the dreadful tidings that darling Alice sank gradually and passed away at half past 7 this morning! It was too awful! I had so hoped against hope.
—Queen Victoria's Journal

LOUISE OPENED HER hand and Leopold's letter fluttered to the floor. "Alice is gone."

Diphtheria had ravaged the royal palace of Hesse and carried off Alice's little daughter Marie, and Alice. While her family had waited and hoped for better news, Louise had been stuck here, unaware of the tragedy until the letters had finally begun to reach her.

"I'm so sorry, Louise." Smack wrapped her in a comforting embrace as tears streamed down Louise's cheeks. "The best are always taken first."

"It seems that way at times, doesn't it?"

Smack handed Louise a handkerchief. Louise dried her eyes before drifting to the window. Outside, a gentle snow dusted the thick woods around Rideau Hall, the trees obscuring the view of the Ottawa River. "I wish I was there."

"Even if you had been, there was nothing you could've done for her."

"I could've been there for Arthur, Bertie, and Leopold. Instead, I'm here."

Not since those first years after Papa's death had she felt so alone. Even then, Arthur and Leopold had been there to help ease the pain, all of them understanding how much Papa's loss had changed their lives. The same would be true for Alice's little children. There would be no loving mother there to comfort them or wipe away their tears.

A knock at the door, and Lorne entered, followed by Major de Winton.

Louise clasped her hands in front of her to face him despite wanting to beat his chest with her fists until he felt an ounce of the pain and desolation he'd brought on her.

"I just heard the news of the Grand Duchess. I'm so very sorry, more so than I can say. She was always kind to me."

Louise nodded, appreciating the real sentiment in his words.

"Major de Winton will make the necessary arrangements for you to return to London and perhaps Darmstadt for the funeral. I must remain here."

"Of course." For a man who'd thought little of what this move to Canada might mean to her and her life, he was extending a great deal of care, and it eased the stiff set of her shoulders, until Major de Winton cleared his throat.

"I'm afraid that's not possible, Your Excellencies." He opened his folio and removed two letters, one opened, one still in the envelope, Mama's wax seal evident on the back. "I received these today, one from Major Ponsonby for me, explaining it is Her Majesty's wish that, despite the tragedy of the Grand Duchess, Her Excellency must remain in Canada. The other is from Her Majesty to Her Excellency regarding the matter."

He handed Louise the letter and she opened it, wanting to tear it to shreds the moment she read it.

Most precious Loosy, Alice's passing is a dreadful hard parting, and on the anniversary of dear Papa's death which has made our grief so much more difficult to bear, but we must not dwell on that; but on the work to do before us—and try and bear up against the trials which beset us in the world, which is only a preparation for the next. Under no circumstances are you to return to England. Despite the tragedy that has befallen our family, your place is beside your husband as he establishes himself as my representative in Canada. Look to him and no other for comfort in your grief.

"I'm so sorry, Louise." Lorne laid a comforting hand on her shoulder, not needing to see the letter to understand the contents.

She shrugged it off and faced him with an icy glare but said nothing, refusing to make a scene in front of Major de Winton.

She trusted Smack with her life. She didn't trust Lorne's secretary, sure he'd been tasked with sending regular updates on Lorne and Louise to Mama.

"I'll leave you. Please let me know if there is anything I can do." Making a dignified retreat, Lorne left, taking Major de Winton with him.

"Mama won't grant me leave to return home or travel to Darmstadt for the funeral," Louise said to Smack. She'd taken refuge in Edgar's arms after Sybil's death, but he wasn't here to hold her, and new tears filled Louise's eyes.

Smack slid Mama's letter out of Louise's hands and dropped it in the fireplace, where it quickly caught and turned to black ash. "She can keep you apart but she can't stop you from caring about those you love, all of them."

Louise laid a hand over Edgar's marble cast of Alice's hands, his gift tragically more prescient than he could've ever imagined. It was a slender connection to Alice, and to Edgar. Through it she felt closer to her lost sister, and drew strength from Edgar to bear this awful grief.

The Legislative Assembly of Ontario was opened on the 10th . . . by the Lieutenant-Governor, the Hon. D. A. Macdonald, who, in his speech on the occasion, pointed out that the increasing trade with England was partially relieving the depression of business. Mr. Macdonald also congratulated the country upon the appointment of the Marquis of Lorne as Governor-General, and upon the advent of Princess Louise to Canada, as being a renewed pledge of the union of the Dominion to the Empire and the throne of Queen Victoria.

—*ILLUSTRATED LONDON NEWS*

The Princess Louise has been holding festivities at Ottawa in honour of the Duke of Connaught's marriage. The Princess had some highly successful amateur theatricals at Rideau Hall, and gave a servants' ball at Government House, when she opened the ball with the Marquis. Tuesday was the Princess's thirty-first birthday, and yesterday was the eighth anniversary of her marriage.

—*THE GRAPHIC*, MARCH 22, 1879

London correspondent of to-day says:—Gossip would have it that Princess Louise is growing tired of her Canadian home already; that, in fact, she is home sick, and wants to return to this country. There is, I hear from Ottawa, foundation for such statement.

—*BELFAST TELEGRAPH*

Rideau Hall, Ottawa, Canada, June 1879

Louise stood on a ladder, paintbrush in hand, adding color to her sketches for the murals in the library. She'd completed the ones on the hallway walls in January before official duties and her eagerness to explore and draw the Canadian wilderness had compelled her outside even in the coldest weather.

"Leopold writes to thank you for the salmon you sent him and tells you to send more the moment you catch them." Smack read Louise her correspondence while Louise worked. "He's quite surprised at you being such a good fisherman and says he can't wait to see you ice-skate when he comes to visit next year."

"I'll be sure to impress him." Heavy summer rain had forced her inside today, and she and Smack worked in the library while Louise finished painting the great blue herons and sparrows she often saw while exploring the river and countryside. There was little she could do about the drab carpets or the imposing stone façade of Rideau Hall, but she lightened and enlivened whatever room she could with her talents.

"Oh dear." Smack clasped a hand to her chest as she turned the letter over, continuing to read.

"What is it?"

"The Prince Imperial. He was killed in Africa."

She held out the letter to Louise, who descended the ladder, set aside her palette and brush, and read Leopold's description of how the Prince Imperial, aching for adventure, had convinced Empress Eugénie and Mama to allow him to enlist in the British Army and take part in the battles against the Zulu uprisings. His squadron had been surprised and overrun, and in the melee, he'd been killed.

"Poor Empress Eugénie, I can't imagine her grief, or Beatrice's. I think she had her heart set on him. I'll write to them both at once." She knew what it was like to be denied the one she loved, but while Louise and Edgar were separated by the Atlantic, protocol, and station, forced into all but the slenderest of communications through Smack and their friends, Beatrice would never know the company of Louis-Napoléon again, and Empress Eugénie had lost the bright future she'd imagined for her son.

The butler cleared his throat, and Louise looked up to see him standing in the doorway with Lady Smyth. Lady Smyth flicked a glance at Louise's stained smock before dipping into the required curtsey, disapproval hanging as thick in the air between them as the smell of paint.

"Lady Smyth, to what do I owe this unexpected visit?" Louise was in no mood to entertain the arrogant woman who'd done nothing but undermine her since she'd arrived. If Louise said the sky was blue, then Lady Smyth would call it green simply to spite her. If Lorne said it was blue, Lady Smyth would say it was the most beautiful sapphire color she'd ever seen. Infuriating woman.

"Lord Smyth is meeting with His Excellency and I wished to pay a call on Your Excellency. We've seen so little of you lately, I wanted to ensure you are well."

"How very kind of you, but as you can see, I am fine."

Lady Smyth glanced past her to the half-finished wall. "Very charming."

"The Rideau Hall library *is* impressive," Louise replied, ignoring the subtle insult to her art. "I hadn't expected so many noteworthy tomes this far from London. George Sand's *Marianne* is a moving story, don't you think?"

Lady Smyth's sallow face flushed. "I'm not familiar with the author or his works."

"Would you like to borrow it?" She slipped it off the shelf

and held it out to her, pressing to see if her curiosity was as stunted as her height. "It's the French version, but of course you speak and read French."

The deep crease between her brows told Louise she didn't, as did her recoiling from the book as if it were a hot coal. "No, thank you. I'm not one of those dreadful bluestockings."

Louise slid the book back on the shelf and turned to face her. She didn't invite her to sit or call for tea. After the news of the Prince Imperial, she didn't wish to lengthen the call or encourage any future unannounced visits. For a woman so concerned with manners and protocol, Lady Smyth lacked the most rudimentary ones.

Lady Smyth looked out the window, her already puckered face drawing in further. "What are they doing there?"

"I've ordered a swath of trees cut between here and the river so we may see it, and enjoy strolls to the water. We'll open it up to the public next spring so they may admire the grounds."

"The public?"

"Those to whom this house belongs."

"It belongs to Her Majesty."

"As Her Majesty's daughter, I assure you she is generous enough to share it with her subjects."

Lady Smyth, seeing nothing to be gained by this topic, switched to another. "I understand you take regular walks through Ottawa in the mornings."

Recent newspaper articles about Louise's morning walks through town and her forays into shops for small purchases had captivated most people, but clearly not Lady Smyth. "I've made sturdy walking boots quite the fashion here because of it."

"Canada does not need a taste for sturdy walking boots, but a preference for silk dancing slippers. You must set the example in your dress and comportment and your marriage."

"I beg your pardon."

Lady Smyth did not flinch but carried on without a blush of shame. "I hate to spread malicious gossip, but it has been remarked upon by many that Your Excellencies do not spend a great deal of time in one another's company, that Your Royal Highness prefers to pursue other interests outside those expected of the wife of the Governor General."

"Who exactly is spreading these rumors?" Louise stepped up to the woman, who had the wherewithal to step back but not stop her chattering.

"Lord Smyth and others have been forced to try and silence certain American newspapermen who aren't as respectful of our institutions and affairs as the English and Canadians. There is a great deal of speculation in the New York society papers about difficulties between you and the Governor General. Rumors from London and whatnot."

"When society pages have no real stories to print, they aren't above making ones up. You were wrong to bring this to me, Lady Smyth, in the guise of being helpful, when all you're doing is fueling malicious rumors. Good day."

Louise picked up her paintbrush and palette and climbed the ladder, turning her back on the woman and leaving it to Smack to ring the bell and summon the butler.

Lady Smyth was gone as quickly as she'd come, but her accusations remained, making Louise's fingers shake so much with indignation and nervousness she couldn't finish the mural.

She gave up, tossing down her paints and tearing off the smock. "What have I done here, to give people such ideas about me? I toured Canada with Lorne, sat through numerous Parliament meetings, and greeted every minster presented to me. I might not attend every event with him, but what society wife accompanies her husband everywhere?"

"She must not have anything else to do but stir up trouble."

Louise wiped the paint from her brush with a rag. "Is she right about the newspapers?"

"I don't know, but the novelty of your arrival is gone. The society pages need news and better gossip to help them sling their rags."

"You're right, of course. I'm simply not used to such vitriol." Especially from the press, who'd loved her in London, where she hadn't done half as much good as she did here, or been half the saint, but she must learn if stories of difficulties between her and Lorne had spread. Mama had banished her from London for the near-truth. If unpleasant rumors were circulating, Mama might extend her exile much longer. "I have to squash the gossip. I can't have it getting back to Mama."

"THOSE ARE DREADFUL, but these are very good. The artists only need proper instruction for them to become first-rate." Louise studied the collection of paintings arranged in the Rideau Hall ballroom with Lady Macdonald.

"They'll immediately benefit from the Royal Canadian Academy of Arts. I heard from the managers today the Clarendon Hotel will be properly ready for the first exhibition."

"Good." Louise had worked tirelessly to establish the Royal Canadian Academy of Arts and to secure a proper venue for the inaugural exhibition in October. "I didn't expect this many submissions."

"You'll help refine the arts in Canada, and Lady Smyth will be pleased."

"Nothing I do pleases her." Louise moved a charming landscape of a farmhouse closer to the window to better examine it. "She paid me a very unpleasant visit the other day."

"I heard. She complained to me about it over tea. I don't blame you for curtly dismissing her. She deserved it."

"Is what she said true? Are rumors circulating about me and His Excellency?"

Lady Macdonald shuffled two small watercolors to a table, her hesitation as much an answer as her words. "There are, among others."

"Such as?"

She moved the paintings again before facing Louise. "A story that my husband behaved indecently with you during the time you were absent from the swearing-in ball. It's been going about since February. I give it no merit, but Lady Smyth and others do."

"Whatever did I do to make them so spiteful of me?"

"You're royal, beautiful, talented, and accomplished, everything they'll never be. Their jealousy is boundless and they strike at you because of it, doing all they can to turn the people and government against you."

"This exhibition will show everyone I'm not the woman Lady Smyth has made me out to be." She would win the people over and outshine Lady Smyth and any other society women who wished her ill.

In Your Royal Highness we recognize a worthy successor to your noble father, the great and good Prince Albert, encourager, in his lifetime, of all that might tend to improve the public taste and advance the interests of the Fine Arts, and whose ideas and work have so largely contributed to the notable revival of art which this age witnesses.

—Speech by The Hon. Mr. Justice Mackay, president of the Royal Canadian Academy of Arts

Ottawa, Canada, October 1879

"I'm grateful and quite embarrassed for your portrait of me to enjoy so prominent a place in the exhibition." Henrietta stood before Louise's portrait of her in a black velvet dress with a lace collar and seated on a red settee. Louise had painted it shortly after Henrietta's arrival in mid-September, and it hung surrounded by a number of Louise's landscapes, including one of Niagara Falls she'd done during a spring tour of Canada.

"You deserve it for all the help you've given me with arranging everything. London doesn't seem so far away when you're here. I'll miss you when you're gone." In less than a week Henrietta would set sail for London. It would be a long time before Mr. Sullivan or Leopold arrived in the spring to enliven the ever-shortening and colder days. Louise had missed Arthur's wedding, Leopold's letter describing the affair of little comfort. Henrietta's letters also stung as she described this year's Grosvenor Gallery exhibition. It was all too much like years ago when Louise had been forced into exile at Balmoral and life in London had continued on without her. Back then she'd had the return to school to look forward to. This time she had no idea when she might see England, her friends and family, and Edgar again.

"What a dreadful painting." Lady Smyth squinted at Mr. Whistler's *Nocturne: The River at Battersea* as if trying to see through the dark London fog he'd painted.

"Is the painter a friend of yours? I can't imagine any other reason for such a piece to be included in the exhibition," Lady Cartwright asked from beside Lady Smyth, neither of them in awe of Mr. Whistler's work.

"He's a great friend of mine, and a well-respected artist who enjoys the favor of such luminaries as Mr. Millais and Mr. Leighton."

The blank looks on their faces told Louise they'd never heard of the artists. For women who wished to broaden their social circle, one would think they would broaden their minds too.

"You were quite friendly with him in London?" Lady Smyth suggested more than she asked, her interest in art vanishing as she resorted to insults in an attempt to drag Louise down to her level, and in front of others.

"No more so than I am with Mr. Albert Bierstadt, who visited us in the spring and taught me to properly draw birds. Unlike some, I'm eager to learn new things and not remain provincial and closed-minded."

"I'm sure you are." Lady Smyth and Lady Cartwright curtseyed to Louise and took their leave, unaware it was Louise who should have dismissed them first, but she was glad to be rid of them. "Insufferable women."

"Don't think of them, think of this." Smack waved her arm at the gallery filled with people eager to admire the art and, unlike Lady Smyth, learn.

"It is grand." In a few short months she'd created something out of nothing, a legacy of her time here, light out of darkness. Edgar would be proud.

"I had a letter from Mr. Whistler this morning," Henrietta said as they continued around the gallery. "He won the libel trial against Mr. Ruskin."

"Good for him."

"It isn't entirely. He was awarded no money to cover his court costs and his debts have forced him into bankruptcy. He's decided to reside in Vienna for a time as the White House is to be sold by his creditors lock, stock, and barrel. It's cheaper for him to live abroad."

"Write to him at once and inquire on some paintings I might purchase for the gallery." She wished she could do more for him beyond this paltry bit of patronage, but she couldn't, not without drawing the ire of Lady Smyth or the attention of people in London, including Mama and the press. *Reynolds's Newspaper* already printed the most scathing things about her and Lorne, every one of them initiating a flurry of stingers from Windsor Castle. It wasn't Louise's fault the radical press didn't admire and fawn over Lorne or that Lady Smyth and others, despite the people's and Lady Macdonald's support, continued to undermine her at every turn.

"Mr. Whistler says Her Majesty has commissioned Mr.

Boehm to complete a full-sized memorial statue for Louis-Napoléon's mausoleum, but there's a great deal of discussion regarding the placement and size and it may not be completed for some time."

Mama would enjoy more correspondence with Edgar than Louise, but she didn't dare write to him. Mama and others still believed she'd strayed with Mr. Whistler. They'd had no hand in Mr. Whistler's current troubles, he'd brought those on himself with his crusade against Mr. Ruskin and the extravagance of the White House. However, silence protected Edgar from any chance of harm, and further separated them. She was trying to make the best of her life in Canada, but without his support, and in the face of constant resistance from some quarters, it was, at times, as hard going as sledges through the winter mud.

Chapter Twenty-Four

That miserable mannikin of a colonial governor, Lorne, it is said, has asked for a battalion of the Guards in Canada, to do honour to his royal better half, babyless Louise! And this at a time when every soldier in England is required either in Asia or Africa! Lorne is fast disgusting all the sensible Canadians by his assumption of royal airs. He wants his brother-in-law, Albert Edward, out there to lower him a peg or two—a process H.R.H. delights in, much to the disgust of Louise.

—*Reynolds's Newspaper*

Rideau Hall, Ottawa, Canada, November 1879

If you spent more time here instead of at the gallery or traipsing through the woods fishing and painting with Lady Macnamara, perhaps I wouldn't receive such bad press." Lorne flung the papers on the desk covered with memos and reports from the all-too-familiar red dispatch box. His office in the round Governor General's Study with the arched Gothic windows and heavy velvet curtains with gold trim was far neater than his study in London, no doubt thanks to Major de Winton. At least the man had one good quality. "Neither would you."

"Not with Lady Smyth undermining me at every turn. Even if she weren't, I wouldn't help you. You took me away from everyone and everything I love to get what you wanted, not having a care for how it'd affect my life."

"I'm sorry I did it the way I did, and that it hurt you and separated you from your family. But you have no idea how badly I wanted this, so much so I was willing to risk and do anything to get it. Surely you can understand that."

All too well, far more than she was willing to admit. The last few years had been nothing but striving to achieve her own goals, and create a life he'd wiped away with his ambition.

She'd never expected to hear an apology for what he'd done. Things must be dreadful if he was venturing into these waters. It softened her anger but didn't douse the hard coal of it still burning in her chest. She'd chosen him from all the others because he held similar interests to hers. Until this moment, she hadn't realized how closely aligned they really were. That very trait, the single-minded pursuit of their desires, might be the real reason they'd never be content together.

"I need your help." Lorne held up a pile of reports. "This is like nothing I've ever handled before, the squabbling ministers, the demanding public, the petty tit-for-tat of one side or the other. You worked with Her Majesty for years, you must know how all this is managed." He set his elbows on the desk and raked his fingers through his hair. "I want to make a proper go of it, not only for me but for the people of Canada.

I'm genuinely fond of them and want to do my best. Please, I need your help."

It wasn't a lie. Louise had seen how he had grown to care for the people and the country, sitting up nights to work, attending parliamentary sessions and cabinet meetings with an enthusiasm he'd never displayed in London.

The strain had even affected his health—he was too thin with worry, though the new slenderness had added a seriousness and maturity to his soft features.

He did need her help, and as much as she wanted to walk out of here and leave him to sort it out, if he failed, the Canadian people more than anyone else would suffer. She couldn't allow that, for she had also grown to have a great deal of affection for this land and its citizens.

"All right. Show me this morning's dispatches and tell me the most pressing issues."

She came around the desk and he handed her the papers to review along with his replies. "I see one problem: You send your answers and thoughts too soon. Mama always waits a day for the first rush of emotion to clear so she can view a matter with a clear head, at least where her ministers and government are concerned."

"If only she were as logical with her family as she is with affairs of state."

"I agree," Louise replied with a wry smile. "It would save us all a great deal of trouble." They spent the morning reviewing minutes, proposals, requests, and difficulties, Louise advising him as best she could in statecraft and the careful handling of egos and personalities. He knew more about the government and its workings than she'd expected, and by the end of the day, the panicked look in his eyes had settled. Together they'd sorted out the issues at hand and determined what needed to be done.

He closed the lid on the dispatch box and sat back in his chair, the twilight outside the windows making his blond hair appear darker. "I feel more capable now."

"It won't last." Louise rose and stoked the fire, bringing the waning flames to life against the creeping cold. "Opinions and issues constantly change as ministers wrangle for positions; however, if you approach them as I've shown you, you'll better manage them."

"I appreciate your help. Might I call upon you again to assist with the boxes and whatever issues might arise?"

"I'll assist you, but for the people and no other reason."

He tapped the arm of his chair thoughtfully. "I understand, but may I ask for a truce?"

"Are we at war?"

"Louise, we aren't exactly at peace, we rarely have been, but we are in this marriage and this position together, for better or worse. I've given it a great deal of thought, and I'd like it if we could be allies, if not friends, work for one another instead of against. Heaven knows what we'll be up against in the future. We should face it together, in our own way."

Better to keep your husband as your friend than your enemy. You don't want him working against you. It could cost you a great deal more than you realize. Alice had warned her in the Darmstadt train station years ago, and she'd been right.

Louise had neglected Lorne and she knew that it had cost her. He was offering an olive branch, and if she accepted it, they might enjoy something of a life together, look out for one another as only a man and wife in the most unusual situation and the most unique family could.

"A truce it is, then, and a promise to stand beside one another instead of against. I'm sure it won't be easy at first."

"We'll figure it out." He stood, took her hand, and raised it to his lips. She squeezed his fingers, making her silent pledge to their new alliance. He'd never be to her what Leopold, Bertie, or Edgar were, but he'd be an ally, standing beside her as she would stand beside him.

"I'll join you tomorrow to review the boxes."

"I'd appreciate that."

She let go of him and made for her room, tired and strangely invigorated. The gaslights illuminating the hallway flickered across the flower and bird murals she'd painted. Her room was warm and inviting, the paintings from her friends in London enlivening the walls.

"You and His Ex were cloistered together for some time," Smack said, helping Louise out of her heavy dress.

"He needed my assistance with government work."

"And you proffered it?" She was as surprised as Louise that she'd been willing to help him instead of allowing him to sink.

"I did." She explained about the apology, their truce, and the moment when Lorne, in telling her how he'd sought this post with single-minded determination, had reminded her of her pursuit of Edgar, school, and art.

"You're a better woman than I am," Smack said. "I wouldn't trust my husband as far as I could throw him."

They sat before the fire, warming their hands. Rideau Hall was as cold as Balmoral, the Canadian winters harsher than even those she'd experienced in Scotland, but no one here was stingy with the coal or wood. The trees she'd instructed removed for the walkway had been chopped up, and helped to warm and brighten her rooms.

She rose and went to the window. Outside, the wide swath of cleared land through the forest glowed with the moonlight glittering off the snow and the Ottawa River in the distance. "There was more to it than Lorne and me understanding each other, for once. For years I worked beside Mama, addressing correspondence, speaking with ministers, reading their notes and papers and her replies. I used to think it a grand waste of time, but today I used everything I ever learned at her elbow to assist Lorne, and I will again."

"Her Majesty will be tickled pink to hear it." Smack laughed.

"I'm not about to tell her. She'd lord it over me for the rest of my life, but for the first time I'm thankful for the education and experience. I used it, for once, not for my benefit, but for the Canadian people."

"Careful, Louise, that sounds quite mature."

She threw her friend a playful scowl. "Smack, you're the devil."

"I'm a practical one, and you are too, despite all the artistic fancy."

"I suppose I am."

The Ottawa correspondent the Hamilton Spectator writes:—I know all your young ladies are dying to hear about the Marquis of Lorne and the Princess . . . She is evidently one of those true, simple, and broad-minded women who treat with silent contempt all affectation, all snobbery, all show, and all pharisaical profession . . . Let the young women of Canada watch the life of this daughter of Royalty; let them imitate her industry, her simplicity, her pure, healthy, useful life, well mental as physical; let them recollect that no life is happy which is idle—that the highest and purest enjoyment in this world is the consciousness that we are constantly employed in doing good and being useful, and that the most wretched of all lives is that of the woman of fashion, or of the girl who spends her time in the whirl of social excitement. The life of the Princess Louise in Canada will, I do not doubt, be a constant and most powerful protest against the enervating, listless, showy life which is, unfortunately, distinguishing American women, and which is also, unfortunately, striking root in this fair Canada of ours.

—*Dundee Evening Telegraph*

Rideau Hall, Ottawa, Canada, February 14, 1880

Louise and Lorne sat in the covered sledge, bundled in furs to ward off the deep winter cold. It still cut through the heavy fur dolman cape she wore over the beaded silk ball gown, and she tucked her hands deeper into her fur muff, shivering in the near-darkness. After a year in Canada, she still wasn't accustomed to the long, bitter winters.

"I never sympathized with Her Majesty's distaste for Drawing Rooms until I was forced to hold them. I don't blame her for not sitting through them. They're ghastly affairs." Lorne adjusted the round beaver hat he wore along with a fur coat to keep him warm until they arrived at the assembly rooms. "I expect the president of the Dominion Rifle Association to be there and press me about my speech. I intend to emphasize the importance of camaraderie between the volunteers of Canada and England instead of this continued separation."

"A wise move." The back end of the sledge jerked as if it'd slid on the ice. Louise moved aside the curtain, noting their unusually quick pace down the long drive from Rideau Hall to the main road. "The driver is in a hurry to get us there."

"I'll tell him to slow down. The roads are icy tonight." He reached up, ready to bang on the roof and call to the man, when the entire sledge shuddered. The screams of horses and men echoed with Louise's as the sledge jerked to one side, toppling over and throwing Louise to the side and Lorne on top of her. The world whirled around her, Lorne crushing her chest as a sharp pain ripped through her ear and head, and suddenly everything went black.

What has happened since I last wrote! The frightful accident to poor dear Louise . . . it seems the horses pulled- and turned the corner too sharply- the sledge went over a heap of snow and upset and the horse ran away and dragged the sledge (a covered one) 400 yards! Poor dear Louise fell on her head and got a severe blow, cut her ear and strained the muscles and sinews of her neck which gave her much pain . . . Lorne was also hurt but slightly . . .

—Queen Victoria to her daughter
the Crown Princess of Prussia

"I DON'T THINK it's wise to make public the severity of Her Royal Highness's injuries before informing the Queen." Major de Winton's whispered voice pierced Louise's fog. The weight of the coverlets on her chest made every pain in her body worse. "We can't have Her Majesty hearing of the accident from the press before we have a chance to apprise her of the situation."

"What is the situation, Dr. Grant?" Lorne asked.

"I suggest she return to England immediately. Her Majesty's physicians are better equipped to deal with the extent of Her Excellency's injuries. I should not like to have responsibility for Her Royal Highness or answer to Her Majesty should the situation turn dire."

"I won't force her to travel until she's strong enough and out of immediate danger. Summon the best doctors, send to New York if you must," Lorne commanded. "We'll wait for their advice."

Louise shifted on the bed, struggling through the fog in her head to hear them and comment, but she couldn't pull through the mud of sleep and pain, groaning in her frustration.

"There, there," Smack soothed from where she sat beside Louise. "Take this. It'll help you rest and ease the pain."

Smack touched a cold spoon to her lips and the sweet laudanum syrup bathed Louise's tongue. She settled against the pillows, one thought rising above the tangle of pain and the pull of sleep. England. She might return to England.

Madame and dearest Mama, Louise . . . must be kept quiet for some time, as any excitement makes the place where she received the blow ache much. The hearing, which was affected, owing to the blow affecting the "auditory nerve," on one side, is much improved, although not yet perfect. My chief anxiety now is that she may for some time feel the effects of fatigue undergone at any place in the form of severe headache at the injured part, but we must hope for the best . . .

—Lord Lorne to Queen Victoria

Rideau Hall, Ottawa, Canada, March 1880

Smack pushed Louise's wheelchair around the grounds of Rideau Hall. Each jostle over the frozen path, every change in the angle of the chair, sent a stab of pain through Louise's head. She wanted to vomit from the agony, but she held it back, breathing in the cold, bracing air, allowing it to settle and strengthen her.

"You shouldn't force yourself to be up and about so much," Smack warned when Louise moaned again at the slight shift in the chair going over a stone.

"I have to. The sooner I'm well enough to travel, the sooner we can go home." Despite Major de Winton and Dr. Grant's eagerness to foist her off on Mama's physicians and relieve themselves of all liability for her care, Lorne had summoned a specialist from New York, along with two noted Canadian doctors, who'd advised against traveling so soon.

She'd been confined to bed for the past three weeks, unable to sleep, the constant buzzing in her ears and throbbing pain in her temples keeping her awake. At last, tired of staring at the walls of her room and seeing no one but Smack, the nurses, her maids, and Lorne, she'd insisted on daily tours around the grounds, forcing herself to improve despite everyone urging her to remain in bed.

Another jostle, and a jolt of pain tore through her head.

"Do you want some laudanum?"

"No, I refuse to rely on it and become more of an invalid than I already am." She could not help but think of Lenchen and her dependence on the drug. She would not let that happen to herself.

Tears of frustration rolled down Louise's cheeks and Smack knelt before her, pressing a cloth she'd dipped in snow to Louise's forehead. The coolness eased the pain but not the throbbing of her ear where the lobe had been torn off by the sledge's runner. She wore a scarf to cover the loss, and avoided mirrors, her swollen and bruised face too unnerving to look at.

"There, there, you're still recovering, and if I know you, you'll never be an invalid. You'll get better, I know you will, and you'll walk over the hills like you did before."

"What if you're wrong? I saw how Mama was with Leopold. She'll treat me no better if I return like this."

"What Her Majesty will do is the least of your worries. Get better and we'll go home. Think about nothing except that."

She dried her eyes, and clasped Smack's hand, grateful for her friend. "You're right. I can't give up. I will get better. I must."

* * *

As for our dear Louise, I cannot honestly say I think her looking well. She suffers so much from her head, and any fatigue or excitement brings it on. She is grown so thin too. It is very distressing that this terrible accident should have shaken her so much . . . she will stay some time, and be very quiet . . . even if she were not delicate as she is now, it would be far too fatiguing for her who requires often days of complete rest and even comfort . . .

—*Queen Victoria to Lord Lorne*

Windsor Castle, June 1880

Louise leaned hard on her walking stick as she slowly made her way down the Grand Corridor. The muscles in her neck that'd been wrenched when she'd been pinned against the sledge floorboards by the weight of Lorne were still stiff and sore and often left her dizzy. The buzzing in her ears from the blow to her temple when the sledge had overturned was gone, and the dreadful headache she'd suffered those first few weeks after the accident had subsided, leaving behind a dull throbbing made worse by too much light or activity.

Sometimes the pain passed quickly, other times it forced her to lie down in a dark room with a cool cloth on her forehead. Today, the light reflecting off the gilded picture frames and the crimson carpets made her head ache but the pain eased as she passed into the dim sitting room.

"You are wearing yourself out by being up so much," Mama scolded when Louise sat with a grimace of pain in a chair across from Mama and Leopold. "You should rest."

"I'll never gain my strength back if I lie about in bed."

"Quite right. Activity is the best thing for Loosy," Leopold said, drawing a glare from Mama.

"We do not need your opinion on the matter. The doctors know best."

"Dr. Jenner agrees with me," Leopold pressed, and Louise knocked his shoe with her walking stick, insisting he stop. A row would do nothing for her head or her healing.

"Have you heard anything more about Leopold's possible fiancé?" Louise asked, turning the discussion to a happier subject.

"We are still in talks with many young women, but Princess Helen of Waldeck and Pyrmont is the most promising candidate so far," Mama announced.

"Not until I meet her," Leopold insisted. "For all I know, she's a boring, bucktoothed ninny."

"With your illness, you will be fortunate if any young woman from a respectable lineage will have you," Mama callously reminded. "Her willingness to consider you at all is in her favor."

"Thank you, Mama, that's most helpful," Leopold sneered. "Perhaps before I marry I might at last gain an independent income and a duchy."

"You know I had to secure Arthur's settlement for his marriage and if I had tried to secure yours at the same time, that awful *Reynolds's Newspaper* and those agitating republicans would have begun their crusade again. Look how dreadful they are to Louise after her accident, starting all sorts of rumors that she came home to escape Canada instead of to recuperate."

Louise and Leopold exchanged a look, the truth known to them but not Mama. Louise was far from well, but when she recovered, she had no intention of returning to Canada. She'd nearly lost her life in the accident. She refused to lose any more of her dreams and love, and nothing Mama could say or do or threaten would change that.

It was bad enough she was cooped up at Windsor, unable to visit London. She hadn't seen Edgar, her studio in Kensington Palace, or her friends since her return. Mama kept a tight rein on all visitors and Louise's movements, limiting her to the castle grounds. Every day Louise walked a little farther along the hallways or rose from her wheelchair to follow garden paths as far as she could before the pain in her neck and head forced her back to her room. She was determined to recover her strength.

"Mr. Disraeli—Lord Beaconsfield, I mean—writes to say he is enjoying his retirement from the premiership. It has given him time to complete his novel," Mama read from a letter. "I would rather have him as Prime Minster than an author, but his health has been so poor lately. Better he rest and get well. Perhaps I will arrange to pay him a call and cheer him up."

Leopold looked to Louise as if to say a visit from Mama might make him worse.

A footman entered with a small tart on a silver plate and placed it in front of Mama.

"Congratulations," Louise offered, having arranged for the treat's arrival. "Today is the anniversary of your coronation."

"Thank you very much for remembering. You are the only one of my children to do so." She shot Leopold a sideways glare he ignored, then glanced up at the ceiling with a far-away look. "Not even the pomp and ceremony of my coronation could match the excitement of my first day as Queen. After years of being under Mama and Sir John's thumb, I was at last my own mistress. My Privy Council flocked to Kensington Palace to take my measure, and I impressed them, none more so than Lord Melbourne. I had believed for years I was capable of so much more than I had been allowed. That day, I proved it."

Leopold rolled his eyes at Louise, who listened with interest. If only Mama could see how little difference there was between her and her children, she might understand them all and ease her tight grip.

Major Ponsonby entered, interrupting Mama's memories. "Your Majesty, Mr. Boehm has arrived to discuss the statue of Your Majesty for the Grand Vestibule."

Louise sat up, despite the ache in her neck, her heart racing with excitement. Edgar was here. "I'll come with you. I'd like to see Mr. Boehm and congratulate him on his appointment to the Royal Academy."

"Nonsense. You are in no state to receive visitors and far too frail to make it from here to the Grand Vestibule. I will give him your regards. He will be most pleased to have them and know you are on your way to recovery under my diligent care." Without further discussion, Mama strode from the room with Major Ponsonby.

Louise grabbed her walking stick, rising too fast and making herself so dizzy she nearly fell back into the chair.

Leopold's steadying grasp kept her on her feet. "Take it slowly or you'll hurt yourself and you'll never leave."

"He's here. I have to see him. Help me."

Leopold offered her his elbow and escorted her from the room. Every step toward Edgar was agony, but she made them, ignoring the throbbing in her temples and the strange light that came over her vision whenever one of her awful headaches was about to strike. She couldn't allow it to stop her from seeing him, not when he was so close.

Their progress was painfully slow as they passed from the private apartments to the State Rooms, Louise stopping every few feet to steady herself and fight back the encroaching pain.

At last, they reached the Rubens Room at the top of the Grand Staircase. She paused to settle herself, and caught the deep tones of Edgar's voice drifting up from the vestibule. Her heart swelled and she tried to hurry forward, but the light and pain nearly doubled her over.

"Loosy, don't, you'll hurt yourself," Leopold cautioned. "There'll be another chance."

"I must see him."

He didn't stop her, but helped her through the increasing agony of her head to the top of the Grand Staircase. The world swam around her as she looked down. There were so many stairs. She started down first one step, then another, wobbling on her feet, hands tight on the railing, until, winded and hurting, she was forced to sit down on the landing.

It was then Edgar came into view. He didn't see her at first, concentrating on Mama, who stood out of sight discussing the placement of her statue. Then, as if sensing her, he turned. Joy followed by worry flashed across his face and he took a step toward her, ready to rush to her and enfold her in his arms, but he stopped. He couldn't come to her, not with Mama so close by.

She leaned against the cool marble wall, frustrated by her weakness, and the knights on horseback flanking the staircase towered over her. If she had the strength, she'd rush into his arms, but all she could do was stare at him. He was the same as she remembered, strong, tall, dark-haired, and sure of himself, while she sat here weak and broken. Shame filled her. She shouldn't let him see her in this state, but he didn't think less of her for her illness, silently encouraging her to stand and be strong.

"Come, Mr. Boehm, we shall discuss the portrait medallion of my beloved Alice for St. George's Chapel."

"Yes, Your Majesty." He took one last look at Louise, forced by Mama's patronage to follow her despite the regret and yearning for Louise she could see in his expression.

I love you, Louise mouthed to him.

He glanced at Mama, then back at Louise, and mouthed, *I love you too*, before walking off to follow Mama, his regretful gaze not leaving hers until he was out of sight.

She closed her eyes and soft tears slid down her cheeks.

"Loosy?" Leopold knelt beside her, the same concern in her voice every time he'd fallen sick over the years thick in his words. "Let's take you back to your room."

She nodded, allowing him to help her rise, to lean on him as they slowly climbed the stairs. Edgar was somewhere in the castle beyond her reach but still in love with her after all their time apart. This, more than Leopold's arm, supported her through every slow, agonizing step back to her room.

Of course after Louise's departure my spirits are not at flood tide. I wish I could think it would be all right to go over to England for a visit, but the effect would be bad here, and I should stick to my post . . . they have beside a very proper opinion that an official should remain at his office, as long as their country pays him to remain there.

About Louise, I must make up my mind that she should have a good long time at home . . . No real rest can be got in Canada, for people expect one to appear everywhere, and are angrily disappointed if the appearance is not made. I told them in a speech lately at Quebec that they must consider her to have been injured in their service just as much as any soldier might be on duty . . .

—Lord Lorne to Queen Victoria

Windsor Castle, November 1880

Louise picked up the hammer and slammed it against the chisel. The strike reverberated through her neck and shoulders and she dropped the tools.

"Bloody hell," she growled through gritted teeth, opening her eyes when the pain subsided. She picked her tools off the floor and laid them on the table despite wanting to sweep every one of them off the top. She could walk unaided around Windsor Castle, and the headaches had eased from nearly every day to once or twice a week, the spasms much shorter and less debilitating than they'd been during those first few months. She could sketch, but she longed to sculpt the way she used to and lose herself in the work.

She abandoned the block of marble, set clay on the turntable, unrolled the leather tool roll, and began shaping the clay with a spatula. She worked for a while before the weakness in her muscles and the throbbing in the back of her head forced her to stop. The half-finished statuette of a dog mocked her and she rubbed her neck muscles, cursing them for not healing as fast as the rest of her.

"I'm glad to see you've returned to your studio," Beatrice said, cautiously approaching.

"I can barely manage it before my muscles fail me. This blasted British cold is making it worse." Chill air sometimes irritated the nerves where she'd been struck along the temple, causing them to burn. She could only imagine how she'd suffer if she were forced to endure a Canadian winter. Thankfully, Lorne had upheld his end of the bargain as her ally, insisting Louise shouldn't return and defending her against attacks in Canada from people who thought she was well and simply shirking her duties.

"Give it time, you don't wish to hurt yourself again and set back your progress."

"How is everyone in Darmstadt?" Louise asked, eager to discuss something besides her health. Beatrice had been visiting Alice's widower and her children with Bertie and Alix.

"As well as can be expected considering their great loss." Beatrice picked at one of the sharp edges of the tools, appearing so much more mature than when she'd begged Louise to help her attend the State Ball. "There were so many people there, including Prince Henry of Battenberg."

"I don't remember him." There were so many young princes

and princesses coming into their majority it was difficult for Louise to keep them all straight.

"He was most charming and reminded me of Louis-Napoléon."

"You know, I never told you how very sorry I am about him, and . . . you."

"I loved him, but he was too much like you, wanting to see the world. When I heard about your sledge accident, I thought the same thing might happen to you, and I couldn't bear it."

It was sincere and very unexpected. "You'd miss me that much?"

"I know we've never been close, but I do admire you and everything you've achieved. It gives me hope, and I sorely need it." She touched the gold jetton pendant of two cupid figures holding hands hanging on a chain around her neck.

It piqued Louise's interest. "Prince Henry?"

Beatrice clasped the pendant with her whole hand, covering it, the flush in her pale cheeks answering Louise's question, but she said nothing, the debate between trusting Louise and the risk of revealing the truth strong in Beatrice's wide eyes.

"You needn't tell me. I understand how hard it is to keep secrets here. Hold on tight to yours, and him."

"I must go. Mama has work for me." She fled the room.

Louise turned the sad clay figure around on its turntable, eager to pick up her tools but afraid to ruin the progress she'd made. Beatrice was right, she must give it time, but she was tired of waiting and resting. Edgar, London, and her old life weren't far away, but it still felt like an ocean stood between her and them.

Chapter Twenty-Five

It seems to me you don't *quite* see *what* I and any Parent, but above *all* the Sovereign (who *can* forbid *any* of her children from going anywhere and have always done so in former days, but I have been far too lenient), object to . . . I have my Position as Sovereign and head of a large and somewhat difficult family to maintain and if such want of respect is allowed—*where* is it to end? It would be a small Republic . . . Let me say once more, it is not the thing itself I objected to—but the *concealment* and the *whole way* in which *it was done* . . .

—Queen Victoria to Princess Louise

Windsor Castle, February 1881

Since you are quite better, it is time for you to return to Canada to be with Lord Lorne," Mama pronounced while she and Louise sat in her study working. Beatrice and Leopold were opening a charity bazaar in Birmingham, leaving Louise to assist Mama. She tried to approach the work with the newfound appreciation she'd developed while working with Lorne in Canada, but every letter sealed, each correspondence composed, smacked too much of those long-ago days of isolation and frustration she'd vowed never to return to. She'd made the same promise to herself about Canada. "I will not. I have a life here I was loath to leave before, and I won't abandon it again. I've served enough penance for you, I won't be exiled and tortured further. Besides, Lorne told you it isn't in my best interest to return."

"It is not up to Lorne, and you will not defy me."

"I will not obey you either. I've suffered enough this last year and endured so much to heal. The English cold tortures me. I won't return to the frigid ice of Canada and risk permanently ruining my health simply to keep up appearances."

Mama clasped her hands in her lap, this calm far more worrying than an outburst. "What exactly do you think you will do here while Lord Lorne is in Canada?"

"I'll return to Kensington Palace and resume my sculpture work." Through slow and steady exercise, she'd strengthened her muscles enough to sculpt for longer periods of time. It was much slower going than before, but it could be done.

"I let your apartments to the Duke of Cambridge on the understanding you would be in Canada for five years. I will not turn him out."

"Then I'll take up my old rooms at Buckingham Palace."

"Not without my permission."

"I'll live with Bertie or Arthur."

"They will not allow it." Louise moved to object, but Mama held up a silencing hand. "There are a number of choice positions and roles I have promised them, ones they will not receive if they defy me as you do, as I have informed them."

"You'd turn my own brothers against me to keep me here like a prisoner?"

"You are free to return to your husband, but if you choose not to, then you will remain at my side. I require a daughter to serve me. Although Beatrice is doing well, she does not have your experience and maturity, and Lenchen doesn't have your savvy with Prime Ministers."

Louise pressed her fingers to her temples, the fog coming before her eyes and the pain in her head building in a way it hadn't done in weeks. She took a deep breath, willing her neck muscles to relax, forcing the dull ache into the background so it didn't blur her vision or leave her too ill to fight.

"It isn't only your future you must consider but your dear friend Mr. Boehm's."

The pain vanished in a swarm of icy chills. "What does Mr. Boehm have to do with this?"

"I know you have a special affinity for him. He is talented beyond measure and quite charming, more so than Mr. Whistler. It is why I favor him with my patronage and will continue to do so if you cooperate."

She knows it's Edgar and not Mr. Whistler I love. Yet she'd carried on with the ruse, ignoring the unpleasant and seeing only what she wished because she admired Edgar's work.

"However, if you defy me, I will cease my patronage of Mr. Boehm and cut off your yearly allowance. You cannot live on Lorne's allowance alone, and the Duke of Argyll's finances are too strained for him to offer more. Either become my assistant or return to Canada, it is your choice, but remember, your security and the happiness of many, including Leopold, depend on your choice. I will not push for his settlement, independent household, or ennoblement if you dare defy me."

"You'd harm your son to strike at your daughter?"

"You thought nothing of Leopold when you carried on with Mr. Stirling. Leopold does not know about it, but I will tell him if you continue with this obstinacy. Also think of your artist friends. There are many in the Royal Academy who owe their titles and success to me and will promote or shun people according to my requests. You could be the ruin of all your friends." She rose and came around the desk to stand in front of Louise. With a headache threatening, Louise could only sit and stare up at her. "You have been selfish in your pursuits, uncaring of how much your desire to have your way harms others. I will teach you to consider them and your position before you think of yourself."

Married children are very often a great trial at first but one gets accustomed to their follies as time goes on and many things right themselves. Still it is very wrong of young people not to listen and take advice for they have no experience. Parents have much to go through—much to bear.

—Queen Victoria to her daughter
the Crown Princess of Prussia

Windsor Castle, March 1881

Louise opened the letter from Dr. James Reid, Mama's newest physician, and read how Lord Beaconsfield, who had been sick for the past month, hadn't improved. Indeed, he was steadily getting worse, and it kept Louise, Mama, and the nation on edge over the fate of their beloved former Prime Minister.

Louise reached up to touch the butterfly pin on her bodice, then remembered it wasn't there. She'd put it away, ashamed at her defeat.

"Loosy, you look dreadful." Leopold walked in with Bertie and sat across the desk from her. Bertie closed the door behind him to give them privacy. Outside, the cold March rain hit the windows, driven by the unrelenting wind making an already dark day darker.

"It's the headaches," Louise weakly explained, ashamed for Leopold and Bertie to see her like this, a prisoner again at Windsor, her life a shadow of what it'd once been. It'd been ages since she'd sculpted or drawn, neither holding any interest for her. Even if she wanted to pick up the spatula or pencil again, Mama commanded nearly all of her attention, leaving little time for anything except the sick headaches when they came on.

"Bollocks." Bertie dropped into the other chair before the desk, his coat open to reveal his tan waistcoat, his middle much thicker since she'd left for Canada. "You aren't sick, you're heartsick."

"Of course I am. I did everything I could to avoid this, yet here I am. I have choices, but all of them are awful. This is the best of a bad lot."

"No, it's not."

"You think I should go back to Canada?"

"Heavens, no. You should stop all this moping about and feeling sorry for yourself. You're worse than Lenchen."

"I'm nothing like her."

"Aren't you?"

"No." She slammed down the pen and the nib popped off, clinking against the wood floor.

Bertie picked it up and held it out to her. "Then prove it."

She took the nib and shoved it back on the pen. "I can't or others will suffer, including you and including Leopold. I'll be the cause of it, the way I was all those years ago."

"What do you mean?" Leopold looked back and forth between Bertie and Louise.

Bertie shook his head, warning her off, but she couldn't keep the secret any longer.

"Mama is holding this over my head, as she is your future if I don't cooperate, but I'm tired of lies and pretending everything is well when it isn't. I'm the reason Walter was sacked."

"I know," Leopold said without hesitation.

Bertie and Louise gaped at him.

"Alice told me the last time she was here. I was furious, but she made me realize why you did it, and I couldn't stay mad. It's the reason I flirted with Alice Liddell at Oxford when I shouldn't have. I wanted to be just another student, not a sickly prince. You did the same with Walter, and Mr. Boehm and your friends, wanting to be like a regular person and not a princess."

"It's not the same. Your flirtation didn't ruin her. Mama is willing to strike at you and Edgar to make me obey, and who knows what she'll do to others." She rose and went to the window, looking down on the garden where Mr. Brown walked with Mama. "I've seen the crushing poverty at the almshouses I've opened. I won't risk Mama ruining my friends' livelihoods or withholding your future because of me."

"I can handle myself," Leopold assured her, "as can Mr. Boehm and the others."

Louise shook her head. "Not against a queen. Henrietta writes to me, but I don't answer, and I don't write to Nino or Mr. Morgan for fear Mama will turn her wrath on them. People treat her requests as commands and if she demands the Royal Academy shun them or people don't patronize them, they'll suffer. I can't allow that."

Bertie snorted. "So you'll ruin yourself instead. A martyr, just like Lenchen. How tiresome."

Louise whirled around, grasping the back of the sofa to steady herself against a wave of dizziness. "How dare you mock and demean me instead of helping me."

"If I thought you were up for it, I'd stand beside you and we'd find a way to make her back down from these ridiculous threats together, but I can't wage war when my ally has already surrendered. Stop withering away in this mausoleum, pining for what you think you've lost, and start fighting again for what you want."

"You're demanding I do things I can't do." She choked on the sob tightening her chest, the muscles in the back of her neck tightening. "I'm in pain, brokenhearted, and grieving everything stolen from me, and not an ounce of pity from you."

Bertie rose and rested his walking stick over his shoulder. "You sound exactly like Mama."

He strolled from the room.

Louise looked to Leopold, his refusal to meet her eyes telling her he agreed with Bertie. "He doesn't understand. He's never concerned himself with his mistresses once he casts them off. I can't do that to Edgar or my friends. I can't see them hurt, or you." Louise sank onto the sofa, rubbing her temples with her fingers. "I don't have the strength to endure it or to fight Mama."

Leopold came and sat beside her. "Yes, you do, you're simply scared. You've never lived like this, weak, at the mercy of your body, afraid it will fail you. It tears at your spirit until you think you'll never be free of the dark moods, but they pass, even if it seems at times as if they won't. If anyone can find a way through this it's you, Loosy."

"Not this time." Louise picked at the cushion button. "We can't fight a queen."

"You're wrong, and I'll prove it." Leopold rose, standing over her, fists clasped at his sides in determination. "Mama isn't as powerful as you think, and you aren't as weak as you believe."

We only wish your happiness and dear Mama's too. Only see for yourself—compare and reflect on all the different circumstances brought to your knowledge and decide for yourself . . . You are no longer a baby. I would not press anything on dear Mama that is distasteful to her—she is easily excited, it would only annoy and irritate her and then you would most likely have a difficult time of it. I trust to all coming right in time as it mainly rests with your own dear self.

—*Crown Princess of Prussia to Princess Louise*

IT'D BEEN A week since Louise's row with Bertie and Leopold, and she'd seen little of them since. After a day with

Mama, she was often too tired to do more than retire to bed with a cold cloth over her forehead. Missing dinners and the Drawing Rooms afterward was the one good thing about the headaches, which had become more frequent in the last week, along with the loss of her already meager appetite. She paused at a looking glass in the hallway, running her hands over her gaunt face and lamenting the dark circles under her eyes. The bodice of her black velvet dress with the satin dove-gray stripes hung much looser on her than when she'd last donned it at the start of her work with Mama. Bertie was right, she was wasting away here, but she didn't have a choice. She refused to see Edgar and her friends suffer.

She pushed open the door to her bedroom, the sight before her making her stop. "What's all this?"

On a table in the center of her bedroom stood a collection of butterfly statuettes and small butterfly paintings propped up against them. Leopold stood beside them, arms outstretched like a showman. "Gifts from your friends who miss the old Louise as much as I do."

He guided her forward and handed her a terra-cotta statuette of a butterfly on a branch by Henrietta. "She's as talented as she is pretty. The others are quite good too, don't you think?"

"They are." She turned over a small carved wooden butterfly from Mr. Morgan, then set it aside in favor of a painting of a butterfly's wings by Nino. The vibrant colors were a stark contrast to the white canvas beside it with nothing on it except Mr. Whistler's large black butterfly signature. There were no encouraging letters this time; they weren't needed, the delicate wings and bodies said enough. Her friends still cared for her as much as she did for them.

"When I wrote, they were all willing to work fast to send these. They're marvelous, but I think this one's the best." He led her to the mantel and the small bronze from Edgar of a horse with a butterfly perched on its withers. The horse's bronze head was turned back to see the butterfly, his nose touching the delicate body. Edgar's love and concern for her was etched in every wither muscle, the pattern on the wings, and the delicate way the horse nuzzled his light rider. It was the only work with a note attached, and she opened it and read the five simple lines from Mr. Tennyson's poem written inside.

We are not now that strength which in old days
Moved earth and heaven, that which we are, we are:
One equal temper of heroic hearts,
Made weak by time and fate, but strong in will
To strive, to seek, to find, and not to yield.

Tears filled her eyes and she covered her mouth against a sob.

"He wants you to leave this cocoon of gloom as much as I and everyone else, and you can, I know it, we all do." Leopold took her other hand and laid a piece of paper across her palm.

"What's this?" She could barely see through the haze of tears clouding her eyes.

"A call for submissions for ideas for a large statue of Mama. It's to be erected in Kensington Gardens for her Golden Jubilee. This isn't exactly what you dreamed of, but you said you wanted to do larger works. This could be your chance, especially since you have the advantage."

"I do." *I look forward to seeing the great things you'll achieve once you learn to use your advantages instead of seeing them as a hindrance,* Edgar had once said. She hadn't seen it then, but she'd caught a glimpse of it in Canada, and again now despite the difficulties between her and Mama. Any other artist who submitted a design wouldn't have the familiarity with Mama Louise enjoyed or the privilege of her rank. She'd used both to assist Lorne in Canada, and establish the Royal Canadian Academy of Arts. She could do it again.

She wiped away her tears with the back of her hand, a spark of life and exhilaration she hadn't felt since the opening night of the Grosvenor Gallery filling her. Bertie was right, she couldn't retreat into a haze of self-pity or she'd be no better than Mama, wallowing in mourning and misery, avoiding life instead of living it, and dragging down everyone around her. Papa had never wanted Mama to live like that. He'd be doubly disappointed in Louise doing it too. She refused to disappoint him or continue to lose more of herself in this misery.

"We'll stand beside you if you stand up to her," Leopold encouraged, his smile matching the one dawning on her lips.

"I don't know how I'll do it."

"You'll find a way."

Chapter Twenty-Six

THE ILLNESS OF LORD BEACONSFIELD. The latest bulletin. The condition of Lord Beaconsfield this morning was not so satisfactory as had been hoped it would be. During yesterday afternoon his lordship left his bed for a short time, and it is feared that this produced a serious relapse.

—*THE GLOBE*

19 Curzon Street, London, April 1881

Louise and Smack alighted from the carriage, noting the somber newspapermen waiting anxiously outside Lord Beaconsfield's home for news. All week the bulletins on his health had been favorable, but Dr. Reid had quietly informed Louise of the truth after hearing it from his doctor friends. Lord Beaconsfield's health was deteriorating, but they wished to keep it from Her Majesty and her people.

Dr. Kidd showed Louise and Smack into the somber home. It was dark inside, the shades drawn and the gas lamps barely flickering in their brass fixtures. The mood matched her deep mauve dress with the small cape and a row of brass buttons along the bodice.

"He'll be heartened to see Your Royal Highness and honored by your visit," Dr. Kidd said as he led her up the stairs. Smack waited in the drawing room for her to return. "He always speaks so highly of you."

"I owe him a great deal."

Dr. Kidd showed Louise into the sickroom. Lord Beaconsfield lay on the bed, frail and thin, and Louise's heart nearly stilled. Dr. Reid was right, he wasn't long for this world.

"Your Royal Highness, I'd rise but I find I don't have the strength today," he said, the rasp in his voice unnerving but his smile as lively as ever.

"Don't fret, I was never one for ceremony." She sat in the chair beside his bed and Dr. Kidd politely stepped out of the room.

"You're wearing my pin." The light she remembered so well whenever he was honored came into his pale expression and gave him new life. It faded quickly, the shadow of death passing over him.

Louise took his hand, working to hold back her tears. "I'm forever grateful to you for everything you've done for me. It's made all the difference to my life."

"Your dear papa would be as proud of you as I am."

"I've done some things he wouldn't be proud of."

"I thought the dying were the ones in need of confession." He chuckled, but it turned into a wracking cough. He lay back against the pillows, the force of it weakening him, and she poured a glass of water and helped him drink.

"I should go, I'm tiring you." She didn't want to leave. This was the last time they'd meet in this life, but she didn't wish to make him worse.

"Don't hurry off, there's something I must say to you, about Her Majesty."

"Would you like her to visit?"

He shook his head weakly. "No, let her remember me as I was, not in this pitiable state, and we both know, if she came here, she'd only ask me to take a message to Prince Albert."

Louise joined his weak laugh with a hearty one. His body was failing, but his spirit still shone. She would miss him a great deal.

"I've always been quick to help you, allow me to do so one last time," he said.

"Of course."

"I know the last year has been difficult for you, and Her Majesty is not an easy person to endure, but you and she are not as different as you believe. It took a great deal of courage for Her Majesty to defy Sir John and the Duchess of Kent's efforts to control her when she ascended the throne. It required unimaginable strength for her to carry on after Prince Albert's death. She may not have done it as you and others might've wished, but she didn't surrender her throne either. You have her will, some might even call it stubbornness, to stand firm against those who wish to dictate your life. She recognizes this quality of hers in you, and respects it, and your strength of will and passion, far more than she's willing to admit. It's why she's always been more lenient with you than the rest."

"You aren't the first to say this."

"But I'm the first you'll believe, aren't I?"

"You are."

He laid his other hand over hers, clasping it tight between his thin fingers. "Draw on your similarities to Her Majesty to help you, and be as forthright with her about your wants and needs as you've been with me. Help her see you two aren't so very different."

"I don't have your talent of flattering her."

"You won't need it. Good luck, Your Royal Highness. I wish I could be there beside you."

She touched the butterfly pin, smiling down on him through a haze of tears. "You will be."

Dearest Mama . . . I trust with time you may find comfort from those around you, who think but of your happiness and good. Ever your dutiful and devoted daughter Louise.

—*Princess Louise to Queen Victoria*

Windsor Castle, April 1881

Louise stood over the open jewelry box on the table near her bedroom window. Outside, the sun shone brightly on the green grass and stone walks of the Windsor Castle garden where Mama and Mr. Brown strolled. It'd been a week since Louise's visit to Lord Beaconsfield, but not a moment had passed without her thinking about everything he'd told her and what she needed to do.

Mr. Brown escorted Mama inside, and a host of gardeners descended on the shrubbery and walks to resume their work.

In a moment, Louise would be expected to join Mama in her study to continue theirs.

Louise peeled back the velvet lining of the burled walnut jewelry box and slid Mr. Brown's letters to Mama out from behind it. She tapped them against her palm, wishing she'd burned them but glad she hadn't. Louise tucked them into the art case Mr. Burchett had given her years ago. The once-clean and stiff leather was full of creases and stains, the supplies inside used up long ago and since replaced. She slipped the strap over her shoulder and made her way through the castle to Mama's study.

"Any more news of Lord Beaconsfield?" Mama asked when Louise entered Mama's study.

"Dr. Kidd's morning bulletin said he slept well last night and is resting comfortably." Louise sat in the chair before the desk, settling the skirt of her cream silk dress with the sprays of roses embroidered on the fitted jacket beneath her. She set the art case beside her, slid out her sketchbook, and removed a pencil from the silver-plated pencil case. She began to sketch Mama, the scratch of lead matching the scratch of Mama's pen on her journal page. The sounds echoed through the red-brocade-walled room, the gold-tasseled curtains pulled back to offer a splendid view of the garden in its spring greenery.

"I am glad to hear it." Mama peered over the spectacles perched on her nose. "What are you doing there?"

"Drawing you. The Jubilee Committee is seeking submissions for a statue of you for Kensington Gardens. I intend to submit a few ideas, perhaps one of you on your coronation day." Louise turned her sketchbook around to reveal a portrait of Mama sitting on her throne, her regal robes draped around her slender shoulders, a scepter in her upraised hand and the crown of state holding down the braids looped about her ears. It was a copy of her coronation portrait, Mama an eighteen-year-old maiden with her and her country's future ahead of her.

Mama set her pen in the stand, laced her fingers beneath her chin, and studied the drawing. "I was so young then. I had no idea of the life I would lead or the joys and heartaches I would face."

"It wasn't easy, was it, insisting on the right to reign while Grandmama and Sir John tried to wrest power away from you?"

"I held on tight to what was mine by right of birth and I won in the end."

"You were strong to stand up to them."

"I was terrified too, but I had to do it." The fondness of happy memories softened the stern set of her lips and eyes. "It was my throne and my life, and I could not allow them to control any of it a moment longer."

"As I can't allow mine to be controlled any longer either." Louise set the sketch on the desk between them, the image of Mama on her throne facing them. "I will not continue as your secretary but will move to Marlborough House with Bertie and resume my sculpting until such time as I can return to Kensington Palace."

The veil of happy memories vanished from Mama's face and she sat back in her chair. "I thought I made my position quite clear."

"I am your daughter. I have the same strength of will and desire for freedom as you. I must be allowed to lead my life as I see fit and to follow my heart as you did with Papa."

"You will do so with Lorne."

"That's not what I mean."

"You are married and will not carry on as if you are not."

"You're a widow who carries on as if she were not Queen." Louise removed the packet of letters from her art satchel and held them up.

Mama went white at the sight of them before narrowing her eyes at Louise. "You dare threaten me with my private correspondence."

"I'm giving them back to you." She laid the letters on the blotter and slid them toward her. "You care very deeply for Mr. Brown, as I do for Mr. Boehm, and I won't be the one who ruins your happiness with a man who adores you, or threaten your place on the throne for my own selfish gains."

Mama leaned forward and slid the letters across the desk to her, fingering the red ribbon, avoiding Louise's eyes. She said nothing as she turned the letters over and over in her hands.

"We're so much alike, Mama, neither of us able to openly pursue our heart's desire but always forced to secretly grasp at what moments of love and friendship we can steal. I won't come between you and Mr. Brown, and I ask you not to come between me and Mr. Boehm."

Mama clasped the letters to her chest and closed her eyes. "I did not think you understood. I did not think any of you did."

"Bertie and the others don't, but I do, as you understand my need for freedom and the things I'll do to achieve it."

Mama opened her eyes, pulled open her desk drawer, and tucked the letters inside before slamming it closed. "If you defy me it will encourage others to do the same, and then where will I be? I might as well not be Queen."

"That's why we're speaking privately. No one need know of this conversation except us."

Mama rose and walked to the window. She stood with her back to Louise, her dark figure framed by the bright light.

Louise rose and joined her, standing silently beside her to look out over Windsor Castle and the countryside beyond. "Do you remember the elation you felt the day you became Queen and could at last sleep where you wished, attend balls, go and see and do what you pleased? Do you remember the rush of life, as if the world had finally opened up to you after being closed and desolate for so long?"

Mama didn't answer, continuing to stare out the window, until Louise thought she intended to ignore her, to give her the cold shoulder until she brought Louise to heel. It would be nothing but terse scribbled notes passed back and forth between them until Louise relented, and she wouldn't, not this time. She wanted victory, but not at Mama's expense, simply her understanding.

Louise waited, watching the birds hop over the grass searching for worms below. She was about to plead with Mama to listen to her when Mama took a breath and answered at last.

"I do remember."

Relief flooded Louise and she gripped the soft curtains in one hand to steady herself. "That's how I feel every time I display my art or patronize artists worthy of my support. I love you, Mama, and until I assisted Lorne in Canada, I never truly appreciated the weight of the crown upon you, and everything it's given and taken from you. I know you understand me and what it's like to sit quietly with a pencil and create something beautiful, or to prove to everyone you're far more capable than they believe. You once gave me the chance to show you what I could do with my sculpting by posing for me. Give me the opportunity to show you everything I'm capable of achieving by allowing me to live my life."

Mama turned to face her, tenderness softening the tightness in her jaw and the stiff set of her shoulders. She stroked the cameo of Papa pinned to the high neck of her dress. "When Papa and I were first married, I jealously guarded my position, giving him nothing but the most menial tasks, afraid he would steal power from me. He made me see I needed him to do more and be more for the good of us and the realm. I see in you his same need and my willful spirit, and sometimes it frustrates me beyond words but I am also in awe of it. I have never told you how proud I was of you at the Royal Academy, or how impressed I was by your work in Canada. I admire your desire to achieve, even if you are still very impertinent." Mama wagged a teasing finger at Louise and the two of them laughed together, breaking the tension. When their humor faded, Mama sobered, less serious than before. "You understand I cannot condone your behavior in public, and you must continue your royal duties."

"I'd be happy to continue them, especially my charity work. I want to help people."

"You must also maintain appearances with Lorne when he returns."

"We reached an understanding in Ottawa and will do as best we can to maintain an acquaintance."

"I suppose that is better than nothing."

"It's the most we can hope for."

Mama studied her a moment, then returned to gazing out at the garden. Sharp dashed about, getting under the gardeners' feet and rolling in the loose clippings. Louise watched the dog, waiting for Mama to say more. Louise had laid herself bare to Mama for the first time, and Mama had responded, seeing their similarities and understanding and embracing them. It didn't mean their difficulties were over, or they'd never fight again, but for the moment, they were at peace.

"I am considering a number of official appointments this year," Mama said at last. "I will make Leopold Duke of Albany and ask Parliament for his annuity. He'll need both when he marries Princess Helen."

"It's been settled? Leopold said nothing to me about it and I haven't seen any letters."

"I do not send all my correspondence through my children," Mama informed her with mock seriousness. "I am certain once he meets her in Germany in November, an engagement will be made. If so, the wedding will take place next year. I will grant them Claremont House for their residence."

"He'll be happy to marry and finally have a home of his own."

"We will see," Mama said, not as certain as Louise. "I also intend to appoint Mr. Boehm Sculptor in Ordinary."

This surprised Louise more than Leopold's possible engagement. "After everything, you'd do that for him?"

"Everything what?" Mama asked with the same feigned innocence as when anyone mentioned a tipsy servant. "His statue of Mr. Brown at Balmoral is a worthy memorial to my great friend, as are the numerous works he's done for so many."

"Thank you, Mama."

"It is my pleasure to reward such a talented man. Shall we return to our work?"

"I thought we might sketch together for a while. I'd like to discuss my ideas for your Jubilee statue. It's such a lovely day, we could sit in the garden." Louise motioned outside to where Mr. Brown kept as watchful and protective an eye on Sharp as he did Mama. She still detested the man, but there was no mistaking his care and concern for Mama and the joy he brought her. Mama deserved such love and affection as much as any of them.

Mama smiled at her. "Yes, that would be lovely."

Chapter Twenty-Seven

There can, however, be no mistake about Princess Louise being a devotee of the wheel. The Marchioness of Lorne is an exceedingly clever sculptor, and sets to work in a most business-like way with her sleeves tucked up and her gown covered with a huge white apron. Lately she has been devoting her attention to animals, and some very successful pieces of sculpture from living models are the result.

—*WAKEFIELD AND WEST RIDING HERALD*

May 1881

Louise studied the maquette of Mama on the turntable, inspecting her progress on the Jubilee statue design. Outside her Kensington Palace studio, the birds sang in the trees and the leaves rustled against the brick. She'd made little progress on the maquette over the last few days, the move to Marlborough House, and negotiating with the Duke of Cambridge to gain access to her studio and to deliver the stone, clay, and supplies, taking most of her time.

Behind her, the large piece of marble she intended to carve

stood in the center of the studio. This would be like no piece she'd ever executed before, and even if the Jubilee Committee rejected it, she'd find a place for it at Windsor or Osborne House. She was eager to begin, sure she'd need more than one try to get it right, but there was plenty of time, a whole lifetime of it, and with Edgar.

She straightened and touched the medal beneath the bodice of her dress. She'd visited his studio the moment she'd arrive in London, only for Mr. Gilbert to inform her he was with Lord Iddesleigh in Exeter discussing a commission. Work on the maquette would fill Louise's time until he returned.

She studied her sketch and the copy of the coronation portrait she'd acquired to help with her work. It leaned against the wall near the fireplace, a guide for her initial clay sculpture. She was shaping the base when a voice behind her made her turn.

"Something grand at last, I see."

Edgar stood in his brown traveling suit, the linen rumpled from the train, the scent of coal and soot still upon him. She didn't care. He could smell like a shepherd and it wouldn't matter. "Edgar!"

Behind him, in the doorway, Smack, with a mischievous smile, trilled her fingers at Louise before backing out the door and closing it behind her.

Louise and Edgar closed the distance between them, their lips and bodies meeting with the passion of years of separation. He was here and she was in his arms, and not an ocean or an empress would ever come between them again.

"I've been so worried about you. If Smack and Leopold

hadn't sent me word, I would've run mad," he whispered in her ear, arms still tight around her.

"Your statue with the butterfly was beautiful, like nothing I've ever seen before. You have no idea the hope it and the poem gave me." She clung to his shoulders, reveling in the feel of his sturdy arms around her.

"I think I have some idea of what it meant to you." He swept her lips with his, the kiss light and tender with his love. They held on to one another for a long time before he finally let go. He slid his hand down her arm to catch her fingers. "What's this?"

He motioned to the block of marble with his free hand.

"My next piece. It will be a large one, and I'll need your help."

He pulled her close, his hand and hers resting over his heart. "I'm yours, in every way imaginable."

For the first time in the history of the world a public monument has this week been unveiled which is entirely the work of a royal princess, for it is the deft chisel of the Marchioness of Lorne which has produced the presentment of England's Queen that will delight the sightseers in Kensington Gardens. The Princess Louise has frequently enriched the sculpture galleries in Burlington House with her talented productions in marble but this latest outcome . . . is stated by those who have had the privilege to pronounce upon its merits to be in the very highest sense of the word an ideal effort . . . Fired . . . by an ambition which refuses to be satisfied with a niche in the Royal Academy, she determined on a creation that should emulate some of the best models of the masters who were her early instructors, and making . . . Sir Edgar Boehm her particular example, she has . . . turned out a statue of her queen mother which will bear comparison with the very best of her Majesty's numerous effigies . . .

—*West Sussex County Times*

London, Kensington Gardens, 1887

Louise tugged the gilded rope, and the cloth concealing her marble statue of Mama on her coronation day slid to the ground. The crowd erupted in raucous cheers, and across the numerous waving Union Jack flags, Louise smiled at Sir Joseph Edgar Boehm, First Baronet of Wetherby Gardens as Mama had styled him. He stood in the special stand erected for the occasion with Henrietta, Mary, Nino, Mr. Morgan, Sir Coutts, the Honorable and Mrs. Percy Wyndham, and the rest of the dignitaries invited to the unveiling. He watched her as he applauded, the pride in his smile echoing in her heart.

Mama sat in the landau parked at the base of the statue, watching the proceedings from beneath her black parasol. Beatrice and her husband Prince Henry of Battenberg were seated with her. Louise, in her Prussian-blue dress with gold edging, the skirt layered at the back over a bustle, and a jaunty hat set at an angle over her hair, came up to the side of the landau and rested her gloved hands on the lacquered side.

"What do you think, Mama?"

"Well done, Louise. Very well done."

About the author

About the book

Insights,
Interviews
& More . . .

Meet Georgie Blalock

Courtesy of the author

GEORGIE BLALOCK is a history lover and movie buff who enjoys combining her different passions through historical fiction and a healthy dose of period films. When not writing, she can be found prowling the nonfiction history section of the library or the British film listings on Netflix. Georgie writes historical romance under the name Georgie Lee. Please visit georgieblalock.com for more info about Georgie and her writing. ॡ

Afterword

Princess Louise lived in an era filled with luminaries in art, government, and business. There were so many people of note involved in her life that it was difficult to decide whom to include and whom to leave out. Thanks to the University of Glasgow's wonderful James McNeill Whistler digital letter collection, I was able to read Whistler's own words to Princess Louise and his son's memories of meeting Princess Louise in Edgar's studio. It brought their relationship to life, and I chose Whistler as the best representative of Princess Louise's many artistic friends. Whistler's letters to and from Edgar were also one of the few contemporary sources that shed light on Edgar's personality.

Joseph Edgar Boehm was famous during his lifetime but has since faded from memory. His personal papers and letters were destroyed by his family after his death, and some think they were burned to hide his relationship with Princess Louise. There is only one biography on Edgar, *The Life and Work of Sir Joseph Edgar Boehm* by Mark Stocker. It is a great book, but the lack of personal papers means Edgar's true personality still remains elusive. Letters between Edgar and Whistler, along with a few contemporary magazine interviews, offered rare glimpses of the real Edgar. As a result, I stayed as faithful as I could to his views on art and work, ▶

3

Afterword *(continued)*

but I took a great deal of liberty with his character, and his wife's.

The novel ends in 1887, but Louise and Edgar remained lovers until his sudden death in December 1890. While Louise and Edgar's relationship was a well-kept secret, his death exposed Princess Louise to a potential scandal. Princess Louise found Edgar's body in his studio, and there are varying accounts of how he died and how she discovered him. Some say she was alone with him when he tried to move a heavy statue and suffered an aneurysm that instantly killed him. Some newspaper reports state that she found his body when she came to visit his studio. The most salacious story is that he died in her arms while they were making love. However the events of that evening played out, Princess Louise was the one who was either with Edgar when he died or who found him shortly afterward. Other than newspaper articles about his passing and her discovery of him, and a brief mention in Queen Victoria's papers about the incident, nothing else survived to offer more insight into the story or the impact of Edgar's loss on Princess Louise. As Lucinda Hawksley notes in her excellent biography of Princess Louise, *Queen Victoria's Mysterious Daughter*, most personal papers and letters from Princess Louise are hidden in the National Archives and no one has been granted access to them.

Edgar's death wasn't the only loss Princess Louise experienced in the

1880s. After a lifetime of illness, Prince Leopold died of an epileptic fit in Cannes, France, in 1884. He had married Princess Helen of Waldeck and Pyrmont in 1882, and they had a daughter and then a son, who was born posthumously. Princess Louise was devastated, and friends and family speak of the great depression she fell into after Leopold's death, one her husband, Lord Lorne, helped her endure.

Princess Louise's relationship with Lorne did hit a crisis point in the 1880s, and they were on the verge of separating. Back then, it was unheard of for royalty to separate or divorce, and Queen Victoria insisted they find a way to quietly work things out. They did, and as time went on, they developed a friendship that served them well throughout the rest of their lives. Lorne never held another prominent government position, but he wrote a biography of Queen Victoria and published his memories of Canada. When Lorne developed dementia, Louise nursed him until his death in 1914. His lack of attention to his clothing and hygiene was a personality trait that some attribute to the very early stages of dementia.

Queen Victoria was a prolific journal and letter writer, but her thoughts and impressions of her fourth daughter were few and far between. One reason for this might be Princess Beatrice's heavy editing of her mother's letters and journals after the Queen's death on January 22, 1901. The letters and ▶

journals have been published and are readily available, but no one knows what delicious stories and intriguing insights about the Queen and her children that Princess Beatrice consigned to the flames. As a result, I had to look to the letters and journals of contemporaries such as Dr. Reed and Major Ponsonby to catch more glimpses of Princess Louise's character and relationships, as well as gain insight into Queen Victoria's relationship with John Brown. The scene where Queen Victoria touched Mr. Brown's leg comes from Dr. Reed's journal, as does Edgar's admission that he'd heard and seen things between the Queen and Her Highland servant while working at various royal residences. Dr. Reed also gives insight into Lenchen's laudanum addiction, which she eventually conquered with his help.

Popular depictions of Queen Victoria often show her as a grandmotherly woman, but she was far from it. She was a queen, she knew it, and it made her very self-centered. She expected to be served and obeyed, and she wielded her power with a heavy hand, especially where her children were concerned. As Princess Louise says in the book, how does one defy a queen? It was a question even Prince Albert was forced to wrestle with. There were times when Princess Louise and her siblings couldn't do anything but bend to her royal will, but they did their best to carve out lives for themselves. Even Princess Beatrice eventually insisted on marrying, enduring six months of Queen Victoria's cold shoulder before finally winning her mother's consent. Like Lenchen, Beatrice still had to serve her mother, but she did gain the chance to have a family of her own. The quotes I included in the book are from Queen Victoria's letters and journals, and I incorporated a few of Queen Victoria's quotes into her dialogue. I did the same with Mr. Disraeli and others where I could.

I remained as true to the facts of Princess Louise's life as possible, but I also took some liberties with the historical timeline, especially the dates of certain artworks and people. For example, Mr. Story's *Angel of Grief* was displayed in 1894, and Rodin's *The Kiss* was first displayed in 1882. Princess Louise's jubilee statue of Queen Victoria was actually unveiled in 1891. The incident with Mr. Corsi and the cigarette was rumored to have happened in the 1900s. I also greatly condensed Princess Louise's time in Canada. Princess Louise did attend openings of Parliament with her mother, but she never opened it herself.

Princess Louise lived until 1939, and I include a brief mention of her in my novel *The Last Debutantes*. She enjoyed an interesting life that included art, travel, philanthropy, and a fascinating circle of friends. Some of her art, and Edgar's *Her Majesty at the Spinning Wheel*, can be viewed on the Royal Collection Trust website (rct.uk). If you are in London, you can see her statue of Queen Victoria in Kensington ▶

Afterword *(continued)*

Gardens or visit her sculpture of the angel supporting Christ at the Colonial Forces Memorial in St. Paul's Cathedral. Edgar's statue of Lord Holland still stands in Holland Park, and his statue of Charles Darwin is at the Natural History Museum in London.

I hope you enjoyed this glimpse into the fascinating life of Princess Louise. For more information about her, I recommend the following books:

Victoria the Queen, Julia Baird
Queen Victoria's Mysterious Daughter, Lucinda Hawksley
Darling Loosy: Letters to Princess Louise 1856–1939, Elizabeth Longford
Victoria's Daughters, Jerrold M. Packard
Royal Rebels: Princess Louise and the Marquis of Lorne, Robert M. Stamp
Princess Louise: Queen Victoria's Unconventional Daughter, Jehanne Wake

Q&A with
Georgie Blalock

Q: Describe Queen Victoria as a parent. On one hand, she seems to be willful and indifferent to the needs of her children, but she also has interesting moments of wisdom.

A: Queen Victoria loved her children in her own way, but that love was heavily influenced by her position as the monarch. From an early age, she was surrounded by courtiers who rushed to do her bidding, and this made her self-centered. She never allowed her children to forget that she was Queen, and she always insisted that they honor and obey her. Prince Albert was the more loving and involved parent. The loss of him was a great blow for the younger children and for Queen Victoria. He'd tempered some of her more selfish impulses, and without him she became more self-centered.

However, being a queen and being involved in world events did give her a great deal of wisdom. She could be as insightful about her children and their situations as she could be about politics or world events. However, she could also dismiss her children's concerns and troubles with shocking callousness, such as her response to Alice after ▶

Frittie's death, in which she stated that the loss of a husband was worse than the loss of a child. Queen Victoria was the most important person in her life, and her children always came second to her interests, needs, and duties.

Q: *Do you think, as an author and researcher, that Louise made the best choice in husbands? Who else could she have married, because, after all, if she had remained single he would have been stuck by her mother's side until she was quite old herself.*

A: I believe that Louise made the best choice in Lorne, but only because she had a very limited selection of available gentlemen to choose from. By rejecting foreign princes, she was limited to available British gentlemen, and not every available gentleman was willing to contend for her hand. Queen Victoria's court was known to be dour and boring, and not everyone wanted to tie themselves to such a demanding monarch. Also, Louise took a long time to make up her mind, and during that time, many contenders married other women. I think that by the time Louise realized she had to marry, Lorne was the best option available and more willing than others to enter into the confines of the royal family.

Q: Do you think there are parallels between any of the younger royals then and now?

A: I think younger royals of today still have to deal with the conflict between following their heart and dreams and fulfilling their duty to their family, nation, and lineage. Although they have a great deal more freedom to marry or divorce and pursue chosen careers, every decision they make is still scrutinized by the press and the people. In the novel, Louise complains that the government and the people have more say in her life and marriage than she does. I think in many ways, this is still true for younger royals.

Q: With the exception of the Prince of Wales—and also Louise—it always appears that Victoria's children were so dutiful. Is this an accurate impression? What made Louise so rebellious out of all the daughters?

A: Princess Louise's elder brother Alfred did his best to live his own life, pursuing his naval career, and through it placed a great deal of distance between himself and Queen Victoria's control. Prince Leopold did his best to defy Queen Victoria and claim his own life, but his frail health made it very difficult to fully escape his mother. If Leopold had ▶

been healthy, I believe he would have followed in Louise's footsteps and been far more rebellious.

Contemporary accounts suggest that Lenchen did not have the personality to disobey Queen Victoria. Neither did Alice and Vicky, who were quite a bit older than Louise and were raised by Prince Albert to fulfill their dynastic responsibilities by making foreign matches.

Princess Beatrice might have been more rebellious if her childhood hadn't been stultified by Queen Victoria's grief. She was four when Prince Albert died, so she never really enjoyed his influence in her upbringing, and her life was dominated by Queen Victoria's mourning. Her willingness to defy Queen Victoria to marry, which resulted in six months of the two of them only communicating through notes until Queen Victoria relented, was the most rebellion she ever displayed. Had she done more of that, she might have enjoyed a life similar to Louise's, but she didn't. She remained the dutiful daughter, even after Queen Victoria's death, editing her mother's journals and letters to portray her in the best light.

Q: Were there any surprises you discovered during the research of the book?

A: The biggest surprise I discovered while researching *An Indiscreet Princess* was how controlling and selfish Queen

Victoria was. She is often portrayed in films as a grandmotherly figure, a reserved and stately queen. Her iron-fisted control of her children, staff, and government was surprising, as was her petulance and capacity for insulting or dismissing her children and their needs. If I hadn't read her journals and letters and seen it for myself, I might not have believed how callous and self-centered she was. ∾

Discover great authors, exclusive offers, and more at hc.com.